Heather Hay was born in Essex in 1946 and educated in Scotland and England. She is married with one daughter and two sons and lives and works in the country. She has kept pigs, goats and chickens. Turning home produce into marketable pies and pâtés was the beginning of a business that led to her catering for Orient Express tours on their trips to Penshurst place, the stately home of Lord De L'Isle in Kent. During this time she started work on her first book, *Country Enterprise*, which was published in 1983.

*By the same author*

**HERITAGE
HONOUR
HEROES
BEAUTY**

# HEATHER HAY

# *Glitz*

**HarperCollins***Publishers*

HarperCollins*Publishers*
77–85 Fulham Palace Road,
Hammersmith, London W6 8JB

This paperback edition 1993
1 3 5 7 9 8 6 4 2

Previously published in paperback by Grafton 1993

Copyright © Heather Hay

The Author asserts the moral right to
be identified as the author of this work

A catalogue record for this book
is available from the British Library

ISBN 0 586 21435 6

Set in Times

Printed in Great Britain by
HarperCollinsManufacturing Glasgow

All rights reserved. No part of this publication may be
reproduced, stored in a retrieval system, or transmitted,
in any form or by any means, electronic, mechanical,
photocopying, recording or otherwise, without the prior
permission of the publishers.

This book is sold subject to the condition that it shall not,
by way of trade or otherwise, be lent, re-sold, hired out or
otherwise circulated without the publisher's prior consent
in any form of binding or cover other than that in which it
is published and without a similar condition including this
condition being imposed on the subsequent purchaser.

# Chapter 1

The newly risen sun floated effortlessly, a blood red Seville orange in an endless panorama of Mediterranean blue. Faint, rose-tinted smudges of sea mist began unravelling, like the veils of a myriad Aphrodites, to lose themselves in the mirrored water.

It was a picture an artist would have praised for classic balance. The horizon was a thin, silvered seam where the sky touched the sea, the watery element an exact third beneath the shimmering line of light.

Charles Freeman leaned back against the highly polished rail designed to prevent him, as owner of the ultra-exclusive, ultra-expensive, fifty metre, twin screw diesel yacht, *Champers*, from falling into the deceptively appealing sea. He stared down contemplatively at his immaculate white 501s; his equally pristine soft kid deck shoes; and the well scrubbed mahogany beneath them that was the colour of lightest honey.

'Shit,' he said softly.

The cigarette that Charles held between his nicotine-stained fingers carried a good inch of ash. He held it slowly out before him, watching, mesmerized, as the inevitable tremor of his hand dislodged the miniature grey column to fall smouldering at his feet. He smiled. A libation of dirt for his far too perfect home that floated serenely on a sea of pollution.

He'd left two girls sleeping in his bed – the term 'bunk' was too restricting a word to describe his sleeping arrangements. The master cabin had been designed by a Frenchman with a penchant for grandeur. *Les filles* were lying in an exotic confusion of red and green silk sheets and black French underwear, recovering from the after-effects of too much champagne, too much lobster, and too much sex.

They were young, hardly out of their teens; they would recover in time for a predominantly liquid lunch and an afternoon spent preening in preparation for another fun-filled night. Yes, Charles thought, they would wake, as always, with their zest for the high-life intact. This time, though, he hadn't. He felt old, but it wasn't age that was his problem. He'd just turned twenty-nine, and he hadn't given a thought to the big three-oh. He was suffering from something far more insidious than the onslaught of time.

The man whom the gossip columnists had dubbed 'Champagne Charlie' tossed the remains of his cigarette overboard and rubbed a tanned hand over the rough stubble on his chin. He'd tried growing a beard a while ago, but his face had itched after a couple of days without shaving. He took his good looks for granted. Men and women alike were drawn to him. His green eyes vividly expressed his strongly felt emotions; friendship and desire made him smile, showing strong, white teeth. His regular features had developed 'character' at the age of seventeen, when, sailing around the Greek islands on a leaky old sloop with half a dozen other youngsters, he'd had his nose broken by a falling spar. It had been set by a doctor smelling of ether and ouzo, who, with alcoholic inspiration, had added a Roman dimension to the boy's profile.

The time displayed on the classically restrained face of his Ebel wrist watch was five past eight, the date 28 March. He made a mental note to remember the time, the place, and the self-diagnosis. Charles Freeman, international playboy, confidant of major millionaires and minor royalty, was a victim of the worst, the most incurable of social diseases – terminal boredom.

He turned slowly to scan the view ahead as he began unbuttoning the neck of his olive green Ralph Lauren polo. It was going to be another scorching day, a spring bonus.

They were entering port, rounding a solid stone breakwater that jutted out to form a protected harbour. Ahead, a raw terracotta hillside garnished with scattered spears of cypress reared up behind a seemingly haphazard jumble of white walls. Red-tiled roofs, green shutters, and a multitude of tiny, geranium-decked balconies proclaimed, from a distance, a traditional Spanish village.

As they passed the outermost buoy marking the route to the anchorage, a different reality was revealed. A vast marina filled the space between a waterfront backed with luxurious Moorish-style apartments and chunky harbour walls devoid of even the memory of fishing nets. Row after row of gleaming chrome and high-gloss fibreglass, the floating toys of the rich, and sometimes famous, rocked gently on the Bergasol scented waters.

The steep, winding paths leading away from the esplanade to private, shadowed courtyards were empty. The only sign of life came from a high balcony, where an apron-swathed domestic shook a defiant, gaudy duster.

'Shit,' Charles said again.

Verité Goode, twenty-seven-year-old freelance PR consultant, reluctantly pushed aside her half-eaten portion of tortellini di ricotta. The chef had excelled, and the dish was one of her favourites, but she had to be a walking advertisement for her own special brand of image creation. She had to half-starve to keep a trim figure; condition her streaked honey-blond hair daily to keep it shining; and work hard on her make-up to bring out the warmth in her hazel eyes and distract attention from what could be considered an over-generous nose.

For two years she had been building her company, 'Goode as Golde', taking on the responsibility for the public personae of a varied list of clients ranging from ambitious MPs to best-selling authors. Using the contacts developed over five years in the retail fashion industry – most recently as head of public relations for a major high street chain – she was certain she was on the route to success.

Her home was a spacious Thames-side flat, shared with her boyfriend Sam, an architect specializing in ultra-modern skeletal structures. They both earned well and spent up to the limit, enjoying weekends in the capital cities of Europe; the best French and Italian cuisine; and collecting 1950s memorabilia.

It was a satisfying lifestyle for someone whose childhood entertainments had been at the whim of a succession of nannies. Verry's parents, Angelique and David Goode, had seldom been in residence at their Knightsbridge home. David was a talented conductor, and had travelled the cultured world with his beautiful wife. A child hadn't fitted in with the order of things, despite being the initial reason for their marriage, when Angelique had been just twenty and the already famous musician thirty-six.

The high spots of Verry's early years had been a succession of visits to New York to stay with her paternal grandmother Sara. Sara Goode was old school Hollywood. Born in 1910, the only child of the owners of a chain of movie houses, she had a vast store of gossipy memories. Only recently, when Irene Selznick, wife of David and daughter of Louis B. Mayer of Metro-Goldwyn-Mayer fame, had died, Grandma Sara had been an honoured guest at the funeral.

Verry brushed her newly washed hair firmly back from her face, fastened it in a pink towelling sports band, and checked her reflection in the mirror. Her cream tracksuit was immaculate, and beneath the cosy long-sleeved top she was wearing a matching cream vest so that she could strip off if she got too hot. Her face was glowing from her regular deep cleanse routine and a liberal application of moisturizer.

She could hear her father's voice downstairs. He liked a glass of milk before his morning run and presumably he was sharing a pinta with Tiddles the cat. It was such a cosy feeling to be spending a few days at her parents' home. She felt like a child again, although in reality there had been few moments of family intimacy in her youth such as the one she had got up so early to enjoy.

David Goode was already jogging up and down the short flight of stone steps leading to the pavement as Verry pulled the wide door closed behind her. It had been raining; the grey paving stones were glistening, and the early spring air felt washed and clean.

'Race you to the park,' David said, and the light breeze tossed the words back over his shoulder as he ran ahead.

Her father's voice was rich and musical. He wasn't tall for a man – five foot eight in shoes – and his body was slight, but he had a presence, the magical aura of the born performer. As Verry watched, he flicked his luxuriant white hair back off his forehead with a shake of his head. It was a gesture Verry knew so well that she smiled. Noted by music critics and colour magazine journalists alike, the 'flick' was one of his trademarks, as was the boyish, almost wistful smile that was so appealing in a man whose performance as a conductor was full of power, strength and mastery.

The streets of central London were almost deserted. A few cabs cruised desultorily; a helmeted policeman walked slowly, his measured pace requiring complete concentration as he stared, mesmerized, at the highly polished bootcaps appearing rhythmically, one after the other, in front of him.

Verry breathed in cautiously. She had a tendency to asthma that, later in the day, would be aggravated by the heavy diesel fumes of the metropolis. The overnight rain had done her a favour in clearing the pollution that had built up over the last few days. As they paused at a traffic junction, allowing a bus right of way, she warned her father that the roads would be slippery. He turned and smiled at her, and she smiled back. They were alone together, and it was a rare privilege.

Hyde Park was green: the grass refreshed, new leaves about to burst into life on the architectural trees. There were sweeps of smart yellow daffodils; the last, tattered remnants of multi-coloured carpets of crocuses. After a while Verry forgot about her breathing and stopped wondering if her muscles would seize up with the unaccustomed exercise. It was a joy to be out; the park had become a private playground for themselves and a handful of other early morning joggers. A few yards ahead, her father was running easily. He moved with the grace of an athlete; it was hard for her to believe that he was over sixty years old.

David glanced back. Verité was running well, keeping up with him nicely, attractive in her well cut, feminine tracksuit. It would be pleasant, he decided, for them to run side by side. He so rarely had company on his morning exercise that he had come close to forgetting her existence. He smothered a pang of conscience. He saw too little of his daughter, his only child. But there were so many demands on his time: the worldwide travel, the all-demanding performances, the image that he worked so assiduously to maintain of a man dedicated to his art. There were his adoring followers, and there was his wife, Angelique, who was so young herself that it was difficult to credit her with a fully grown daughter.

He slowed so that Verry caught him up.

'Are you OK?' she asked jerkily, between oxygen-charged mouthfuls of air.

David nodded. Another few hundred yards or so should see the end of the indigestion that had been bothering him since he'd woken up. He'd had a couple of spoonfuls of magnesia and discussed his problem with the cat before they'd set out.

The traffic was building. Verry was beginning to be uncomfortably aware of the fumes, and she wasn't surprised when her father's hand went to his chest. He faltered a little in his running, coughed a couple of times, and then, giving her a brief, reassuring smile, resumed his normal pace.

The magnificent façade of Buckingham Palace ahead of them set David to thinking through the rehearsal he was to attend that afternoon at the Albert Hall. He was giving a concert there on Saturday night, at which the Princess of Wales would be present. It would be his particular delight to produce something really spectacular from the orchestra for her enjoyment.

He began humming softly to himself, working on timing, building to the great, pounding climax where he would lose himself amongst the surging music. He stumbled, his breathing constricted, so close to the final few bars that his mind carried them on, heedless of the sudden pain.

'Daddy!' Verry reached out and caught hold of her father. He looked strange, his mouth wide open as if the air was something he had to devour. As the colour drained from his face, the lips writhed bluely back. She tried to pull him to a standstill, but still he faltered forwards, and then he was clutching at his chest, falling . . .

She knelt, shivering, beside him on the cold, damp

pavement so close to the palace gates. David Goode, maestro, lay twisted, his once elegant figure belittled by the majesty of its setting, whilst music – swelling glorious sound, the most perfect performance he had ever experienced – engulfed his senses until, at last, the beloved art became more insistent than life itself.

The limpid waters of the Mediterranean were warm, close to blood heat, as Charles sat, cross-legged, on the sandy sea floor. The rhythmic sound of his breathing, magnified by the lightweight aqualung strapped to his back, was soothing. The headache he had developed on board *Champers* was slowly starting to fade.

A vivid yellow outboard floated some twenty feet above him. Its flat bottom had trapped bubbles of air that shone like marbles. Staring upwards he could make out two small feet trailing over the dinghy's side, gently splashing the water, sending silver streaks across the blue. The two girls sunbathing in the miniature vessel had become noisy that afternoon, over-excited by the Bucks fizz he'd had served at tea. The strawberries had been good, the cream light and fluffy, the meringues crisp and white. Without his headache, after his own version of afternoon tea *à l'anglais*, he would have felt like sex. That would have nicely filled the gap between mid-afternoon and early evening, when he could have busied himself dressing for a night at the casino. He was due some luck on the tables.

He needed a new business deal, something to occupy the portion of his mind he liked exercised. There were times when the opportunity to be the ultimate entrepreneur – the dipper in and out of other people's business lives in pursuit of a quick buck – could be distinctly seedy. The current economic climate had presented chances to make fortunes to those prepared to frequent grimy factory clearances, trauma-filled property salerooms, or simply keep in touch with the international company liquidators; but, for Charles, it was all too sordid. He liked to support his jet-setting lifestyle by living off his wits, not other people's misery.

What were the girls' names? They were Italians, twins, goodtime girls out to find themselves husbands or sugar daddies. Charles had no intention of filling either role. Rosetta? Was that what one of them was called? As he tried, not too hard, to remember, he looked around him. The ostensible purpose of his trip to the bottom of the sea was to catch some supper. He had brought with him a sharp stick, a metal lobster pot, and thick leather gloves. There were rocks off to his left, ideal hunting grounds for crustaceans. Attached to the woven wire basket was a small red balloon which he could release if he required assistance; simply slipping its knot would send it bobbing quickly to the surface.

Rosetta and Rosalie, he remembered now. They were extremely pretty, with dark skin, rosy cheeks and long, curling hair. They were also, when he felt like it, great fun, as happy to share one man as he was to enjoy their quick-fingered talents.

There had been nothing of interest for him in that morning's papers. No hint between the lines of the financial pages of a sweet deal to be done with his inimitable style and panache; no name of friend or acquaintance well positioned for an assisted 'kill'. If he hadn't been underwater he would have sighed with irritation. As it was . . .

He reached forwards, pulled the string, and detached the balloon.

Rosalie was wide awake, dipping her small, chubby toes in and out of the water and watching the sparkling drips fall back into the sea. Her sister slept beside her. They were both slick with sun-oil, their size eight bodies glistening like gilded pastry in the sun. Rosalie studied her breasts critically. You could never be too careful. There was a pool of Bergasol in her tummy button; she dipped a finger into it and then stroked the protection over her nipples. They reacted instantly, stiffening to the touch. At that moment, the red balloon surfaced with a liquid pop. She glanced quickly at Rosetta. The elder twin by twelve minutes had finished up drinking straight champagne at Charles's tea. With luck, Rosalie thought, her sometimes too constant companion would be asleep for ages.

Charles watched the small boat begin to rock – that would be the girls getting into their breathing apparatus. He straightened his legs, easing out a touch of stiffness, then he raised his arms and stretched. A small shoal of tiny fish scattered around him as the surface of the sea broke open above him and shafts of light flashed like tamed lightning as the girl entered the water. She duck-dived immediately, her hair floating like dark seaweed as she looked first left then right. Finding Charles, she kicked her flippered feet expertly and made straight towards him, wondering how long her sister would stay asleep.

The blue light made their tanned skin seem pale. Charles reached out and took Rosalie's hand, pulling her towards him. Putting his arm firmly around her waist and digging his feet into the sand he spun them both round and round while her hips swung to an unheard lambarda beat. He could feel her sunwarmed skin pressed up against him. After a few minutes he pushed the girl gently away, and she looked at him, puzzled, trying to understand what he wanted. He used his hands to show her and with a quick smile she understood.

The tiny triangles of material were tied high on each hip. Slowly, making sure he savoured every movement, she tugged at the little bows, first one, then the other. She paused for a moment, letting the water keep the fabric pressed close against her, until with a sharp tug she removed the garment altogether. They both watched it float slowly, twistingly upwards, the dancing strings like the living tendrils of a sea anemone. Even when it reached the surface, Rosalie kept her face turned away from Charles. She wanted him to play with her.

He swam towards her, where she was suspended upright in the water, her feet kicking gently. He reached out, slipping his hand between the slim thighs, feeling the young muscles tightening. He moved his hand upwards, briefly touching the soft, tantalizing hairs before slipping back down the soft smooth skin. Swiftly, Rosalie used her hands in a sculling movement to lower herself in the water, so that once again he was touching her where she wanted. She felt his cool fingers move against her warmth and she twisted to face him. She was aching to kiss him, to feel his tongue in her mouth, and the fact that underwater it was impossible made her want it more. She threw her arms around him, and he wriggled out of his bathing trunks; she positioned herself carefully, then swiftly, holding tightly on to his muscular arms, she forced herself down.

It was as Charles entered her sister that Rosetta awoke. She looked around. There was the red balloon, the scrap of floating orange close by the boat. She quickly pulled on her aqualung and poised for only a second on the edge of the dinghy before tumbling backwards into the water to join them.

Slowly, contemplatively, Verry twirled her gold Cross biro between finger and thumb. She'd spent almost a quarter of an hour doing nothing, just sitting at the Davenport in the corner of her mother's elegant drawing room. It was ten forty-five, the middle of Wednesday morning. On a normal day she should have been at work.

She glanced down at the doodles she'd been scrawling

on a sheet of cream vellum notepaper. 'PR' – the two letters stood out amongst a montage of meaningless whorls.

'Private relations,' she whispered. Her life had been thrown into turmoil.

The telephone beside her rang and she picked it up quickly.

'Verité?' The husky voice of her American grandmother was instantly recognizable, despite a crackle on the line.

'Mother's out of danger. She's back home – upstairs, asleep.'

'How she ever could . . .'

'The doctors didn't think she really meant to kill herself. You know what they say – an attempt at suicide is a plea for help.' Until the day before yesterday, that had seemed just a hackneyed phrase. Suddenly, it was a concept she was depending on, but she still hated the trite way it had come out.

'I'll be with you on Friday, Verité. And don't say you don't need me, because you do. You're a working girl, and your mother's going to need twenty-four-hour attention – she can't be left for a minute. Whatever they say, she might just try it again – you know how much she enjoys a scene. You have got rid of all the other pills in the house, haven't you?'

Verry rubbed tiredly at her eyes. Her grandmother probably wasn't going to be any help, just someone else who'd need looking after. She was over eighty.

'Gran,' she started. It would be so much easier without her, but she couldn't bring herself to say so. 'Let me know when your flight gets in. I'll come and collect you.'

'You just stay with your mother.' The strength flooded back into the husky voice, the fear that an old woman wouldn't be wanted replaced by the normal autocracy of the matriarch. 'I can get myself a taxi, and some damn fool will take care of my luggage, they always do. That's one of the bonuses of getting old – one of the few.'

There was a click on the line, and Verry was left staring at the receiver in her hand. No 'goodbye', no ordinary family salutations. Friday, she thought suddenly. She would have to send details of the memorial service by special courier. If only her mother had not insisted on having it so soon.

The beautiful inlaid desk was crammed with unpaid bills – they would have to be dealt with as soon as the will was proved. Each tiny dovetailed drawer contained a small mountain of paper. It would take hours to create order out of the chaos. She should be working, stirring up good publicity for her clients, furthering her career, smothering her grief, but this was a task she could not delegate.

'PR' – the letters stared up at her again. Amongst her mother's crumpled papers one of Verry's early business cards looked fresh and purposeful. She picked it up and felt the smooth, cool surface, enjoying the brief, happy memories; she could hear her mother beginning to move around upstairs.

It was about to start again, Angelique's tears and tantrums, the railing at fate for leaving her alone. Her mother had never been there when she'd needed a shoulder to cry on. Why, then, did she feel so overwhelmingly that it was her duty to take care of the neurotic wreck of a still hauntingly beautiful woman?

'Here, cabbie,' Sara Goode said imperiously. 'Pull over right here.' She was breathing heavily. The strain of her overnight flight from New York was beginning to tell on her eighty-plus-year-old constitution, but to her immense satisfaction her spirit was as indomitable as ever.

The driver stopped the meter and reached back to open

the door for his elderly passenger.

'I haven't finished with you yet, young man.' Sara peered shortsightedly at the great expanse of steps stretching upwards between herself and her destination, the vast ornamented doors of St Paul's. 'I want you to wait here for me.'

He began to complain; the traffic, the ever-prowling traffic wardens . . .

'You do as I want, and I'll give you a twenty-five pound tip. That's a lot of money just to sit and wait a while. Now, do you still want to deposit an old lady and her luggage in the middle of nowhere?'

He laughed. The 'luggage' was alligator, old but still impressive, and he thought she was good for the fare, including the promised tip; but the magnificent Wren cathedral was hardly 'nowhere'. They were in the heart of the City of London – some would have said the heart of the universe. 'OK,' he said. 'You win.'

'And mind you look after this little chap properly.' Sara thrust the handful of animated fur she'd been holding through the open window and on to the cabbie's lap. 'Jasper's his name, and I reckon he'd appreciate a drink.'

'Hey, lady, is this thing housetrained?' But he looked in vain for a reaction as the diminutive American began slowly mounting the steps.

He sighed. There was a collection of nobs standing at the top of the steps, and the press were hanging about as well. He reckoned himself a bit of a music buff, and he vaguely remembered hearing it was David Goode's memorial service today. Come to think of it, the old girl looked a bit like the famous conductor – same loads of hair, although hers was an unlikely palomino blonde, and she certainly had style. She was the first customer he'd ever had who'd made him stop off at Harrods on the run in from the airport just so that she could buy herself a pet. Over an hour he'd waited with the warm, furry creature now snuggled on his lap. It was panting, a bit like the old lady. They made a good pair: obvious class, and obvious bother. He wondered again if the dog knew where, or more importantly where not, to spend a penny. A sudden tapping on the window of his cab was his signal for the off. At least it was a policeman telling him to move on, and not some flighty female traffic warden. The actual law went in for warnings first and tickets second.

It took a couple of minutes to pull out into the maelstrom of delivery vans, bicycle messengers, ponderous red buses and other cabs working all hours, like him, to make a bob in the recession. He'd find a bit of grass to give the dog a walk, and come back for the old girl in half an hour or so. The fare was going to be something monumental. He was smiling contentedly at the thought as the little dog's bladder finally overflowed.

Having eventually reached the top of the steps, Verry's beloved grandmother paused for a few moments before making her inevitably impressive entrance.

She was no stranger to 'occasions'. Growing up in and around the Hollywood lots, she was a classmate of the young Buddy Schulberg, who later wrote a series of notable screenplays including the brilliant *On the Waterfront*. At seventeen, she married Laurence Goode, a thirty-year-old producer, and within a year gave birth to a son, David. The child was the only fruit of their union.

On her stately passage down the aisle to join her daughter-in-law and granddaughter at the front of the Cathedral, Sara acknowledged the murmured sympathetic greetings from either side. It seemed a long way to walk.

\* \* \*

'But, Mother, you have to eat something.' Exasperation made Verry's voice harsh. She forced a smile to her lips, but it was an effort. She leaned over the forlorn figure huddled in the chair. 'Nobody can live on martinis alone.'

Angelique tilted her head back so that the soulful, deep, tearless eyes stared up into her daughter's. 'But that's what I am – alone!' she whispered huskily.

Verry straightened abruptly. The deliberate misunderstanding convinced her that her mother was still putting on an act. It was as if the reality of David's death hadn't yet penetrated the veneer. The black Armani, the wisp of black veil trailed between the widow's hands, was still a performance, as had been the so-called suicide attempt, timed to perfection to allow Verry to rush to the rescue.

'Be an angel,' the so-thin wrist arched in a swan's neck seemed too frail to bear the weight of the Lalique crystal, 'and get me another little drink, darling. I will eat, I promise, but not yet. Anything, the slightest morsel, would choke me, I swear it.' Angelique's slender fingers gripped fiercely at her throat and for a moment she did look sick, pale and haggard, but the effect was only fleeting.

The vast kitchen echoed hollowly, resonant as a shell now that the staff had left, fleeing from Angelique's emotional outbursts. Verry pulled open the door of the double larder fridge and stood for a moment, the cool air dousing her rising temper. She was tired, her head ached and her hands were trembling. She wanted to be tucked up in a chair being pandered to herself. She'd said a final farewell to her father today, supported her mother and at last seen her grandmother off to bed. She wanted Sam with her, fussing around, making one of his 'little' omelettes, holding her hand, stroking her brow. Instead she was the nursemaid, acting out her new role in her mother's life.

'There's damn all food in here,' she shouted out. Tears were very close to the surface, her throat hurt unbearably, she was desperate to curl up in a ball and go to sleep. 'I said there's damn all food in the fridge.'

'Don't blaspheme, darling, today of all days.'

Verry spun round. Her mother stood in the doorway, still holding the shred of black veil to her eyes. 'I'm sorry there's nothing for you to eat. I don't suppose anyone thought of it. I don't suppose anyone thought you'd be hungry . . .' She let her words trail off, an accusation. 'Will you drink a cocoa if I make some?'

'Cocoa.' Angelique's voice became even softer. 'Dear, darling David used to make me cocoa. In the strangest places, even on the hottest nights. Brazil, Cape Town . . . so many happy, happy memories.'

Memories that Verry couldn't share, the years she'd spent out of sight at boarding school, on holidays with friends and acquaintances, with Grandma Sara. 'I'll take Gran up a cup as well. Would you like yours in the drawing room or are you going up to bed?' She turned, but Angelique had left and only the scent of lilies remained, expensive, surreal.

'Damn!' The ice-cold milk bottle slipped through her numb fingers. 'Damn!' she cried for the mess on the white tiled floor, 'Damn!' for the overblown service that had been yet another performance in her life, 'Damn!' for the death of her father. Damn! Damn! Damn! for the little dog, Jasper, that had come sniffing round her feet at the spilt milk and sent the offended Tiddles screeching out through the cat-flap.

Angelique tugged the duvet higher round her throat. She longed to be cocooned, enveloped in warmth, but deep inside she was chilled. She was so confused she couldn't sleep, despite the pills, despite the alcohol that all evening had done nothing to dull her nerves. Verité was heartless, she'd decided. All that fuss about food. Angelique laid a cool hand on her own flat stomach.

She had kept her figure, improved on it since her youth, since her one venture into motherhood. She ran her fingers over the smooth contours of her leg. Her skin was expensively soft, her knee was small, the bone of her shin narrow. His *petit oiseau*, David had called her. He had loved her delicate bones, the long azure vein that ran just below the surface of the skin along the inside of her thigh. She could imagine him now, kissing that line of blue, his thick head of hair hiding his face. She would watch him, fascinated, as he traced the route upwards . . .

In the room above Angelique, Sara lay awake. She'd drifted off to sleep almost as soon as she'd come upstairs, but then woken abruptly as if disturbed by a sudden noise. At first she thought it might be Jasper, but then remembered that after making a puddle on the bedroom carpet he'd been banished to the kitchen. After a while she'd realized that it hadn't been a sound that had woken her, but the silence. The house had the thick, dense stillness of expensive carpeting under over-polished furniture, the heaviness of a multitude of oil paintings hung on damascened walls.

Sara was missing home. She would have welcomed the hum of her air-conditioning, its cheerful warbling that kept her company in the dead of night. Tucked up in her own posture-sprung bed she could have listened to the world begin to waken. The water pipes started to hum with liquid life at around five-thirty. That was the Samuels, the family two flats below her; the husband was working out of town on some new housing development. He was an engineer and had his office on site. Mrs Samuels had said it made her mad that he kept the same hours as the labourers. The traffic outside would begin to pick up around seven and by then the plumbing would have subsided into the background; then it was the sound of the mailman. There might be a nice, newsy letter from an old friend. Yes, Sara thought as she sat up, she certainly was missing home.

There were two books beside her on the bedside table. Angelique had obviously chosen them with her usual care for appearances. The first was a recent biography of Ludwig van Beethoven, looking as if it had never been opened. Beside that lay a beautifully bound folio of ballerina sketches by Degas. Sara laid her hand on the watered silk cover. The bedside light threw theatrical beams, making craggy mountains of her knuckles, a whole landscape of her wrinkled skin. She stared in disgust at her nails. Their subtle peach polish looked hideous against the maroon fabric beneath them.

Sara sighed. Growing old was such a bore; her dear David would have hated having to come to terms with it. That was her one consoling thought. She moved her shoulders irritably; it didn't do, at her age, to cry. She had decided on the flight over that to show grief would be in bad taste. David would have hated it. He would have wanted her to be at her very best. 'Be serene, mother.' She could almost hear his voice. 'There is nothing so becoming to a woman in this world as serenity.'

Then why – she slammed her hand down sharply – why on earth had he married such a silly, self-centred creature as Angelique? He, the artist, should have been bolstered and protected. Instead he had been the one to provide emotional support, to be there, calm and loving, through tirades and tantrums. Sara had feared, at the memorial service, that Angelique would make some kind of scene. Had there been a coffin, she would probably have thrown herself on it, or something equally mortifying.

In the public eye Angelique had been the perfect

widow, alabaster pale, slender as a wand, swaying gently with grief. Even the final decorous faint had been performed as etiquette demanded, with Verité at hand to help her slide gracefully on to the pew. Verité, her grandmother thought, had looked appalling, her face like putty, her hair escaping from under a seriously strange hat. The poor child's eyes were ravaged; there was real grief there.

Sara sighed again, a habit she had got into since living on her own. She rather liked it; it made her feel in sympathy with herself. Her dear David had left a daughter who adored him, even though she'd seen precious little of him; a wife who worshipped herself but would come to miss the man who had made her the centre of his world; and a mother who whilst mourning the loss of her son was showing an equanimity that would have been envied by her peers – the few of them that were left.

'Oh, David,' she muttered savagely, 'oh, David,' and then she buried her face in her hands, her shoulders heaving, fat tears forcing their way through her fingers. 'Why did it have to be you?'

## Chapter 2

Charles breathed in tentatively. It hurt. He lay very still, his eyes closed. He had spent the night vainly trying to will himself into blissful, all-embracing sleep, and failed miserably. Now, wincing, he sat up.

'What a bitch!' he muttered with feeling as he padded through to the bathroom. He twisted his torso painfully so that he could scrutinize his bruises in the full-length smoke-tinted bathroom mirror. They were obligingly lurid. Grape purple merging into navy blue marked the distinct outlines of several ribs, while a sunset red streak stretched across his abdomen.

He brushed his fingertips over a particularly evil black lump and grimaced. He was very sorry for himself. Even the nurse in the casualty department hadn't been all that sympathetic. Her main concern had been to get him to admit he'd been drinking, and – the final indignity – the doctor's hands had been cold. All that pain and there hadn't even been any broken bones to show for it.

He pulled down a lower eyelid and glared balefully at his reflection. His stomach growled ominously, reminding him he'd thrown up last night's dinner. 'Bitch,' he muttered again, but his mood was lifting.

In a few minutes, after the water-pick had livened his gums and the mouthwash reddened the basin, he was almost smiling. At least she'd been true to type. Charles was a great believer in categorizing 'his' women and he liked nothing more than being proved right. From the very start he'd decided the highly strung Amanda made love like an electric eel – pulsing, writhing, wrapping him up in her long, slim thighs. He'd found it stimulating – for a while. It had been during that 'while' that he'd lent her his town car, an acid yellow BMW soft-top. It had been when he began to discern a certain slithering in her technique that he'd suggested, quite subtly, that she might like to return the vehicle. Apart from anything else, the repetitive use of taxis was making him feel like a tourist.

Amanda had returned the vehicle all right, but in her own particular fashion, all sparks and shocks. He'd been walking away from the Waldorf, his arm snugly around Priscilla, the sweet little thing he'd discovered at a ball in aid of some hospital or other. It had been simply chance that he'd looked up, for one moment, out of those melting blue eyes and seen the yellow peril hurtling towards them. He'd done rather well, he considered – thrown Priscilla into the arms of the astounded doorman, then leaped heroically across the bonnet of his car. They'd come to a shuddering halt, Amanda laughing, her lips drawn back, her eyes flashing. He'd never realized until that moment that her mouth was too wide for her narrow face with its high, slanting cheekbones.

The Thames was sparkling, short grey waves lapping at Victorian granite as half a dozen sea gulls mewed and swooped where an old man threw scraps on to the water. Charles felt better. He breathed in the Embankment air: the heady mixture of traffic fumes and ancient river never failed to invigorate him. The soreness was still there in his chest, but the stiffness was wearing off. He began to stride out. He was heading towards lunch and he was hungry. Also, he was intrigued. Powerful women did that to him, and Hilary Milland was nothing if not powerful.

Red carpet led from the pavement on to the gently swaying pontoon that stretched to the floating restaurant. There were flowers in hanging baskets rocking with the tide, a natty nautical awning forming a canopy overhead. A white-jacketed waiter bowed silently, indicating the way. It was strangely quiet on board and Charles glanced briefly at his watch. It was a couple of minutes past one; he was right on time.

He turned a final corner into a wide, gently rocking stateroom and Ms Milland was before him, holding her hand out in greeting. He'd glimpsed her once or twice in the past, but knew her face from press photos. She had pale, almost white hair, a fine high brow, widely spaced intelligent eyes and a slim, patrician nose. There was also the hint of laughter, and Charles realized it was directed at him. She'd booked the entire boat, and it was such an amazing gesture that he had let his surprise show. The restaurant was empty, the usual ranks of tables and chairs removed so that the shining teak deck was revealed in all its glory and the solitary table, laid for two in the very centre of the floor, seemed to float on its own reflection.

'I thought we should have a little privacy,' the woman who – gossip said – made money where macho men wouldn't dare explained.

Charles smiled. 'Obviously,' he said. Then he grinned, and finally burst out laughing. He loved it. He loved her poise, her style. She must be fifty-five if she was a day and she reduced all the other women he knew to giggling schoolgirls.

'Our business interests don't overlap, you see.' Hilary paused for a moment as the waiter poured the Chassagne Montrachet. It was an '85, difficult now to get hold of. 'That's becoming increasingly rare. Thanks to the recession too many of the big guns have spread their nets wide. It was a mistake, of course.'

'Personally, in time of storm I batten down the hatches and stick to what I'm best at.'

'Wine, women and . . . ?'

'Not song, I can assure you.' Charles dabbed at the corners of his mouth with a napkin. 'Singing isn't my strong point. I reserve it for the shower.'

'You've got the chest for a singer.' Hilary spoke slowly, running her eyes over the broad expanse of white shirt front. 'I'd like to hear you sometime.'

Charles almost choked on the innuendo and the sudden intake of air reawakened his bruises. He exhaled slowly, counting to ten. 'What made you phone me?' He had verbally underlined the 'me'.

'I saw you last year at Cannes, with someone I do business with. Someone I respect, whose judgement I accept.'

Charles raised his eyebrows in query but she briefly shook her head.

'It doesn't matter who it was, except that he said you could be useful to me. You have a wide net of Mediterranean contacts, and that's what I need right now. So far my action has been mainly in the States, but following through to Europe seems to make sense. There's always money to be made in times of flux. And then there was the personal thing.' She raised a hand for the waiter and they remained silent as the fish course was removed.

'The personal thing?' Charles echoed her words.

'You turned me on,' she said simply. There was no awkwardness, nothing of the ingénue; her eyes remained straight and level, locked with his. 'I just looked at you and I was buzzing. My escort didn't know why, but it turned out to be his lucky night.'

'I have to admit, I've never met anyone like you before, Hilary.' Charles reached out, taking the narrow, manicured hand in his. It was a gesture that seemed to be required.

'They made me and then threw away the mould.' Hilary laughed, her eyes crinkling at the corners, genuine amusement lighting her face. 'So how about it? A nice no holds barred business relationship with a little fun on the side?'

Charles paused. He didn't want to turn down the business, and certainly not the pleasure, but there was just a wrinkle of discomfort. He squeezed her hand and was saved by the arrival of the main course, a Châteaubriand served with a Mouton Rothschild. He had the definite impression that she was building him up.


Angelique swept tearfully into the drawing room. 'Nothing,' she cried. 'I have been left with nothing. I'm penniless, quite destitute. Poor darling David. It must have been the worry of it all that killed him.' She collapsed gracefully into a damask-covered armchair, a tiny square of richly embroidered muslin pressed to her eyes.

Sam followed her into the room. He shrugged his shoulders at Verry and Sara who, on Angelique's instructions, had not attended the reading of the will. 'I didn't go in with her,' he said in answer to the continuing query in Verité's expressive eyes. 'Your mother went into the solicitor's office on her own, and when she came back out he was half carrying her. I gather it's pretty bad.'

Angelique was murmuring into her handkerchief. 'Tragic,' they heard her say. 'Such a waste, such a terrible waste.'

'What is it, Mother?' Verité went to sit on the arm of the chair. For a moment Angelique seemed about to tell her to get off, but then she subsided, once more, into tears. Verité leaned closer. 'What is this about? Daddy was rich. I don't understand . . .'

'He was a gambler,' Angelique said bitterly. 'It was his great, ruling passion, and now finally it's been the cause of his death. Everything – the house, the money – he'd wagered it all and lost.'

'Rot,' Sara announced firmly. 'David never bet on

anything in his life. He had much too much sense.'

'If you believe that,' the widow said tremulously, 'it proves you didn't know your son at all. I'm not talking about backing horses, or any of the other common things – David was anything but vulgar – but he took risks all the time. He backed hunches, he backed people, and until now . . .' Her voice trailed off. Then, regaining her self-control, she asked Sam to get her a drink.

Sam. Verité watched him as he busied himself making them all extra dry martinis. He wasn't at his best in a crisis, but he was so kind, so considerate, and she was so fond of him. 'I'll have to stay here tonight,' she said, half to him, and half to herself.

'Surprise, surprise,' he muttered. He was standing close enough to Sara for her to hear and understand. Verité's lover, like Verité's grandmother, had a premonition of disaster. Angelique, who had chosen to keep her only child at more than arm's length for as long as either of them could remember, was now going to be the clinging vine. Watching Verité now, her arm around her mother's slender, drooping shoulders, her young face drawn by concern, both of them found it very easy to imagine the capable daughter taking over her father's supportive role.

'No,' Sam said loudly into the telephone. 'I won't hear of it, Verité. And I want you back here, now, where you belong. That woman . . .'

'Please don't go on any more, Sam. I need your help, your sympathy, not a lecture. I have to do this. Mother can't possibly fend for herself.'

'Bullshit.' Generally, he tried not to swear, but there was a time for everything. 'And I don't care what you say, I will not agree to sell the flat. It's our home.'

'I can't afford to keep it.'

'You can if you live in it, with me. Nothing's changed

for us with your father's death. Angelique's not an old woman. She'll have to sort herself out.'

'She can't.' Verité's voice was almost a wail. 'She's never had to earn her own living; she wouldn't know where to start. I have to provide her with a home.'

'For Christ's sake,' Sam said despairingly. 'You're not going to listen to me, are you? But it doesn't matter, because she'll act true to form just like she always does, and you'll have to see sense in the end. I won't help you over this, but I'll always be here if you need me. Meanwhile I'll do everything I can to stop you throwing what we have away.'

She put the telephone down slowly. She could imagine the flat now, light and spacious, the ideal backdrop for the original Bakelite phone, the Tiffany lampshade. Her mother's drawing room was like a museum. The furniture was exquisite, mainly French, and it would all have to be sold, to pay off her father's debts.

Verry slowly stirred two sweetener tablets into her black, decaffeinated coffee. 'You're sure you want to stay on in England?' she asked. She and Sara were sitting either side of the oval pine table in the kitchen. It was only eight o'clock in the evening, but Angelique had already gone to bed.

'Quite sure, dear,' Sara said firmly. She would stay with Verité and her mother for as long as it took. 'And I won't be a hindrance. I may be old, but I'm not potty or anything. It's a shame I'd already given your father the money your grandfather left me, but when David got the chance to buy the lease on this place it seemed the logical thing to do. After all, it's Knightsbridge, isn't it?' She nudged her coffee cup more firmly on to its saucer. She couldn't believe she'd misjudged her son for all those years. 'But I think I'd better keep my apartment on, just in case. You could stay there yourself if you go to New York on business; having your own place is so much nicer than being in a hotel. Meanwhile I can feed myself over here, and pay for the odd little luxury, but as far as capital is concerned . . .'

'It'll be lovely having you with us.' It would certainly leaven Angelique's company. 'I've found a cottage in Chelsea that looks ideal. It's small but it has four bedrooms, and the agent says the owners are hard-pressed so they'll take a low offer.'

'Poor souls. But as they say, it's an ill wind. Now let's get back to business.'

Verité smiled. She loved her grandmother. 'The bank is going to help me buy the cottage, on the understanding I'm selling the flat.'

'But you're not.'

'Sam will come round to my way of thinking in the end. He has to.' She looked momentarily worried. 'I don't have any choice. I can cut down on a lot of expenses – the frivolous ones – but I can't afford two mortgages.'

'You know I don't approve of you taking on Angelique?'

Verité nodded. 'You've made your feelings quite clear, Grandma. But Mother has to be provided for.'

'It's not your job.'

'It is if there's no one else to do it.'

'I wonder just how clever you could be, Verité, if you were given the chance.'

They both watched as Tiddles came cautiously in through the cat-flap, checked that Jasper was asleep in his basket, and then made her way to the food bowls.

Verité got up to pour some crispy, fish-shaped cat nibbles. 'Is that a rhetorical question,' she asked, 'or are you leading up to something?'

'If someone came along and gave you the opportunity

to make enough money to set your mother up independently, so that after a while you could go back to living your own life, just how far would you be prepared to go?'

'How long a while?' Verité sat down again and sipped at her coffee. 'And exactly what is this opportunity you're about to try and sell me?'

'Verité! It doesn't suit you to be cynical.'

'No, Grandma, I'm not a cynic, I'm tired, that's all. And I have to get back to work tomorrow, get things going again.'

'I expect you could put things on hold for a while, couldn't you?'

'Not in PR. A couple of days off and you're yesterday's news. I'm worried about making up the time I've lost recently.'

'Your father's death gave your own persona a boost.'

That was true. Verry nodded, and tried to smile, but gave up the attempt. 'Sick, isn't it?' she said.

'I want you to give me a year of your time. In exchange, I'll give you the rights to my manuscript, to the entire kit and caboodle, the biography, and everything else that's in it.'

'Grandma!' Sara's memories were a family legend, accumulated over half a century: the glossy fragments of early Hollywood, her close friendship with the Selznicks.

As if reading her mind, Sara said, 'Irene went out and did her own thing, you know. After all those years married to David, she went on to produce for the theatre, and she was a great success. She wrote too, quite well.'

'I know, Grandma.' Verité had read the two elegant autobiographies. 'And I think your offer is wonderful, but publishing is in such a state that I'm not sure this is the time . . .'

'I'm not talking about the book – at least, not as a stand-alone project. I'm talking about the movie. There's a whole synopsis in there for *Viva Europa* – the one your grandpa always reckoned would make him a fortune.'

The one Sara's husband hadn't made because he'd died too soon, as Sara's son had. Verité realized suddenly how very brave her grandmother was being. She reached out and squeezed her hand. 'But I don't know anything about films,' she said.

'Well, I do. I know the worth of a good, simple plot, and – most important of all – a concept. Four young unknowns, that's what the story revolves around. With your PR ability you could make them into overnight stars, and if you had them well tied in to an agency contract you would be looking at serious money. And of course you know about films, Verité. It's in your blood. Your grandpa must have told you more about the business than any of these young producers knows today.'

She'd been a child, walking hand in hand with the bear-like, cigar-smoking first-generation American. What, if anything, of their talks could she remember?

'How else can you ever get a life of your own again?'

Sara had always been great on the punchline. Verité got up and walked towards the kettle. 'How about another coffee?' she asked. After all, the night was still young.

'The story in there is as valid today as it ever was.' Exasperation made Sara's voice hoarse. She was determined Verité would do what she wanted. 'Sure, some of the scene-setting is dated, but the concept is as fresh as ever.'

'I didn't say that it wasn't.' Verry sipped cautiously at her scalding coffee. They'd stayed up late, and now she was finding it a struggle to wake up properly. 'But you know as well as I do how long film projects take to get off the ground, and I don't have that time. Whatever I do has to be pretty well instantly rolling. I'll have to convince the bank I'm on to a winner for a start.'

It was cosy in the kitchen. They'd kept the blinds closed from the night before, the central heating was going full blast and Sara had got muffins baking in the oven. It would be the perfect start to a Sunday, Verry thought, if only Sara weren't so persistent.

But Sara was determined to have her say. 'It depends how you go about it. You've got to be the motivator, the guy who gets things done. Then people start to react at your pace, and the bank'll get the message.'

'It might be an idea to get an opinion on the whole manuscript, see if there's a market for it as an autobiography. We'd have to get an agent, though.'

'What?' Sara's hands clutched at air in her obvious horror. 'Your grandpa would turn in his grave. Fifteen per cent for nothing. Look here, Verité, we'll be making a start by taking *Viva Europa* out of the manuscript; there's no point in throwing it in with my life story. You get on with the movie, and then if you can't place the book with a publisher I'll do it myself.'

'Nothing you do would ever surprise me,' Verry laughed. 'But I'm sure you're wrong about Grandpa. I think he would have sucked on one of his big fat cigars and said that eighty-five per cent of something is a lot more than a hundred per cent of nothing.'

Sara snorted down her nose, slid off the high stool she'd been sitting on and made her way to the oven. She walked slowly, her stately progress masking the stiffness that was now permanent. She'd seized up for good, and she knew it, so she wouldn't bother with the freaky exercises that were all the rage back in the States. She reckoned that being a lady meant acting like one.

'You want to get yourself some new clients,' Sara persevered. 'Just like the story, four bright young things all ready and eager to do whatever it takes. And that'll make great entertainment, Verité, watching some healthy young animals strutting their stuff. There could be all sorts of fun and games.'

'"Strutting their stuff"!' Verry laughed. 'Grandma, you have no idea how that sounds.'

'If it sounds funny to you, my girl, it's because you've picked up too many of your mother's old-world ways. When you used to come out to us every year you were a regular little American, and we just loved you for it. You had so much go . . .' Sara's voice drifted off. She could almost see them, the twelve-year-old child and her adoring grandpa, arms round each other, running through the snow. She sniffed aggressively. That was another of the mean things about growing old: your mind kept playing sneaky tricks on you.

'I really would love to have a go at it. I can't think of anything I'd rather do right now than get into a new field. And I've always been interested in films, in who's in them and why. That was inevitable, I suppose, with you and Grandpa.'

'I could write you a nice new synopsis,' Sara said eagerly, her voice a little muffled because she was peering shortsightedly into the oven. 'You could get it typed, and we'll jazz it up with a glamorous cover and some nice glossy photos inside. But you've really got to have those young people, you know. They're the key. You get them signed up in a decent contract and then start doing your stuff. You're good at getting your clients noticed – and I'm not being biased.'

Verry began pacing the floor. 'I know the story says four young unknowns, but I think it would be better a different way.' She was gesticulating with her empty cup. 'The most difficult thing is starting someone off. It's always a long shot, seeing if the press bothers or not. But if I selected people who were already quite well known, already justifying media coverage, then we could just add to that. The trick is' – she paused a moment, standing in the centre of the kitchen, her eyes fixed unseeingly on the Schreiber units ahead of her – 'to use celebs from other spheres. They mustn't be in films or TV yet, but they'll have to want to be – to want desperately to be.' She started walking again, her housecoat flapping wildly around her slender ankles.

'You know, that's a good idea. Apart from anything else, it would give those kids a reason to sign up with you, wouldn't it? If you can promise them a stab at the really big time you're going to get your deal. And make sure it's twenty per cent.'

'I think that might be a bit – '

'No,' Sara interrupted forcibly. 'You just tell them that you only get what you pay for in life. They won't appreciate you if you come cheap. Besides, you said yourself it's going to take a lot of doing. Your expenses are going to be pretty interesting.'

'I'll have to be careful, but there must be ways. The media PR bunch are pretty nifty at making impressions on the cheap.'

'Then crib a little. It never hurts to watch what your competitors are up to. So, what do you want with these muffins? Butter, jelly?' She was feeling great. At last Verité was beginning to see things her way.

Angelique didn't join them until almost lunch time, by which time the drawing room floor was strewn with Sara's manuscript.

'Drink?' Angelique asked. She had made her way straight to the sofa table and was looking down at the bottles arrayed on its polished surface. 'Sherry, Sara?'

'I would love one.' Sara sat back in her chair, rearranging the cushion behind her so that it took some of the pressure from the small of her back. 'Have we been busy here.'

'Verité, a sherry for you too?' Angelique appeared not to have noticed the chaos beneath her feet. She was wearing slate grey, a neat tweed jacket and matching culottes with toning tights and shoes, her hair drawn back in a complicated pleat fastened by tortoiseshell combs. She was still wearing tinted glasses and it was hard to read her expression.

'Verité is working on the manuscript,' Sara said unnecessarily, irritated by her daughter-in-law's manner.

'How nice for you.' Angelique sipped at her brimming glass of Tio Pepe. 'How nice for you both.'

'Mother.' There was concern in Verité's tone, and, she hoped, a warning. She was trying to prevent a scene, one that Angelique was clearly dressed for.

Angelique turned her head to catch the thin rays of sun struggling through the heavy net curtains. Her lips were pale rose, a perfect example of art helping nature, and they moved neatly, economically, as she spoke. 'How long is it since you started that book, Mother? Thirty, forty years? Yes, it must be all of forty years.'

'Forty-eight,' Sara said drily, and Angelique's head snapped round so that she could concentrate on her mother-in-law. 'I remember David commenting that I must have started right after you were born. That dates it perfectly. We must remember to use that fact, Verité, when we do our press launch. It adds a nice touch, to tie the book's conception to your mother's.'

To Verry's amazement Angelique laughed, a genuine sound of amusement. The reaction didn't faze Sara, who had long ago given up being surprised by Angelique. 'There's someone coming to view the house later on this afternoon. I'd be grateful if you would show them round, Verité – I really don't feel up to it.'

Sam had been going to pick her up after lunch. She'd have to call him. 'Of course I will.'

Sara made a face, but the other women feigned not to notice.

'Are they serious buyers, do you think?' Verry asked. It was an effort showing people round, and so far there had been no one willing, or possibly able, to pay the asking price.

'I don't know, and I certainly don't care. After all, every day I stay here I am at least warm, and have a roof over my head.'

'Stop it,' Verité burst out. 'I've said I'll sort things out. You mustn't talk like that – it's not fair.'

'Poor Verité.' Angelique stood, effortlessly unfolding her elegant legs, and Sara envied her painfully. 'You always did have the ability to fantasize. Now, if you'll excuse me, I'll leave you two to your games. You will tidy up, won't you, before these people come, just in case they are the ones?'

A whole twelve hours spent with Sam, away from Knightsbridge and the tension that emanated from Angelique – Verry felt like a new human being. 'Hi ho, hi ho,' she sang loudly, if slightly off key, 'it's off to work we go . . .'

'Do you mind?' Sam's voice was muffled by the bedclothes he'd pulled over his head. 'It's obscene to be so cheerful this early in the morning.' He didn't want their time together to be over so soon, he wanted her back in bed.

It was eight-thirty. His artistic bent refused to function before ten, so there was no need for him to get to work for ages. Verry carried on humming as she put the finishing touches to her make-up, translucent powder applied overall with a fat, soft camelhair brush and a final slick of lip gloss. She walked jauntily to the side of the bed and bent to ruffle Sam's hair.

'Stop that,' he yelped. 'There's little enough on top as it is. Don't discourage any last struggling sprouts.'

She was laughing as she made a quick breakfast – wholemeal toast and coffee, decaffeinated for Sam, the real thing, thick and aromatic, for herself. She was going to be living dangerously from now on, so she might as well hit the caffeine. They ate, as always, at the small circular pine table under the skylight in the pitched roof. A watery sunlight filtered on to the table, showing up Sam's pallor.

'Too much booze,' Verry said around a generous bite of toast. 'I thought you were giving it up.'

'Cutting down, to be exact.' Sam sniffed suspiciously at his drink. 'This isn't Bovril, is it?'

'Nope.'

'God, please don't sound so cheerful, not today.'

Sam's words were an echo of her mother's that awful day of the memorial service. 'Not today . . .' Verry felt the chill begin to take hold of her again, but she wouldn't let it, couldn't let it. She had too much to do. 'Why not today?' she asked.

'Because I have the most appalling piece of work to produce. I hate the spec, I hate the company that wants it . . .'

'But you love the money.'

'This is true.' Sam's face creased into an unwilling smile. 'And I do have to admit that they pay well. Philistines they may be but at least they're not mean with it. What's your day?'

'Today,' Verry leaned back in her chair, the bentwood curve pushing comfortably back against her shoulders, 'is the beginning of the rest of my life.'

Sam watched guardedly. He was aware of the fragile

state of her emotions, didn't want to talk her into a corner. 'And so?'

'And so I have to get a move on.' She stood up abruptly, her chair squeaking on the quarry-tiled floor. 'See you later?' She had to manage another night at the flat.

Sam nodded.

'I'll bring in supper.' A quick kiss on a bristly unshaven cheek – funny, she thought, how hair grew on Sam's face and not on his head – and she was gone.

The Production Centre was a few blocks north from Oxford Street. Verité took the tube to Bond Street and walked up. It might not give her the ego boost of hailing a cab, or a companionable chat to start the day, but it was a whole lot cheaper. There would be no money coming in from her existing clients for a year at least. She'd subbed her business to a one-time competitor. In the middle of the night she'd woken sweating at the thought of the risk she was taking, but there was no time for panic. She was well aware that for what she had in mind she would need every penny she'd got, and then some.

There was a reasonable entrance from a reasonable street. It wasn't exactly Knightsbridge, but then, she reminded herself, this was the nuts and bolts area of media production. The centre provided offices complete with receptionist and basic facilities at a reasonable rent to those involved in TV/film projects – and that could cover a multitude of sins, although the thin walls probably put paid to the casting couch. Smiling at the thought, Verité surveyed her own ten by ten space in the 'heart' of London.

The white-painted walls were dotted with Blu-Tack left by a previous occupant, looking so like old chewing gum that she couldn't bring herself to touch it. A girl was coming in that afternoon, a youngster eager to break into the glamorous world of showbiz. It wouldn't do to disappoint her too much, especially as she was prepared to work for a pittance. The receptionist supplied the whereabouts of a florist and an off-licence. No furniture so charming as flowers and bottles, Verité thought with a smile. The real quote, as she knew quite well, was books, and with that in mind she also bought a dozen glossy magazines.

A couple of giant bunches of white daisies soon glowed from the tops of the two back to back desks arranged in front of the window, while a couple of dozen assorted bottles – three Chianti, six bubbly, some red, some white – and a dozen Paris goblets filled up shelves intended for files. Verité arranged the magazines so that they fanned artistically on the low glass-topped table. All that remained to be done was a liberal spray of Christian Dior's Dune around the room. God bless the duty free, thought Verité, and gave an extra squirt for luck.

## Chapter 3

Why was it that only Paris, on a sunny spring evening, could make him feel so good? Charles drummed his fingers happily on the black leather covered steering wheel of the metallic blue Citroën XM he'd hired as soon as he'd landed at Orly. The radio was playing something by Verdi, a light frothing complexity of notes that filled his ears and submerged his senses. He was even delighted to be marooned in the centre of the inevitable 18.00 hours Champs Elysées traffic jam – it was the ideal introduction to a night *à la France*. He had caught the tune now and hummed along for a few bars.

Ahead of him, like the colossal legs of some mythical hero, the Arc de Triomphe straddled a perfect arc of pristine blue sky. At the base of the monument a zephyr breeze tugged playfully at the eternal flame, the memorial for the unknown soldier. Charles slipped the car another few feet forwards. All over the world, it seemed, *le soldat inconnu* was recognized by the same evocative phrase.

It was his father who was remembered here, on this beautiful evening, with young lovers on the boulevards, older ones dressing for the evening, dinner at Maxim's, perhaps. There was a girl behind him, driving some open-top sports car, very *à la Brigitte*, dark narrow sunglasses, a few metres of white chiffon wrapped around her hair and then tied around her slim throat; she even had the pout. He smiled in the driving mirror and she turned her profile, a neat, practised gesture showing the lift of her pert rounded chin.

*Le soldat inconnu* – what was the point of taking life

seriously, if all it got you was a spurt of flickering flame? It might not even have been in France that his father had died, although his mother had liked to think so, for, as she'd said so often, it had been Jean-Paul's home, his first love. Had he cared for the country of his birth more than for his woman? Charles had sometimes wonderered why it seemed his mother didn't mind a nation as her husband's mistress. Closer now, the Arc rose imperiously above him, demanding attention, dominating the waves of petroleum-rich air.

He could no longer see the flame. He thought ahead to his evening. Hilary was in Paris, and they were to dine together, somewhere chic and intimate. He hadn't told her that his father was a Parisian. It would, he felt, have spoiled her 'take' of him. She had him categorized as the ultimate English gentleman. The fact that he spent most of his life on board his yacht she found charmingly eccentric; anything more cosmopolitan would complicate things, and Charles liked his life uncomplicated.

The snarl up in front of him suddenly dissolved; there seemed to have been no rhyme or reason for the last few hundred yards of chaos. He glanced once more into his rear-view mirror. The girl was gone – Brigitte Bardot had accelerated away to meet her Jacques or Alain. One final glimpse of the flickering flame. How different would life have been if his father hadn't died? 'Special duties.' On bad days Charles thought that meant spy; on good ones, security. He concentrated on finding somewhere to park. Hilary would be waiting; she was always those essential couple of minutes early.

'Hilary, you look stunning.' Kiss, kiss, kiss, two for Paris, the third for being lovers on the most beautiful, most classically calm and perfect of evenings. 'I didn't tell you, did I, that my father was French?'

\* \* \*

'Something elegant.' Verry ran an appreciative eye over the magnificent cars displayed before her. 'And colourful. A good red possibly, yellow at a pinch.'

'A very feminine concept.' The pin-striped salesman smirked. Colour first, make second, price last.

The showroom was a temple to polish. More than thirty specialist vintage vehicles were on display. Every available square foot of the prestigious Park Lane showroom, with its white marble floors and plate-glass view of Hyde Park, was occupied by expensive 'wheels'.

'It has to seat four.'

Another professional smirk. 'A family car?'

'No, no children – four adults, although they don't have to sit all that comfortably. It's the look that's all-important.'

'All our cars are beautiful.' The salesman's tone had become doubtful. He'd analysed the punter's clothes – necessary to keep the riff-raff out of an exclusive show-room – and Armani was hardly downmarket. The manner was right, too, but he was a little concerned by all this emphasis on appearance.

'They certainly are. They even manage to surpass Bugsy's descriptions.' Bugsy – the salesman relaxed. Bugsy Maclone owned the business and was responsible for the idiosyncrasies of his customers. 'I think I have just the thing,' he said as he gestured to Verry to follow him.

Sara adjusted her spectacles so that they sat more securely on the bridge of her nose and said firmly, 'It's about time we got down to brass tacks, Verité.'

Her granddaughter laid aside the typewritten sheet she'd been reading. It was a page of what Sara referred to as her 'new script'.

'There is far too much fuss made, these days, about the simple project of making a movie,' Sara continued.

Verry smiled wanly. It was past eleven o'clock at night, she'd put in a full day at the office trying to get the wheels in motion and struggling to get her bimbette to function like a secretary, and she couldn't agree that anything about the film business was simple.

'I mean it.' Sara's voice rose. 'In the early days people like Selznick were starting a new film every Monday and rolling a finished one into the cinemas every Friday.'

'Today's audience is more sophisticated . . .'

'Today's audience is made up of people, just as it was then. Don't get too complicated – that's the trap they're all falling into. A simple, fast-moving plot and a competent director, that's the bottom line.'

'I'm not actually aiming to produce the film myself, Grandma. I keep telling you that.'

'And you're wrong.' Sara reached out for the glass of whisky and soda that was fortifying her well past her normal bedtime. 'Look at all the work you're putting in. You've got the script – or at least you will have pretty soon – you're working on getting the principal actors, and you've even got that Bug creature to lend you the car.'

'Bugsy, Grandma, as in Bugsy Maclone.'

'Thank you for correcting me, dear.' The sarcasm wasn't diluted by the large mouthful of drink Sara had just taken. 'But I shall always think he reminds me of a beetle – it's something about the set of his shoulders. Now, where was I?'

Verry wanted to go to bed, but felt she couldn't while her grandmother was still working. Angelique had gone upstairs hours ago; they could faintly hear the soundtrack of the black and white video she'd taken up with her. Verité began trying to distinguish the words, and when Sara spoke again it startled her.

'I'm going to start writing memos. It's what David did all the time, and it certainly didn't do him any harm. It's a good way of keeping a record, and it might just help me stop forgetting what I mean to say.'

'My father wrote memos? I don't remember that.'

'Not your father.' Sara looked momentarily flustered. 'I meant David Selznick. It was his trademark, writing memos, he did it to everyone. And they were clever. Your grandfather kept some of his for years.'

'Selznick produced *Gone with the Wind*, didn't he?' Verité asked. Her interest was roused and she felt less tired. 'How do you think he would have liked to do the sequel?'

'Gone with the Wind Two?' Sara laughed, a low, earthy sound. 'I think he would have had some pretty pertinent things to say about the casting. What a hype that was. The way he played it had us all buzzing for weeks.'

'Who would you have chosen for Scarlett?'

'Now or then? If you mean then, at the time I desperately wanted it to be Katharine Hepburn. She was – is, rather – such a fine actress. The film wouldn't have been the same, of course. Your sympathies would have been quite different, because however spoilt Katharine had acted you'd still have been on her side. I never was with Vivien. She deserved everything she got.'

'My, my.' Verry laughed. 'You certainly didn't like her. So who's today's candidate for your displeasure?'

'The best actress to play Scarlett now?' Sara paused contemplatively, then shook her head. 'It's no good asking me. I'm an old woman.'

The statement upset Verry. She had become used to her grandmother saying that age was no impediment, merely a reason for people to give you their seats in buses – except, as Verry never pointed out, Sara didn't go anywhere by bus.

'Let's get back to your movie.' Sara had no intention of letting the conversation slip away from her pet subject.

'All you have to do now is raise the money, and that's not beyond a clever girl like you.'

'Thanks for the vote of confidence, Grandma. But I've already borrowed up to the hilt.'

'So, there's no extra risk in going for more. Let's face it, if things do go wrong, you don't have a cat in hell's chance of clearing what you owe. If you're going to go for broke then at least do it in style.'

It was clear that Sara was sincere. It was only when she really wanted something that she allowed her speech to become cluttered with colloquialisms.

'It's certainly an interesting thought, but I just don't see how I could raise the money.'

'Start by lowering your budget – the real budget, I mean, not the inflated one you're going to put out to the market, the one they're going to chip away at. Do some chipping of your own to start with. Cut away the excess. There's always something. Plan to do your location shots on the cheap, *cinéma vérité* all over the place.' Sara paused, then she continued, 'I'd never thought of the link before. *Cinéma* "vérité" gives you a nice little PR latch.'

Verry stood up, came round to where her grandmother was sitting, put her arms around her shoulders and squeezed gently. 'You are a darling,' she said. There were tears in her eyes, and her throat felt tight. 'I just wish there was some way I could promise to do it, for you, for all the belief you have that I can.'

Sara stared down at the script she was working on. Her sight was blurred. She would have given anything to be twenty years younger, to be able to play a more active part, to give the help that was so badly needed. She swallowed before speaking. 'You will do it, Verité. You're like your father, a born performer. Just go out there believing in yourself and you're more than half way there.'

\* \* \*

Verry picked up her briefcase from where it lay beside her on the seat of the taxi just as, several hundred miles away, Charles Freeman leaned heavily on the polished chrome rail of *Champers* to survey the stultifying panorama of yet another Spanish luxury resort. For Verry, the door to her future opened quickly, and with a flourish, as the cab pulled to a stop and a top-hatted commissionaire saluted a greeting. It was as she stepped on to the high-gloss marble floor of the London Hilton's luxurious reception area that Charles flicked yet another half-smoked cigarette in a perfect parabola above the exotic flotsam of the harbour.

Verry gave a receptionist the names of the four visitors she was expecting over the next two days. Charles began to wonder what he would have for breakfast.

For them both, the morning had begun. For them both, there was one glittering beacon on the horizon, one Mecca drawing them onwards – Cannes, the film festival *par excellence*. It would be the chance to shine, to do fast, effective business and then shine again. It was the opportunity to become immersed in the heady mix of hacks and harlots that brought back the swingers, year in, year out, to search for the ultimate sensation.

The foyer of the London Hilton gleamed opulently. A cluster of dark-suited Japanese businessmen chattered animatedly as their pile of Louis Vuitton luggage was silently ferried past them.

'Ms Goode?' A slim, blond-haired young man rose quickly from his vantage point on an overstuffed, tapestry-covered sofa. He extended a tentative hand towards the woman he had recognized from the press coverage of her father's funeral.

'Dirk, how nice to meet you at last.' Verry squeezed the proffered hand warmly. The pop-star was even more beautiful in the flesh than on the small screen. His finely chiselled features showed off a perfect skin and he wore his dark plum Jean Paul Gaultier suit with casual grace.

'I have a conference room.' Verry allowed the words to drift over her shoulder as she strode towards a waiting lift. It was important that she stamped her own personality on the meeting. Over the next two days she had to set up the basis of the biggest business deal she had ever attempted. Fame she'd secured in plenty for writers and models, tycoons and politicians. Now she had to go for the big one, a deal that took her right to the top. PR. Her world, and she intended to use it. There hadn't been, as far as she knew, many women moguls in the film business and she thought it was about time to redress the balance.

'Cool scene.' Dirk Solo rolled the words around on his tongue. His greeting grin, that Verry correctly surmised displayed several thousand pounds' worth of orthodontics, would have sent his teenie-bopper fans into ecstasy.

Verry smiled more restrainedly. 'I'm glad you like the venue. I thought the Hilton might be a bit passé for a pop star.'

'A Hilton is never passé,' the almost impossibly handsome young singer said seriously. His face was a perfect oval, his eyes Celtic green, his ultra-blond hair swept back off an unlined brow, but his mouth, Verry was interested to note, was surprisingly firm. 'These places have a kind of unique sincerity. They're designed to be used by people who appreciate them. By that I mean they're for us Americans, and we're the nation that expects hot to be hot and cold to come complete with ice.'

Verry clapped her hands lightly. 'I didn't expect philosophy from a pop singer.'

'Don't knock the music business, lady. It's done me very well and the fact that I'm here today doesn't mean that singing isn't still my first love. But I've cut the apron strings from the good old US of A and set off on my own, and you may be just the person to help me. On the other hand, I've knocked about in business long enough to appreciate' – he softened his words by another dazzling grin – 'that it's just as likely you're not.'

'You've read the script?'

'Sure, and I appreciate what you're trying to do. I like the tie-in with your granny, and I like the fact that each of the four parts in the film balances so perfectly that there won't be any bitchiness – at least not from me. I know I can't expect to be *numero uno* straight off.'

'You're each *numero uno* in a manner of speaking. After all, there's nobody with any more clout in the film. I'm glad you liked the synopsis. It's based on experience. My grandparents knew dozens of Hollywood's best-loved stars.'

'OK, OK.' Dirk held up his hand. 'I've already swallowed the package. It's not me you have to convince, it's the money men. And that's the only thing you haven't said so far: that you've got your finance set up and ready to go.'

'If you're talking about production finance, I haven't said I've got it because I haven't.' Verry kept her voice level and the expression in her eyes serene and confident. 'All we need at this stage of the project is development money, and that's all taken care of.' Sara writing the script, Sam coming up with a few grand against Verry's equity in their car, plus – the most important ingredient – the overdraft at the bank. It was too late to regret the fact that she'd always lived up to the hilt, and the cash she'd got together was as good as – probably better than – most of the other kites being flown out there.

'I reckon you must know if you can afford it or not. You'd be a mug to sign me up for something you can't provide, and you don't look like a mug to me.'

'Thanks for the compliment,' Verry said dryly. 'The deal, as you know, is half reasonable expenses plus fifty per cent of everything I bring in for you on the film side over the next three years, against your salary. I assume you've had someone go through the contract?'

Dirk nodded, and a lock of shining hair fell forward over his eyes. 'Naff haircut,' he muttered. 'That's the first thing I'm going to change.'

'Not too much.' Verité frowned. 'You don't want a new image, just a new slant.'

'Sure, boss lady. Anything you say. And I'd love to spend all day listening, but you know how it is. I've got this pad to look over. I'm just dying to spend some of my ill-gotten gains.' He reached inside his jacket pocket and pulled out an envelope. 'It's all in here, signed, sealed and delivered.'

A warm flush of delight spread up Verité's throat and she was relieved she'd worn a polo-necked blouse. She didn't want her first signing to think he'd pulled his agent.

'Fleur Montford to see you.' The immaculately coiffed receptionist appeared briefly to make her announcement before disappearing back to her desk in the corridor.

The Hilton's system was working perfectly and Verité felt calm and at ease as her next potential client, the model who had launched an entire beauty range with her distinctively English style, came into the boardroom.

'Do come in and sit down,' Verry said. 'Would you like some coffee?' She was surprised at the girl's presentation; less than low-key, it was practically non-existent. The black leggings worn with black tunic and wrap-around dark glasses were *de rigueur* for fashion models between shoots, but the beaten up green hunter jacket and scuffed brown jodhpur boots made her look as if she'd hitchhiked up from the country. Even the perfect, translucent skin stretched over immaculate cheekbones didn't relieve the impression of the farmyard.

'A glass of water would be nice.' The girl's voice was low, beautifully modulated; another surprise to go with the clothes. 'Was there some reason we didn't meet at your office?'

Verry poured iced water from the vacuum jug and kept her back turned to her visitor as she replied. 'I like to meet prospective clients on neutral ground.' It was as well she had, this time, she thought, because so far the model wasn't making a good impression.

'I just wondered.' Fleur took the proffered glass and sat gazing down into it, slumped in the chair with her long slender legs stretched out in front of her. 'I'd like to be able to do that, to just abandon all the usual day-to-day stuff and take off to somewhere different. I think that's why your offer attracted me.'

'Think? You mean you're not sure why you came to this meeting?'

'I know why I came – I came to find some reason for getting up in the morning.'

'I'm sorry, Fleur, but you've lost me. You sound as if you have nothing else to do with your time, but you're a successful model, you're highly paid . . .'

'And shatteringly bored. Have you any idea what a pain it all is? I'm trotted halfway up a volcano for a photo-shoot in front of several million gallons of boiling lava. Can you tell me why that should make the girl on the street buy BO-basher that smells of roses?'

'It's about image, isn't it? It's glamour . . .'

'I know all that.' The words were tumbling out now. 'And I know it makes lovely, glossy pics. I just don't see why it has to be *me*. The early stuff was different – all terribly, terribly English. I could understand that; after all, it's what I am, so I was just able to go on being me. Then suddenly I was meant to be a *femme fatale* and go along with all that kind of crap.'

Verry raised an eyebrow at the expletive but thought she was beginning to understand the outlandish clothes. They were a statement of identity. 'If you go into films you'll be pretending all the time.'

'But that's all right.' Fleur stood up abruptly and pulled off her jacket. 'Because then I shall actually be being different, I'll have a part to play.' She paused a moment and then laughed. 'A part to play. That's good, isn't it? You have to understand – what I'm doing now is about someone else going through the motions. I contribute no more life to it than a blow-up doll, and I probably get a lot less fun out of it than the doll would. That last bit's tacky, but you must get the idea.'

'It sounds as if my offer must have come at just the right time.'

'Just "in" time.' Fleur pulled off her dark glasses. Her periwinkle eyes were widely spaced, her gaze clear and honest. 'I think I was about to go off at half cock. And since the Fleur range is produced by my cousin's firm I could never let rip about what I really felt. Volcanoes! I ask you.'

Verry smiled. The girl had a directness that she appreciated. 'Was it very hot?'

'Hot? It was absolutely scorching, I was terrified, and this complete dumbbrain of a photographer kept saying, "Just another step back, dearie, just another one." I could smell my hair singeing. As you said, your offer came just at the right time. I'd love to have a crack at getting into films and I'll do anything it takes.'

'Except balancing on the edge of live volcanoes?'

'I might even do that, for a good bit of dialogue, and as

long as the script has some birdbrained photographer who just happens to slip.'

'But what exactly *is* a collateral warranty?' Verry asked. It looked as if their precious evening together was going to be fraught.

Sam had rushed into their flat muttering the words like a mantra. With his hair awry, his rain-splattered Burberry unbuttoned and flying back from his shoulders, she thought, affectionately, that he looked like an agitated beige bat.

'Don't ask, just don't ask.' Sam collapsed into his 'thinking chair', the black leather chaise-longue on the sculptured chrome frame. He stared distractedly up at the ceiling and said very loudly, each word clipped and distinct, 'God give me strength.'

Verry put the kettle on and began getting the ingredients together for Sam's favourite reviver after a hard day at the office. She had sliced an unwaxed lemon and taken the honey jar from the cupboard before Sam became, once more, aware of his surroundings.

'Don't bother about the hot toddy,' he said. 'Just bring me the whisky bottle.'

Without a word Verité did as she was asked. She also brought two glasses and the soda siphon.

'I am in serious shit,' Sam announced to his glass as he began to down its contents.

'Because?' Verry was kneeling beside Sam and had begun to take off his shoes. They were soaking wet, as were the bottoms of his trousers.

'What would I do without you?' Sam reached out and laid his hand gently on Verry's hair.

'Take your own shoes off?' She smiled. 'Come on, it can't be as bad as all that. Have a hot bath . . .'

'What's the time?' Sam jumped off his seat and peered down at his watch. 'Quick, turn the box on. Jesus, I bet I've missed it already.'

It took them several frantic seconds to find the remote control that for some inexplicable reason had found its way to the breakfast bar.

'BBC 1, quick,' Sam shouted down at the black plastic box when at last he held it in his hand.

He glanced up at the television as a picture of a football pitch took shape. He pressed another button, and a news presenter was earnestly talking straight at them. There was no sound. Verité snatched the control and pointed it at the screen.

The television burst into full life. '. . . Mid Park tenants' action committee is even now trying to raise sufficient funds to take the matter to court.' A meaningful pause. 'And now over to Julie.'

'I have missed it. God damn!' Sam smashed his glass down on the floor and Verry stepped back quickly to avoid the flying glass.

'Sam, for goodness' sake calm down.'

'Or what, or bloody what? All these years, all this hard work – I can't bear it. My reputation is going to stink, and the poor bastards whose flats are falling down round their ears aren't going to get a penny piece. Ask me again what a collateral warranty is. I'll tell you. It's what my bloody ex-employers should have taken out: an insurance policy that would have covered them and me.' He started pulling at his tie, unbuttoning his shirt.

'Skyline, you mean?'

'Yeah, Skyline.' Sam was now ripping off his socks, dropping them on to the floor beside him. 'Bloody cheapskates. That's why I left them. Always cutting corners.'

'It's to do with the Mid Park development?' Verry

followed Sam as he stalked towards the bathroom. He was unbuttoning his trousers as he went and she was picking up the trail of clothes.

'Why did it have to happen now?' The shower was running hard. Sam had turned on only the cold water, and he stepped quickly under the deluge and began stamping about. 'I'm so close to the Dutch project, so damned close.' He adjusted the temperature control, allowing himself a touch of warm, before rubbing hard at his face and the muscles at the base of his neck.

Wordlessly Verry pushed up the sleeves of her jumper, squeezed some liquid soap on to the palms of her hands, and started massaging Sam's back.

'If only I hadn't made such a thing of it. It probably wasn't even necessary for my presentation to go in heavy on Mid Park, but I'd still got the model showing all the innovation, the clean-cut lines, the sparseness of structural detail. I paid a lot to get that model done – it was what persuaded Skyline to go for it. And it's not my design that's at fault.' He turned towards Verité and she began soaping his chest. 'The fault's somewhere in the concrete. If only they'd taken out the warranty it could all have been dealt with at reasonable speed. Just because they didn't and the tenants are out on a limb some journalist started calling for an investigation. Now everybody's going to lose out on this one.'

'Arms up,' Verry instructed.

Sam stood with his arms above his head as she soaped him. He had his eyes closed and after a while began opening and closing his mouth. 'Goldfish impersonation,' he announced.

Verité could feel his shoulders relaxing under her soapy hands.

'Like to come in here with me?' he asked hopefully.

'No way.'

'Spoilsport. You might as well pass me a towel, then.'

'Is it really that bad?'

'Worse.' Sam knotted the towel round his waist and stepped out on to the cork bathmat. 'I was so keen to get all the kudos going on that design; the press won't have forgotten. I'm going to carry the can, and it's going to be full of something very smelly.'

'The people in Holland might not even get to hear of the problem . . .'

'They called my office. Someone's been in contact with them already, a journalist from *The Economist* wanting to know if they were happy to go ahead with my design "all things considered". Of course, what he really meant was, "Whoopee! You load of cheese-eaters won't have heard anything yet, so I'm going to get the first quotable quote about bigmouth Sam Cairns coming unstuck." I should never have made that speech at the architects' dinner. It made me into a duck in a shooting gallery.'

Verry didn't know what to say. So far Sam had orchestrated his career to perfection. A modernist pure and simple, he had become something of a contentious figure at a time when press sympathies lay with the Prince Charles school of architecture. Meanwhile, he had developed his own following. The open, airy interiors he created from glass, steel and reinforced concrete were warm and economical, and until now had proved longlasting. 'There's only one thing that's going to make you feel any better,' she said softly.

He threw himself on the bed and lay back, the towel unravelling. 'Come on, then,' he said. 'Spoil me.'

With the two signed contracts from the day before safely in her Hermès briefcase, Verry allowed herself a light lunch before embarking on what she hoped would be her last day at the hotel. She ordered smoked salmon – no brown bread, no temptation. She hoped her stomach wouldn't rumble through the afternoon; it was ethereally hushed in her temporary sanctum, thanks to wall-to-wall Wilton and a profusion of wood panelling.

Jesse Standing appeared promptly at two. Six foot one, well muscled, and with a glow of health under his smooth, ruddy skin, he looked exactly what he was – a successful middleweight boxer in his mid-twenties. He had fought his way up to where he was making money, and where he had the time and space to think about his future. The commentators always said he had 'it', he told Verité jauntily, and he wanted to spread 'it' around. He thought the best way of getting paid to do that was to hit the big silver screen. He was grinning as he signed with Verry's gold pen.

With a spare few minutes before her last appointment, Verry telephoned home and spoke to her grandmother. She confirmed Angelique was resting, watching another old film on the video, sipping the inevitable ice-cold dry martini.

Three thirty arrived, and Verité had everything ready. Slowly, her watch recorded the passing of three forty, ten to four. By five past four she had started thinking through her second-string list of prospects.

Shakira Keenes arrived exactly one hour late. She swept in on a cloud of Yves St Laurent's Opium. Her olive skin glowed, her dark hair swept in a sculptured curve on to her immaculately made-up cheek. She had a cold, she said huskily, and, surprised by the total lack of apology for unpunctuality, Verry found herself offering consolation instead of receiving it. Shakira was friend and confidante of the rich and famous, and the aura of scandal that surrounded her final signing, Verry hoped, would give added spice to her 'pitch'.

* * *

It was done.

Signing a contract with 'Goode as Golde' had committed each of the four to parting with fifty per cent of their film earnings for the next three years, dropping to thirty-five per cent after that time, or when individual earnings topped £500,000, whichever was the sooner.

In return they were each guaranteed a salary of £50,000 p.a. plus half approved expenses.

Now there really was no time to spare.

## Chapter 4

Angelique reached slowly forwards and laid her fingers on the full-length bathroom mirror; it was cold to her touch. The atmosphere in the minute room was dense with steam from her leisurely shower but the mirror was bright and clear. That would be Sara's doing. She was so – Angelique searched for the right word and smiled when she found it – her mother-in-law was so *capable*. There must be some amazing, miracle invention that Sara had contrived to apply to prevent the mirror steaming up. Angelique continued to survey her naked reflection. All in all, despite the acute thinness that she sought for and achieved, she would rather have faced her image mist-shrouded.

There were two bathrooms in the Chelsea cottage, one on the first and one on the second floor. Both were tiny but cleverly planned, fitted with classic white units, white tiles and gold taps. Angelique had the top floor, and in hers she used the dark maroon towels from the Knightsbridge house. The effect was luxurious despite the bijou size of the room.

Angelique walked through to her bedroom, still naked, her dark hair hanging in strings over her shoulders. It would be almost too much of an effort, she thought, to decide what to wear. The doors of the fitted cupboards that faced her filled one wall. They had been covered in fabric that matched her curtains, which in turn matched the wallpaper. If she could have summoned the energy, she thought, she would have had a dressing-gown made of the same fabric. Then she could have disappeared entirely. Deliberately she had kept her furniture to a minimum. There was some satisfaction to be obtained, she had discovered, from feeling a martyr. The bedroom was soulless, the production of the yuppie turned interior designer employed by a property company trying to keep afloat by churning out what they believed were mini-versions of the stylish establishments their clients had left behind. One thing Angelique did find comforting was the fact that she wasn't alone in her reduced state. Thanks to the past few years of recession the entire street seemed to be populated by those who'd known headier times – witness the number of big Volvos parked outside.

By nine o'clock, bathed and breakfasted, Sara had taken over the drawing room. Her manuscript was spread about in piles. Those on the circular Georgian table occupying the centre of the floor were chapters about her early memories. Hollywood as it was fabled, the stars of the silent screen in and out of her parents' home – and beds if memories other than her own were to be believed. Surprising herself, the older Sara got the more she hoped that what she had once thought of as libel was true. Her parents had been happy, and stayed together until the end. It was nice to think they'd enjoyed a sexual freedom Sara had never allowed herself, except for . . .

She pulled her thoughts together quickly. It wouldn't do to let herself drift off again. There was so much work to be done. The script for Verité had to be perfect, and there was something she'd written, a part of her youth, that she was determined to find and let Verité consider. It wasn't yet in *Viva Europa*, but it was a good idea, and just right for today.

It took two hours to find. Holding the typewritten sheets close to her eyes, she studied the words. It was just as she'd remembered, taking her back to the house near the beach, the rough dirt road leading to the half-dozen weekend homes of the Hollywood greats.

In her memory she travelled past the first – Mae West's, scene of those unending parties that spilled over from one day to the next – then past the second, and at last she reached her destination. The pages lay limp in her hand; she didn't need to read any more. Turning into the house, parking in front of the garage block. She was young again, in a print dress, pink roses on white, her hair tied back in a pink ribbon. 'Sugar Candy Baby' her beau had called her. She was eighteen, and he wasn't much older. His father was a projectionist, supporting a wife and five kids on the edge of poverty. But Billy was going to be different. Billy, their eldest son, had been to college; he was going somewhere. He had a driving ambition: he wanted to direct, to produce, to make his own movies, and they all thought he would. For a moment the present-day Sara, with the accumulated knowledge of her years, saw through sweet Billy. He had courted her because she was the boss's daughter; her father employed his father. Her father could make – or break – a young producer setting out on his own. She'd been too much in love to understand that at the time and then after Billy died so tragically it hadn't seemed right to question his motives. The spell was broken. She sighed, a quavering, tired expelling of air, and laid the papers down. She would make a hot drink to fortify herself before reading the words she'd written over half a century ago, when she'd been a different person.

'Angelique?' she called out as she crossed the hall to the kitchen. 'Would you like some tea?'

'I'm just going out.' Angelique appeared at the head of the short flight of stairs. She was wearing tight-fitting black leggings with a voluminous jumper, and her hair was tied up in a pink silk tie-and-dye scarf. Over her shoulder she carried an African woven basket.

It was so unlike her daughter-in-law's usual ultra-sophistication that Sara was surprised out of her normal equanimity to ask, 'Where on earth are you going dressed like that?'

'Dear Sara.' Angelique almost ran down the stairs. Her white trainers were trimmed to match her scarf. 'We're living in Bohemia now, you know. In our little garret. And I've nothing to do, I'm likely to die of boredom, so I thought I'd become an artist. I used to paint – well, of course, you know I did.'

There was a short, awkward silence as both women remembered the villa in the south of France, and the young man who'd visited, the holiday tutor. For once David had been annoyed with his beloved wife. There had been arguments about the modelling, Angelique posing for the painter, then he for her. And the villa littered with their efforts, depictions of naked flesh propped against the walls, a scandalized maid. Sara had been staying with them while her husband did some business in Paris. She had been in turns amused and bemused, and then finally furious when she'd found the two, naked as had become their habit, but not painting – certainly not painting.

'And where exactly will you have your studio?' she asked dryly now. 'After all, you're the one who keeps saying how small this house is.'

Angelique felt her hard-won good mood fade in an instant. 'You should talk. Look at the mess in there. You've had that damned rubbish spread about ever since we moved in. Look at it! Tatty old sheets that should have been thrown out years ago!' She strode into the room and kicked at the orderly piles, and the typewritten pages, like autumn leaves, began to float. There was a sharp tearing sound as she scuffed her foot over the tallest pile of all.

'Stop that! Stop at once!' Sara was appalled. 'How dare you?'

Angelique was in her element now. She moved in a flurry of staccato movements, her legs stretched and supple, dancing nimbly between the furniture as the papers flew higher and higher.

Sara was gasping, anger making her short of breath. She clutched at her chest as she stooped, trying to rescue as many precious pages as she could. A red mist floated into her vision and she felt sick, until suddenly Angelique came close to her and with the strength of desperation she caught the destructive dancer, holding fast the arms that were still struggling to rise and whirl.

They hadn't heard the door open, or even Verry's sharp intake of breath as she surveyed the chaos. It was Sam who acted, walking over to the two women locked in their strange embrace, separating them, pushing them into chairs. He began to pick up some of the papers, his face hard. Verry bent to help him but he stopped her abruptly.

'No. This is one mess you won't clear up. Go up and get changed; have a bath.'

'I'll make some tea.' Verry turned away. She was so tired she could cry. She'd just got back from France, where she'd been up until two in the morning trying to get some kind of deal going with the satellite TV people. Sam had been waiting for her at Heathrow, with a lecture about how she should return to living with him. He'd talked all the way back in the taxi: how Angelique was a leech, how she'd never make a life for herself if she didn't need to because Verry was providing one for her. And how Sara was suffering, too; that had been the worst bit. He'd said Sara was looking older, frailer, from living with Angelique's tantrums. Verry had rebelled at that and said that Sara wanted them to be together, it had been her idea, and she was loving working on the film project. It had given her a purpose, a new lease of life.

And they had come home to this.

Verry spooned tea into the pot, laid a tray with cups and saucers, milk and sugar. The kettle boiled busily for a few seconds, then it clicked off, and sat there waiting. She simply didn't have the energy. There would be a grand scene and she just couldn't face it. She pulled her jacket a little more tightly around her, rubbed the backs of her hands over her eyes, and then walked out, into the hallway, out of the front door and on to the street.

'So.' Salim Abu Dann waved an immaculately manicured hand to encompass the Mercedes limousine in which he rode, the elegant Belgravia apartment he had just left, and his destination, a private Cessna jet waiting at Heathrow. 'How do you like my world, Shakira?'

'Like?' Shakira laughed, a low, liquid sound that she had worked hard to perfect. 'I love your world, Salim. I really feel it's where I belong.'

The Arab smiled and it lifted folds of fat at the corners of his mouth so that his eyes became even more deepset. The girl was hooked and he was satisfied. It would be interesting to see how she reacted from now on. He didn't think she had misinterpreted his manoeuvres. He had, occasionally, been wrong before, and there had been scenes, tantrums even, from several of the young society girls he had trawled into his net. But he thought this one knew the score.

Salim's plane was sleek. Long and low, it was a shark amongst whales emblazoned with crude commercial insignia. A man Shakira took for a steward stood at the head of the short flight of gleaming white steps, ready to see them aboard. A well-cut navy blue suit enhanced his slender physique and olive skin, and she wondered what other duties he performed for his employer. After last night she doubted that Salim's tastes would hesitate to cross the gender divide.

'We have another guest joining us,' Salim said as he advanced ahead of her into the plane's luxurious interior. The sound of their footsteps was absorbed by the thick-pile carpet, and all outside noise had been cut off the moment they'd entered the main cabin. 'In the meantime, Bruno will bring us some champagne.'

It was Dom Pérignon, served cool, in thin crystal flutes. Shakira settled herself on a blue velvet-covered sofa. The cabin's decor was opulent in texture but restrained in colour: more navy and white. She was pleased she was wearing scarlet.

'To you.' Salim raised his glass. 'And your beauty.'

Shakira imitated his gesture, her red nails glistening against the ice-coloured glass stem. 'And to you.' She paused for a second to sip at the chilled liquid and then, staring all the time into those black, unfathomable eyes, she took her calculated risk and added, 'And your money.'

The Arab exploded. Champagne spurted from between his pursed lips as he began to choke, but the sound turned quickly to laughter. It was genuine amusement – the first unguarded emotion Shakira had seen him display. 'I knew,' he spluttered, 'I knew I was right. You understand the game. We shall go a long way together, you and I.'

A low buzzer sounded, followed by a respectful voice announcing the imminent arrival of the final passenger. Shakira laid her glass down on a perspex-topped table and reached for her handbag. It was time to check her lipstick.

'He is important to me, this one,' Salim said as he stood. 'I will make it worth your while.'

Shakira nodded. She studied her reflection in the tiny glass held in the palm of her hand. There was a moment of unease, a fleeting sensation of nausea, but it passed as she breathed in deeply and then slowly exhaled. She'd made her own way so far and she was going a lot further. Everything in life had a price, and she was prepared to pay for what she wanted. She was glowing as the thickset Italian entered the cabin.

Dirk sat in the plush cinema foyer, disconsolately sipping a Diet Coke. Why did these 'Meet your idol' competitions always get won by some dimbo chick aged fourteen? Still, it was part of the job, and he did as the kid requested and pulled out his Swiss Army penknife. The one he always carried, the one he'd used in New York to frighten off a gang of would-be muggers – two down-and-outs to be exact, but it had given the press a field day.

'Is that why they call you Dirk?' Wide-awake blue eyes expertly made-up, a rosebud pink mouth so perfect that if she'd been any older he'd have suspected collagen implants. Baby blonde hair and that heady scent of hero-worship. She was a fan.

He wasn't going to give her the reply she wanted about his name, the one she was bound to have read in some tabloid. What she was after was a repeat of the response he'd made to Claudia Cardinale. Dirk reckoned the film star should have known better than to ask the question. His reply – inspired by too much booze and too close proximity to the seriously famous – had been that it was because his prick was so pointed and lethal. She'd said she had already assumed it was something to do with his implement and simply wondered if it had been some reference to speed. The whole table at Del Monico's had fallen about laughing.

Dirk signed the proffered photo, supplied by the magazine's publicity department. It was the one his ex-agent had been so proud of, his hair so pale it seemed white in the 1930s-style shot. In profile, he looked moody; soulful, she'd said. He sipped the fizzy drink he'd ordered to keep the kid company and tried not to think about his ex-agent or how she'd developed his image.

Christ, he could still blush at the memory of her first go at bleaching his hair. They'd been in some tacky bedroom in a backstreet hotel in Memphis. In those days he'd been the lead singer with the Grapes. What a bunch! That had been another joke. Anne-Margaret had dyed his hair, going through what felt like twenty different colours – 'tones' she'd called them in her inimitable backwoods accent. He hadn't wanted to change the colour of his hair – brown was fine. He thought he looked a bit like Duane Eddy. But she was pushy. It made her seem much older than he was, although they'd both been nineteen when they'd first met.

The kid was talking about her friends at school, how they'd envy her for meeting the real Dirk, in person.

He could summon up Anne-Margaret's face any time he wanted to. The round cheeks; the short, thin nose that flared disdainfully at the end; the narrow mouth, so expressive when she was angry; grey eyes like a cat's, that changed colour with her mood. Just before she'd got him his first record deal she'd cut off her shoulder-length black hair and shaved her head, because she'd reckoned it made more of an initial impression, him with his shock of stand-up platinum and her with none at all. There wasn't anything she wouldn't do to further his career, as long as he sang the way she wanted – heavy metal with a touch of heart, she called it. Even the smell turned her on, sweat and leather overlaid with lager. He'd had to drink can after can of the stuff to replace the rivulets that poured down the inside of his skin-tight trousers.

He shivered at the memories and the fan giggled, thinking it was the ice cubes in his drink.

Finally a better class of teeny bopper had been clever enough to drive a wedge between him and Anne-Margaret. That gap had exploded into a rift when he'd gone to Sweden. It was a two-week holiday before the start of his first decent foreign tour – Europe on marginally more than a shoestring. To celebrate he'd hit Nordic crumpet like there was no tomorrow and Anne-Margaret, afire with all she'd achieved for her protégé, had given him an ultimatum. He was to drop the Abba lookalikes, stop messing around with catchy, swinging numbers played on a piano and get back to the fundamentals. Rock meant rock in Anne-Margaret's book, hard lumpy bits and all.

The fan went off with the woman from the mag. She kissed him goodbye, full on the mouth. He could taste her toothpaste.

The European tour had been a disaster. He'd ended up so drunk on some Scandinavian ferry that he'd slipped on the car deck and broken his leg. And that had been the turning point. He'd gone into black denim, slashed up to his boxer shorts on the leg with the plaster cast. Surprising himself, he'd kept his hair blond; it seemed part of him now. He'd balanced himself on a tall stool, tucked a guitar under his arm, and let himself go. It jelled. There was no rhyme, no reason, but the paying public loved it. The surgeons kept him in plaster for five months, his new record company for another three. That Christmas Anne-Margaret sent him a card, inside which she'd written, 'Congratulations on the most effective hard-on in the business.' He hadn't laughed. He still didn't think it was funny.

Charles bit hard into the wilting stalk of celery he held contemptuously in his fingers. He was angry; he was starving hungry; and he was bored. He did not enjoy poetry.

'The wind, felt upon the senses of the sky . . .' The voice droned on as yet another 'volunteer' aired his meaningless, rhymeless drivel. Beside him, Hilary stood apparently entranced.

'The wind . . .' Much more celery, Charles thought, and the wind would be audible.

Around them a hushed gathering of middle-class, middle-aged middle managers nibbled meaningfully at a profusion of green and white stalks, and sipped occasionally at chunky glasses containing khaki-coloured puréed vegetables.

It was a 'cleansing'. A 'meeting of those interested in preserving a calm and tranquil mind in a sea of chaos'. The words revolved around Charles's head, memorized from the handouts sprinkled liberally around the Blackheath flat.

Hilary had unexpected sides to her character, he was deciding. He could not see at all where the current evening's activities fitted in with her globe-trotting, money-making lifestyle.

It was approaching midnight as they drove away across the Heath. A blue-white light flashed intermittently in the distance, warning low-flying aircraft of the bulk of Canary Wharf. Charles found it comforting. It made him think of airports, warm places, good food.

'What did you think?' Hilary was sitting back in the passenger seat, her eyes closed, her face relaxed. 'Tell me honestly.'

Charles laughed shortly, a bark of sound. 'I couldn't even begin. Where the hell am I going to get something to eat?'

'Does big boy fancy a Big Mac, then?'

'A big anything, with chips and tomato sauce.' Charles broke into a groan. He was so hungry he was in pain, and he wanted a drink. But the streets were deserted, the neon lights dimmed.

'Never mind, my darling.' Hilary reached out and caressed his thigh. 'Aim for home. I've got something hot that just can't wait for you.'

He was very close, he knew, to blowing it entirely. He was fond of her, and they did have a very good working arrangement developing, but one more reference to sex when he was suffering and he'd tell her to piss off.

'Mummy has just what you want,' Hilary breathed.

'Look!' He slammed his foot on the brake and turned to face her, red in the face, veins standing out like cords on his neck.

Hilary laughed out loud. 'Mummy has bacon, fried eggs and hash browns that just can't wait . . .'

Verry took the brightly covered synopsis out of her briefcase. Carl Thomson, Managing Director of Funda Europa, adjusted his tortoiseshell-framed glasses more firmly on the bridge of his nose and watched his visitor's neat fingers at work. He liked a woman who was efficient.

'*Viva Europa*.' Verry laid the brochure down on the huge desk with a flourish.

Thomson's office was impressive. It had been planned that way. From the cream carpet, buttermilk walls and dark teak desk to the original oil paintings it combined New World money with Old World taste, and that suited exactly Funda's function in the marketplace: gathering in investments from the USA and channelling them into a multitude of European ventures.

'You are aware that we haven't funded a film project before,' Thomson said in his low, modulated, cosmopolitan accent.

'Your assistant made that quite clear, Mr Thomson. But he also said that you were always willing to listen to a well-prepared proposal.'

'That's true.' The financier reached forward and picked up the brochure, weighing its twenty pages in his hands as if that would help him assess its value. 'So tell me, what makes this different from all the other thousands of scripts going the rounds?'

Verry smiled. 'For a start, this project isn't "going the rounds", as you put it. You are the first funding source we've approached . . .'

Thomson interrupted smoothly, 'So it's early days, and we're the first.'

'It would be nice to discover we could do business together and you were also the last.' Verry laughed lightly. 'I think you'll appreciate the market research. There are figures on the public's interest in Europe . . .'

'You will have found your British pro-Common Market lobby useful there.'

Verité thought quickly. Thomson was obviously given to interrupting, and she didn't want it to break her flow and make her forget to make some important points. It was just as well, she realized, that she'd brought a spare copy of the proposal with her. She pulled it out of her case. 'Perhaps it would help if we went through this together?'

The meeting took exactly an hour; both of them were practised at keeping to a busy schedule. It ended with the financier seeing her to the door, where he shook hands warmly and thanked her for her professionalism. He said that he would study the proposal at length, and put it around a few of his people to get a kickback on content. He finished by saying that their business ethos made it very unlikely that they would fund the entire project themselves, and she would be well advised to seek some other parties interested in joint ventures.

Verry stepped out on to the Brussels street on a definite high. Everything had gone beautifully. He'd kept the extra copy of the synopsis to canvass his second opinions. As for co-funding, she'd expected that. She felt really great. The tempting smell of chocolate, the magical velvety mixture of vanilla and cocoa, wafted from a glossy confectioner's just ahead of her. She walked in quickly before her conscience could change her mind. She deserved a reward.

Verry tugged at Shakira's jacket, vainly trying to make her sit down. She was embarrassed by her companion's shouting, although she needn't have been because almost everyone in the crowded sports hall was doing the same.

'But I just love it, Verité.' Shakira laughed.

Around the two young women the fight fans were going wild. A few rows ahead of them the boxing ring was swarming with bouncers, cameramen and officials. Somewhere, hidden in the mêlée, were the two bantam-weight boxers who had just had the capacity crowd raising the roof.

Verry could have groaned with exasperation, but she didn't bother. Shakira, still on her feet cheering like the rest, wouldn't have heard.

'Ladies and gentlemen, please return to your seats . . .' a red-faced, evening-suited master of ceremonies bellowed into his microphone, but nothing was going to quell the enthusiasm until the two fighters left the ring, and it looked as though the crush of admirers was going to slow that process down considerably.

Verry pulled again at Shakira's jacket. Powder-pink Chanel trimmed with the inevitable black and garnished with gilt buttons, it was hardly, Verry thought, the usual run of fight fan's gear. 'Shakira, for heaven's sake calm down.'

'You must have enjoyed it too.' Shakira was flushed as she flopped down on to her seat. 'That was manic. I'm so thirsty, I think I must have sweated pints.'

'Just don't even say the word sweat,' Verry pleaded.

'My clothes are going to reek when I get out of here. This place smells.'

'I know.' Shakira leaned back, stretching her legs out as far as they could go in the cramped row. 'And it's a brilliant smell – blood, sweat and tears all mixed up with ambition. I can't wait for the next bout.'

The crowd around the ring was clearing slowly. A moving swarm, like bees around their queen, clustered around what were presumably the boxers heading back to their dressing-rooms.

Verry would also have liked a drink, something long and cool, but she didn't want Shakira wandering among the crowd. She had no idea what the girl might get up to.

The whole point of the evening had been to get the feel of the event so that when Jesse next fought Shakira would be able to play her part: the agonized girlfriend squirming unhappily in the front row. Unfortunately, it was now apparent that left to her own devices Shakira would, on the contrary, be the ultimate fight fan screaming for blood. The way she'd looked when the referee had stopped the fight had been murderous. Verité thought Shakira's only saving grace was the fact that she'd been cheering the underdog.

The last bout was a disappointment to everyone. It lasted under a round, and the boxer who ended up lying on the canvas for the count of ten seemed to have slipped over more than been knocked down. It lived up to everything Verité had suspected about fixed fights, and judging by the catcalls around her her opinion was shared by the majority.

They pushed their way into the good-natured, slow-moving queue clogging the aisle as the lights over the ring behind them dimmed. Jesse had promised he would be waiting for them outside. On their gradual progress towards the exit Shakira started chatting to a couple of young men. Smartly dressed in dark grey business suits, wearing flamboyant designer silk ties and chunky gold bracelets, they were apparently regular boxing followers, recognizing Jesse and teasing him about his two glamorous girlfriends.

Verry was pleased. It showed how well the Shakira/Jesse partnership was going to work.

'This really happened?' Shakira sat on the edge of her chair, leaning forwards, her eyes fixed on Sara's face. 'It's not just something you made up?'

'Even if it was – and I promise you it's not – you still have to agree it's a good idea for the film,' Sara replied.

'Verité doesn't think so.' Shakira pinched a strand of her dark hair between a finger and thumb, and began twisting it round and round. 'But I think you're right, and it would make a great scene. It's such a good concept, and so visual.'

Sara watched her visitor with affection. She was a strange girl, obviously as promiscuous as a cat but still very sweet, and apparently happy to spend time with an old woman. This was her third visit in a fortnight. Sara spoke her thoughts out loud. 'It does me good to talk to you.'

'That's because I'm not family. You have to love Verité and Angelique because they're so closely related to you, and you do love them even if sometimes they're hard to get on with. Me, on the other hand, you can take or leave. It's often easier that way.'

Sara sipped her tea. 'Is that how you feel about men, Shakira? That it's safer not to fall in love with them?'

Shakira nodded her head emphatically. 'Love is dangerous for a woman. It puts her at a disadvantage, makes her vulnerable. I've been there, I should know.'

Sara waited to see if she wanted to say more, but when

Shakira did speak it was to return to their earlier conversation.

'Do you think that apartment you wrote about was unique in Hollywood circles?'

'I wouldn't be so naive. There were love nests all over the place. There was more sex going on there than movie making, and I can tell you, they made thousands of movies.' Sara chuckled, pleased with herself. 'No, there was a thriving trade in pornography, and I'm sure a lot of it ended up framed and hanging on walls. Just the thing to provide the necessary titillation for an executive tired from a day on the lot and looking forward to a few hours' pleasure with his latest starlet.'

'But your apartment had the works . . .'

'Not *my* apartment, Shakira,' Sara laughed. 'I just visited it the once, when I was very young. The difference was the standard of the stuff there. It was all fine art, real masterpieces. Thousands and thousands of dollars' worth of paintings hanging on the walls, stunning marble statues in the corners – it was like a museum. I think that's why I wasn't disgusted. I mean, at that age I could very easily have taken fright and run. But it was all so beautiful. You had to look closely to appreciate the technique, and then of course you appreciated exactly what technique you were admiring. I did run in the end; my boyfriend Billy drove me home. But I took a pretty good impression away in my mind.'

Shakira looked thoughtful as she asked, 'Would it be possible to bring that out in our film? The quality of the art?'

'That's what bothers Verité. She says it would just look tacky, and that's not the kind of film she wants to make.' Sara felt a sudden pang of conscience. She was sounding disloyal. 'She's right, of course. We never set out to go for an X certificate. This is a fun film, genuine entertainment, but I still don't think that's a reason not to hint at what was going on, as a pointer to the producer's character.'

'It's such a good idea.' Shakira's voice was soft, almost caressing.

'You're not to think about going out and setting up somewhere like that yourself, Shakira.' Sara laughed uneasily. 'It could get you into all sorts of trouble, and I wouldn't like to think I'd been responsible.'

'I don't think it would get me into trouble. Handled correctly, I think it could get me into all sorts of success.'

'I wish I hadn't told you now.' Sara sounded irritable. She was worried, and she felt unpleasantly like a madam in a brothel.

'Thank you for the tea.' Shakira stood up gracefully. 'I won't tell Verité about this. She wouldn't like it if we'd talked about the scene behind her back.'

As she watched the girl get ready to leave Sara was conscious of a growing feeling of annoyance – with herself. She'd been too ready to show off those early pages. They read so well, not exactly titillating but more inspirational. An invitation to imagine what it might really be like to enjoy the ultimate sensual experience in such a setting. Suddenly it seemed tawdry, and that was just how Verité had seen it.

# Chapter 5

'What now?' Dirk asked petulantly.

'A tandem ride?' Fleur was watching a young couple riding their shared bicycle cautiously over the damp cobbles.

'You must be joking.'

'I was. There's heaps to do here in Amsterdam.' Fleur's voice tailed off. She didn't actually think there was a lot that she and Dirk could do together and enjoy. It would have been better if they'd stayed in the hotel.

'I think Verité should have planned this better.' Dirk pulled up the collar of his leather jacket and hunched his shoulders. Just looking at the slick grey waters of the canal made him feel cold inside.

'It's only for a few hours,' Fleur said appeasingly and then stopped abruptly. It wasn't up to her to keep the pop singer happy. 'Do whatever you want, you don't have to include me. I'm perfectly happy. I'll go off and get a coffee.'

'Aha.' Dirk smiled for the first time that morning. He'd only been up for a couple of hours so he hadn't been miserable for very long, but he preferred being happy. He grinned widely, exposing his perfect, gleaming teeth. 'So you do enjoy a little "coffee", do you, Fleur? And I thought you were such a goody-two-shoes.'

'What on earth are you going on about?'

Dirk put his arm cheerfully around Fleur's resisting shoulders. 'You can drop the little miss innocent act with Uncle Dirkie. Come on – we'll go somewhere I know.'

Fleur planted her feet firmly and refused to take another

step. She was just as tall as her escort and unless he used force, she was immovable. 'I assume,' she said sarcastically, 'that when I said "coffee" you thought it was a euphemism. A euphemism is . . .'

'Yes, I know,' Dirk said edgily. 'And if you didn't mean you were going for a quiet smoke in one of Amsterdam's multitude of "coffee" shops then you're even more of a prude than I took you for.'

'I'm not a prude!' Fleur felt suddenly, inexplicably upset. It didn't matter to her what Dirk thought. 'It just so happens I'm not into drugs.'

'Don't like because you haven't tried.'

'Yes I have,' Fleur flared. 'You're not the only person who's been fêted and admired, you know. There are loads of sycophants in my world too, always ready to sympathize about how stressed it all is and offer a little help.'

'Euphemism, sycophants? You swallowed a dictionary today, or what?' Dirk was feeling a great deal better for having aroused some emotion in Fleur. He had the feeling that given the right encouragement she might even turn into a human being.

'Fuck off,' she snapped, spinning round in his grip so that he staggered. They were close to the edge of the canal and Dirk grabbed desperately at a tree to stop himself from falling in. 'Fuck off,' Fleur said again, this time so loudly that a group of raincoated tourists turned round to look. 'And go and blow your mind on your own.' Then she walked away, her head held high, looking every inch of her five foot eleven.

'It's not going to work,' Dirk said emphatically. 'Fleur and I together are a definite no no.'

Verry studied her nails. She had paid for the entire trip to Amsterdam, the flights, the hotel, right down to the photographer who was to be on hand when her two clients emerged hand in hand from a nightclub in the early hours. 'Aristocrat model clubs with US pop-star'. She had no intention of allowing her efforts to be wasted.

Fleur watched Verité. She had had several hours in which to think since the morning's argument with Dirk, and now appreciated that something had to be salvaged from the trip. She asked, 'Why can't Shakira go around with Dirk? It seems much more natural. She could fly over and be here in a few hours.'

'No,' Verité said firmly. 'The whole point is that you and Dirk aren't an obvious couple. You're different.'

'I'm a bit of rough,' Dirk leered. He was beginning to feel cheap, exploited.

'I'm willing to try again,' Fleur said.

'Charming.' Dirk's face twisted in a sneer.

Verry studied the expression. He really shouldn't do that, she thought. It made his eyes look almost sunken, but it wasn't the right time to tell him.

Dirk had leaned forwards so that he could talk right into Fleur's face. 'You nearly dump me in a canal,' he said, 'and you're willing to give me one more try. Thank you very much.'

'I think we're going about this the wrong way.' Verité kept her voice calm. 'Why don't you both act the part? That's what you're going to be doing a lot of in the near future – acting. So it will be ideal practice. Dirk, you play the part of boy in love with girl, and Fleur vice versa. Improvise.'

'Myself I'm into method.' Dirk sneered again, but it had less of an effect on his eyes because he was actually considering what Verité had said.

'Fleur?'

'OK.' Fleur's voice was clipped. She was trying very hard not to react to Dirk. She wanted so much to take him down a peg; he thought he was so special for having what he liked to call 'street cred'. Suddenly, she remembered something that Sara had told her and smiled.

'Right,' Verry concluded. 'We're in business.'

Dirk wore a white silk shirt. It was, as he said, very Errol Flynn: full sleeves, a standup collar and worn open to the waist. His trousers were leather with fringes at the ankles, very, as he said, Adam Ant. The final touch he added reverentially: a golden St Christopher on a long chain, it hung halfway down his hairy chest. Fleur's eyes glazed over.

Verité was finding her role the hardest of all. She could see Fleur over-reacting to Dirk and she wanted to laugh. Of the two of them Dirk's acting was the better. He had never, since she had first met him worn anything so outrageously 'pop'. It was his way of getting back at the girl he thought too stuck-up for her own good.

Fleur was wearing a simple black shift. Made of clinging crêpe de chine cut high and tight on the thigh, it would photograph brilliantly. At first she had been wearing pendulous crystal earrings but seeing how Dirk was dressed she had hurried back to her room to change into large, gold, pirate hoops. Then, as she said with saccharine in her voice, they made a pair.

They were to dance close, Verité had instructed, to sit snuggled up when they weren't dancing, and when they appeared at the witching hour of midnight – early for ravers, but about right for a couple aiming to share the same bed – they were to be arm in arm, cheek to cheek, ready for the photographer.

Considering how badly it had started off, Verité was more than delighted with the results. British papers picked up twice, the music pages of a bottom end of the market tabloid, and to her special pleasure Dempster in the *Mail*. The Dutch papers had three pictures, all based on the music side. The one photo appearing in France was full colour, and the caption featured Fleur. There could well be more over the next few days.

It wasn't too difficult to change the flights so that Fleur left the hotel two hours before Dirk was likely to wake up. That seemed, to Verité, to be the best way to avoid a possible scene. It was very doubtful if Dirk could be controlled for the entire trip back to London in close proximity with his supposed lover. And if any photographer happened to pick up on their arriving separately at Heathrow it would look as if they were acting clandestinely, making their affair even more romantic.

Fleur was sucking strong mints when she knocked at Verité's door to say goodbye. She was quiet and restrained, so Verité followed suit and did not refer to their last meeting. That had been when Dirk had dragged his companion into Verité's suite shortly before one A.M. Fleur had been giggling hysterically, Dirk had looked as if he was about to hit her, and Verité had hurriedly stepped between them. The singer was pale with fury. He had played his part, acted the attentive, doting lover, and in return Fleur had – he'd spat the accusation – breathed garlic all over him, making him want to throw up all evening. It was the age-old trick, played by film stars who didn't like men putting tongues down their vulnerable throats as the cameras rolled and the crew looked on.

It had taken half a bottle of Bols to get Dirk calm enough to go to bed. He would need to wear dark glasses to face the world next morning. Verry was not looking forward to the trip back, but all in all, she thought, her effort had paid off.

Charles sipped at his freshly squeezed orange juice, took a generous bite of his *croissant au beurre* and shook the pages of the *Financial Times* noisily. 'Are you finished in there yet, Hils?' he called out.

There was no reply from the en suite shower room that had been occupied for the past twenty minutes. He wanted to get up and get dressed, but he had no intention of walking the few metres along the companionway to use the guest facilities on board his own yacht.

The newspaper he was reading was three days old; he'd picked it up from an ex-pat Brit who ran a small supermarket at the French marina they'd used to refuel yesterday evening. So far he hadn't found anything of any special interest except that several articles pointed to a resurgence of interest in international ventures hyped by ecologically friendly PR. It reflected the trend of the financial pages in the French newspapers he'd been reading recently; it even tied in with the recipes in the UK Saturday Review sections – they'd all been for celery. Charles laid his paper down abruptly.

'Hils!' he shouted.

Hilary stepped into the state room. She was wrapped in one fluffy white towel and was rubbing her hair dry with another. She looked irritated. 'Do you have to keep bellowing at me when I'm in the john?' she asked.

'Sorry,' Charles apologized perfunctorily. His mind was working at speed on the jigsaw he was just putting together. 'I never took you for a green freak before that evening at Blackheath. Then I thought I must have been wrong, but I might have guessed there was more to it than concern for our planet.'

'So.' Hilary sat down on the small round stool in front of the dressing-table. 'The penny's dropped at last, has it?'

'You might have told me it was business. I thought we were meant to be involved together in that.'

'The business that we do together is very well defined, Charles. You give me introductions and I pay – very handsomely, I might add – for any that come off. I didn't need any help from you for my little bit of do-gooding.'

'Do-gooding my arse,' Charles said furiously. 'Why the hell did you drag me along on that evening if you didn't want me to get involved?'

'I enjoy your company.' Hilary smiled and stood up, letting the towel fall to the floor. She had a good body, the result of hours of her private fitness instructor's expensive time. 'I still enjoy your company, as I hope you enjoy mine.'

'There was something about the way you said that – it sounded almost like a threat.' Charles was lying stretched out on the bed, a fine linen sheet stretched over his stomach and the bulge that Hilary was studying closely.

'It's not like you to take a threat lying down, Charles.' She laughed softly, a dull red glow at the base of her throat. She raised a hand to her lips and slowly, lasciviously, licked the tip of her middle finger.

Charles lay very still; he had no intention of reacting. He reminded himself how well he knew her body, that there was no reason for the sight of her naked to turn him on.

Hilary was still licking slowly. She put the finger into her mouth, pursing her lips, sucking. All the while she was staring at Charles, at the growing evidence of his arousal. The flush had spread up her neck to her cheeks; her eyes were narrowed. She slid her feet apart on the soft pile carpet, and her ginger-blonde pubic hairs glistened from the shower. She tipped her pelvis back so that, without having to move his head a centimetre, Charles could see the pink wetness of her. Her hand seemed to flicker as it travelled down her body, touching her breasts, pausing to savour the hard, risen nipples, stroking the smooth flatness of her stomach. Charles was mesmerized. His own hands, as if with a life of their own, moved to what had now become the throbbing, erect sign of his desire. Hilary laid the very tip of her finger on the tiny swollen clitoris that so inspired him. As she pressed harder she groaned, a low animal sound that brought Charles swiftly to his knees, reaching out towards her.

'And this is Angelique, my mother.' Verité was inexplicably nervous. It didn't actually matter whether Dirk got on with Angelique or not. She had invited him home to meet her family as part of getting to know her signings.

'You didn't warn me she was beautiful.' Dirk held on to Angelique's proffered hand.

'"Warn"?' Angelique smiled. 'That's a funny thing to say.'

'I like to be prepared, have my act ready before I meet somebody special.'

Sara laughed approvingly. 'You carry on like that, my boy. That's just what she needs. I'm Granny, by the way, though you don't call me that, you call me Sara.'

Dirk took the old lady's hand in his left. He now had both women in his grip. He gently engineered them towards the sofa, manoeuvred himself between them, then sat down, and they had no choice but to do the same.

Not, as Verry could see, that they had any wish to do otherwise.

'I've heard a lot about you' – Dirk turned his head to look at Sara – 'and your husband. I've been reading up on the early days in Hollywood. I think I would have enjoyed it.'

Sara adjusted herself into a more comfortable position, tucking a well-stuffed cushion into the small of her back. 'I think you would have enjoyed yourself very much indeed in those days, Dirk. If you'd come out to us with all that charm you would have been just smothered by starlets, they were so desperate for some fun.'

'That's not *meant* to be an insult, is it?' Dirk asked. 'The "desperate" bit, I mean?'

'Verité says you're going to be in films,' Angelique said.

Dirk turned away from Sara. 'I'm glad she's so positive to you. To me it's always that I "might" be.'

'Verité is very careful what she says, Dirk. She never commits herself unnecessarily.'

Verry turned away to pour some drinks. Her mother always managed to make her feel ill at ease. However cautious she was being with her promises, she still felt that each of her four was convinced they were on their way to a brilliant acting career. If it didn't come to anything she thought they might be difficult.

Angelique was speaking softly, Dirk leaning close to her to hear what she was saying. Sara looked at Verry and grimaced. She'd been all set to enjoy a nice little tête-à-tête with their visitor and her daughter-in-law had changed the tone.

'Mother.' Verry handed Angelique a martini, then gave one to her grandmother and finally to Dirk. Normally she would have served the older woman first, but she'd felt it was time to interrupt Angelique's performance. She was beginning to be embarrassed by the atmosphere developing on the sofa.

'Cheers.' Dirk touched his glass first to Sara's then briefly to Angelique's. Why was it, Verry wondered, that the latter, almost negligible chink of glasses, seemed so intimate?

Shakira was ahead of Fleur as they walked into the crowded room. They were stepping into hotel splendour at its best – Louis Seize furniture, floor to ceiling rococo framed mirrors reflecting a wall-length buffet heavy with formal delicacies displayed on aspic-coated silver. A well-stocked bar was set off by a sparkling array of glasses.

The setting could have been a flagship hotel in any one of a dozen European capitals except for the uniquely French scent of the cigarette smoke drifting up from the predominantly male gathering – Gauloises were back in fashion yet again – and the sulky, Sacha Distel look-alike waiters.

'You see? I told you it would be a grand affair,' Shakira said delightedly. 'Definitely no slumming, Fleur.'

'I didn't mean to imply . . .'

'No, of course you didn't. In no way did you give the slightest hint that you thought I was inviting you to some kind of orgy.' Shakira moved sinuously further into the room, insinuating herself through the narrowest of gaps between Armani suits worn with Gallic panache. The crush was thickest ahead of them, in front of floor-length windows draped with antique gold silk.

'I only said I don't like crowds.' Fleur picked up a glass of orange-coloured liquid as they made their impeded progress past the bar. She sipped cautiously – it tasted like pure orange juice.

'This isn't a crowd.' Shakira paused, then stood on tiptoe, trying to see over the mass of shoulders ahead of her. 'It's a party. Eureka!' She gripped Fleur's arm tightly and pulled her through the crush.

'Ricci!' Shakira threw her free arm around the broad neck of a swarthy, red-faced middle-aged man already the centre of attention of half a dozen beautiful young women.

'Darling!' The Italian forced the word out around his fat cigar, disengaged himself from a tiny blonde Cindy doll and squeezed Shakira tightly against his chest.

Fleur watched, mesmerized, as wet, full lips, still encompassing the Havana Royale, planted themselves on Shakira's smooth cheek. She tugged her arm, trying unsuccessfully to disentangle herself from her companion's grip.

Shakira's voice rose above the surrounding hubbub.

'I've brought you a present, Ricci. A real live English aristocrat.'

At this point, Fleur knew from past experience, only instant departure could save her from acute embarrassment, but she was hemmed in.

'My dear.' The cigar was gone in an instant, the bimbos dispersed. 'I am charmed.' Ricci plucked her arm from Shakira's grasp and held her fingers lightly in his wide, hairy hand. His grip was dry and cool, the ritual kiss to her knuckles the faintest sensation.

Shakira raised her expressive eyebrows in an 'I told you so' gesture. The crowd around them thinned, the decibel level dropped to a sophisticated hum, and it was almost possible to hear glasses tinkling. Miraculously the gathering in the Grande Suite Napoleon had become exactly what Shakira had promised, a top level business reception. A place to see, and be seen. A place to make contacts.

Verry slammed the door of Sam's Toyota Land Cruiser closed behind her. She breathed in deeply and the taste of the chill country air was like iced Perrier.

Pencombe Place, Fleur's family home, lay before her. In the bitter-lemon spring sunlight the sandstone walls glowed apricot. It was massive, dozens of diamond-paned windows stretching away on either side of a castellated portico surrounding a studded oaken door. The vast circular gravel sweep in front of the house was almost full of cars, and a young boy, whose flaming mop of red hair caught the sun like a beacon, was efficiently organizing the parking. Fleur must have been watching for her agent's arrival, because she came quickly, striding from a narrow side door. Dressed in olive green corduroy plus twos, a camel polo-necked jumper and matching long socks, she looked, as she was, totally at home.

She greeted Verité with a kiss on each cheek and said,

'It was nice of you to drive down.'

'It was nice of you to ask me,' Verité smiled, and then looked suddenly startled as a great roaring sound broke the rural stillness.

'They're on the other side.' Fleur gestured towards the twelve foot high wall leading away from the left hand side of the house. 'In the paddock over there. They've just started inflating the balloons. We'll go down a bit later, but come and have some breakfast first.'

The food was as splendid as its setting. In the baronial hall – Verry was sure she recognized it from a recent Robin Hood film – trestle tables were laid with platters of smoked salmon and mounds of steaming brioches. There were bowls of fluffy cream cheese, others of gleaming scarlet strawberry jam, and a dozen bains maries piled high with scrambled eggs. Several men and women were helping themselves to food, all 'smart casual' in dress and obviously determined on enjoying themselves. Black and white uniformed staff moved about quietly and efficiently.

'You don't have to ask the obvious question,' Fleur said with a laugh, 'because I'll tell you anyway. We don't have food like this every day of the week.'

'You disappoint me,' Verry smiled.

'All this is laid on by the hospitality company. They charge top rates for their ballooning extravaganzas, so it's all done beautifully. They always give us a few freebies because they think it keeps us sweet – which it does, of course.'

Verry picked up a plate from the buffet and helped herself to a couple of slices of the translucent smoked salmon before spooning some creamy scrambled egg on top. Fleur picked up a brioche in her fingers and bit into it. 'You can always tell family,' she laughed. 'They're the ones that eat as if there's no tomorrow. Bengy always . . .' She broke off suddenly, her expression changing swiftly from delight to dismay.

'Fleur, whatever's the matter? Are you all right?' Verry laid her hand on the girl's arm. The colour had faded from her cheeks, and she looked faint.

'I'm sorry.' Fleur blinked slowly, as if she was recovering from some terrible shock. 'I'm fine really. I'd just forgotten something, for a minute.'

Verry was still concerned, but since she didn't find Fleur easy to get close to she thought it was best to begin eating her breakfast.

Fleur began talking quickly. 'You're in a basket with the press photographer. He's after some particular effects, so I thought it would give you a better flight than' – she lowered her voice theatrically – 'the one the plebs are doing.'

Verry smiled pleasantly. Fleur had made a good recovery but was obviously still unsettled. They were both relieved when a leather-jacketed balloonist, complete with World War I goggles and flying helmet, came into the hall to announce imminent take-off.

The paddock was full of the sound of the balloons filling with gas, and the sight of the flames roaring up into the cavernous interiors of the brightly coloured envelopes. There were over a dozen balloons in all the colours of the rainbow, even a giant champagne bottle inflated and ready for the off.

It was a perfect morning, the air still, hardly a breeze to shake the yellow and brown leaves on the parkland trees. Standing in the basket next to the photographer, who was urgently rummaging through his equipment, Verry had leisure to look around. They were on a gentle slope; behind her sheep-dotted fields led up to distant, dark green woods. In front verdant paddocks stretched down to a river, slow moving and silver, reflecting the sun like a mirror.

There was a flurry of activity as they took off, the overwhelming noise making it hard to think, and then they were sailing in a multicoloured flotilla making its majestic way across the sky. Verry experienced a fleeting moment of panic, a sudden realization that she didn't really like heights, and then fascination took over. A flight of ducks winged past a few dozen feet away, seemingly unconcerned until a sudden burst of the gas jet sent them wheeling. Verry was pleased that she was with the photographer. The balloonist and his assistant were paying him all the attention and she was free to look around and convince herself that it really was fun.

They began to ascend slowly, then quite rapidly, and the cows and horses they sped over became smaller and smaller. The countryside changed to brown fields, and they passed over a tractor busily driving backwards and forwards like a picture from 'Toy Town'. The air was getting colder and Verry zipped up her anorak. It was one of her mother's good thermal skiing jackets, and it was just as well she was wearing it. She shivered briefly, but forced her shoulders to relax and started to get warm. The champagne bottle was floating some way behind them, if anything even higher up. Verry hoped whoever was in that was wearing something warm too.

The photographer began gesticulating forwards. Verry put her hands to her eyes, shielding them from the sun's rays so that she could see, ahead and below them, a medieval castle floating on its mirror image. She recognized it as Leeds Castle. The advertisements said it was the most beautiful castle in the world, and from her bird's eye view Verry was inclined to agree.

It seemed they were going down for a closer look. They

started to descend quite quickly, and Verry crouched down, not wanting to see the speed at which the ground was coming up to meet them. Soon it was impossible for her to ignore the pace of their descent any longer, as the horizon rose above the rim of the basket and enlarged at an alarmingly rapid rate.

There was a remarkable degree of activity in the basket and she seemed always to be in the way. The photographer became more and more insistent and Verry wished he'd shut up – how important could a few pictures be anyway? Then she realized that his over-emphatic gestures were born of panic. He was as frightened as she was, perhaps even more so, and he'd been ballooning before.

They hit the trees a few hundred yards from the moat surrounding the castle. The first contact was little more than a brush, a sweeping noise of branches on the bottom of the basket as they careered along. Then came a jolt and Verry felt her neck jar painfully, though they still seemed to be moving very fast. She was clutching on grimly now, squatting down in the corner she had been forcibly pushed into. She couldn't have moved voluntarily; she was frozen with fear. After the jolt, they bounced a few feet into the air, and for a glorious few seconds Verry thought that they were going to float clear. Then, in a sickening plummet, they fell.

When the basket tipped Verry rolled out. She felt her shoulder collide with something hard, she was aware of her arms and legs flailing hopelessly, and then with a bone-shaking thump she stopped falling. She lay spread-eagled, her eyes closed, her ears supersensitive to every sound: the leaves settling around her, the faint whisper of the wind in the tree tops.

'Maid Marian, I presume.' The loud, masculine voice so close at hand made Verry jump. Opening her eyes, she struggled to focus. There was a bump on the back of her head and she felt decidedly sick.

'Champers?' the voice enquired. 'Straight? Or – even better for shock – the Freeman special, a cocktail fit for the gods. Spot on considering you've just fallen out of the sky, don't you think?'

Verry's eyes focused at last. A few feet away from her a supremely Savile Row vision of the sporting gentleman sat cross-legged on the leaves. In one hand he held a magnum of champagne, minus its cork, in the other a glass.

'Got the brandy in my pocket, if you'd like,' he offered helpfully.

'I feel sick.' Verry struggled into a sitting position. They were on the edge of a wood, somewhere above them she assumed the balloon still sat in the tree tops, and ahead Leeds Castle lay contentedly in the sun. 'I am going . . .' She managed to lean sideways – away from her would-be gallant – before depositing her breakfast amongst the leaves. After a while she could sit up straight again.

'I came down after you. My ship's the big one of these.' He waved the champagne bottle. 'Your flight companions are all OK; they've toddled over to the cafeteria *là-bas*. I wouldn't advise it in your case, though. I believe they serve chips at this time of day.'

'Would you please leave me alone.' Verry was surprised at how steady her voice sounded, weak but not wobbly.

'Wouldn't dream of it, never abandon a damsel in distress.'

She had nearly been killed. The realization came flooding over Verry and she shivered. Then she felt her cheeks burning with anger as she realized how very nearly everything had ended.

'I don't know who . . .' she began and then she looked a bit harder. 'You're Charles Freeman, aren't you?' She recognized the face from the society columns.

'At your service, and you're Verry Goode. That surprised you, didn't it? But Fleur told me all about Goode as Golde. Very good, Verry, very good.' He laughed. It was a pleasant friendly sound that went with his handsome, charming face.

'Sod off,' Verry said. She said it viciously, using every ounce of her fury at having been so nearly consigned to oblivion.

Charles stared, the smile almost fading from his face. He was tempted to say something about admiring a woman with spirit, but all things considered he didn't think it would be a good idea.

'Take your damned champagne and go away and drown in it.' She was struggling to her feet, trying to avoid standing in the embarrassing, steaming mess beside her.

Charles didn't say a word. Slowly, he tipped up his bottle of fizz, poured a splash into the glass he was holding and raised it in salute before touching it to his lips. Then he turned and walked away through the woods. All in all, he was quite pleased with his exit.

She shared a minicab back to Pencombe with the photographer. It was very quiet, nobody else having yet returned. The boy with the red hair was sitting on the fence bordering the drive, and when he saw them he grinned around a mouthful of bread stuffed with what looked like smoked salmon. Verry was first out of the cab. The cool air blew on her face, a cloud crossed the sun and the house ahead of her was in shadow. It would be cold inside, she decided, cold and damp. In the winter winds would blow in the corridors, there were no doubt bats in the attics, and there would be woodworm in the furniture. She walked towards the Toyota. There was the faintest smell of car fumes from the assembled horsepower. It made her feel better. Poor Fleur, she thought. Having spent the journey back from Leeds Castle contemplating getting rid of the girl who had committed her to the balloon, she now saw the tragedy of so vibrant a creature being brought up in the country. It was cold, draughty, dangerous – she thought of a lot of other words during the four-mile drive to the bypass that would connect with the M25 to take her back to civilization. By the time she'd reached the Thames she was aware that all she needed to feel better was a hot bath and a telephone. She would be productive today, she just felt it.

## Chapter 6

Angelique reached out, picked up the tortoiseshell comb lying on her dressing-table, and began to comb her hair. It was still damp from her shower and the widely spaced teeth of the comb separated the well-conditioned strands into dark cords. She had been considering having it cut. Since David's death she had noticed more grey than ever during the few days that she allowed it to show at the roots before having them coloured. Staring hard, she could already see where it was growing in. It made her hair look thinner, it made her look older.

With a sigh she reached for the scissors. She began on the left hand side, took a line just beneath her ear and snipped. A dark, curling lock fell on to her shoulder and then down to the floor. It was amazing what a difference a few inches of hair made, she decided. The right side was more difficult, since her left hand shook too much to use the scissors safely, and she had to bend her wrist around to be able to use her right. Perhaps, she realized, she should have gone to the hairdresser's, but she just hadn't felt like it.

It took over half an hour to achieve a fairly even result all the way round. By now her hair was almost dry and she kept shaking her head, swinging her hair so that it flew out sideways. She rather liked the overall effect, but there was something wrong at the front. Her normal swept-back style looked harsh with her hair so short. Perhaps a fringe? That was much more difficult than she'd expected.

Rewashing and conditioning occupied some more of her

morning. She applied a generous handful of mousse, then blow-dried her hair leaning sideways to achieve volume.

The finished effect was dynamic, young and vibrant. Angelique surveyed it critically. It made her face look tired and old. She would need to change her make-up, so she began rummaging in the centre drawer in front of her. There were dozens of lipsticks and a colourful collection of eyeshadows. She selected a bottle-green kohl pencil for outlining her eyes, to throw up the iciness of their grey; then she patted charcoal shadow on top of her lids and carried it out to the corners. Somehow that emphasized the fact that the rims of her eyes were red; brown eyeshadow calmed that a little. She chose a tawny blusher and applied it generously. It underlined her unusually high cheekbones and reminded her why she didn't normally use colour on her face: she felt it made her jaw look too long. Staring in the mirror, her reflection verging on distraught, she recognized the expression from Van Gogh's self-portrait. However much David had admired it, that painting had always unnerved her. It was possible that lipstick would help. She chose a reddish orange with a matt finish that slid on smoothly, filling the tiny lines around the edges of her lips. She hadn't noticed before what an unkind light her mirror reflected.

After two vodka martinis her new look still didn't seem any better so she smothered her face in cold cream, smearing the colours into a pastel goo, making her eyes look even redder. It hurt, pressing hard with tissue to remove every scrap of paste. Around her hairline greasy patches stuck to her scalp. She ran a hand through her fringe because it felt itchy on her forehead. The hair instantly fell forwards again, so she clipped it back savagely with a bobby pin.

Lying on the bed Angelique stared up at the ceiling. She felt hot and sticky, as if her skin couldn't breathe. She inhaled deeply on her cigarette and began to cough, a harsh, retching convulsion that made her roll over and curl up into a ball. Her chest felt raw inside, so she poured the next vodka neat and drank it down in one gulp. The initial fire subsided to a warm glow and she pulled her knees up to her chest, cradling her head on her arm. She wished she hadn't cut her hair. Thinking of the dark strands filling the waste basket she began to cry, warm wet drops that fell on to her arm and ran down into her fingers.

'But that's wonderful,' Verry enthused into the telephone. 'It's the red Bugatti we can have, is it?'

'That's what you wanted.' Bugsy laughed. Pleasing a pretty woman always made him feel good.

'I promise we'll look after it.'

'You'd bloody better.' For a moment Bugsy was serious. 'It's worth a packet.'

'I'll even have it valeted before we bring it back. I'm sure we'll get some excellent press coverage – I'm calling a photo-shoot in London next month. With the four well-known faces and the story of them driving to Cannes in the actual car we're going to use for the film we should get most of the dailies – with the usual proviso, of course: failing acts of war, or God, or Elizabeth Taylor.'

'Give me as much warning as you can of the date for that, Verry. I'd like to invite a few of my customers along. Where are you doing it?'

'Trafalgar Square, I hope. I've got to go and do a proper recce, but we should be able to sort something out without the traffic police getting too agitated.'

'I'll lay on some drinkies, and a few exotic nibbles. Perhaps we could have a cavalcade . . .'

'Better not,' Verry interjected quickly. 'Just the one pretty car, otherwise we'll risk clouding the issue.'

'You're the expert.' Bugsy paused, there was the sound of rustling paper, and then he continued, 'You couldn't do me a favour, could you?'

Verry made a face. It would be embarrassing to have to refuse any request of Bugsy's considering he'd just put a hundred thousand pounds' worth of car at her disposal, but she hoped the favour wasn't of too personal a nature.

Bugsy continued rustling paper. 'You couldn't let me have some shots of your model girl, Fleur Montford? Only I've got this friend who thinks she's something special . . .'

Verry suffocated a giggle. Bugsy presumably fancied Fleur from afar; he was sounding like a schoolboy. 'Of course,' she replied. 'I'll get her to sign a glossy. What's your friend's name?'

'No need to bother her that much. Just a photo or two would be nice.' He sounded wistful, but cheered up briskly. ''Course I'll get to meet her at your photo-shoot, won't I? Then I'll be able to give my pal all the gen.'

'Yes, Bugsy, you'll get to meet her,' Verry agreed. 'I'll be in contact when I've fixed a date.'

To have the car settled was a great relief, and an excellent PR move. She was going to announce – at a glitzy press-call – that the British film industry was being given a well-deserved fillip courtesy of a Hollywood script some fifty years old. She would give a brief outline of the plot: four young people determined on stardom, presented with a challenge by a film producer who could change the course of their lives. Equipped with nothing but beautiful clothes, an expensive car, and their ingenuity, they were to motor from London to the Riviera via several of the capitals of Europe. It was the Grand Tour with a difference. They were to arrive at pre-set venues – some of the finest restaurants in the world – where the film producer would be ready to wine them, dine them, and send them on their way. They would each leave London with ten pounds sterling, and they were to hand the same amount back to the producer at their final rendezvous on the coast of the Mediterranean. Verry had interpreted the challenge to suit her cause. Her foursome were to make their way to Cannes and the film festival, where she intended to find her distributors for *Viva Europa* and, if the gods were willing, make some more money contacts. She would see them off from London, meet them in Paris, and then at the end of their trip.

There was much to do before the press-call, including giving up her office at the Production Centre. She didn't have time in the day to go there and crack the whip over her still incompetent secretary, nor had she the inclination to find herself a new one. She could work just as well from home. The next thing to do was find some publicity-hungry designer to provide the glamorous clothes for her people. The telephone rang just as she was about to pick it up and dial her contact at *Vogue* magazine.

'Verité?' It was Sara's voice. 'Thank goodness you're there. There's been an accident. It's your mother – she's . . . oh, dear, hold on.'

Verry held the telephone receiver tightly. It seemed ages before Sara's voice came back.

'Come home. Come home right away, Verité,' she said, and the line went dead.

'You're sure she wouldn't be better in hospital?' Verry asked. The doctor was packing his bag in the narrow hallway, having left his patient upstairs in bed.

'Positive. Very bad environment for someone in her condition.' He was youngish, Verry supposed about thirty. He had thinning ginger hair, a pale freckled face, a strong Scottish accent and a disapproving expression. 'She should have had someone with her. So recently widowed, and clearly highly-strung, and of course she's tried this before.'

'My grandmother had just gone to the shops. She'd been in the house all morning.'

'Not good enough from now on. And you'll need a baby alarm.' He looked irritated by Verry's obvious non-comprehension. 'Wire her room up with an intercom. Cheap enough, you can buy them at Mothercare. Then you can keep an ear out all the time. With practice you can interpret very well what's going on without invading the patient's privacy, or rather without her being aware you're invading it. But we don't want a repetition of this. She was lucky to have been so sick early on. That would be the neat spirit – it had turned her stomach.'

Verry felt as if her own stomach was turning as she asked if her mother was sedated.

'Only by the after-effects of what she'd taken. She'll be sleeping on and off all day, and hopefully a bit of the night too. But you'll have to be on hand. Even if you can afford it I wouldn't recommend a nurse. Your mother needs affection – and to have cut off her hair, too.' The doctor shook his head woefully. 'She's a bonny woman. It's a tragedy.' With a final, meaningful look at Verry he left, promising to come back within twelve hours.

How on earth would she manage? Verry felt trapped. She had to continue with the film project; her mother had proved, in the most dramatic way possible, that she needed a secure future. Somehow Verry would have to cut her own role in the trans-Europe trip. She wouldn't have time to set up Continental press coverage now, just as she wouldn't have time to gallivant to the luxurious restaurants she'd been so looking forward to. The drive to Cannes would have to be even more of a 'spoof'. The foursome would start in London, cross the Channel to France and then motor down through the Alps to the

Riviera. That would give Verry a precious week to chase up more potential sources of finance, and somehow look after her mother – at least there was Sara to help there. She and her protégés would meet up at Cannes, ready and bright for the film festival where, if some more hard work paid off and they achieved a blaze of publicity, she might just place her project.

The doctor had only been gone twenty minutes when Verry heard the crash from the kitchen. She ran in. The last whole teacup off the tray was still spinning on the floor. Sara lay awkwardly in a litter of broken china, her arm bent at an unnatural angle on top of the tray, while milk dripped slowly from her skirt on to her leg.

'No.' Fleur spoke softly but her face was determined. 'I won't give it up, Bengy. It's not fair of you to ask me to.'

Bengy Michaels leant against the wall of the great hall at Pencombe. The chill of the stone through his loosely hanging green Harris tweed jacket did nothing to cool his temper. His face was gaunt, the flesh on his large frame wasted, but he was still a big man, and looked even bigger because he was angry. 'I will not have you gallivanting all over Europe in the company of some tart.'

Fleur remained silent; she was pale but composed. She was used, by now, to her fiancé's rages.

'Have you any idea what that slut's reputation is?' Bengy continued, his mouth twisted with rage.

'You seem to think you have.'

Bengy raised a hand aggressively, then without warning his mood changed. 'Fleur,' he begged, 'Fleur, my darling, don't go. Don't leave me alone.'

'It's not for long.' Fleur felt guilty. Bengy and her home were inseparable, yet it was he who was making her throw herself into the film project. Truthfully, she didn't relish the idea of travelling for several days in the company of three near strangers, but if that was what it took to give her a chance of a new life, then she would do it. Only the new life had no place for Bengy, and he kept saying he'd have no life at all if it wasn't for Fleur.

'I could come with you,' Bengy said, his voice lifting, enthusiasm colouring his face like a small boy's. 'I could travel just a little behind you – we could meet up at the stops, the hotels . . .' His voice tailed off as Fleur shook her head.

'I need to get away, Bengy. Please understand.' Fleur had been so in love with him, once. It seemed a lifetime ago, before Bengy's riding accident, before his leg had been so horribly broken that he would never walk without a stick again, before his nature had twisted too, so that he was smothering her.

It was very quiet, the thick stone walls absorbing any of the outside, country sounds. There was nobody else in this part of the house, the area that in summer would be open to the public. In the dusty silence the vast antique tapestries hanging on the end wall seemed dull and lifeless. Even the medieval courtier forever offering flowers to his lady-love looked lacklustre, as if the gesture he performed had staled through force of habit. There were two full suits of armour displayed beneath the tapestry. Their owners had been shorter than Fleur. As a child the relics had frightened her, given her nightmares; now they made her think of Bengy. He was like those knights of old, trapped in an unyielding shell that restricted his movements, made him clumsy. He was pushing himself away from the wall, using his stick as a prop so that he could get his balance. How could she leave him, she thought? How could anyone with even an ounce of sympathy leave someone so pathetic? And yet pity couldn't be a substitute for love. She stepped beside her fiancé and he put an arm around her, squeezing her briefly. There was never any more than that. The passion of their earlier days had turned into a platonic relationship that left Fleur nervous and insecure and Bengy angry with all the world but most of all with himself.

'Shall we go into the gardens?' Fleur asked. 'It's mild enough for a walk down to the river.'

They would make slow progress, admiring the first of the rose buds, tinged brown by the frost, but still bravely struggling for life. There was a froth of apple blossom on the trees in the orchard; the leaves just starting to burst forth. It was, for a little while, as if there was no outside world, and for that time Fleur could be almost content.

Jesse Standing, successful middle-weight boxer and would-be film star, was about to eat lunch. Verry watched in amazement as the calories piled up. It was Jesse's father's treat. The old man had appeared briefly to escort Verry and Jesse into his club, the Wig and Pen, that was so pleasantly placed at the top end of Fleet Street, exactly opposite the law courts. The club member had ensconced them at a table, organized drinks, menus and service, and then with a cheerful wave disappeared, as he'd said, 'out back'.

A whole four-pound chicken, roasted to a perfect crispy gold and then halved, formed the centrepiece of Jesse's plate. Around the edge was a ring of mashed and roast potatoes, in a deep line across the centre lightly boiled cabbage shone with butter. Peas and carrots completed the picture, and gravy had been expertly ladled over all by the waiter.

'Dad never eats,' Jesse explained as he sprinkled salt over his food. 'Not in public, anyway. That pheasant all right for you? It doesn't look much of a helping.'

'It's enormous,' Verry protested. 'I shan't even manage to finish it. How does your mother keep up with feeding you?'

Jesse grinned. 'She loves it. Cooking's her forte, and it's just as well, because there are four more like me at home. I've got three brothers, and none of them's under fourteen stone. My sister's tiny, but she still eats like a horse – more so now she's expecting twins.'

The waiter returned with a bottle of champagne – vintage. 'From them upstairs,' he said. 'With luck for the next fight.'

Jesse nodded his appreciation and went on eating steadily as the foaming drink was poured. 'Ladbrokes own this place,' he explained. 'The boss is a friend of my old man's. Nice, isn't it?'

Verité nodded her agreement. It was very nice, with the cosy atmosphere of Tudor panelled walls and the manly bonhomie of the small bar area. Bobby Charlton, hero of several generations of football fans, walked past their table and tapped Jesse on the shoulder in greeting before disappearing into the cigar-scented interior.

'What exactly does your father do?' Verry asked.

Jesse tapped the side of his nose. 'This and that. At least, that's what he'd say if you asked him. His main business is fruit and veg. His company has a lot of hospital contracts.'

'Are any of your brothers in the business?'

'All of them. They run a truck each. Three beautiful Mercs we've got – makes a good-looking fleet parked side by side at the yard. Sis runs the office, but she's going to take a couple of months off when the babies come along so Mum'll handle it then. It's a real family firm.'

'And you didn't want to join?'

Jesse looked surprised. 'But I'm in it. I do the market in the morning. Suits me, being up bright and early. Job's over by ten, so I've got all day to train. On the run up to a fight one of my brothers takes over, but I usually turn out just the same, go jogging round the market.'

'You are amazing,' Verité said feelingly. 'I have to say I thought you were a bit like a prize racehorse. Whenever I've seen you it's being dropped off by your father's Mercedes, and you always look so well-dressed. I thought all you did was work out in the gym, perhaps interspersed with a few manicures.'

Jesse looked down at his immaculately kept hands and laughed out loud. He'd finished his main course, and was sitting back happily. 'Boxer's fortune, good hands. You know you make me laugh, you career women. Don't get me wrong, Verité, I'm not being rude or anything. But I've met a few London girls, none so grand as you, but getting there, and they all get flustered by the thought of a bloke making his bread before their day starts. It seems to worry them that I might be missing out on sleep. I'll make you a bet. I reckon you don't ever go to bed before twelve. Am I right?'

Verry nodded. She felt relaxed; the food had been excellent, and Jesse's cheerful view of life was a tonic.

'Well, I'm in bed by nine every night, so if I get up at four, then we're getting about the same hours a night, right?'

'You don't honestly go to bed at nine?' Verité looked disbelieving.

Jesse grinned sheepishly. 'Well, no, I don't, not often. But the theory works.'

'What does your family think about your wanting to go into films?'

'My brothers want to meet' – he began ticking the names off on his fingers – 'Michelle Pfeiffer and Madonna, and it's Tom Cruise for my sister. My mum says it'll be a good reason to inspire me to detrain when I give up the game. She's seen too many of Dad's mates go to flab when they give up. Dad doesn't say much. His love's the boxing, but I've had a fair crack at it, and I'm going to do better before I finish, so I reckon he'll be happy. If it does work and your scam comes off, they'll have to get someone to cover for me, but I wouldn't like it to be anyone permanent. I'd like to go back in the end. It's in my blood, being with my family.'

'Because it's been such a good lunch I'll overlook the fact that you called my venture a scam. It's nice to see you've got your feet so firmly on the ground.'

'It would be hard not to, at my weight. Now surprise me and choose a nice gooey pud. You've eaten like a sparrow so far.'

'Flowers' – Dirk placed an enormous bunch of red roses on Angelique's bed – 'chocs and . . .' He looked back quickly, checking that Verité hadn't yet followed him into the room, then whispered, 'Something to tuck under your pillow.'

It was a silver hip-flask.

'You're sweet.' Angelique's voice was weak. She lay limply and her face was pale, but she was smiling.

Verry walked into the bedroom. 'Well,' she said, surprised. 'You've achieved something I couldn't. What on earth did you do to get my mother to smile, Dirk?'

'Just my innate personal magnetism.' Ignoring the strategically placed chair, Dirk sat down on the edge of the bed.

'Verité,' Angelique whispered, 'be a darling and get us all some coffee.'

Verry looked meaningfully at the pop-star and left. She'd told him, earlier, as they'd stood in the hall, that her mother was to be kept calm, she wasn't to smoke or have any alcohol. Those had been the doctor's instructions. He had also left a diet sheet containing dozens of suggestions for light, nutritious meals. Angelique refused to consider it, saying she didn't feel like eating.

'The flask.' Angelique had propped herself up on one elbow and was reaching to where Dirk had tucked his most welcome gift.

'Here.' Dirk leaned across to help her. He smelt of expensive cologne and Angelique breathed in appreciatively.

By the time Verry returned with a tray of coffee and biscuits Angelique was sitting up, the pillows fluffed up behind her head, and the opened box of chocolates on her lap. She was chewing contentedly.

'Knew she'd like soft centres,' Dirk said smugly. 'So do I.' He reached over and helped himself to one. There were already several missing from the box.

'How did last night go?' Verry asked. Dirk had been performing at a charity event at the Savoy.

'Good gig. I was the main event.' He laughed. 'That really got up the nose of the Italian they'd got in to do some opera.'

'The diva,' Angelique said. 'She's a diva. That's the same as saying you're a pop-*star*.'

'She was all right, actually – her voice, I mean. I wouldn't have minded if they'd suggested a duet. It's been done before, mixing pop and classic. It works.'

Angelique leaned forward, obviously interested. 'It was Jenny Jones, wasn't it? She sang with Carreras.'

'Domingo,' Dirk corrected.

Angelique nodded and reached out to take the cup Verry offered.

Verité asked if she would like a biscuit and wasn't surprised by the refusal. She was, however, amused by Dirk's insistence that her mother took one.

'Dunk it,' he said, demonstrating with his own. 'But

you'll have to be quick – these are a bit crumbly. Gingernuts would be better. You should get some gingernuts, Verité. Ange would enjoy them.'

Angelique obediently dipped her biscuit into the steaming coffee and ate it. Verry watched the performance in a bemused silence. Never, in her life, had she heard her mother referred to as 'Ange'. It was quite unreal, she thought, Dirk's casual mateyness and Angelique's total acceptance of it.

Dirk stayed for an hour, during which time he chatted animatedly to both Verry and her mother. When he left he said he'd be back the next day, and suggested that Verry might like to use his visit as an opportunity to get out of the house. As he put it, it would be a relief from being cooped up.

'But you can get to Rome in two and a half hours from Heathrow,' Shakira said authoritatively. 'Private Cessna, door to door, no hassle.'

Jesse yawned, picked up a cream eclair from the elegant plateful provided by the London Waldorf, and said sarcastically, 'Thanks a bunch. You might be able to pick up these perks from your wealthy friends, but for me it's a question of scheduled flights, slow-moving customs queues, the whole bit. It's only a chat show, after all, and it doesn't work out timewise. I'd never be back here in time for the launch.'

'What if I can fix it?' Shakira bit into her coffee eclair. The cream smeared on her lipstick and she licked it off slowly.

'All the TV station's prepared to cough up is the first class flight. I'm not sure what that's worth . . .'

'I don't mean money,' Shakira said contemptuously. She looked around. The Palm Court lounge was about half full, the balcony on which they sat apparently being the most favoured area, since all of the tables had been taken. Below them, on the pale marble floor that formed the setting for the regular Friday *thés dansants*, there were still vacant seats. She watched a couple walk in. They looked American, expensively dressed, elderly, tired and, the husband particularly, belligerent – it wasn't easy for them to catch the eye of the frock-coated waiters.

'You mean you want my body!' Jesse laughed loudly, attracting attention from nearby tables so that Shakira looked cross.

'You could do yourself a lot of good if you dropped that act,' she said.

Jesse raised his eyebrows, but didn't comment.

'I know a lot of very influential people. You're the kind of person they like to meet. A sports star, especially a boxer, businessmen find exciting.'

'And their wives,' Jesse said. It was impossible, at times, to tell what he was thinking. Several boxing journalists had commented on his poker face.

'And their wives,' Shakira agreed. 'If you ever win the British Championship . . .'

'I couldn't sit here without a minder. I'd have a posh car waiting outside, and I wouldn't have to consider sweet-talking some overweight gangster so that I could hitch a flight on his private jet.'

'Salim isn't overweight,' Shakira said, letting the word 'gangster' stand.

Jesse poured them both some more tea. They were drinking a delicate Darjeeling with lemon. There was a strainer to catch the leaves, an extra jug of hot water. The boxer liked the ritual.

'If you were the champion you'd be very glad to know my friends. They would save you a lot of bother.'

'I can take care of myself.' Jesse was watching the newly arrived American couple too. They wanted breakfast. It seemed they were staying at the hotel, that they had just checked in having arrived from the airport. It was lunchtime in the UK, but biologically it was their breakfast time, and they wanted bacon and eggs. That, the husband was announcing loudly, was what they'd come to England for.

Shakira sighed. She and Jesse had been paired off by Verité in the search for more publicity. Despite the hyped romance, their relationship was platonic, and it looked as if it would stay that way, but they could make a logical double act if only Jesse would let her steer him in the right direction. He was being difficult. 'You're too macho,' she said.

'Thanks.'

'I didn't mean it as a compliment.'

'I know. Finished?'

Shakira looked longingly at the last remaining eclair, which was covered in dark brown icing, and nodded regretfully. 'Yes, I've finished. Chocolate brings me out in spots.'

They walked side by side down the foyer stairs and out on to the pavement, where they stood waiting for the green uniformed, top-hatted doorman to hail them a cab. Jesse found a pound coin in his pocket to hand over as a tip. When the cab arrived he saw Shakira into it ahead of him, winked at her and then stepped back.

He wanted to walk, to clear his head. It was possible to live very well on the admiration of the money men, he knew that as well as Shakira did. He reckoned that she didn't mind selling her body for the good things in life. It didn't bother him, because he didn't fancy her. However, he thought he might come round to liking her. She wasn't so different from him. They were both banging away hard with the attributes God had given them. He was pleased with the pun. He thought he'd phone Shakira later on; she'd probably think it was funny too.

'Don't cross me, Charles,' Hilary said softly.

They were standing side by side at the rail as *Champers* sailed into port.

'I always think Cannes at night is a beautiful sight.' Charles kept his eyes focused on the fairy-lights strung up along the promenade ahead of them. 'How long will you be away? Three days, four?'

'That's entirely up to you. I want you to promise me . . .'

'Stop.' Charles spun round to face her. 'Not another word, unless you want this to be the end. Is that what you're angling for? For us to have a bloody great bust-up so you can stalk off and leave me to whistle for my share?'

Hilary struck out instantly. She never controlled her strongest instincts, and her open hand caught him full on the cheek. 'I've slept in your bed, you bastard, and you bring it all back to money.'

'Slept?' Charles's voice was ominously calm, his eyes glittering in the light filtering through the porthole from the cabin beside them. 'It's not like you to be shy, Hilary. I think screwed is much closer. Screwed like a stoat.'

She swung her hand back again, but this time Charles caught her wrist in a vice-like grip. 'You might at least leave like a lady,' he said, and then, dropping her arm, as if having touched her at all had offended him, he walked away to the bows, where a member of the crew was standing, a boathook at the ready.

It was three in the morning, and Charles still sat at his desk, from where he'd heard Hilary leave at just after eleven. There was a pile of paper to his right covered in his handwriting, the sheets a chaos of jottings. He'd spent hours noting down every bit of information he could remember that Hilary had let slip about her proposed European operation. It was to be modelled on something she'd come across in the States, a kind of ecological Weight-Watchers, members paying an annual subscription to belong, and then a weekly fee for attendance at the detoxifying sessions.

The Blackheath evening had shown him the depth of commitment available, and everyone present on that night was committed to bringing in at least six new members over the year. As soon as there were sufficient numbers a new cell would be established, and so on *ad infinitum*, with a percentage of the spawning's fees going to the founder group that in turn paid into the top of the pyramid's coffers. As Hilary had once said, there was no need for the successful entrepreneur to look for anything new, just pick out the thriving bits and pieces of established ventures and put them together. The parts that didn't remind him of Weight-Watchers made him think back to the water purifier boom.

Eventually he began to write neatly and methodically as he composed a prospectus for the Green Machine. Hilary's enterprise was called Green Air. It would please him to take the rug from under her feet. He felt soiled by having been used by her, and it wasn't a sensation he enjoyed or forgave.

It was full daylight and the odour of baking bread was drifting across the marina when Charles put down his pen and stepped out on deck. The outline was finished, and for the contact he had in mind it was ideal. He would go for fifty thousand dollars up front, and then five per cent of the long term business. He would settle, if pressed, for three and a half per cent, and forty grand for starters, but one thing he was determined about was to get his share paid in dollars. The lire that his prospect worked in was too volatile.

A girl was riding towards him on a bicycle, her long legs pedalling enthusiastically, blonde hair swept back in a single plait. She was wearing a blue and white Breton jumper and minuscule white shorts that showed her Ambre Solaire tan off to perfection. Even at several hundred yards he would be prepared to bet that she had perfect white teeth, shining blue eyes and wasn't a day over twenty-one.

He rubbed at the stubble on his chin. She had a couple of baguettes in the basket perched jauntily over her front wheel. She slowed to a halt beside a yacht moored a few berths away. He narrowed his eyes as he watched her park the bike, then expose two perfect ellipses of neat brown bottom as she bent to tie a shoelace. It would be a great pity if she was spoken for.

He heard her call out as she jumped aboard, 'Papa!' Her voice was high pitched, Parisienne, he thought. An old man stepped out and took the proffered bread. Charles's scenario expanded. The poor child was marooned with aged parents. It was his duty to rescue her, to offer some light entertainment. He was whistling as he went off to shave.

## Chapter 7

'So why did you sign up with Verité, then?' Dirk ran a fingernail down the centre of Shakira's naked back.

She was lying on her stomach, stretched full length on the bed, a narrow white towel laid over her buttocks. It was how she'd been when the departing masseuse had let Dirk into her flat. She had her arms folded under her head and was watching her visitor as he stood beside her. 'Because there is a chance she will achieve something I can't do for myself, without getting in the way of my other activities. Also, she is paying very generous expenses.'

Dirk smiled. 'I think I can make a good guess at your "other activities", as you put it. I don't think you're one for letting your attributes go to waste.'

Shakira shrugged. 'You know the motto for people like us: live dangerously, for tomorrow you may go to seed.'

Dirk let the tip of his finger rest lightly on the lowest part of Shakira's spine, just before it rose again beneath the skimpy covering. 'Your skin's good,' he said objectively. 'Despite the tan.'

'You don't approve of sun worshippers?' Shakira rolled over on to her back. Her breasts were full, the nipples brown, like hazelnuts.

'Don't do that.' Dirk stepped back quickly, raising both hands as if in surrender. 'When I arrived you said no hanky-panky, but you can't lay it on the plate like that and expect me to keep my part of the bargain.'

'You'd like some, then?' Shakira smiled. She enjoyed the open admiration of the opposite sex. 'Maybe someday, when we've got time.'

'Time?' Dirk ostentatiously stared down at his watch. 'You give me five minutes – less. With those tits, thirty seconds.'

Shakira lay back, totally relaxed. 'Then I definitely wouldn't enjoy it. When you have time to please me, and I'm in the mood to please you, then maybe. Maybe for hours, maybe even for days. Please, pass me the robe.'

Dirk handed over the midnight blue silk dressing-gown that had been hanging on the back of the bedroom door. He turned away as Shakira stood up to put it on. He wanted her so much it hurt. His trousers were always cut high under the crotch, and now he was being strangled. Pushing a hand deep into his pocket he tried to juggle his balls loose, but he was so turned on he was worried he'd come in his pants if he touched himself any more.

Shakira walked through to the sitting room and went straight to a small antique cabinet that she opened to reveal half a dozen bottles. 'Like a drink?' she asked.

Dirk opted for a Bacardi Coke. He reckoned he needed something sweet. They sat facing each other, one on each of the two matching Habitat sofas that flanked the pseudo-Georgian fireplace.

'Who pays for this pad?' Dirk asked.

'A friend.'

'It's well positioned.'

Just off the King's Road, a two-roomed flat plus bathroom and kitchen. It wasn't as special inside as he'd expected, though. It had no real character.

'It's only temporary. The last place I had was beautiful, but there were complications.'

Dirk suspected that there often were complications for those living in flats provided by other women's husbands.

'I have somewhere new in mind, somewhere very special. With luck it'll come off, but even if it doesn't I've decided to move from here. Most of the other tenants only stay a week or two, a month at most, and I don't like that atmosphere.'

'Why did you ask me over?' Dirk got up to refresh his drink. Shakira was only sipping at the Armagnac she'd poured herself.

'I thought it would be a good idea to have a chat, sort out a few ground rules. We'll be spending a lot of time together over the next few weeks, but most of it will be with the others. When we're paired off I'll be with Jesse and you with Fleur.' Shakira paused. She didn't have women friends. 'What do you think of her?'

'Who, our resident model?' Dirk could see the danger signals; Shakira was ready to turn into a scratching cat if he said the wrong thing. He laughed derisively and said, 'She's certainly tall.'

A delighted flush spread over Shakira's face and she laughed out loud. 'I knew we'd get on, you and I. I'm hungry. How about a takeaway?'

'You going to change your mind about the hanky-panky?'

Shakira shook her head.

'Then we'd do better to eat out.' He stood up.

'But Verité said we weren't to be seen out alone together.'

'What Verité doesn't know won't hurt her. There's a nice little bistro not far from here where we can go in the back way. Nicco's a mate of mine. Come on, put some clothes on, cover up those bee-eautiful tits before you do me an injury and let's go eat. I'm fucking starving.'

'But you can't drive up there,' Dirk announced.

Along with Jesse and Fleur, he was studying the street plan Verité had spread out on her dining room table.

'It's taxis and buses only,' Jesse agreed as his finger

traced the one-way road running north around Trafalgar Square.

The door closed quietly as Sara left the room. She had been sitting beside Shakira on the sofa, but had decided to go and find an aspirin. Her arm always hurt as it got towards evening.

'That's the whole point.' Verry looked at the four faces studying her. Shakira was expressionless, Dirk irritated and the other two, Jesse and Fleur, puzzled.

'Will you please explain?' Dirk asked, his voice modulated to sound bored. He felt Verité was trying to score points off him.

'I actually want the car stopped. The best photo-call in the world will only pick up a couple of slots if we're lucky . . .'

'But us all getting arrested is something different,' Jesse interrupted.

Verité laughed. 'Not arrested, just stopped. It'll be the driver who gets booked if anyone does.'

Shakira stubbed her half-finished cigarette out in the ashtray on the coffee table in front of her, and asked, 'And the driver is?'

'Me,' Verité said, surprising them all. 'I'll collect the car from the showroom, pick you four up and then drive us once round the block, so to speak. Then I'll drop you off in front of the photographers. That's agreed with the police, as long as I don't take long over it. Then I'm to drive off and park somewhere legal, and come back when the call is over. When I do return it's to pick you up, speed being of the essence again. You may have guessed that it won't go quite as I've explained. But I don't think we'll really foul up the traffic any more than it is usually.'

'You're taking a chance,' Jesse said. 'If the fuzz get shirty there's no telling what they might charge you with.'

Taking a chance – Verité's smile was genuine. Risking a fine and an endorsement on her licence was small fry compared to the rest of what she had on the line.

Sara had got accustomed to the plaster cast on her right arm. She had it supported by a sling made from a Hermès scarf that Angelique no longer wanted. Angelique, it appeared, was changing her image.

'Grandmother mine,' Verry said sweetly as she brought in the tray containing their lunch: scrambled eggs on toast topped with a generous dessertspoonful of chopped parsley stirred into fromage frais. 'How do you feel about getting involved in a little skulduggery?'

Sara gave a beaming smile. 'I knew today was going to be interesting. My stars said so.'

'I want you to hijack a taxi,' Verry announced.

'I'm sorry, Verry,' Sam said around his breakfast toast, 'I'll be in Holland.'

'But, Sam, you promised! I'm relying on you.'

Sam rolled his eyes but didn't say anything, reaching instead for a second mini-packet of cornflakes. Feeling he was acting the rat made him hungry, but he had no intention of becoming involved in what he mentally referred to as the 'Nelson's column fiasco'.

'This is going to make things very difficult.'

'More difficult than your never being available has made life for me, I suppose?'

'That's not fair. You know how much I'm trying to get through in a day, and now Mother's confined to bed . . .'

Sam sucked his cereal and milk in loudly.

'Oh, Sam,' Verité said despairingly. She'd managed to make a night at the flat. For the time being they'd agreed to differ about the benefit of putting their shared home up for sale and they'd spent twelve wonderful hours together, only six of them in sleep. Now he was spoiling it.

'Move back in here,' Sam said firmly. 'Then she'll get up quick enough.'

'The doctor says . . .'

'The doctor enjoys getting his stethoscope under her nightdress.'

Verry struggled to control a giggle as she stood up and began clearing the table. She piled the mini-cereal packets that Sam had made his choice from on to a tray, then began stacking the cups.

'Stop that,' Sam said, and stood up himself. He checked his watch and said, 'It's just past eight. We've a good half an hour – more if I sprint to the office.'

Verité chuckled delightedly. 'You'll be in no condition to sprint.' And she stepped into his arms, tipped her head back and looked up into his eyes. For a little while she could forget. Forget the rapidly rising overdraft at the bank, forget Angelique waiting to be waited on, forget the whole *Viva Europa* venture.

Verry had been right. Sam hailed a taxi when he left the flat at ten minutes past nine. So did she.

The weather was perfect. As Verry got out of bed sunlight was already drying the overnight dew on the roof opposite her bedroom window. She could hear Sara moving around already, although it was just before seven. Four hours to go before she was to collect the car.

'Verité.' Angelique opened the door without knocking. 'What are you wearing today?'

'Mother!' Verry spun round from her dressing-table in surprise. Angelique hadn't come down from her room in almost two weeks.

'I assume you've bought something new.' She walked

towards the wardrobe. In thick black tights and a polo-necked sweater her body looked unformed, like that of a twelve-year-old child.

'Actually, I thought I'd . . .'

'Excellent.' Angelique held the short black sway-back coat out in front of her. 'I knew you wouldn't want it.' She started walking back towards the door.

Verry almost said something. She thought about it, but the look her mother gave her silenced her. She had been going to take the Max Mara coat in case it turned cold. Its shape was very flattering – as her mother had no doubt noticed. It appeared Angelique was intending to come to the photo-call. That would be Dirk's doing.

Sara stood at the bottom of the stairs and called, 'Breakfast!' She too found Angelique's appearance downstairs remarkable, but she didn't say so. She'd learned long ago that there was nothing Angelique enjoyed more than evoking surprise.

'You will drive it carefully, won't you?' Bugsy's hand lingered on his car. Now that it was time for it to leave the showroom he was having second, if not third, thoughts. In fact, if it hadn't been for the dozen select corporate clients he had lined up to take along to watch the show, he would have backed out of his agreement. Once the car's part in the trans-Europe drive was in the newspapers he would have to stick to his bargain. He knew it, and Verité knew it, so once the car got to Trafalgar Square he was irrevocably committed.

'Fleur's looking forward to meeting you,' Verité lied blithely. 'She's fascinated by vintage cars.'

Bugsy took his hand off the deeply polished red paint as if it were hot. 'You mustn't be late, and neither must I. Got a fleet of taxis to take us up there, since you said just the one special motor.'

Verry waved brightly. She'd been given a few lessons on how to drive the powerful sports car, but this would be the first time she'd ventured out on her own.

The traffic was dense, but moving. She eased the nose of the Bugatti cautiously out into Park Lane and the chauffeur at the wheel of a dark blue Bentley flashed his headlights to indicate he was giving her space to pull away from the kerb.

Verry had wrapped a lightweight silk scarf around her hair, and was wearing a short, tent-shaped yellow woollen dress that she'd bought from Ines La Frenais's shop in Paris. It was very chic, as were the almost flat matching pumps. She had been going to wear black tights, but seeing her mother's all black outfit had decided on white ones instead. They were opaque, very 1960's Biba, as were her sunglasses: large, tortoiseshell-framed ones with very dark lenses.

One of her unwritten rules had always been that the PR specialist never made her own PR. The time had come, however, when in order to succeed she would have to break a few rules. If the film project was to take off she would have to become at least as well-known a personality as her 'famous foursome'.

This was the beginning. As she turned east, the Bentley swung off west behind her, the driver giving her a salute on his horn. She waved a response. It was like being given a good luck signal.

'I've just come down from *Le Manoir aux Quatr' Saisons*,' Shakira said, her French accent as impeccable as her English.

The short, trench-coated journalist leaned hard on her shorthand pencil as she took notes. 'And who was the gentleman I saw in the limousine just now, the one that brought you here?'

'A relative,' Shakira smiled – demurely, she thought, but the journalist interpreted it as smarmily.

'Not another of your fiancés?' The woman had stressed the 'another' and suddenly she had Shakira's full attention.

'What does that mean?' she snapped.

'Nothing, nothing.' The reporter was smiling now, busily jotting down the symbols that would turn into her article with hardly any editing at all. She'd had her slant ready before she began her interview.

Jesse was watching the two women from the vantage point where he was having his photograph taken for *Boxing Weekly*. He was sitting, legs apart, on the corner of the vast marble plinth supporting one of the great bronze lions. The sun was bright, but it was cold for the end of April. Apart from the fact that he suspected two of his most important appendages were in danger of freezing off, he was happy.

The four subjects of Verry's photo-call had arrived separately, as per the final plan. Fleur and Dirk were standing close to the base of Nelson's column talking to Angelique, who was the only one of Verité's family to have arrived so far. A couple of young girls, PR gophers whom Verité had 'borrowed' from an old friend, were on hand to greet the press.

So far, Verry's timing was working perfectly. She was taking a tremendous chance, she knew, in not being there at the beginning herself, but she was determined to get the maximum effect out of the car. She drove past the neo-classical Sainsbury Wing extension of the National Gallery, and breathed in sharply. The closer she got to her destination, the more her stomach was tying itself in knots. She could see Fleur, in a vivid red coat as promised, and that must be Shakira, wearing a slim green suit.

The statue of Nelson brooded more than a hundred feet

above his motley crew of pigeons and tourists; the wide stone pillar supporting his small grey figure was a great, disproportional phallic symbol. Verry struggled to hold on to her concentration. The traffic was milling around, messengers on bicycles darting up her inside, cars and taxis overtaking everywhere. She was close behind a bus that was belching filthy black diesel fumes all over the shining bonnet of Bugsy's car. There were still a few minutes to kill, so she indicated left and drifted round the corner, past the black Victorian railings of the National Portrait Gallery. She had it all worked out. A couple of right turns and she'd be back on Charing Cross Road, ready for the final few hundred yards.

Angelique was shivering. It was her first day out of bed, the clothes she wore were lightweight and a sharp breeze was whipping across the open space. A faint spray from the fountains travelled on the most aggressive gusts.

'You shouldn't have come,' Dirk said. He was worried about her. She should have been tucked up somewhere warm and cosy. He wanted to put his arms around her and cuddle her warm, but not with all the eagle-eyes around. That would really confuse them.

Shakira strode up to join the group. She looked very angry, vivid red patches bright on her cheekbones. 'That cow,' she spat. 'Bloody ugly dyke . . .'

'Careful.' Fleur looked round anxiously. She didn't want a scene for the photographers. She had been surprised at how nervous she'd felt on the train journey up from Pencombe that morning. Photo-shoots were her way of life, but this time, because it was the start of something special, she was on edge.

'Liked the limo.' Dirk grinned at Shakira. 'I thought Verry said we were to be low-key arriving.'

'That was low-key – for me.' Shakira's mood was

recovering. 'You have to feel sorry for someone so unattractive.' She was watching her interviewer, who was now talking earnestly to a photographer.

'Make way for steam.' Jesse jogged towards them. He was wearing an impeccably cut navy wool suit with a faint white stripe, which showed off his shoulders to perfection. He looked over at the clock tower between them and Charing Cross station. 'Almost time.'

'Ten, nine, eight . . .' Verry counted under her breath.

Two policemen were waiting at the kerb, close to the spot on the south side of the square where she had arranged to pull in briefly.

'. . . three, two . . .' She pulled up at the constables' feet.

As arranged Shakira and Jesse jumped straight into the back seat. The pack of pressmen followed hard on the heels of Dirk and Fleur, who, hand in hand, were running towards the car.

Verry opened the driver's door and stepped elegantly out on to the pavement. Her size five grossgrain pumps were perilously close to the strengthened toecaps of the taller policeman's size twelves.

'You can't actually stop here, madam; that was . . .' he started to say.

'I'm so sorry,' Verry gushed. 'I didn't think I was going to get here at all. They did tell you about the débâcle, didn't they?'

Fleur sat behind the steering wheel, while Dirk risked life and limb in the fast-moving traffic as he dashed round to the passenger side. Photographers began taking shots, several of them streaming on to the road in front of the parked car.

The older of the two policemen stepped out after them and held up a hand to slow the passing traffic.

'You'll have to move on.' The constable standing beside

Verry was becoming agitated. He glanced over at his colleague, who was looking angry. Traffic had begun slowing to a crawl as drivers paused to watch the action.

Shakira and Jesse were sitting up jauntily on the back of the car, Shakira busily crossing and uncrossing her luscious legs like a latterday Marilyn Monroe.

'Move on now, miss.' The policeman bent down to speak directly to Fleur. 'Move on right away, or I shall have to . . .'

He was catcalled by half a dozen of the photographers. As he went to reach into his pocket for his notebook there was a loud, sarcastic cheer.

Verry laid her hand on his arm. 'I'm so sorry, officer. It's all my fault. The whole thing's gone wrong.' She could see Bugsy and his party, holding champagne glasses, a couple of mini-skirted waitresses in full black and white parlourmaid outfits complete with frilly caps handing round canapés.

Responding to Verry's look, Fleur began to get out of the car. Dirk followed her, and then, as Verry got back behind the wheel, Jesse and Shakira stepped back on to the pavement. With a few more words of apology, and a brief, apparently flustered wave, Verry pulled out into the traffic again. Her final glimpse was of Bugsy looking puzzled, but he wouldn't be confused for long, she thought.

Twenty minutes later, during which well-orchestrated time the foursome would be posing for shots – draped around the lions, feeding the pigeons, balancing on the edge of the fountain – Verry was loitering in the traffic in Regent Street. With a murmured prayer she finally began the circuit past the art galleries once again. It was all up to Sara now.

They were still there. That was the first and most important fact that registered with Verry: the press were still in full attendance. Suddenly a red taxi darted in front of her, standing out from its black fellows. Her grandmother was in the cab. Verry could see her hair, the wonderful silver-blonde confection at its amazing candyfloss best. The taxi indicated right, towards the taxi-only lane. It went very slowly and deliberately, and Verry followed.

'Hey!' The policeman's bellow was followed by a piercing blast on his whistle as she entered the forbidden road.

Several hundred pigeons, their wings clapping like rifle shots, whirled up into the air. It couldn't have been better. The photographers ran, cameras bouncing, towards the vivid red car that miraculously for them was brought to a complete standstill when the taxi it was following slewed sideways and halted.

Verry smothered her smile of triumph and managed to look concerned as she stepped on to the road. There was now a cacophony of horns as traffic behind her was forced to a halt. Her foursome ran towards her, the two men vaulting the waist-high stone wall forming the eastern boundary of the square, as the two girls ran the short way around the end of it. They quickly met, to dispose themselves artfully around the car. The older policeman had now brought out his notebook, while his partner was speaking into a walkie-talkie.

A very large, puce-faced taxi driver emerged from the stationary cab and walked meaningfully towards the group being so eagerly snapped from all directions. 'Oi,' he bellowed and instantly became the centre of attention. 'You blue-boys gonna help me move my cab or not?'

Sara made her own way across the square, taking charge of Angelique en route. Together they hailed another taxi, one that was not obstructed by the fracas behind them. Sara instructed it to take them to the Ritz. She felt they'd earned a pick-me-up.

* * *

They made the front page of the *Evening Standard*, in colour. The jaunty caption said it all. 'Enid Blyton lives again. Famous Five start their adventures with a little help from the boys in blue.' The photo was marvellous, the policeman, as Sara said, being a very handsome boy himself. Verry looked as if she'd stepped straight off the Champs Elysées. Shakira was quite beautiful, Verry said, caught looking full-face into the camera. Jesse came over as very big, very strong, all beef-cake – 'with brains' Verry added quickly. Dirk's picture must have sent his fans into ecstasy. By the time they'd finished in Trafalgar Square there had been nearly a hundred screaming teenyboppers hounding him. Fleur was in profile, the perfect English rose, and the car – Bugsy must have been in tears. There was only the merest glimpse of glossy paint; certainly not enough to identify the make, the model, the year, all the things he'd told Verry to make certain were taken note of. But these were early days.

Verry raised her champagne glass. 'To the Famous Four,' she said.

'Five,' Sara corrected, and they all drank.

The big, beautiful car swept effortlessly up the winding road leading away from the Alpine village where they'd spent the night. Dirk was driving. It was bright and sunny and he had insisted they had the roof down, despite the rapidly dropping temperature as they climbed out of the valley.

'I'm freezing.' Shakira wriggled further down in her seat beside the driver. She turned to glare directly at Dirk who was studiously ignoring her.

'So am I,' Fleur agreed from her position at the back. She had to shout to be heard over the wind whistling around them. 'Jesse is too. Come on, Dirk, pull in and let's get the hood up.'

Dirk's only answer was to change gear, double declutching noisily.

As they climbed even higher Fleur's face became white and pinched. Jesse put his arm around her shoulders and pulled her close to him. At first she felt stiff and unyielding, but then she allowed herself to relax and snuggled closer to his warmth.

After a while, there was snow all around them. As they reached the first summit, they caught glimpses of the road ahead snaking amongst a seemingly endless vista of craggy mountains.

Dirk was feeling good. It had been stuffy in their hotel last night and he had felt claustrophobic in the enforced company of the other three. Fleur had kept on about how it was cheating according to Verité's rules for them to have paid a hotel bill, and it was driving him mad that she and Jesse seemed to think they had to take that seriously. They were now aiming for the chalet Shakira had laid on, where they would stay for three nights before driving the whole way to their next rendezvous in one go. It wouldn't be too bad as long as they took it in turns to drive.

Dusk came suddenly. Even with the car hood up the air was so cold that it felt crystalline. As the last fiery streaks faded from a gunmetal sky it felt as though the temperature dropped a rapid ten degrees. Jesse was at the wheel.

'It's not far now.' Shakira was checking the map by the light of a pen torch. She had a set of typewritten instructions on how to reach their destination. 'Only another couple of kilometres or so.'

Twenty minutes later they saw the sign, a shining wooden nameboard proclaiming 'Edelweiss' and decorated with several painted versions of the flower itself.

Dirk grimaced and expostulated, 'How kitch can you get?' When he spoke he felt as though he were stretching his face muscles. Despite his thick jacket and the heater going full blast he still felt stiff and chilled inside.

The house was straight out of a fairy story. Tyrolean carving dripped almost as thickly as the snow around the edges of the roof. There were tiny balconies underneath each of the upper-floor windows, also iced to perfection. Lights shone from the windows, orange and warming. As the car stopped they caught the smell of woodsmoke.

Shakira had a key. It was clear from the directions that if they arrived after dark there would be no one to greet them until the following morning.

'This is amazing.' Fleur pulled off her gloves as soon as she stepped into the vast, pine-lined room and quickly began unravelling the scarf wound round her throat. 'It's like something out of an old Bing Crosby film. I bet there's a musical box somewhere that plays "White Christmas".'

'And I thought you aristos were meant to have good taste,' Dirk groaned. 'Give me a David Hicks interior every time. All this decoration makes me want to puke.' He walked up to a window surrounded by painted wreaths of white and blue flowers.

Shakira began to hum. She was smiling, happy now that they had stopped motoring. 'Edelweiss, Edelweiss,' she sang, and laughed when Dirk flung a cushion at her. It too bore the white flower emblem.

Jesse kept opening the multitude of pine doors leading off the living room until he found the kitchen, another confection in wood and paint. The fridge was disguised as a woodsman's larder. Inside were eggs, butter and several large portions of Swiss and French cheeses. Behind another painted door he found a six foot tall deep freeze, in which were stacks of individually wrapped steaks, ready breaded escalopes of veal, and bags of ground beef. He started pulling out packages.

'I've found the booze,' Dirk shouted. He'd also opened

131

several doors until he'd found one leading to the cellar. A few steps down brought him to a white-painted, vaulted room lined with wine racks, nearly all of which were full. He selected a few bottles at random, and looked approvingly at the labels. They would have graced the very top of any classy restaurant's wine list.

Shakira had taken her boots off and was rubbing her stockinged feet in front of the fire. Fleur stood a few feet away holding out her hands to the blaze. 'This is better,' she said.

Shakira kept on massaging her toes. 'I thought last night's stopover was the pits – there weren't any en suite bathrooms at all at that place. I can't bear the thought of sharing a bath with a perfect stranger.'

'You didn't actually have to get in together,' Fleur laughed.

'Funny ha ha. But talking of a little light lust, you and Jesse seemed quite cosy this morning.'

The colour in Fleur's cheeks was heightened by the fire; she could feel them glowing. 'It was the only way to keep warm. Dirk should never have insisted . . .'

'What's this?' Dirk came back into the room, his arms full of bottles. 'You're not taking my name in vain again, are you, Fleur? I'm beginning to think you must have a nanny complex. To anyone else I would have said mummy complex, of course, but I bet you were brought up by . . .'

'Shut it.' Jesse spoke quite softly, but there was something in his voice that made Dirk raise his eyebrows and glance over at Shakira, who was looking complacently at Fleur.

They had steaks for supper, with straw potatoes from the freezer and a delicious mayonnaise Shakira made in the food processor. Rich with virgin olive oil, it was tangy with lemon juice and subtly underlined with garlic. There had been an iceberg lettuce in the crisper drawer along with tomatoes, cucumber and celeriac, so Fleur had assembled a salad as Jesse had laid the table and Dirk had started sampling the wine. There was no television or radio, but there was a CD player and a selection of discs. Dirk put on one of his favourites, 'Nightbreak', which he'd recorded in LA last year.

## Chapter 8

Charles looked again at the invitation on his breakfast table. It had been waiting for him on board *Champers*. If he'd come back from Paris last night as planned he would have been tempted to take it up; as it was he'd caught the early morning flight back and got on board just after eight. Abu Dann was well known for the extravagance of his entertainments, and more importantly for Charles, the quality of his guests. There was always someone new worth cultivating. Last time it had been an American beef baron who was pulling out of Chile and the rainforest mêlée. The timing had been just right for Charles to suggest participation in a joint venture in Spain where polytunnels and irrigation were turning desert acres into intensively productive vegetable farms.

Abu Dann was arranging transport from Geneva airport to the skiing lodge in the Alps, but Charles would have to leave immediately if he wanted to get there, and there were other things he had to do.

Fleur woke suddenly, as if some sound had broken the silence. She sat up, fumbling with the switch on the bedside light. It was a relief when she could see the room around her. Her heart seemed to be beating unnaturally fast, as if she'd been running. She must have been having a nightmare, she thought, but she couldn't remember what it had been about. There was a glass of water on the bedside table and she sipped it slowly. The food they'd had last night had been very rich. She looked at her watch; it was five-fifteen. If she hadn't thought it would disturb the others she would have got up and made herself a cup of coffee.

The book she'd brought up from the cosmopolitan selection in the living room was in French. Last night she'd thought it would be a good exercise to read it, but now she would rather have had an English novel, something light and entertaining. After several slow pages she gave up, turned the light off and lay down again. When next she woke it was morning, sunlight was forcing its way around the edge of the curtains and there was the sound of a car just outside.

'Salim!' Shakira sounded delighted – and surprised. Jesse, the only other member of the group who had got up early, was not deceived. All along he'd been waiting to discover some reason why Shakira had been growing steadily more hyped up and he reckoned that the middle-aged fat Arab was it.

'I am pleased to meet you.' Salim held a hand out and Jesse shook it. 'I am quite aware that one must be careful of a fighter's hands, so don't worry. I shan't squeeze too hard.'

Jesse smiled with his mouth, but his eyes were expressionless. Shakira was using him and he didn't like it.

'Shakira has told you about our little party here tonight?'

Jesse shook his head. From the corner of his eye he watched Shakira slip upstairs.

'Just a few friends, some good wine, some music. It will be fun for you in the middle of your journey. The car is going well?'

'The car's fine.' Jesse was thinking, working out the right move.

'Verité Goode's friend Bugsy will be here this evening. I'm sure he'll be pleased to hear that his motor is performing well. I am thinking of buying it after the film is made. It may well be the start of a collection. Shakira may have told you that?'

'Shakira isn't always all that talkative.' Jesse's mind was made up for him. If Verité was involved then he'd go along.

The caterers arrived in a small fleet of Citroën vans, the once convex roofs of which had been customized to look like the pitched roofs of Tyrolean lodges. Dirk, as he muttered to Jesse, thought his puke level was being tested to the limit.

The food they carried into the kitchen was for hearty appetites: vats of steaming meats in rich tomato sauce, stacks of latkes. Salim was amused by the golden potato pancakes – they were, as he said, a good Jewish staple.

The Arab had brought with him a mobile telephone. The lodge did not have a land-based phone, as he explained, because they were liable to break down in the winter. Ensconced in front of a blazing fire he made a succession of international calls. At about twelve o'clock he got around to dialling Charles's mobile number.

'Charles, it's Salim,' he said. 'How nice to speak to you. I assume I've caught you en route. Where are you now? Some little Spanish airport on the east coast, or are you still in Paris?'

'I'm afraid I'm stuck in the Med. I didn't get your invitation until this morning.'

There was a short pause. Salim had learned over the years that disappointment had to be exaggerated to carry well over the airwaves. 'Charles,' he sounded desolate, 'you are going to come to my party. You must. I've gone to so much trouble.' He made it sound as if all the organization, the flowers now arriving by the vanload, the pastries from Geneva, the chocolates from Belgium, were all for one special guest. It was a game they both knew how to play, and it was Charles's move.

'Funnily enough, I was talking about you the other day,' he said, stretching the truth only a little. 'There's a bit of business I might have to put your way.'

'You see, you must come to the party. Catch a plane now.'

'I can't, really.'

'But you can, I insist. Look, I shall arrange it all for you. Just tell me the closest town to where you are, and I'll have you picked up by chopper.'

'I'm not flying in over the Alps,' Charles said dogmatically. Some things he did for kicks; risking being cremated in a sardine can was not one of them. 'I remember the last time.'

Salim laughed, a warm sound that carried well. 'We no longer use the landing pad here, you will be pleased to know. It was blocked by a little avalanche a few months ago and it didn't seem worth clearing. No, my dear Charles, I'll have you driven in from Geneva. Now come on, go and pack your bags and I'll see you tonight.'

Charles was intrigued. Salim was clearly determined that he should attend his gathering. There had to be money in it. 'OK,' he said, 'you're on. I'd be delighted to come.'

Fleur surveyed her reflection in the full-length mirror gracing the centre of the baronial-sized wardrobe in her bedroom. Her dress was of chiffon, hanging from thin satin shoulder straps to drape seductively over her hips and swirl just above her knees. The colour, on the blue side of turquoise, made her skin look like marble and her eyes seem almost navy blue. She wasn't pleased with the result. There was an air of vulnerability that it had seemed clever to enhance at home but now, in the midst of strangers, was unnerving.

In another guest bedroom, Jesse adjusted his black bow tie carefully. He felt like a dog getting ready for Crufts. He was getting fed up with playing a part, appearing to escort Shakira whom he couldn't fathom and increasingly didn't want to. The knock on the door was a welcome interruption.

'Ducky, you look beautiful,' Dirk lisped. He enjoyed sending the fighter up. 'And we'll have to be careful, meeting like this in your loverly boudoir.' The accent was vintage Dick van Dyke.

'Piss off.'

'Now don't be like that. I'm all alone. Fleur's doing a complete make-over on herself, and Shakira, well . . .' He got bored with his act and let his voice drop back to its normal level. 'She's doing a make-over on our genial host. I offered her the chance to give me a quick one, but she turned me down. There's no accounting for tastes.'

'It's none of our business what she gets up to.'

'It is if it's obvious. Verité wants the two of you looking all lovey dovey, so the fact that she's a quick lay for anyone with a gold card and a Rolex makes it all a bit iffy.'

'That's a filthy thing to say. You want to wash your mouth out.'

'Want to make me?'

It was ridiculous, and they both knew it. They weren't going to fight over someone neither of them cared much about, but the trip was getting to them both.

'You see, I told you you could make it.' Salim beamed an effusive welcome to Charles.

'Your invitation said seven-thirty for eight. It appears

I'm early.' Charles stepped out of the cold and into the brilliant interior.

'What's an hour between friends? Let me take your coat. I'll show you to a bedroom where you can freshen up and get changed. There are some bright young things about the house somewhere whom you might like to meet before the fun begins.'

Charles exchanged his black polo-necked jumper and black slacks for his black dinner suit. He remembered Hilary saying he should branch out, try something different, perhaps follow the American fashion and wear a patterned jacket, but the very thought made him cringe. He shot his cuffs the requisite inch, revealing just a glimpse of Tiffany diamond-set cufflinks. They had been a gift from Salim, a year or two ago when he had been newly arrived in England and Charles had arranged for him to rent the right country manor, go to the right race meetings, chose the right trainer for his brand new string of thoroughbreds.

'And this is Fleur Montford,' Salim said completing the introductions.

'Hello, Charles.' Fleur stepped forwards to kiss him on the cheek.

He was pleasurably surprised. They had first met at the ballooning event at Pencombe, and briefly once after that at a charity ball at the Grosvenor. He said, 'You look beautiful,' and was aware of six foot two of middleweight glowering at him. He vaguely recalled that the gossip columns had been full of Fleur and the pop singer. It seemed, despite her demure appearance, that she played the field.

By eleven o'clock the designer gathering in and around the chalet was buzzing. A German pop group was performing in a thermal-lined marquee that, with the living room's wall-wide patio doors fully opened, formed a twenty metre extension for dancing. A complete bar had been set up flanking the door to the kitchen, from where a continuous stream of hot canapés appeared carried by girls in full Tyrolean costume and pink and white doll make-up.

'But I don't want to,' Shakira said again. She and Salim were alone in her bedroom where he'd been trying to persuade her to join him in smoking a joint for what felt like hours.

'It's just like a cigarette. Why the fuss?'

Shakira shrugged her shoulders. She knew he thought she was being tiresome, but she'd been drinking and she didn't like what happened when she mixed drugs with alcohol. 'I'm not a prude,' she said.

'How could I, of all people, think that?' Salim laid his hand gently on Shakira's arm. He was at his most charming, his most urbane. 'I just want you to relax, to be yourself. Going around with those others has tied you up in knots. You're not my fun girl tonight.'

'Anything else. I would do anything else you asked me.'

'But I don't want anything else. I just want you to be the star, to shine.'

It would be so much easier to agree. So far Shakira had refused her sponsor nothing. That was how she thought of him, as her sponsor. He was providing the money for the new flat, he was talking about a car, he had provided the Azzedine Alaïa dress she was to wear that evening.

'Just try a little.' Salim put the cigarette to his own lips, breathing in the perfumed smoke. 'You see, there's no harm.' He offered it to her, maintaining eye contact, keeping his voice warm and low.

Shakira's hand was trembling as she took the joint. She was angry with herself, now, for making too big a deal of this.

'You see, it's so easy.'

She nodded. Even with the first few breaths she was more relaxed.

'Just a little more, then we will join the party.'

Charles had made his contact. Bugsy Maclone was eager to hype up the vintage car market. The world-wide recession in luxury goods had hit his business hard. Today, a good example of a moderately rare car was going for under a hundred thousand pounds; there was a long way to climb back up. The dealer had explained that he already had his own PR campaign under way. For example, he'd said, gesturing to where Fleur and Dirk were dancing together, it was his Bugatti parked outside. But he accepted that such publicity as the tour achieved would only be marginally beneficial to him. If the film became a reality there would be much more of a bonus. In the meantime Salim had convinced him that someone like Charles Freeman could help re-establish the social chutzpah of owning such a vehicle. Salim was suggesting that the Bugatti stay on at Cannes for Charles's use, in exchange for trailing Bugsy's name under the noses of the assorted rich and almost famous who still frequented the Riviera.

Jesse stood, a glass of Glühwein in his hand, watching Fleur. She moved rhythmically in counterpart to Dirk's staccato action. Half a dozen languages were being spoken around him, and he wondered fleetingly what his brothers would have made of the evening. He gave himself the answer: they would have said it was naff. And it was. Despite the loud music, the gyrating couples and the overflowing food and drink, there was something missing. It wasn't a party, it was a stage show.

'You're not dancing,' Charles commented. Business done, he had made his way to where Jesse stood.

'Not my scene.'

'I'm surprised to hear that. I thought it was all "Dance like a butterfly, sting like a bee".'

'Do you have a problem with boxing or something?' Jesse asked belligerently. He'd had several glasses of the sweet sticky drink the girls were pouring out and was feeling bolshie.

'No problem.' Charles raised his glass in a mock toast.

Jesse thought about hitting out. He reckoned Charles was taking the micky and he didn't like it. He watched the glass go to his potential opponent's lips, noted the foaming contents, and was surprised out of his bad temper. 'That's not beer, is it?'

Charles nodded. 'It's Czechoslovakian lager, and it's a lot better for the liver than that muck you're drinking. And, of course, it came out of a can, so it's a lot more difficult to doctor. Some hosts will go to remarkable lengths to make their parties go with a swing.'

'Christ, I could murder a pint.' Jesse abandoned his half-full glass on a small side table and looked around for the source of the amber nectar. That was when he saw Shakira.

She looked stunning. Standing in the centre of the living room she was the focus of a group of admiring males. Her dress was the same shade of café au lait as her skin; it was moulded to her, swathed over her right shoulder and split up the left side from the knee-length hem to her waist. There was nowhere any underwear could have been concealed: her smooth, bare hip exposed no panties, her erect nipples no bra.

The music in the marquee changed. The pulsing beat became slow and romantic and by mutual consent Fleur and Dirk left the floor. They walked to where Jesse was standing at the entrance to the living room, his back towards them.

'Jesse.' Fleur tapped his shoulder. 'Could you be an angel and get me an Evian with a dash of orange? I can't face the crush at the bar.'

It was Charles who answered her. He had been standing to one side, also watching the group around Shakira. 'I think you're going to have to wait a while for your drink, Fleur. This, if I'm not mistaken, is going to be the high spot of the evening.'

Shakira had stepped up on to a pinewood coffee table. She was smiling dreamily, singing softly to herself. Someone had put on the CD player. Dirk's latest hit pulsed out and Shakira began moving in time to it. She was carrying a chiffon scarf that matched her dress, and now, holding one end in each hand, she began to caress her body with it. Slowly, languorously, she slid it down her upstretched arms and wound it round her neck, and all the time she danced.

'She's stoned!' Dirk said in amazement. He'd always found her so self-contained. In a strange way she was a private sort of person, but the display she was putting on now was very, very public. Perhaps, he thought, her behaviour was due to the quality of stuff on offer. He'd been smoking the Arab's 'specials' himself, and hadn't felt so good in ages.

Salim had gravitated to the edge of the crowd who were now clapping in time with the music, moving to its rhythm. 'I enjoy your singing,' he said to Dirk. 'I find it stimulating.'

'So does she,' Dirk said emphatically. He couldn't take his eyes off Shakira. It was his music and she was at one with it. He felt the beat, the power, begin to take him over.

'Here.' Salim handed the singer the joint he had been smoking. Dirk sucked in hungrily, once, twice, then he bent, trance-like, and removed his shoes. His eyes fixed on the writhing figure before him he stepped forwards. Jesse reached out to stop him, but Salim caught and held the outstretched hand. 'No,' he said sharply.

The music changed. It was another of Dirk's songs, one he'd written years ago, when he'd been very young, sad, and lonely. He stepped up on to the table with Shakira and the crowd sighed with pleasure. He began to dance, his hips fitting to her movements. She wrapped the scarf around his body, pulling him towards her until they moved in perfect rhythm.

Salim's voice was so low that Jesse had to struggle to hear the words. 'I suggest you don't do anything, Mr Fighter. I suggest you just stand very still. If you don't want to watch you can always close your eyes.'

Jesse glared down at the Arab. He went to take a step forwards. The situation was getting out of hand; someone had to protect Verité's investment.

A short sharp jab from behind caught him under the kidneys. He spun on his heel to face his aggressor and then froze. It was Salim's driver, the man they'd been introduced to as Bruno, still in dove-grey uniform complete with peaked cap. He looked very smart, very competent, right down to the six-inch filleting blade that was the business part of the knife he held in his leather-gloved hand.

Dirk was euphoric. He'd never felt this way before. He'd been close on many occasions, but something had always just eluded him. This time the music was perfection, loud enough to fill his brain with sound but still leaving him room for sensation. His audience was with him, every step of the way. Shakira was his mirror image, his other self. She began, slowly, to peel off her dress. It slipped down off her shoulder, revealing the swelling of her breasts, then inching over the white-brown skin that he instinctively knew would smell of camellias. He moved closer, he had to touch her; she reached out, her dress clinging, just skimming her nipples. She began unbuttoning his shirt.

It took a while for Charles to become aware of the tugging at his sleeve; he had leaned back against the wall, allowing the performance to wash over him. He'd seen 'skin' acts before, but this, he was sure, would be something unique.

'Charles, please.' Fleur was desperate. 'You have to stop this. It's wrong, it's . . .'

'You want to see me lynched?' Charles forced a light laugh. He was aroused, taut inside; he wanted to watch, could hear the music drawing them on, pulling all of them towards the climax.

'This isn't what we're here for.' Fleur couldn't think what to say. Her senses too were pulverized by the sound, but she found the sensation hateful.

Salim had worked his way through the crowd to stand beside Fleur. He was very close to her, looking sympathetic. 'Come,' he said, 'I'm afraid our friends are a little carried away. I know somewhere quiet, where we can be in peace.'

Fleur recoiled from him as she would from a snake. Stepping back quickly she collided with Charles, whose arm went instinctively around her.

'There is nothing to fear.' Salim held his hands out in apparent supplication.

For Charles the spell had been broken. He gripped Fleur more firmly, and smiled at Salim as he spoke. 'We'd love to take up your offer – together, if you don't mind.'

They made a slow progress around the edge of the room, Fleur's face buried in Charles's shoulder. Salim's expression was set and hard. As they reached the stairs he gestured abruptly for Charles to go up, and then stayed himself to watch.

'But you made love, Shakira, out there, in front of them all.' Fleur was crying. She couldn't help it. She felt deeply ashamed, as if all four of them had been involved.

Shakira put her cigarette to her lips. She was cold, chilled through now that the manic excitement was over, the crowd gone, the four of them, with Charles, in sole possession of the living room. 'Not love, Fleur. We didn't make love, we had sex. There is a difference.'

Jesse slumped dejectedly in an armchair. He hadn't been able to do anything except stand and watch. Worst of all, despite his anger he'd been turned on, and now his feeling of earlier impotence was tinged with anticlimax.

'Tell her the difference, Dirk,' Shakira instructed haughtily. 'Explain to Fleur that only love can be intimate.'

Dirk threw his half-smoked cigarette into the fire. 'Fuck off,' he snarled and stalked out of the room. He felt cheap.

Charles would happily have left the little gathering, but Fleur had begged him not to. He sat watching the flickering flames licking the logs in the grate, wishing he was back on *Champers*, alone. 'When do you resume your trip?' he asked.

'I can't.' Fleur looked at him unbelievingly.

Jesse stood up. 'Stop over-reacting,' he said roughly. 'It was a party, and some of the guests got a bit carried away, that's all. Don't tell me you haven't ever been at that kind of do before. Christ, it's all over the newspapers every time your upper-class mates just about have it off in the middle of the Savoy dance floor.'

'That's enough.' Charles spoke softly.

'Who the hell do you think you are?' Jesse pushed his

146

face close to Charles's. He was steamed up, boiling over with the aggression that the chauffeur with the knife had invoked.

'I think I'm the person who . . .'

Whatever Charles had been going to say was interrupted when the door flew open with a crash. Dirk stood in the doorway. He held a whisky bottle in his hand and his face was pale, his eyes red-rimmed. He was looking at Shakira. 'Wannanother fuck?' he said.

'No thank you,' she replied primly.

He stared at her for a moment, seemed about to say something and then turned round to walk away. Instead he came staggering into the room backwards. After him came Salim's chauffeur, pushing the singer in the chest dismissively.

'I am to drive you to the airport,' he said to Charles.

'No hurry,' Charles said blandly. He might not want to feel responsible for the Montford girl, but he did.

Salim hurried into the room. 'My dear Charles,' he gushed. 'You really must leave now, much though I would enjoy your company. There are things to do, places to go.'

Charles had a low anger threshold. He could disguise his fury but not prevent its growth. He breathed slowly before saying, 'I may well leave with these young people.'

'There is no room in their car.' Salim's voice was rising. 'Besides, they will be here a little longer.'

'No,' Fleur interjected. 'I will not stay in this house another minute. None of us want to stay here, none of us.' In her dislike of Salim, she had allied herself once again with her companions.

'Shakira stays,' Salim announced. 'So, unless you want to leave her behind . . .'

Shakira stood up quickly. For once she looked anxious; she had had enough of Salim's manoeuvrings for a while.

'No,' she said. 'I also want to leave.'

Salim struck out, his open hand catching her across a cheek. He hit so hard that she fell back into the chair.

Jesse took a short step forwards, his left fist already in motion. It came from low down and rose like a power-hammer to hit their host on the very point of his chin; he was lifted an inch off the ground before falling backwards, to lie still on the floor.

The chauffeur had been taken by surprise. It was a few seconds before his hand went to his pocket, but he was too slow. Charles gripped his wrist and pulled it up behind his back in a savage arm-lock. 'The four of you,' Charles snapped. 'Leave now. Don't bother to pack, just clear off, go on. Now.' He barked the last word like an order.

They drove off in a flurry of snow flung up from the ground by their spinning wheels.

Fleur was driving. She didn't want to, but Dirk was looking like death, Jesse was nursing his bruised fist and Shakira . . . Fleur kept blinking away tears. The wind was cold on her face, though the sun was bright. She should have been wearing her dark glasses, but she'd left them behind in the rush. Shakira was sitting in the passenger seat beside her. She was sobbing, convulsively, unrestrainedly. Fleur thought it must be with fear.

It was several hours until Charles reached the airport. He had attended to Salim, seen him settled and comfortable, and, Charles hoped, reconciled to the turn of events. Now, Charles used international directory enquiries to get the telephone number he wanted. On the first dialling it was engaged. After a few minutes he tried again.

'Goode as Golde,' a tinny voice said.

'Verité Goode, please. This is Charles Freeman calling.' There was a short pause. Then the same voice, even more metallic, said, 'Mr Freeman, what can I do for you?'

'Verité?'

'This is Verité Goode, I repeat . . .'

'Please don't bother. This call is not a request for you to do anything for me, Ms Goode; far from it. I just thought you might like to know you have a few problems.'

'Problems?' Verry's voice was clipped. She remembered Charles Freeman with irritation. She didn't have the time or the energy to put up with his social posturing.

'Your four young protégés are somewhere in the middle of Europe, careering along in the cold and the dark, being hotly pursued by an extremely annoyed middle eastern potentate. If I add that his annoyance was fired by sex, fuelled by a punch on the chin, and not exactly helped by a weeping Honourable and a seriously pissed pop singer you might begin to get my drift. I suggest you call your little convoy home, or at least meet them en route.' Charles was beginning to relax; he was enjoying himself. 'May I also suggest . . .' But he was talking to an empty line. He was smiling as he hung up. The rather attractive Ms Goode was nothing if not constant in her antagonism towards him.

They spent two nights en route for Cannes, both at modern, featureless, three-star hotels that catered for the tourist just one step up from economy.

There were basic bathrooms en suite, televisions and coffee making facilities in the bedrooms, but only minimal room service. Shakira didn't really notice. As soon as they'd checked in, she'd gone to her room with a bottle of vodka she'd got Dirk to buy for her. In the mornings she'd appeared ready for the road, well wrapped up, head scarf wound around her hair, dark glasses already in position.

After Fleur's initial three-hour stint Jesse had done

most of the driving. He'd been glad to have something to do, to take his mind off the toothache-like niggle of having been faced down by the Arab's chauffeur. Charles Freeman had convinced them all that they should make for their final destination straight off.

Arriving there early for the festival, they would have to maintain anonymity until Verité arrived. Jesse had tried phoning her London number half a dozen times, but always got the answerphone. He couldn't think of a message that covered their situation, so he hadn't left one.

Verry had left Sara in control in London. She was to forward any messages to the hotel in Cannes where Verry intended ending up. Meanwhile, she was going to fly to Geneva and try to trace the others from there. She had an Alpine address that Shakira had given her, a place where they were going to stay for a few days, and she intended to start there.

Sara had plans of her own. It was time, she believed, to do something about the manuscript. There were dozens of publishers out there in the marketplace. Never mind the much hyped downturn in the book trade: if a clutch of editors had been vying with each other to pay multimillions for Margaret Thatcher's memoirs, then there had to be some of them left with money to spare for what, Sara said to herself, was probably a whole lot more entertaining.

The *Writers' and Artists' Year Book* that Sara found on Verité's shelves was as good a place to start as any. She sat down with a pencil and paper and began going through the list of publishers. She totally ignored the legend 'Unsolicited manuscripts not accepted' – how could they know what they might be missing? She thought it was up to an ambitious author to make her point. A couple of days in a taxi should cover most of the options. With her list of potential publishers, she began going through an A to Z of London streets, creating an itinerary. Getting the legwork done was fifty per cent of winning the ballgame, her husband had said. It would be good to have something positive to tell Verité when she got home.

Since leaving Edelweiss, Fleur had had time to think, and plenty to think about.

Jesse had insisted she sat in the back next to Dirk when she'd given up driving. He thought they should keep as much as possible to the charade invented for them by Verité. At first Fleur had kept as far away from the singer as possible, wedging herself in the corner of her seat. He hadn't seemed to notice, sitting hunched down, chain-smoking one Gauloise after another. He hadn't said a word on the first day. They'd driven fast, pushing the Bugatti harder than before, stopping only to buy food they could eat in the car. Fleur kept remembering the Arab's chauffeur, the sneer on his face as he'd tried to reach for what she'd assumed was a gun. After a while she convinced herself that she had over-reacted, that he was just a 'heavy', the accoutrement of a nervous man of money, not a psychopath ready to murder them all.

It was after an overcooked dinner in their first hotel that Dirk had taken her aside, out of Jesse's hearing. 'I want to talk to you,' he'd said. 'Alone.'

They'd gone to an empty television room littered with dozens of vinyl-covered chairs lined up in front of a thirty-inch screen.

'I want to say I'm sorry,' he said.

Fleur didn't want to think about the party any more. She replied quickly, 'That's OK, honestly. I think we should just forget it.'

'Hold on – don't fly off at half cock. I don't want you to get this wrong. I'm not apologizing for what I did – if you ever get to know me, you'll understand that's just par for the course. But I am sorry you got frightened. That bastard that sniffs around after Shakira is an evil bugger.'

'I didn't know I could feel that kind of fear.' Fleur spoke slowly, exploring her own emotions. 'I've been frightened before, for someone I loved who I thought might die, but it wasn't the same. This was all-consuming, leaving no room for any other feeling at all.'

Dirk's lips twitched at the corners. It was the first time he'd felt like laughing all day. 'Just shows you're normal and the ass you care about most is your own.'

'No, not mine. I wasn't frightened for me.'

'Something tells me you weren't all fired up about yours truly, so who?' He paused as if lost in thought, then continued, 'You still worried about that other guy, then?'

Fleur flushed. 'Well, no. I mean, he's fine. We all are.'

'How do you know? You called him up on the phone since we left him with those creeps?'

Fleur didn't say anything. She would be happy for Dirk to suppose she'd fallen for Charles Freeman.

But realization had dawned and Dirk was suddenly in his element. 'Oh, I get it. No wonder I haven't had any luck trying to charm the pants off you! You've been horny all along for that great hunk of beefcake.'

There were a thousand things Fleur wanted to say. She opened her mouth to speak, and then a slow smile replaced the fluster. 'I wouldn't put it quite like that,' she said.

'I'm forgiven?' Dirk held his hand towards her and they shook hands formally.

'On one condition.'

'Whatever you say.' Dirk's tone was bright. He was almost his usual self again.

'That you agree to rescue Shakira from that sticky little man. You could sweep her off her feet . . .'

Dirk held his hand up. 'You can stop right there. Shakira and I just don't jell. However it looked the other night, that was just what she said, pure sex. As for sweeping her off her feet, that's not my scene. I'm a shit, pure and simple. I don't like it when the American press say so, but I don't mind saying it myself. If you and Jesse make a number then bully for you, but this little foursome doesn't break into two neat pairs, despite all our glorious leader's planning.'

Thanks to the excellent directions she'd been given in the last village, Verry easily found the house she was looking for. Someone was brushing snow off the wooden nameboard at the roadside, so she slowed her rented silver-grey Alfa Romeo to a crawl and then pulled up beside him.

'Yes, this is Edelweiss.' The man was wearing a charcoal-coloured, thickly padded anorak and matching ski pants. His dark hair was slicked back from his forehead, his smooth olive skin glowed with moisturizer, and he wore mirrored sunglasses.

'I'm looking for some friends of mine,' Verry said. She had wound down the car window and ice-cold air flooded the interior. She shivered as she continued, 'Two men and two women. They planned to stay here for a few days.'

'Go on up to the house,' the man instructed brusquely. 'There will be someone there to help you.' His English was excellent; only the slightest sibilant accent, which Verité couldn't identify, revealed it wasn't his mother tongue.

She drove slowly up the winding driveway. It had been well swept after last night's fall of snow and her heavy-tread tyres bit reassuringly into the gravelled surface. As she rounded a final shoulder of mountain the house was revealed a couple of hundred yards in front of her. She was impressed by its size and amused by its extravagant decoration, but disappointed by the fact that there was no fire-engine red Bugatti parked outside.

The front door of the house opened as soon as she stepped out of the car. A man stood framed by the ornate pine architrave. He called out, 'Good morning, Ms Goode. Do come into the warm. It's very chilly this morning.' He rubbed his hands together briskly as if to emphasize his words.

Verry paused for a few seconds beside the car. There was no reason for her to be surprised by the recognition, she told herself; if the others had stayed at Edelweiss they would inevitably have mentioned her name. She smiled and hurried up the short flight of steps.

'Come on in. Come and stand close to the fire.' Salim walked his guest towards the fireplace where fat pine logs were blazing merrily, then gestured to the open door to the kitchen where a young girl in a frilly apron was cooking. 'Antoinette will bring us some hot drinks.'

'That's very kind, Mr . . . ?'

'I am Salim Abu Dann, a friend of Shakira's.'

Verry noticed that her host wore tinted make-up. There was a line of it at his jaw, and looking closer she could see the reason for the camouflage: a blue-green bruise that led up to the cheekbone. 'She told me she was staying here for a few days. I'd hoped to catch up with her.'

Salim smiled apologetically. 'I'm afraid they've already gone. Driven away in that beautiful car. I can't tell you where they are now – in fact, Shakira had forgotten something and I sent Bruno to look for them, but no luck. You don't know where they are staying, then?'

'I have no idea where they'll be until they were scheduled to reach Cannes the day after tomorrow. I'll leave to meet up with them there.' As she spoke Verry was remembering what Charles Freeman had said on the telephone. This, presumably, was the irate Arab, and the bruise had been Jesse's work. She shied away from thinking about the sexual connection. 'I'll take whatever Shakira forgot, and give it to her.'

'There is no need,' Salim said, then paused as the girl brought them mugs of steaming hot chocolate and laid down a plate of home-made *langues du chat*. 'I too shall be at Cannes for the festival. You know, I am beginning to feel that there is a degree of inevitability in all this? Their journey towards their future, your pursuit. If I shared your religion I would say it was almost biblical.'

'I'm sorry?' Verry laid down her mug. The drink was too hot. 'I don't follow you.'

'It's not important.' There was a silence that was long enough to make Verry feel awkward before he continued, 'I had a friend of yours here the other evening, the charming Bugsy Maclone. We had quite a fun time. It's a pity you weren't here. I shall see you get an invitation to my next little gathering.'

Verry smiled politely. She doubted whether she would accept the future offer of hospitality. She didn't think she would like it, just as she didn't like her host's effusive speech and gestures combined with his expressionless eyes.

'I am very interested in Shakira's career – if there are any strings you feel I could pull . . . ?'

'Thank you for the offer.' Verry stood up. 'I'll bear it in mind. Meanwhile, I think I should get going. It's quite a drive until I reach my next stop.'

Salim escorted her to the door. Outside, the man with the mirrored glasses was just giving her windscreen a final polish. The rest of the car shone like glass.

'My dear Bruno,' Salim purred. 'He really is quite

compulsive about cars. That is one reason why I am considering making a collection of vehicles through your friend Bugsy.'

'Perhaps you should start with the Bugatti we're using?' Verry had reached the bottom of the steps. She was trying to disentangle herself from Salim's grip, which had apparently been applied in the name of safety but had about it a growing sensation of grope.

'Ah yes, I have done so. I own it already, as of yesterday. I do hope you have told your young people to take care of it.'

Verry felt a flicker of anger. She didn't want this man involved in her business.

'I have arranged for Charles Freeman to use my Bugatti after you have left Cannes. That will help your publicity, I have no doubt. He has just the right profile – that exciting mixture of class and decadence, so essentially English – to bring your proposed film to the attention of the people who matter.'

As Verry drove away she glanced in her rear-view mirror. Master and servant stood side by side watching her leave. They were very still, seemingly part of a landscape that had grown suddenly menacing with the abrupt change in the weather, the grey light and the first flecks of snow.

Fleur wrapped a skimpy towel around her hair; she had knotted another, marginally larger version around her body. She was still wet from her shower. She frowned as whoever was at her door began knocking again. 'Who is it?' she called out.

A gruff voice with a heavy French accent answered, 'Room service.'

She hadn't expected such a quick reaction. She'd only

phoned down for more bath-towels a few minutes ago. She looked vainly for something more to put on, but everything apart from what she'd been wearing the morning after the party had been left behind at the chalet. She hadn't had a chance to shop for replacements yet. Standing behind the door she opened it a little and said, 'Just put them down on the floor.'

To her surprise a bouquet of red roses was shoved unceremoniously through the gap. As she bent to look at the card a male voice said, 'Happy Christmas,' the door was pushed wide open and she staggered back across the room.

Jesse stood, his arms full of packages, his hands gripping half a dozen carrier bags. He was grinning widely.

'But it isn't Christmas.' Fleur adjusted her towel more firmly. 'You might close the door. Anybody in the corridor can see me like this.'

'Your every wish is my command.' Jesse hooked the door with his foot and kicked it closed. 'Presents,' he said and began letting the boxes fall, one by one, to the floor.

'You've been shopping.'

'Ten out of ten for observation. Here, try this on for size.' He held out a cellophane bag that contained a cream cashmere wrap.

Fleur threw it round her shoulders. It felt wonderful, soft and silky.

'And this.' Jesse was squatting on the floor, tipping out the contents of the multicoloured bags and boxes. He threw her a silk shirt followed by a matching skirt; there were packets of tights, several pieces of richly embroidered white satin underwear.

'How on earth did you know my size?' Fleur asked. She was growing increasingly amazed as she checked the labels.

'Easy.' Jesse grinned and held his hands cupped as if they were holding a pair of oranges. 'Closed my eyes and imagined.'

Fleur looked down so that he couldn't see her blush. 'I must owe you a fortune.' In checking the labels for size, she had also seen the designer names.

'I told you, it's Christmas.'

'But . . .'

'No buts.' Jesse took two quick steps towards her.

Fleur was confused by his proximity. The bed was close behind her, pressing into the backs of her legs, and she could feel her cheeks getting redder and redder.

'I phoned my manager. I've got the fight! They've offered me a crack at the British Heavyweight Championship! Can you imagine' – he put his arms around her – 'what this means to me, to my mum, my dad?'

'Don't,' Fleur whispered. She looked up into his eyes. 'Let me go.'

'Let you go? You still don't understand, do you?' He bent towards her. She tried to turn her face but he took hold of her chin.

Their lips touched.

'Fleur,' he whispered. 'Have you any idea what you do to me?' His fingers touched her neck, strong, commanding, and yet so mesmerizingly gentle.

For the first time in days Fleur was really warm. She didn't feel the towel slip off her head, was hardly aware of the damp hair touching her back as her head tipped. He was kissing her again, her lips were parted, his tongue flicked briefly between them. She was aching with longing, her arms around his neck pulling him against her. The knot of the towel above her breasts pressed against his chest, and, fumbling, he undid it.

'Jesus, you're beautiful,' he said. He stepped back, looking at her body, the slim hips, the long, long legs that had been driving him crazy. She had tiny breasts. He cupped one in his hand, bent to kiss the rose-tinged nipple.

He picked her up effortlessly. She, who had always felt so tall, so awkward, was lifted like a child and laid gently on the bed. She shivered briefly at the touch of the chill coverlet beneath her, but then Jesse was beside her, stroking the white skin as he'd imagined doing for so long.

Fleur put her hand to his face. She'd stopped thinking, everything was sensation. His smooth palm slid effortlessly over her stomach; she parted her legs as he touched the dark, curling hairs. She lay back, her eyes closed.

He kept saying her name, over and over again. She started to speak and he kissed her lips. All she wanted was here. He came into her when she was ready, and they moved, each striving for victory, each, in the end, winners.

# Chapter 9

Verry slammed down the telephone. That was the third call she'd made since waking up that morning at her hotel in Cannes. Each one had increased her conviction that the place for her group to pick up publicity that evening was going to be on board Charles Freeman's yacht. Her last conversation, with an old friend who was doing freelance journalistic coverage of the festival, had made it clear that they were the most coveted invites on offer.

Verité skipped through her Filofax. She remembered Charles flicking his visiting card on to the ground beside her just before he'd walked away through the woods at Leeds Castle. She'd picked it up and filed it as a matter of habit.

The number marked *Champers* rang and rang. She redialled and held on for five minutes but there was still no reply. There was no point in ringing his UK number, and there was only one possibility left, listed as his carphone. That took a considerable time to connect, and when it did it was engaged. She sipped at a glass of iced Perrier while she counted to thirty and then tried again. This time, after two rings, Charles Freeman picked up the phone.

'Hello?' His voice was just as she'd remembered: laid-back, plummy, cynical, and all in just one word.

'Is that Charles Freeman?' She didn't wait for an answer, she knew perfectly well it was. 'This is Verité Goode. We spoke a few days ago.' There was a crackle on the line. 'Hello? Are you still there?'

'I'm still here. Where are you?'

'I'm in Cannes. First, thank you for your call the other day, I did follow up on it, but there really wasn't any problem. Second, I wondered if I could prevail on your famous hospitality.' She was making herself feel sick, but she poured on the professional charm. 'Your party tonight . . .'

'My dear Ms Goode, "Goode", as I seem to recall, "as Golde", you don't mean you're prepared to put up with some of my company, do you? The lengths you PR girls will go to for a bit of publicity. At least I assume that's what you're after – an increase in profile, a few glossies in the mags?'

There was a pause which Verry ended by admitting, 'Yes. That's precisely what I'm after, and I know it's a cheek my calling you, but, as they say, those who don't ask don't get.'

'Now that's funny. My mother always said it was "Gimme gimme doesn't get". Still, I suppose Mother can be wrong sometimes.'

He was going to play ball. Verry closed her eyes with relief.

'I will do the impossible for you, and extend my precious invites by another three, I'll have them sent round. Where are you staying? The Majestic or the Carlton?'

Verry murmured, 'The Carlton.' Three invitations. Even she hadn't got the gall to ask for more, but three!

'This is on one condition, my dear Ms Goode. You have to come yourself. I'm not amused by "bright young things", at least not in mixed dozens. So you just toddle along, and who knows, it might be worth your while. I might just need my image given a little building. *A bientôt*, Ms Verry, very Goode.'

'I thought we'd draw straws.' Verry was acting very professionally, avoiding making eye contact with either

Fleur or Shakira and so, hopefully, avoiding a scene. 'Each of you girls takes one from this bunch, and whoever has the longest goes to the party, and takes their escort along with them.' She held the handful of drinking straws out above the woven wire table top of the chic beach bar.

Dirk stood up suddenly, making the dregs of the coffee in the bottoms of their dumpy china cups tilt wildly. 'No need,' he said. 'It's all arranged, Verité. This is Fleur's evening, hers and Jesse's. And there's no need to look so po. It doesn't have to compromise your pairing off. But Shakira and I have other fish to fry.'

Shakira was also standing. 'We'll see you back at the hotel. Don't worry about us, Verité. There'll be lots of other occasions where we can shine over the next few days.'

Verry watched them walk away, and then looked over at Fleur. 'I think we should go and have our hair done,' she said, and laid a couple of notes on the table to cover the bill.

Jesse was almost dressed when Dirk came to his room. The pop-star was walking on the balls of his toes, looking bouncy and full, as Jesse would have said, of fight.

'Howya doin'?' Dirk asked, and shifted a wad of well-chewed gum from the inside of one cheek to the other. 'You any good at tying these friggin' things?' He, like Jesse, was wearing a dinner jacket, and he had a strip of black tie hanging loosely round his neck. 'I'm hopeless. I was even slow at tying my shoelaces.'

Jesse pulled at his own immaculate velvet tie, which shot back into place on its elastic.

'That's the pits.' Dirk grinned, and pulled out of his pocket a small, beautifully wrapped package. 'I knew you needed class, so here you go. Good luck token.'

It was a tie like Dirk's, raw silk, a living black. They

stood side by side facing the mirror trying to tie them and then gave up and stood face to face as they tied each other's.

Shakira walked in and giggled. She was wrapped from her shoulders to the floor in a pale blue velvet evening cape. 'I never took you for a bender, Jesse.' She laughed. 'Dirk I wouldn't be too sure about, but a great big boxer who goes for the guys, I think that's stretching even my imagination a bit far.'

They collected Fleur, who was dressed in an ankle-length fuchsia tube that showed her model figure to perfection, and then made their way to Verry's room. She opened the door to their knock and it was the first time she had really appreciated their cohesiveness as a group. The impression was so powerful that for a moment she couldn't think what to say. She felt suddenly very much on her own.

'Shakira and I just wanted to wish you lot luck,' Dirk said. He leaned forward and kissed Verité's cheek, and then Fleur's. 'Those who are about to die,' he quoted inexplicably, then, holding Shakira by the hand, he walked away.

Verry stepped out into the hotel corridor to watch them leave. She wasn't too bothered about their holding hands, for they were walking purposefully, looking like confederates rather than lovers. They arrived at the waiting lifts, Shakira stepped in ahead of Dirk, and then they were gone.

'Time for a glass of bubbly before the off?' Jesse queried. He was looking at the bottle of Krug sitting jauntily in an ice bucket on Verry's side table.

'Absolutely not.' Verry smiled. 'That's for later, when we return in triumph.'

She surveyed her protégés. Fleur's dress rose high at the neck. She wore no jewellery except crystal earrings that cascaded on to her shoulders, and her hair was swept up away from her face in an almost Egyptian bouffant style. It gleamed with condition. Verry had been greatly relieved to find that Madonna wasn't going to turn up at Charles's party – the American superstar wasn't arriving in France until tomorrow – and now she was sure they could deal with the rest of the opposition.

Jesse looked powerful, in command of his body and himself.

Verry was wearing floor-length Armani velvet. At first glance it was a deceptively simple black dress with a demure, rounded neck. In reality it was totally backless, brilliantly cut over the shoulders to reveal, on movement, a hint of naked breasts. 'Come on,' she said. 'Let's go sock it to them.' Her voice was uneven. She felt quite emotional, very proud of her signings who certainly, tonight, looked like the film stars she so much wanted them to be.

The yacht was a blaze of lights; pink and white sparks of brilliance had been draped from stem to stern and wound around the mast. Living up to its name, the vessel seemed to float on a sea of bubbles, a reflection of fairyland. Even the weather seemed to have been ordered for the occasion. It was a balmy, perfumed night, and the waters of the marina lapped lazily in time with the music that drifted from the state room. To Verry's surprise it was Chopin, a piece, she was sure, conducted by her father. She stood for a moment watching the brightly dressed crowd on deck, looking at the massive bouncers about to scrutinize their tickets, glancing round the bay, at the myriad lights. She looked everywhere, but nothing took her mind off the music.

Jesse took both women by the elbow. He felt great, on top of the world. He didn't give a damn, for the moment, whether the film project took off or not; he was just going to enjoy the party. Besides, although he'd stick to his bargain with Verité, his future lay, as it always had, in his fists. Fleur looked at him and smiled. They were careful how they behaved together in public, but in private they were reaching heights of passion he'd never even guessed existed. There was only one cloud on his horizon: he wished he knew how Fleur really felt about him. He was sure she was holding something back, a minute portion of herself. Tonight he felt strong enough to make her completely his.

'My goodness!' Verry stepped back quickly, her stiletto heels clipping Jesse's toes.

They had reached the deck, taken a few steps forwards and suddenly, out of nowhere it seemed, a giant black cat had appeared in front of them.

'Bloody hell,' Jesse muttered, surprised out of his equanimity. 'That's a bloody panther!'

Ignoring them totally, the lithe, ebony feline padded forward towards the prow. It wore a collar of diamonds and was held by a long – too long, in Jesse's opinion – golden chain. The animal's escort was a magnificent black woman, as sleek and sinuous as the animal itself; her melon-shaped breasts were bare, while around her neck hung a matching diamond collar and a length of leopard-patterned chiffon was wound around her hips.

'Bloody hell,' Jesse said again, and then he laughed. There were three photographers trailing after the vision like bloodhounds. 'What some people will do for publicity.'

'Good evening, Fleur.'

She turned to the man who spoke her name.

'May I say you look very beautiful? Every inch the English rose.' Salim Abu Dann let his eyes travel slowly over her body.

Jesse moved quickly to stand between his woman and the Arab.

'And the impetuous Mr Fighter.' Salim smiled. 'Somehow I knew we would meet again.'

Verry was frowning. She didn't like the tone of Salim's voice, which was somehow far more menacing than the panther. She stepped around Jesse and held out a hand in greeting. 'I remember you said you would be in Cannes. Are you here for business or pleasure, Mr Abu Dann?'

'Please, don't be so formal. Call me Salim.' He caught the proffered hand and carried it to his lips. 'For me, business is also pleasure. Perhaps one day you will have reason to understand that.'

Verry was about to pull her hand from the soft yet threatening grip, when she heard Charles Freeman laugh beside her.

'Do put her down, Salim,' he said easily. 'Ms Goode as Golde has the power of the press at her beck and call. She could be a very powerful adversary if she chose. I'm sure you wouldn't like to be at the centre of a sexual harassment exposé.'

Verry smiled. Salim had dropped her hand as if it were red hot. She turned to thank her rescuer, reminding herself as she did so not to fall for his much vaunted charms.

It was as she looked up at him, trying to think of just the right thing to say, that she first became aware of the sound of an approaching helicopter. It seemed to be coming very close to the yacht, the noise of the rotor blades rapidly obscuring the music and chatter.

Charles stepped to the rail and craned forwards, his hand shielding his eyes from the glare of the fairy lights as he looked up. There was a sudden commotion as half a dozen dinner-suited minders made their way to the rail, amongst whom Verry recognized Bruno. He was holding a small revolver he had pulled from inside his jacket.

'Wait.' Charles's voice was imperious. He held his hand up, keeping the bodyguards under control as the chopper swung into view.

From the nearby quay a pair of spotlights shone out, lighting the night sky in criss-crossing arcs of yellow before they found their target.

Verry cluched at Jesse's arm in surprise. She could see Dirk sitting in the open doorway of the helicopter. He looked utterly relaxed, his legs swinging backwards and forwards. His shirt collar undone, his black tie dangling loose, he was the very picture of decadent elegance. In one hand he held a microphone. There was a moment of static, and then his voice came booming out. Verry grinned. It was well done. They were watching Dirk sing, but actually hearing the prerecorded version of his newest hit. She began tapping her foot. This was mega-publicity-grabbing stuff. After a few moments, the second spotlight, which had been making patterns on and around the flying machine, dipped and finally focused. There was a general gasp of surprise from the watchers on board *Champers*. Standing just in front of Verry, Charles laughed out loud and clapped his hands.

Shakira was a living blaze of jewels. She hung suspended beneath Dirk, her shapely body glowing and glittering in pure Versace. From her neck to her navel was a sheen of crystal blue, each nipple a blaze of purple, her feminine triangle outlined to perfection by a matching cluster of gemstones. She moved languourously in time to the music, her face alight with pleasure.

'Very good, Ms Goode,' Charles boomed beside Verité, 'very good indeed.' He put his arm around her shoulder in an apparent burst of enthusiasm, and she looked up at him, startled for a moment by the noise and the excitement. He bent swiftly and kissed her full on the lips. In an instant he had let her go again and was leaning over the rail, applauding as the helicopter manoeuvred closer.

As owner of *Champers* he was the first to help Shakira on to the deck. He embraced her warmly, then greeted Dirk, who slid athletically down the rope as the helicopter hovered, a giant gleaming dragonfly, above the boat.

The couple's reception was rapturous. A bevy of flashlights illuminated the deck, and a flurry of activity on the pontoons announced the arrival of a massive press contingent.

Charles stage-managed it all brilliantly, arranging Shakira and Dirk artistically on the prow of his boat, calling for the landbased spotlights to be shone on them. All the time he was laughing and joking, all the time Verry was accepting the congratulations – even Salim seemed genuinely impressed – and all the time she kept reminding herself that Charles Freeman had had no right to kiss her like that, no right at all.

By ten o'clock the following morning Verry had every available newspaper spread around her on the floor of her hotel suite. Photos of Dirk and Shakira were everywhere. The French dailies had had a field day, and a news agency had spread their coverage worldwide.

'Pretty cool,' Dirk said for about the twentieth time. He acted as if he were in a daze. He kept saying he'd never really thought they'd pull it off, never thought it would go so smoothly.

'I still can't believe you had this all planned and never said a word,' Verry said to Shakira.

The three of them were on their own; it hadn't seemed in the best taste to wake the others to show them the wall-to-wall coverage. So far the only mention Verry had found of Fleur and Jesse was in Nigel Dempster's column, and he'd skated close to the wind by wondering whether Fleur, a professional model, had enjoyed being upstaged by Shakira, a talented amateur.

Shakira was being uncharacteristically quiet. Verry had seen her speaking to Salim on board *Champers* but had no idea what the conversation had been about. Her onetime admirer might merely have been congratulating her on the act, but somehow Verry didn't think it was that simple.

Dirk got up from the capacious sofa and walked towards the door. 'I'm gonna rouse up Jesse,' he said. 'I reckon I owe the guy a drink.'

Shakira looked at Verry, and asked, 'Shall I go and get Fleur?'

Verry nodded. She was disappointed that Fleur hadn't received more coverage – she would have photographed spectacularly – but there was nothing that could be done about a *fait accompli*. As the door closed behind Shakira her telephone rang and she picked it up quickly.

'Verité?' It was Charles Freeman. She hadn't had a chance yet to telephone and thank him.

'Hello, Charles.' She laughed awkwardly. 'This is a little embarrassing. It should be me calling you, since I . . .'

'No problem. I'm an early riser – I've been ringing people since six this morning.'

'Then I'm very glad you didn't start with me. But I would like to say a tremendous thank you.'

'The coverage is something else, Verité. And I'm not surprised, I for one had never seen anything quite like it.'

There was something odd in the tone of his voice that made her ask, 'You didn't mind what happened, did you? I mean, I hope you don't think it spoiled your party?'

'Spoiled it? By no means. Whatever I had planned couldn't have achieved that level of excitement. It was first rate. There is one thing that's bothering me, though.'

The tone that so irritated Verry had crept back into his voice. 'And that is?'

'Tell me something, did you ever meet Theo Cowan?'

Verry frowned; she felt she was being toyed with. 'Not met. I've heard about him, though – he was "Mr Cannes", wasn't he, in a publicity sense? Handled Michael Caine, Peter Sellers . . .'

'He was the only man I know who could walk into a roomful of real stars and get greeted by all of them by name. He knew the ropes out here, and I mean really knew the ropes. Just how much is your suite costing you?'

'I beg your pardon?'

'Look, I don't quite know why I'm bothering with this myself. But I do know I'm getting increasingly bothersome vibes about how much this caper is costing you. That performance last night must have taken at least fifty grand, I can't even begin to think of the palms you must have greased to get all the clearances necessary, and since you're not in the local clink this morning you must have coughed up all round.'

'You seem to be under some misapprehension. Last night's "performance", as you call it, was nothing to do with me. Therefore, I have done no "greasing", given no backhanders. And I, like you, am at a loss to know why you're concerning yourself with my finances. Once again, thank you very much for your hospitality last night. If you'll excuse me, I have a lot to do this morning.' She put the telephone down carefully, daring it to jangle and further inflame her aggravated nerves.

Dirk walked into the room without knocking. Shakira was close behind him as he announced, 'Jesse isn't in his room, and neither is Fleur. Neither of them came back to the hotel after the party last night.'

* * *

After two hours of driving around the town, telephoning all the top hotels, and even ringing London to see if a message had been left with Sara, Verry admitted she was worried.

She dialled Charles on board *Champers*, and as soon as she spoke he could hear her concern. 'Did you see Fleur leave your party last night, or Jesse? They may well have been together.' She had left them at two-thirty, going back alone to wait for the early morning papers.

'There will be hell to pay if you've misplaced Britain's big boxing hopeful.' Charles laughed, but he wasn't amused, he was thinking hurriedly.

'Will you check with your crew?' Verry asked abruptly.

'Of course. Are you at the hotel?'

Verry confirmed that she would be staying in her suite for the next few hours and he rang off.

Within half an hour he was knocking at her door.

'Charles!' Verry stood in the doorway, wearing a cream track suit, her hair pulled back in a ponytail. She looked quite severe, and annoyed to see him. 'I didn't expect you to come over.'

'And obviously didn't want me to.' He stepped around her to get into the room. 'This must be costing you a small fortune. Still no news, I assume.'

She shook her head, and the ponytail bobbed aggressively from side to side.

'I don't think he's got them.'

'What? Who? Who do you think hasn't got them? Where do you think they are?'

'I, as well as you, I expect, thought Salim might be involved, so I have been to visit our oily friend. He has a yacht – almost but not quite as beautiful and prestigious as mine. I should explain . . .'

'Please,' Verry interrupted, 'just tell me what you know.'

'As I said, I'm pretty sure he hasn't got them. He even managed to look surprised when I suggested he might know the whereabouts of the man who knocked him out cold. Bruno was mooching about on deck looking aggrieved, so I assume he's been told to keep his hands off your big boy for the time being. So, no I don't know where your little friends are, and the best thing we can do now is go down to the terrace for a drink.'

'Don't be ridiculous . . .'

'I am never ridiculous, Verry. Granted, I like to be a little light-hearted at times, but I am never foolish. Now, I suggest you slip into something less comfortable and more suitable, and then I'll give you an hour or so of my sought-after company while with luck this very Agatha Christie mystery of the disappearing heiress clears itself up without any help from Hercule Poirot.'

Verry settled herself on the empty seat at the empty table in the most prestigious spot in Cannes at twelve-thirty on a sunny May morning. 'How on earth did you manage this? The terrace is always crammed to overflowing.'

'A little trick the aforementioned Theo once taught me.' He sat back, adjusting his sunglasses more comfortably as without apparent instruction a waiter appeared and dispensed two glasses of foaming kir royale. '*A votre santé*,' he said and downed half his glass in one long swallow.

'Why do I get the feeling that you're about to continue your lecture?' Verry asked. After a few sips of her drink and under the admiring, speculative glances of the surrounding crowd, she was beginning to relax.

'Because I am.' An uplifted arm brought a refill for both their glasses. 'Theo was a great success here because he was so clever. He could create publicity out of nothing. Or at least, if not from nothing, from a whole lot less than you're spending. Take this table. I have it booked for months ahead every year, and it costs me considerably less than it would to throw a drinks party in any of the chi-chi bars. Look at it this way: if you had done the same, on day one people would see you sitting here, which is not so remarkable; on day two – and bear in mind that on each of these days you've invited three, maybe four of the prestigious journalists or possibly money-men you want to woo – on day two they ask the waiter who is that pretty girl.'

Verry smiled, as she was meant to.

'Day three, they're saying I see Ms Goode is here again, and by day four you're an established part of Cannes, its folklore and ritual. It's easy, and so much less effort than entertaining thirty or so people a night, when you wouldn't get the ones you want to come anyway because there are so many other exotic bun fights on offer. See what I mean?' Charles leaned back in his chair and waved a greeting to some old acquaintances who were regretfully turning away from the full terrace.

'Thanks for the lesson.' Verry smiled. 'But now, I think – ' She began to stand up, but Charles waved her down into her seat again.

'Hold on to your hat,' he grinned. 'This is when the trip starts to get choppy.'

Verry followed Charles's gaze. Coming towards them, blue blazer flapping, was a very red-faced Englishman walking rapidly, and awkwardly, with the aid of a stick.

Verry could tell he was English by his voice. It was very loud, very upper crust and it was bellowing, 'Ms Goode, Ms Goode, I want a word . . .'

'Bengy.' Charles stood up and gestured expansively. 'Come and join us, old boy.'

'Don't you "old boy" me.' Bengy clutched at the back

of a chair for support as he waved his stick aggressively.

There was an amused buzz of conversation on the terrace. Scandal was always a welcome diversion.

Bengy's voice carried distinctly. 'Where's Fleur? I've been to her room and she's not there. The maid says she doesn't think she stayed in the hotel at all last night. What the hell have you done with my fiancée?' The final question was roared in Verry's face.

Charles regained his seat, leaned back and said calmly, 'We kind of hoped you might tell us. After all, as you said yourself, you are engaged. If anyone should know where she is it's you, Bengy.'

'How the hell could I know? Fleur doesn't even know I'm here.'

'My point precisely,' Charles drawled. 'Damned funny engagement if you ask me.'

Bengy raised his stick again. He was too hot, and very bothered. 'It's all your fault.' He glared down at Verry. 'All this damned film nonsense. It hadn't entered her head until you put it there.'

'I don't think that's quite right,' Verry said softly. 'Fleur told me she'd been thinking about getting into films for quite a long time. It's inevitable that she would have considered it, after all. Lots of European models . . .'

'Tarts!' Bengy bellowed. 'Tarts and whores, all those strutting fashion mannequins . . .'

Charles was smiling lightly, but he didn't look amused. 'Including, by implication, your fiancée. You know, I'd be very careful who you slag off so loudly. This isn't exactly a private place, and libel suits are an extremely expensive hobby.'

At a table nearby an extremely elegant middle-aged woman stood up and walked purposefully over to where the Englishman stood. 'I think your comments are disgusting,' she said in smooth, Paris-accented English. 'You are a boor. If I were a man I would strike you, and if I were one of these "whores" you refer to so freely I would spit on you. As it is I despise you.'

There was a ripple of applause. Charles kept clapping after it had ended and the woman had walked, very beautifully, away. 'It just doesn't seem to be your day,' he said calmly.

'If you give me a number to call,' Verry said as she took a small diary out of her handbag, 'I'll get Fleur to ring you when she gets back.' She held her pencil poised above a blank page.

'I'll give you until three,' Bengy blustered. 'Three this afternoon, and then I'll be back. You tell her, you just tell her . . .' His words trailed off. He was still very red in the face, and sweat glistened on his brow and around his neck above his tightly buttoned blue shirt.

'I'll tell her you're here,' Verry said.

They sat silently as he stumped off, then Charles stood. 'Come on,' he said. 'You need to get away from all this.'

Dirk pressed the lift call button again. He wanted some company and thought the bar would be the right place to find it. He was feeling a great sense of anticlimax after last night. If it had been a gig he would have gone on partying round the clock, hit some good stuff and been spaced out long enough for the euphoria to gradually fade. As it was he needed a good drink, a good screw, or preferably both.

The lift doors opened. 'Jesus,' Dirk said with feeling. In front of him stood Fleur and Jesse, arms around each other, still dressed in last night's finery. The only real difference in their appearance was that Fleur wore a wreath of freesias in her hair and Jesse's shoulders were sprinkled with confetti.

'Hi!' Jesse grinned inanely, and then began to sing. His

voice wasn't totally tuneful, but the words were clear, 'Here comes the bride, here comes the bride.'

Fleur disentangled herself from the encircling arms and stepped towards Dirk, holding her cheek towards him. 'You may kiss me if you like. Come on, Dirk, wish us luck.'

There was a commotion behind Dirk as Shakira ran along the corridor towards them. 'You're back,' she called out. 'Thank goodness.' She slowed to a halt, her expression of utter amazement starting Jesse off again.

'You mean . . .?' Dirk said. 'Oh, my God. Or even worse, oh my Verité. I don't think this was part of the script, kids.'

Shakira flung her arms around Fleur. 'I'm so happy for you,' she whispered, 'so happy.'

'Champagne, champagne.' Dirk capered about, his earlier disillusionment forgotten. 'We gotta party, jeez have we gotta party.' He shoved them all towards the lift. 'Ground floor, my man,' he instructed a startled-looking fellow guest who had been trying to go up to his room on the fourth floor.

Bemused by the goings-on, the stranger did as requested and pressed the requisite button. He was still standing in the lift when the delirious foursome danced out into the foyer. It just showed, he thought, as he pressed button number four for what he hoped was the final time, the weird things these film people got up to. His lady wife, who had won the all-expenses-paid week for two at the glorious Cannes film festival courtesy of her favourite home economy magazine, was going to have yet another exciting episode to put in her postcards to the folks back home.

'I didn't know you knew about Fleur's being engaged,' Verry said. She had assumed when Charles had arrived personally, and at speed, to help in the search for Fleur that he had a romantic interest in her client.

She and Charles were sitting opposite each other at a friendly, almost naively simple bistro that he had steered her towards on leaving the terrace bar. Verry was aware that the peasant earthenware plates and rustic furniture were a blind – her menu had displayed no prices at all, so it had to be absurdly expensive.

Charles picked a chunk of crusty bread from the basket between them and broke it in his fingers. 'It was through Bengy that I first met the Montfords. That was before his accident.'

Verry accepted the piece of bread he offered and queried obligingly, 'The accident?'

'Your bête noire used to be a great horseman: master of the hunt, all that stuff. He was a nice enough chap, a bit hearty, very county. Very dashing, I suppose, to a girl like Fleur, who in those days had set her sights no higher than helping her grandmama run the stately pile. He's a fair bit older than she is, so he bided his time and then tally ho they were engaged, the family delighted, etc. etc. Unfortunately he followed that up with a set-to with a train. At least, he and his horse did, and not surprisingly they came off worst.' Charles was smiling as he spoke, keeping the tone of his conversation light and trite, if not the subject. He wanted to entertain his luncheon guest, take her mind off the scene that he was certain was boiling up for her later. 'They thought he was on the way out to begin with, so I suppose it's a bonus that he's as all right as he is. But that limp is permanent, and his nature's changed. Now he's a miserable sod most of the time, when he's not ranting and raving.'

'Fleur got into modelling through a relation of hers, didn't she? The woman who owns Body Beautiful? She's a cousin, I believe.'

Charles nodded and began pouring out the rough, local white wine provided in a litre jug dripping with condensation. 'That's Marie Jopling – Sullivan as was, before she married the property developer. She based the entire Fleur perfume range around your Fleur. It was a definite long shot, but it paid off. Now, can we stop talking shop, and get down to choosing some lunch? They do excellent calamari here, or perhaps you'd like pasta with a fish sauce? In either case it'll be reeking with garlic – at least that'll keep friend Bengy at arm's length later on this afternoon.'

Dirk's party had overflowed on to the terrace, where the happy couple were the centre of an impromptu wedding reception. The hotel was providing non-stop champagne, there had been several trays of assorted canapés, and a trio of gypsy musicians had been corralled in off the street. Fleur was exquisitely happy as she waltzed in her husband's arms. He completed her world; she was content at last.

The shout carried over the spiralling violin. 'Fleur!'

She recognized the voice, but for a moment couldn't place it.

'Fleur!'

It was Bengy. Her face crumpled. Jesse looked round. Singling out the man in the blazer, he knew instinctively who it was. He handed Fleur into Dirk's arms and walked towards his adversary.

'You bastard!' Bengy raised his stick and swung it down viciously.

It was only Jesse's training that saved him from a smashing blow on the collarbone. His hand shot out, caught, and held, the quivering weapon.

'Let go!' Bengy shouted. 'Let go and face your punishment like a man. That's my fiancée you've been mauling in public. Let go of my stick at once, I say.'

'She's my wife,' Jesse said softly. He tightened his grip and spread his legs to take the twisting and turning that Bengy was using to try and break his hold. 'My wife,' he repeated.

Bengy looked stunned. 'I don't believe you,' he blustered. He twitched half-heartedly at his would-be weapon.

'Ask her.' Jesse turned his head, looking back to where Fleur stood hesitantly. 'Come on,' he called. 'Come over here and tell him.'

Fleur took a step forwards, her eyes fixed on Jesse. She was drawing her strength from him.

The squeal of brakes on the road outside seemed to wake her from a dream. All that was real was Jesse. 'Jesse,' she said, holding her hands out towards him as she began to run across the terrace.

The crack of the shot was a whiplash of sound. Jesse spun round, staggered, and fell, taking Bengy with him.

Dirk brushed Fleur aside. He was shouting, but she wasn't aware of the words. There was red on Jesse's shirt, a patch of growing scarlet on the white. She reached tentatively towards him.

'Fleur.' It was Bengy. 'Help me up.' He was struggling, Jesse's weight across his hip. 'I can't get up.'

'Don't move,' Dirk snapped. He had slipped his hand inside Jesse's shirt and was trying to stem the bleeding with his wadded handkerchief.

'Jesse.' Fleur had hold of her beloved's hand. It was so cold that she began rubbing his fingers. 'Please, Jesse, talk to me. Don't go away. Jesse . . .'

She was still kneading his hand when the ambulance arrived, screaming to a sideways halt with inimitable French panache. The white-jacketed medics didn't turn a hair at the sight of the couple in crumpled evening dress, the woman garlanded with flowers, the man unconscious, covered in blood and pinning another man to the ground with the weight of his body. On inspection the second man was uninjured, although writhing in pain.

It was, after all, Cannes, and it was the film festival. It might even turn out to be a well-orchestrated publicity stunt. The medic whose girlfriends told him he looked like Tom Cruise kept a professional smile hovering around his shapely lips, just in case.

## Chapter 10

The doctor was very young, very charming, and obviously used to being discreet. 'He's been lucky,' he said soothingly.

The hours of tension had taken their toll. Relief left Fleur weak and she slumped against Verry. They had waited late into the evening in the brilliantly lit hospital waiting room that smelt of exotic flowers and strong antiseptic.

'He was honestly hit by a bullet?' Verry asked. She still couldn't believe what the policeman had said.

'But of course.' The doctor was suddenly very Gallic. 'What else could have made such a wound? The bullet hit him at an angle and slid across the ribs. As I said, he has been fortunate. He will have a considerable scar, but no long-lasting damage.'

'Will he be able to fight again?' Fleur whispered.

'Fight? Oh, I see. I suppose so.' The man of medicine shrugged dismissively. 'Don't worry. I shall patch him up so that he can go back into a boxing ring and have his brains knocked out by a less immediate method than a bullet. There is no point in your staying any longer; the patient is sedated now. Come back tomorrow.' He relented a little and smiled sympathetically at Fleur. 'Not much of a way to begin your honeymoon.'

There was a contingent of press waiting for them in the hotel foyer. Verry held Fleur close as they ran the gauntlet of the flashing bulbs and shook their heads to the shouted questions. This would get Fleur in the dailies all right,

Verry thought sadly, but for all the wrong reasons.

Dirk was waiting in Verry's suite. He got up as they came in and poured them each a generous scotch on the rocks. 'I called the hospital,' he said. 'Told them I was his long-lost brother, so you don't need to fill me in on the news. He's one lucky son of a bitch. I thought he'd had it this afternoon. It looked a fuck of a mess under his shirt.' As he handed Verry her drink his hand was shaking. He'd never been much good around blood.

'Have the police been to see you?' Verry asked.

'Sure, and made it clear they didn't approve of gangster-type shootings in the middle of their prestigious circus. They were dying to blame it all on me, as the convenient, available American.'

Verry sipped at her drink and smiled tiredly. 'Don't get paranoid, Dirk. I don't have the energy to act the shrink tonight.'

''Nother drink help?' The singer held the half full bottle of scotch up in the air and waved it about as he spoke. 'Now you aren't going to like this, boss lady – Jesse in hospital, Fleur for all we know tubbed up . . .'

Fleur slammed her drink down on the coffee table. 'How dare you! We didn't get married because I was pregnant, we got married because we're in love, and it was the only way to make sure we couldn't be messed about by anyone, ever again.'

'Cool it,' Dirk advised. 'Save all that sob stuff for your family. The point I'm trying to make is that something gives me the idea that neither you nor Jesse are going to want to throw yourselves wholeheartedly into the film project now. And the other pertinent point, as far as our glorious leader is concerned' – he looked meaningfully at Verry – 'is that Shakira has shacked up with Mr Shitface himself again. Some girls just never learn.'

'How could she?' Fleur's face was white with fury as

she almost leaped out of her chair. 'It was that revolting little man's chauffeur who shot Jesse. My God, he might have killed him.' She stopped talking abruptly, disconcerted by Dirk's rolling about on the sofa. He seemed to have been overtaken by hysterics!

'You take the biscuit,' he spluttered. 'Seriously, Fleur, you are completely and totally unique.' He raised his voice and rounded his lips to emulate her ringing, bell-like tones. '"That revolting little man's chauffeur" – *chauffeur*. Jeeze, the guy's a killer, a hired gun. Only the British aristocracy could refer to a hood like that as "the chauffeur".'

'For heaven's sake.' Fleur sat down again. Dirk's amusement had taken the wind out of her sails. 'Whatever you want to call the creep it must have been him who shot Jesse. Did you tell the police you thought so?' Her last question sounded accusatory.

'Did you?' Dirk retaliated.

'Stop it, both of you,' Verry said calmly. 'Fleur didn't say anything to the police because she was too distraught. Dirk, if I guess right, said nothing because he didn't like their attitudes. And I . . .' she paused for a moment, working out how to phrase her thoughts, 'I didn't say anything because I wasn't involved in your fracas at the chalet.'

Fleur almost reacted to the word 'fracas', but she was too tired to keep taking offence.

'Did Shakira leave me a message?' Verry asked.

Dirk shrugged his shoulders. 'Just that she'd see you back in England. They're off on some cruise round the bay in his yacht. It's called *Aristotle* – that's meant to make you think he's a Greek.'

'So it looks as if I'll have to concentrate all my energies on you, Dirk.' Verry forced herself to look enthusiastic but she couldn't manage to feel it. It looked as if she was down to twenty-five per cent of her stock-in-trade.

'I gave you a head start,' Dirk said. He had risen and was topping up the drinks in their glasses. 'You can follow up on the coverage from the other evening. Is it worth bringing in the shooting? It might well come over as mysterious and enticing.'

Fleur muttered 'For heaven's sake' into her drink, but Verry said, 'I don't suppose we can sit on the connection. Anyway, you're right. It might add a bit of spice. Fleur, is Jesse going to want to carry on with the film project, do you think? And what about you?' She couldn't ask outright if the girl was pregnant, but the thought had crossed her mind.

'I just want to go home,' Fleur said, her lips trembling. She was clearly on the verge of tears. 'And I don't even have a home to go to – I mean, one where I can live with Jesse. I share my flat with two other girls, and he lives with his family. We were going to spend our first few weeks back in London in a hotel while we looked for somewhere. But now Jesse'll probably be in hospital, and I – I – ' She stood up quickly and ran out of the room.

'Let her go,' Dirk said as Verry got up to follow her. 'She needs a good howl, just like she needs to grow up.'

'That's a bit hard.'

'Life's hard. You should know that. It looks as if you're going to be landed with all the hassle and only one marketable product. That wasn't how you had it planned, was it?'

She shook her head emphatically. 'It certainly wasn't. But we'll make the best of it. I think anyway that you were always the most likely person to pick up some actual business out here. Music business, that is. There are some Italians looking for someone to do a prestigious cameo part. Rock-star revisited, that sort of thing.'

'Thanks!'

'Don't underestimate what a slot like that can do. It brings you to the public's attention in a new light.'

'Not if I was playing a pop singer it wouldn't.'

'Look, it's only something I've heard about. Don't start pulling the part to pieces without even knowing what it's about.'

'Shakira's boyfriend told her he thought you didn't know the ropes.' Dirk's expression was unreadable.

'What ropes are we talking about, precisely?' Verry kept her voice steady.

'The set-up out here. He comes every year. He says publicity is about PR girls running round the town before nine in the morning. He says business doesn't actually get done here, just contacts reaffirmed.'

'He says a lot, your friend.'

'He's not my friend, but I think he might just have a point.'

Verry was silent. Abu Dann had probably made the same comments as Charles Freeman, only less politely. She'd worked out for herself that she'd put too much emphasis on this part of her project. She should have simply been at Cannes to make contacts, not shown herself to be desperate to pick up anything.

'So,' Dirk said, 'when do we meet with these mafia guys, then?'

'The Italians, you mean? I thought you reckoned I was on the wrong track with them.'

'I didn't say that. What I said was that I think you've still got things to learn about the film business. It doesn't mean I don't think we can get somewhere, working together, so let's get this clear: I do still want us to work together.'

'Something tells me there's more to this little chat than meets the eye.'

'That's part of my charm, babe – the hidden depths.

Let's just say I have reasons for wanting to continue our business relationship, so I'm prepared to put up with a few wrinkles.'

'How very considerate of you,' Verry said sarcastically. 'And what if I think we should break it off? I'm not sure, listening to you, that it wouldn't be better for us both just to walk away.'

Dirk spoke consideringly. 'That wouldn't be very clever. Not with all the money you've sunk in this venture so far.'

'And?'

'And what?'

'Well, there's got to be something more, hasn't there? I can't believe that you want to stay on with me because of the money I've laid out.'

'Not just your money.' Dirk had laid stress on the 'your'.

'You mean the helicopter stunt? Who exactly paid for that, you or Abu Dann?'

Dirk smiled slowly, like a cat that had got the cream. 'You really don't know, do you?'

Verry waited. She had been tired earlier, but now she had got her second wind. She was prepared to talk all night, if that was what it took to get to Dirk's bottom line.

'You're not making this easy.'

'Why should I?'

'Because' – Dirk stretched, one arm after the other, as high as he could reach over his head, loosening his neck muscles; it had been a long day – 'because of your mother. We have a thing going.'

'God, how romantic.' Verry almost spilt her drink in her anger. 'A "thing". Some sordid little love affair . . .'

'The only word you have right there is love.' Dirk was so quiet, so calm, that it silenced Verry. 'I love Angelique, and she loves me. She proved it by setting up the stunt for me. It was all her idea – the helicopter, the spotlights on shore, everything. She didn't know when we could do it, but she was sure there would be some time that was just right, and she paid for the lot, right down to Shakira's schmalzy costume. So you see that's why we have to make your scam work – because it matters to her, and she matters to me. She matters more to me than anyone in the world – even more than I matter to myself. Don't look so shocked. You'll feel that way yourself some day.'

'She paid? My mother paid for everything?' Verry was finding it hard to breathe, her throat was so constricted. 'But she couldn't. She has nothing. That's why I'm here – that's why I've done all this.' She gestured dazedly at the luxurious room around her. Unconsciously she echoed Charles's words. 'Have you any idea how much this costs?'

'I don't know where you're coming from with all this "mother has nothing" crap. Your mother's no pauper, although it wouldn't make any difference to me if she was. What she has is class, real class, and I haven't had much of that in my life.'

'You'll have to excuse me.' Verry spoke formally, as if she were talking to a stranger. 'I'm very tired. It's been a long day.'

Dirk heaved himself up off the sofa. 'Sure,' he said. 'I could do with a few hours' sleep myself. Then we can get cracking first thing. Keep up with all those PR girls pounding the early morning streets, eh?'

Early morning streets – Verité's thoughts were drawn back to her father, running in the park . . .

'I'll see myself out,' Dirk said. Verry had taken it hard about her mother, he thought. It was understandable, in a way. After all, she might take it as an insult that he didn't fancy Verité herself. She was so much closer to his age. He cast a look over her, just in case he'd got it wrong, but there was no buzz, only a grudging admiration for the way she kept motoring on, however deep in schtuck she was getting herself. He was going to be the big hero and get her out of the mire. Angelique would appreciate that. It was a pity she hadn't come to Cannes with them. He walked slowly back to his room. He could certainly do with a screw. He contemplated ringing down to the porter's desk. He reckoned they'd be able to fix something up.

As he passed room 409 the door opened and a girl came out. She was young, not more than nineteen. She wore scarlet leather, a matching mini-skirt and blouson jacket. Her long blonde hair was damp at the ends.

'Late night?' he asked. Working girls always won his sympathy.

She nodded, pursed her pale lips and shrugged her shoulders. '*Cochon*,' she spat at the door. 'Fat pig,' she translated in heavily accented English. 'He is snoring like the animal he is.'

They'd walked on together, Dirk towards his own door, she, apparently, towards the lifts. He raised his eyebrows as he put the key in the lock, and she shrugged once again, this time with a smile. '*Tu as du whisky?*' she asked as she followed him into the darkened room.

The deck heaved gently. The Mediterranean was a placid lake, and *Aristotle* was moving at half speed as they approached the harbour.

Salim laid his hands reverently on Shakira's soft shoulders. They were bare; her dress, a slip of cobalt blue satin, had been moulded to her figure by an expert. 'You are beautiful,' he said. He bent to kiss her nape where the upswept hair exposed a cluster of tiny, sweat-dampened curls.

'This place is beautiful.' Shakira was gazing at the view ahead of them, at the myriad white and terracotta houses that climbed the cliff side as it reared up out of the calm blue sea.

It was a vista of wealth. The yachts moored at the marina ahead were substantial; serious money toys. She longed to be out there, to play where the stakes were high.

'I am very proud of you,' Salim said.

He too was surveying the approaching port. He had business interests to attend to that evening. He had no intention of taking Shakira with him on his round of calls, but he wanted her malleable when he returned. She had a unique ability to arouse him and she was aware that he needed sex. He was stressed; a taste like iron spoiled his food. Only immersion, total and complete, in the unparalleled depths of his sexual fantasies would restore him. He smiled at his thoughts. There was already a stirring in his loins. Shakira became aware of it and leaned back against him. She was very skilful, very accomplished, and he knew that she wanted to be taken out that night; to be fêted, to enjoy the recognition that would certainly come after her Cannes triumph.

She would have to be placated.

'A present,' Salim announced. 'I have a little something for you.'

Shakira turned to face him, so that he was aware of her mound of Venus pressed caressingly against him.

'Later,' he laughed. 'Not so impatient, my little one. Later, we shall have endless time.' He reached slowly into his top pocket, felt the end of the cool golden strand between his fingers and began, slowly and tantalizingly, to pull.

The giving of presents could be made into an art form; there was so much more excitement to be had from the gift of jewels than the simple handing over of a box. Shakira watched the stubby fingers, saw the quality of the golden clasp, and began to smile, her lips parted so that he could see the moist, pink tip of her tongue.

'Salim,' she breathed, but he shook his head.

'Wait,' he said. 'I am going to give you a lesson.'

She hardly heard him. Slowly, the first diamond appeared, fat and glistening. Rose-cut, it caught and reflected the sun's rays, shining blue, then red, a living fire. One stone, then the next, and then the next . . .

'You have captured the Riviera, my dear,' Salim said softly. 'Encapsulated its unique joys, its heady beauty, its sensuality: the smell of warm flesh mixed with the most expensive perfumes. Unfortunately, the Riviera is not for sale and I cannot buy it for you.' He laughed, his eyes fixed on the tremulous mouth, the tangible greed that invoked a sheen on her upper lip, as later he would make her sweat with longing.

'It's superb.' Shakira held the necklace in the palm of her hand.

'The designer called it *La Rivière*. It is a play on words, because he himself comes from Cannes, and because to a jeweller a *rivière* is a string of jewels, a single strand.'

'How can I ever say thank you?'

Salim stroked the tender cheek. 'You will find a way, you always do, my precious. You know, I am not often captivated for long, but there is something about you that continues to please me.'

'We are very alike,' Shakira said. 'You and I, we are both prepared to give anything in return for what we want.'

'Alike?' Salim smiled.

It was the first mistake Shakira had made. She had no concept of how far he would go to achieve his aims, no way of understanding. He ran his finger across her luscious mouth, down the warm, throbbing throat. She was, after all, an innocent.

The fact brought a new thought to mind, a surprising one. 'I will see you later.' His fingers reached to circle the slender neck. 'I would like you to be wearing *La Rivière* when I return. Only *La Rivière*.'

Shakira nodded.

'I may not be alone,' he said as he stepped down into the small powerboat that would take him to shore, leaving the business of mooring and registration to his skipper.

Shakira nodded again. There was always a price to pay. She wondered how much the necklace was worth. Fifty, sixty thousand pounds? Not enough for the flat she wanted in London. She would have to be especially generous with her favours when Salim returned. There was still so much he could give her.

There had been an intriguing message waiting for Verry when she got home from Cannes. She had quickly run through her answerphone tape, jotting down half a dozen phone numbers. There was nothing unexpected, except . . .

She dialled the *Daily Tabloid*'s number and asked for Angus Mackay. He was their relatively new editor. She'd known him quite well a few years ago. They hadn't actually gone to bed together, but the thought had been there once or twice.

'Verry.' The remembered Scots accent was loud in her ear.

'A voice from the past,' she laughed. 'How are you, Angus? Your message said you called yesterday. I would have phoned back sooner, but I've been away. Had you given me up for lost?'

'I never gave up on you, Verry.'

Verry laughed again. 'So what prompted the call?'

'A bit of auld lang syne, you could say. I have the feeling I might be able to do you a favour. Are you still shacked up with that architect fellow?'

'Does the favour hang on my answer to what I might see as a leading question?'

It was Angus Mackay's turn to laugh, a sound thickened with cigarette smoke. 'No, you don't have to worry, Verry. I'm not after your body – at least not on this call, I'm not quite mean enough to chat you up on your own phone bill.'

'The answer to your question is yes, I still see Sam – not as much as I used to but only because I'm so busy.' There was a niggling sensation of guilt that it didn't matter enough to her that she and Sam had to engineer time together.

'However busy you are, I think we should meet. How about a drink this evening?'

'Your usual hang-out?' Verry remembered the smoky city pub that Angus had frequented when he was a cub reporter. It had become his second home.

'Seven-thirty. If you're a good girl I might even buy you a pie.'

'I'm always good, Angus.'

'What a disappointment. See you later, Verry. And by the by, bring along a couple of PR packs on Dirk Solo and that girl Shakira, will you?'

Verry held the receiver against her ear for a few minutes after the connection had been broken. Angus's final request had set her thinking. His editorial policy was clear. He was in the business of selling newspapers – millions of newspapers – and he wasn't above using scandal to achieve his aims.

Angelique chose that moment to make her way downstairs and walk into the living room. She smiled vacantly at her daughter and picked up the magazine she'd been looking for.

'Hello, Mother, it's me. I've just come back from

Cannes, remember?' Verry said sarcastically.

'Hello, darling.' Angelique's voice was distant. She appeared still to be half asleep.

'It's coming up to six o'clock in the evening, Mother. The rest of the world has put in a day's work already. Do you think you could pull yourself together enough to answer a few questions for me?'

Angelique perched on the arm of the sofa. She was wearing a housecoat of padded silk, and the soft swirl of pinks and white was extremely flattering. She swung her foot, the delicacy of her slender ankle accentuated by the drifting pink feathers on her high-heeled mules. She let her gaze drift around the room for a few seconds before focusing on her daughter.

'Dirk says you paid for his helicopter stunt.' Verry had intended to be subtle – on the flight back to Heathrow she had planned how she would draw her mother out on the subject, but now that they were face to face she was having to struggle desperately to control her anger.

'Dirk told you that?'

Verry nodded. 'He said that even after forking out all that cash you're still well off.'

'If Dirk said I paid, then it must be true. Dirk doesn't lie.'

'Mother!' Verry felt sick. 'Talk to me like a human being. Do you still have some money? Was all that business with Daddy leaving you penniless a lie?'

Angelique stirred, the feathers on her slippers fluffing up. 'I do think it's time you stopped saying "Daddy", Verry. It sounds affected in someone your age. I would prefer you to say "David" or, if you must, your father.'

'My father that art in heaven,' Verité said bitterly. 'All right, Mother, I'll admit defeat. I give up for now, but it's not for ever. I have to go out. I have to follow up a piece of business that your lying has got me into. I have a shrewd suspicion it's going to be nasty, probably smutty, and it's going to involve your beloved Dirk. But please don't worry. I'll sort it out, as I've sorted out everything else for you, Mother – or should I say Angelique?'

She didn't hear Angelique's response – if there was any. There was just time for a quick shower and change of clothes before setting off for the appointment with Angus. She took the requested PR packages and left the house without talking to her mother again.

'You look well, Angus.' Verry stood up as the editor made his way into the bar. It wasn't true. His features had coarsened, he wasn't going to age gracefully, but it was a relief that he'd arrived. She didn't like being in a pub on her own; the smoky, beery atmosphere seemed to bring out the lechers in force.

'You look beautiful, as always. A little tired, perhaps.' He looked critically at the dark smudges beneath her eyes. 'But it so happens I find that rather sexy.'

'I brought these.' She proffered the glossy packs. 'If you want any more information . . .'

'I know the score.' Angus flicked through Shakira's write-up at speed, only pausing when he reached the full-length photo that made up the last page. 'In-depth interviews two a penny, fuck just a little more.'

Verry flinched. 'That's a rotten thing to say.'

'Not far off the truth. She's nothing more than a high class slut. Speaking for myself, I'd rather have a gutter hooker any time. At least they just ask the going rate for the job. Her type' – he tossed the folder down on to the beer-stained table between them – '"wants everything that's in your wallet and a good time too."'

'Your new job hasn't softened you any, Angus.'

'Not likely to, my dear. There's more smut out there than down the chimneys at dear old Battersea power station. You should never have taken this sort of people on, Verry, if you're going to act the shrinking violet.'

'Why did you ask me here?'

'To do you a favour.'

Verry sat silently. She challenged Angus with her eyes, trying to egg him on to get to the point, but the newsman was too old a hand. He sipped at his double brandy, the corners of his lips lifting fractionally, but the expression in his muddy brown eyes never wavering.

'Want another drink?' he said eventually.

'No thank you. I have to get back for supper.'

'No drink, no steak pie? I suppose that means you don't want to be beholden to me, does it? Home to Sam for supper and sex? In that order, I wonder, or . . .'

'Angus,' Verry said softly, 'you don't have to spin this out. We used to be friends; I didn't even know that we'd become enemies. Please just say what it is you want to tell me, and then I'll leave you to drink in peace. I've had a long day.'

'Haven't we all, dearie. But you're such an ice maiden I'd hate to see you lose your cool. I'll come to the point.' He put down his empty glass and gestured to the barman for a refill. 'One of my journalists has done a nice piece on your Dirk. Very nice, I have to say – in-depth, according to our definition of that vastly overused phrase. We've charted the rise to fame, the changing habits. Some of it's cribbed from the American press – they hate his guts out there, you know. You should have considered that before signing him up. Shit sticks whatever brand of disinfectant you use.'

'I know all about his relationship with the American press, Angus. But he's grown up a lot.'

'Spare me the crap. I don't need the sell – I'm never going to buy his records, and he's never going to screw my mother.'

The colour drained from Verry's cheeks. It was what she had dreaded. 'What are you getting at?'

'The piece is called "The seven ages of man". We're working on the subtitle, but it'll be something like "The subverted tastes of a rock-star".'

'Go on.'

'This may well be obvious to a highly educated girl like yourself, Verry, but the seven ages we're referring to are the ages of crumpet our hero enjoys. At the top of the heap, winner by a mile, is your ma. Forty-nine we've got her down as, coming on fifty.'

'You make me sick.' Verry actually felt nauseated. She'd already started to imagine the scenario, how her mother would react.

'I wouldn't throw up yet, if I were you. Save it for the biggy. Because at the other end of the scale we have sweet Samantha, our Barbie doll look-alike whose mum named her after Samantha Fox. Being a clever girl, like I said before, that should give you a clue to the kid's age. She's pushing fourteen and she's prepared to swear to being the love of dear Dirkie's life. Touching, isn't it.'

'What do you want?' Verry whispered.

'Cooperation. In the words of the immortal archbishop, what do I ever want except a helping hand? I'm not yet committed to run with the Ages piece. What I would prefer is something political, a touch of parliamentary spice to bring us a little more upmarket.' He smiled. 'I see from your expression that you doubt our ability to capture the ABs. But you'd be surprised at our readership, Verry. Not much we print goes unnoticed.'

'I asked you, what do you want?'

'Shakira Keene has a liaison with one of the most charismatic Tories this government possesses. It just so happens that his PR image is based on his stability. He's the ultimate family man: two black labradors, a couple of kids, the Range Rover with the mud-splattered wheels. You get my drift. In reality he's a kerb-crawler, a groper of women MPs, and all the rest of it. He was introduced to your Ms Keene by a wealthy Arab, as part of a very iffy deal involving development of friendie's constituency. They shrouded the whole kit and caboodle in environmental crap and got away with permission for an entire new town. Millions isn't in it.'

'You want an interview with Shakira?'

'I want the works. I want our MP photographed in sixty-eight of the sixty-nine positions. I want him clutching her close in some dusky night club, her jerking him off in the back of a London taxi. Don't worry, Verry, we'll do it tastefully enough. Black patches over his face and hers, something like a "hunt the ball" competition.' He laughed drily. 'Quite applicable in his case, since he reckons himself a real cock man.'

Verry stood up. She looked disgusted.

'Take your time,' he advised. 'Think it over. You've got a couple of days – let's say Thursday evening at the latest. I'll be in here as usual, and you can let me know what you've decided. If you don't show, we'll run with our first piece. Being friends and all that, I thought you'd appreciate the offer.'

Verry picked up her handbag and walked, head high, out into the cooling evening air. She couldn't let it get to her, couldn't allow herself to panic. She had to go through everything logically. Her mother would be at home, expecting Verry to pick up where she'd left off.

It felt a long time before Verry saw a vacant taxi. The city streets were bleak, the yellow lighting cold on grey stone. She had been so furious with her mother about the deceit over her father's money, not to mention the affair with Dirk so soon after her father's death.

Verry leaned forward. 'Can you pull over by that

telephone box?' she called to the taxi driver. She had to speak with Shakira.

There was no reply from the new number the girl had left on Verry's answerphone. Traffic thundered by and the perspex box quivered as she held on, willing Shakira to come in, to answer the call. Nothing.

There was only so much she could achieve in a day. She would go home and face her mother, find out the truth about the inheritance her father had left her. Later she would try Shakira again. Tomorrow Dirk should be back in London. There would have to be meetings, questions.

The taxi pulled up outside her own front door. She looked at the little house that was home for the three generations of women. If everything collapsed what on earth would happen to Sara? Verry had to know her mother's situation. She walked purposefully up the path as the gate clanged shut behind her.

'That's it. I can't take another minute of this silly evasiveness.' Verry stood up and walked away from the table where she'd been eating supper with her mother and grandmother.

Sara watched, registering the stress in Verité's face, the tautness of her mouth, the pallor under the make-up. There would be tears before bedtime.

'I simply cannot understand, Mother' – Verry turned to look at Angelique, who was sitting calmly, still nibbling at the odd morsel of stir-fried vegetable – 'how you could have put me through all this. Have you any idea how much money this film venture is costing me?'

Angelique shrugged. 'It doesn't really make any difference what you've spent, you've said as much yourself. If you fail you can only lose what you've got.'

'Lose!' Verry was shouting, her pent-up anger making

her over-emotional. 'Who the hell's said anything about losing? But that's what you want me to do, isn't it? You want me to fail, to have to go back to scratch and start at the bottom.'

'Don't be silly,' Angelique murmured. She was looking down at her plate as she spoke, at a lightly browned shred of red pepper streaked with soy sauce. 'Of course I want you to be a success. What mother doesn't want her daughter to do well?' She speared the piece of vegetable with her fork and carried it to her mouth.

Verry laughed bitterly. 'A mother who never really wanted a child in the first place. A mother who did everything she could to keep that child out of sight and out of mind.'

Sara stood up ponderously. 'That's enough,' she said. 'You'll both regret this when you've cooled down. Come back to the table, Verité. We might as well sort this out between us now. For a start, we have to know how much money Angelique actually has.'

'*Have* to know?' Angelique looked at her mother-in-law, her head tilted mischievously to one side. 'I wonder? I don't really think it's any of your business.'

Verry walked over to her mother, leaned over and spoke forcibly into her face. 'It is my business. You said you had nothing. That was why I gave up the agency and set this whole film project in motion. I was doing well before that. Everything I've done since Daddy died, I've done for you.'

'How touching,' Angelique said, her voice totally devoid of feeling. She carefully laid down her fork, wiped the corners of her lips with a napkin, and then pushed her plate a fraction of a centimetre away.

Sara wanted to slap her.

'Mother.' Verry got down on her knees. She didn't

want to sound aggressive, she wanted to try and understand. 'Just tell me why you lied. There must have been some reason.'

'The reason is she's greedy,' Sara snapped, her patience at last exhausted. 'Get up, Verité. You're not a little girl any more. You're a grown woman, and so is your mother. She's perfectly capable of looking after herself.'

'Oh, but I'm not,' Angelique said softly. 'I never have been and that was how David liked it. Your beloved David, Sara, made me into what I am today. If anyone should feel responsible for poor, incapable Angelique, it's you. He was so afraid I'd become a managing, overpowering, domineering busybody like you that he did everything for me.'

'Daddy adored Grandma,' Verry put in quickly.

'Your dear daddy was terrified of his mother, Verité. That's the truth, and she's always known it, and encouraged his fear. Tell her, Sara. Explain how you only had to pull the strings and David would come running back to you from wherever he was, whatever he was doing.'

Sara had begun to cry. She dabbed ineffectually at the scalding tears, feeling let down again by her age. She never would have cried when she was younger. When she spoke her voice was muffled. 'We all know you'll be apologizing for this tomorrow, Angelique. That's your only saving grace, the fact that your nastiness doesn't last. But I just wish you wouldn't be so unkind.'

'It's not unkind to tell the truth,' Angelique said petulantly. She knew as well as they did that she would be begging their forgiveness tomorrow. She enjoyed the ups and downs of her emotions, loved wallowing in them. It was as invigorating to her as good wine.

Sara's tears were drying. She had thought of something very satisfactory to say to her daughter-in-law. She spoke slowly, wanting the import of her words to be well understood. 'It's probably the change that makes you so highly strung these days, Angelique.'

There was complete silence. Verry hardly dared breathe. Her mother's whole life was based on youth, on agelessness, and now, with Dirk around, it was even more essential that she maintain her Peter Pan myth.

'Don't be silly.' It was Angelique who broke the silence, her voice high and nervous.

Sara said nothing, just smiled knowledgeably.

Angelique blundered on. 'That's an old-fashioned concept. It's outdated, it's . . .'

'Germaine Greer wouldn't agree,' Sara said smugly. 'I have her book about getting to fifty upstairs. I bought it for you, actually, for your birthday. I like to choose my presents to suit the occasion and we must celebrate this particular birthday in style. It's an important milestone in any woman's life, my dear.'

'I'm too young for the change,' Angelique whispered. She looked despairingly at Verry. 'I am, aren't I, darling? Tell Sara I am.'

'It's all right, Mummy.' Verry put her arms around the narrow, quaking shoulders, laid her cheek on the shining hair. 'It's all right.' She couldn't think what else to say.

# Chapter 11

Verry quickly checked that she had arrived at the address she had written down in her Filofax. Standing on the steps of the handsome, red-stone Sloane Square building she had a row of four bells to choose from, each with an illuminated name plate beneath the high-tech intercom fitted into the wall. Flat three had no name in the space provided, but three was the number that Shakira had left on the answerphone. Verry pressed the button. After a few seconds she heard the microphone switch on, but there was no further sound apart from a faint buzzing.

Verry said, 'Hello? I'm looking for Shakira Keene.' She waited a few moments, and then, with a barely audible click, the door beside her swung open.

The hallway was luxurious. Lustrous camel-coloured carpet stretched from wall to wall, and then up the wide staircase. A large, ornately framed mirror hung above a side table bearing a famille rose bowl piled high with pot pourri. A discreet brass plaque arrowed flats two, three and four upstairs. The bannister was polished mahogany, and there were several gilt-framed paintings on the walls.

The first floor had a spacious landing, on which a large, rounded brass bowl containing a standard bay tree stood like a sentinel beside the heavy door that presumably led to flat two. One more flight of stairs, the treads expensively wide and shallow, and Verry had reached her destination. As she put her hand out to press the recessed bell the door swung open.

'Hi,' Sam said. He was pale, his hair fluffed up as it always was when he got worried.

'Sam!' Verry stepped forward as he ushered her in. She was confused. The situation was unreal, dreamlike. 'I didn't expect to see you here!'

'Welcome back.' Belatedly, he kissed her on the cheeks. It was the greeting of a friend, not a lover. 'You didn't phone me last night.'

'Something came up.' She was emerging from her daze. 'What on earth are you doing here? This is the address Shakira gave me.'

'She's not here.'

Out of the corner of her eye Verry was aware of a door closing down the hall.

Sam had also been aware of the movement. He said again, 'She's not here. She really isn't.'

Verry looked around her. The interior decoration of the flat was heavy, and surprisingly traditional. There were large, dark oil paintings on the walls, marble statues in the corners.

'I'll tell her you called.'

Verry stepped around Sam. There was something about the painting on the wall behind him . . . She spun round quickly to say something to him, then looked more closely at the statue to her right. It was of two figures entwined, a man and a woman, locked in embrace. The woman's legs were twined around the man's sinuous thighs, his hand clutched her breast, and he had entered her body. The sculptor, a master of his art, had caught every pulsing vein.

'You'd better go in there.' Sam gestured for her to walk on into the room he had just left. It was a formal drawing room with Regency sofas, heavy, opulent drapes, flowers in bowls, and more art. The walls were covered in masterpieces – erotic masterpieces.

'I don't believe it,' Verry said. It was her grandmother's memory come to life. 'This is just like . . .'

'Yes. It's based on Sara's story. Just like the good old Hollywood days.' Sam laughed, but it was a hollow sound.

'What are you doing here?' Verry asked, and then smiled mirthlessly herself. 'I'm sorry. That's a silly question.'

'Shakira really isn't here. It isn't her in the other room.'

Verry nodded an acknowledgement. 'I'm sorry for interrupting you, Sam.' She turned to leave.

'You've been away so much,' Sam said plaintively. 'You know I've missed you.'

'Funny way of showing it.' Verry would have liked to get mad, to shout, rant and rave. Instead she felt empty, devoid of feeling.

'I could come with you now,' Sam offered. 'We could leave here together.'

'I don't think so. You will arrange for me to have my half of the flat money now, won't you.'

'The flat?' Sam queried confusedly.

'Go to hell,' Verry said shortly. The more she looked at the paintings on the walls the more sickened she became. There were graphic scenes of rape, of carnal acts between men and animals, men and other men. It was all in the style of the masters: rich antique oils, Italian marble. Whatever the value of the works on the walls, the flat was a bordello, and it had come about because of her own grandmother and her memories of the love-nest of some depraved film producer of long ago.

Verry didn't wait to get home before finding a telephone. 'Angus? Just to check that you'll be at the pub this evening. There's no point in hanging on until tomorrow. I want to get this over and done with.'

This time it was Angus who'd been waiting. 'I was about to give you up, Verry,' he said. 'It's almost nine.'

'I had a lot to do.' Verry sat down on the wheel-backed

chair and breathed in deeply. 'If you're going to offer me a drink I'll have a bloody Mary.'

Angus had his own brandy topped up and considered the woman sitting waiting for her drink. He'd fancied her once – still did, if he let himself admit it, even though he disapproved of women working in a man's world. She was wearing a short skirt. Her legs were good; not spectacularly so, but well shaped, and she'd got a neat ankle. He looked up to her face to find she'd been watching him, and, somewhat disconcerted, carried their drinks to the table.

'I have a trade,' Verry said after her first sip. 'I have a piece that your readers will love, in exchange for the Dirk story that will only end up getting you into court.'

'I don't like threats.'

'Not a threat, Angus, a promise. I've been to see your Barbie doll, and her mother. There's nothing in the story. The girl wanted to get her picture in the papers, and you'd offered the mother money to back up what was clearly a put-up job. It's cheque-book journalism at its sickest.'

'You bought them off,' Angus said admiringly. 'You've turned human at last, my dear. How much did it cost you?'

'Not a penny,' Verry said, and took another mouthful of drink.

'And I thought you never told a lie,' Angus mocked.

'No money changed hands, and never will. I simply got them what they really wanted, the chance for little miss birdbrain to get her picture in the papers. An innocuous fashion feature on the girl in the street and her mum. I still have friends in newspapers, you know, Angus, just as I have enemies.'

'I drink to your myriad abilities.' Angus raised his glass. 'You mentioned a trade?'

'In exchange for your guaranteeing to me – in writing –

that you will never publicly link my mother's name with Dirk.'

'I get the politician?' Angus crooned into his glass.

'No, absolutely not. Shakira utterly denies even having met the man, and she will stick to that denial. What I have to offer is much more titillating than an old-hat scandal.'

The *Daily Tabloid* took six thirty-second TV advertisement slots during Sunday evening's prime time viewing. The voice of a well-known classy actress reached several million living rooms. She spoke seductively of the mysteries of the ages, of the power of aphrodisiacs, of titillation of the senses, and on the twenty-eighth second the word 'erotica' was left hanging in the air.

The series of photos ran for a week, aided by articles by psychiatrists, psychologists and gynaecologists as well as artists, writers and assorted sex objects. The interior shots of Shakira's onetime flat provided a magnificent source of entertainment. It was, from Angus Mackay's point of view, a great success.

It was from Verry's point of view as well, until, on the Friday, the last article was run. It was the climax, a piece on how sex ruled the leaders of power and industry. Featured, centre page, was a photo of the MP. The occupant of a neighbouring flat, so the article ran, had recognized the regular visitor. Verry felt cheap. Shakira cried and said it wasn't true that she'd slept with him, just as it wasn't true she was back with Salim as Fleur had accused her of being. Sam phoned to offer condolences and that gave Verry the opportunity to ask him to arrange for her things to be sent over from the apartment they'd once shared.

It was a relief when Saturday came.

\* \* \*

'Dirk?' Angelique's voice was soft down the telephone.

'Hi.' He pushed himself up on to one elbow and checked his watch. It was half past seven. He hadn't got to bed until two in the morning.

'I've been dreaming about you.'

'Good for you.' Dirk punched his pillow into shape. 'Have you any idea what time it is?'

'It's bedtime,' Angelique murmured. 'You and I are in bed, and we're together.'

'Weird.' Dirk lay back and closed his eyes again.

'I want to touch you. I want to hold you in my hands.'

Dirk stirred. He was starting to feel warm. 'Don't stop.'

'I want to kiss you.'

'Where?'

The abruptness of the question made Angelique blink rapidly, but she didn't take long to answer. 'On your mouth,' she said. 'To begin with. I want to force my tongue between your lips.'

'And then?'

'And then I want to lick you, trace the line from the corner of your lips to your ear. I want to move my tongue in and out.' She paused for a moment and then said, 'Can you imagine that? Can you imagine the warm, wet flickering?'

Dirk's affirmative was a moan of pleasure.

'What are you doing?' she asked quickly.

Dirk's voice was breathy. 'I'm holding my cock in my hand, and it's big and it's throbbing, and it needs you, here.' His eyes were closed and he reached out, as if to take her hand and guide it to him.

'I am there,' Angelique said. 'I'm there with you, I'm touching you.' She was longing for him to touch her, to feel the hard little button that would send tremors of feeling coursing inside her.

'Touch your breasts,' he whispered. 'Stroke them. Feel the nipples.'

'They're hard,' Angelique cried.

'Just like me.' Dirk opened his eyes. He was so horny he was going to explode. 'Grab a taxi over,' he said.

'Grab your balls.'

Angelique's words so surprised him that he did as she said, and slid his palm beneath the hot, full orbs.

'What are you doing now?' he breathed.

'I'm going to make coffee.'

'What?' Dirk sat bolt upright. 'What the fuck did you say?'

'I said I'm going to make some coffee. Decaff, preferably. Would you like some?'

'Jesus F. Christ.' Dirk staggered up off the bed. He had the biggest hard-on of his life and it was meant to be a joke. 'Where the fuck are you?' he bellowed into the phone.

'Downstairs, darling, just outside your front door. Haven't you ever heard of the mobile telephone?'

He was downstairs in less time than it took for Angelique to run the tip of her tongue over her lips in delighted anticipation.

'Charles!'

Charles Freeman hesitated in mid-stride. He had just left his hotel and was intent on absorbing some soothing Parisian ambience before making for the airport. He did not relish company.

'Charles, what a surprise.' Hilary was breathless from running the few yards to catch him up. 'I was sure it must be you – there aren't that many beautiful men walking the streets at this godforsaken time of year. Why aren't you at the coast?'

'Hilary.' Charles considered her – the immaculate white

culotte suit, the expensive suntan, the restrained yet clearly expensive gold jewellery, the apparent enthusiasm at seeing him again. 'It's been a long time.'

'Three months, two weeks, a few days, but who's counting?' Hilary laughed. She looked embarrassed, as if she'd been trapped into admitting that she'd missed him.

'So, what are you up to?' He kissed her, once on each cheek.

She hesitated a fraction, as if she'd expected a third embrace, the continental confirmation of intimacy, then she answered 'This and that. I'm still involved with environmental marketing. We're spreading into Italy shortly. And you, Charles? What are you doing? Tell me everything you've done since I saw you last.'

It was clear that she wasn't going to be easy to get rid of. There was a café a few metres away, its striped awning offering to protect customers from the worst of the sun.

'A drink?' Charles asked.

There was enough in selecting a table, ordering coffee, and generally settling into their seats to occupy a few minutes. Then, cradling her cup in her hands, Hilary said: 'I couldn't get to Cannes. I knew you'd be there. Did I miss a lot?'

Charles watched a young woman walk by with a miniature apricot poodle on a lead. It and she were identically coiffured. 'It's always amusing,' he said lightly. 'This year was no exception.'

'I saw a photo of you in *Tatler*,' Hilary persevered. 'You were with Fleur Montford.'

Charles smiled. He had no intention of prolonging the conversation.

'It's such a coincidence us meeting like this. Someone was talking to me about you just the other day. Someone who wanted to know where you were and what you were up to.'

Charles raised an incurious eyebrow.

'Ask me who it was.' Hilary tried to look coy, failed, and repeated, 'Go on, ask me.'

'Very well, Hilary.' Charles replaced his coffee cup on its saucer. 'Satisfy my scarcely containable curiosity and tell me exactly who this fan of mine is.'

The uninterested tone registered and a swiftly suppressed look of anger crossed Hilary's face. 'It was Salim Abu Dann. He'd been trying to get in touch with you, and none of your people seemed to know where you were.'

Charles had had no contact with the Arab since Jesse had been shot. It seemed that no one had implicated Salim's driver in the shooting and the whole affair had tailed off. 'Where was he when you saw him?' he asked.

'Paris. He's staying here. Isn't it odd that we three' – she laughed shortly – 'three of the most definitive "savoir-faires", should be stuck here at this time of year? It must be fate. We must all meet up for dinner tonight . . .'

'No, thank you.' Charles stood up, dropped a note on the table to pay for their drinks and stepped back into the sunlight . . . 'I have a plane to catch this afternoon. It's been nice seeing you.' It had been inevitable, he thought, that he would not tell her the truth. He'd been too well brought up to tell a woman he despised to clear off. It was at times like these that he considered refinement a handicap.

'This afternoon?' Hilary was quickly on her feet. 'Then at least we can have a few hours together.'

'Hilary.' Charles turned to face her. 'I really would appreciate some time on my own. I have a lot on my mind.'

'Remarkable.' The anger now showed plainly. 'As I recall you never had much – mind, I mean.'

Charles shrugged. 'Water off a duck's back, Hilary. We don't have anything left to say to each other. Let's just be civilized about this, shall we?'

'Civilized?' Hilary was walking beside him, almost running to keep up with his long strides. 'That's a damned funny thing for you to say.'

He turned off the main thoroughfare. It was becoming embarrassing. Hilary was shouting, her voice echoing off the tall stone façades on either side of them. Her words would be trickling in the open windows, insinuating themselves into elegant apartments, causing amusement among the few civilized beings left in Paris in August.

'You're a bastard, Charles Freeman, a lying snivelling rat. You took everything I gave . . .'

A green municipal van was coming slowly towards them, part of the great Parisian clean-up campaign. Charles thought fleetingly of the apricot poodle.

Hilary caught his arm. 'Say something, you bugger.' Her face twisted with hate, she looked old and spiteful. 'I can sort you out. I have friends who can put you on the spot, Mr high and mighty.'

'Oh, Hilary,' Charles said in exasperation. 'Just leave it alone. Go away. We didn't part friends – ours wasn't that kind of relationship. Do us both a favour and clear off.'

'Bastard,' she repeated, her voice high and bitterly mocking.

Charles stepped into the road. The pavement directly ahead of him was being hosed down, a high-pressure jet washing the summer dust of the city into the drains.

'Parasite,' Hilary cried. 'Leech, bloodsucker . . .'

Charles jumped swiftly back on to the pavement, pulled the hose out of the hands of the startled worker, and turned to direct the jet.

She was standing there, her mouth open, ready to spew more vitriol, the look of anger turning to disbelief. The jet of water caught her in the stomach and she staggered back a few steps. He quickly found he could adjust the flow to a nicety and Hilary was transfixed, like a rabbit caught in headlights. Within seconds she was drenched, her hair plastered over her forehead.

Slowly Charles lowered the hose and passed it back to the gibbering Frenchman. Reaching into his wallet he extracted several high-denomination notes, not bothering to count them before handing them over. With a parting *'Merci, monsieur'* spoken in a deliberately thick English accent, he considered the transaction completed.

Hilary stood very still, a steady trickle of water dripping off her clothes to join the spreading puddle at her feet. Conscious of a satisfactory sense of justice administered Charles touched his fingers to his temple as a gesture of farewell, turned slowly around, and resumed the solitary stroll that would occupy the time until his flight.

Charles ran briskly up the short flight of steps just inside the gleaming mahogany front doors of the London Waldorf. He nodded to a green-uniformed porter, acknowledged a wave from the barman glimpsed through the leaded-light doors leading to his usual haunt, the leather-chaired Club bar, and strode into the Palm Court Lounge. He looked around. Most of the tables were taken, and he smiled as he sighted his quarry. A woman sitting nearby leaned over and nudged her companion who also turned to admire the gentleman standing, suavely, in the doorway.

'Charles!' Verry stood up to greet him. 'What an amazing coincidence meeting you here.'

He bent to kiss her cheek. 'Not really,' her visitor said smoothly. 'I had them ring me. I knew you held meetings here.'

Fleur buried her face in her napkin to stifle a giggle. She and Verité had been enjoying a quiet cup of coffee together and catching up on outstanding business. She'd never seen her agent so flustered.

'Would you like some coffee?' Verry offered, gamely trying to act as if this kind of thing happened to her every day of the week. She held up a hand to attract a waiter's attention.

As the summoned assistance approached Charles raised his voice to travel the short distance across the marble floor. 'The bill, please.' He looked down at Fleur. 'I'm so sorry to break up your meeting, but this really is quite important.'

Fleur kept her eyes away from Verité as she replied, 'That's absolutely fine, Charles. I'll pick up the tab, don't worry.'

He leaned over the table to kiss her on both cheeks, then taking Verry firmly by the elbow he led her back out on to the street.

'Is this a kidnapping?' Verry asked. 'Should I be fighting back?'

'Only if it gives you a buzz.' Charles was marching them over the road towards the front taxi in the rank. 'Personally, I prefer my women compliant.'

Verry almost tugged her arm away at that. She didn't like the proprietorial 'my women'. On the other hand, she doubted very much that Charles's interest in her was romantic. She wasn't his type.

Charles settled himself comfortably and then turned to face his companion. 'I assume you keep a travel bag packed at home?'

Verry raised her voice, and said distinctly, 'Will you pull over to the kerb, please, driver, and wait a few minutes.' She then reached forwards and slid the glass courtesy panel closed.

'Masterful,' Charles breathed. 'Or should I say, mistressful?'

'I don't suppose this is news to you, Charles, but you

are the archetypal chauvinist,' Verry said. She was quite calm now, quite in control.

'Of course. It's my trademark. Being magnanimous, however, I am prepared to make a few concessions in my chauvinism. For example, I have actually admired a fair bit of your campaign, and I'm renowned for being unbiased in my business dealings with either sex, in that I'll happily make money off either. The most damning evidence against me is probably the fact that despite the occasional put-down I will continue to open doors for even the most terrifying of females until the day I die.'

'If you've quite finished, would you mind explaining why I'm here?'

'You're on your way to your sweet little Chelsea hideaway, so that you can collect the aforementioned travel bag.'

'Because?'

'Because we are en route to the airport, to catch a plane to take us to sunnier climes. It is rather a disgusting day out there, don't you think?' He peered through the rain-splashed window at the pewter-streaked streets. 'When we touch down it will be to the scent of mimosa. What more can I say?'

Verry's patience was being stretched to its limit. She said coldly, 'You can say what on earth this is all about. And please don't bother with the whole, unexpurgated version. A few lines will do fine.'

'Two words will more than suffice – your Arab. Is that enough?'

'Salim Abu Dann? I wouldn't exactly call him my Arab, but what's he doing now?'

'What he is about to do is dump a lot of something unpleasant on your lap. When did you last speak to Shakira?'

'A little while ago. She owes me a return call. We have

to discuss whether she's going to go ahead with her film ambitions.'

'I wouldn't hold your breath waiting for her to ring back. She's shacked up with lover boy again, only this time he's showing her off legit. He's become fiancé number five, or is it six? You know, I really would like to find out what she's got. It must be something quite special.'

'She could have told me herself,' Verry said irritably. 'It could have been embarrassing not knowing.'

'Embarrassment is a mild emotion compared to what friend Abu Dann intends you to feel, Verry.'

Verry instructed the taxi driver to move on and then waited for Charles to continue.

'He's targeted your grandmother – who, incidentally, I gather is quite a woman. He, like me, has had a search done on her previous press coverage. There isn't much, but what there is is top drawer. The most recent piece is a photo of her with the Selznick family after Irene Selznick's funeral. She's old Hollywood, American "class". My God, how I hate that word.'

'She's written her life story,' Verry said slowly. 'It's very readable . . .'

'From what I gather, it could be dynamite. A lot of the story you handed to the *Daily Tabloid* has been picked up worldwide. Salim has the perfect follow-up: the fact that the whole erotic idea was Sara Goode's.'

'Don't,' Verry interrupted. 'Don't go on. You don't have to. Why on earth would he do that? What point is there?'

'The main point is easy: to whitewash his beloved Shakira, who will be written right out of the script. The scenario fits beautifully. You can bet your bottom dollar he's even managed to get Granny's name on the lease. He'll let it be known that she laid on the flat for the rich and famous to come and go – double entendre totally intended.'

'My grandmother was really excited yesterday. She said she'd found a publisher at last.'

'The plot thickens,' Charles said blandly. 'And here we are. I'll wait in the cab, shall I? I don't think there's time for family introductions. Our plane takes off in less than an hour.'

'You look surprisingly good like that,' Charles said.

Verry turned away from him, leaned her elbows on the gleaming chrome rail and surveyed the blue horizon. 'I apologize for not having the correct gear,' she said drily, 'but I have to admit to not being an habituée of flashy yachts, and you didn't give me time to buy anything new.'

'*Champers*,' Charles said in the tone of an aggrieved lover, 'is not "flashy". And I was not trying to imply that you were incorrectly dressed. I often wear denims myself, and have even been known to sport the occasional breton jumper.'

'A la Gaultier?' Verry laughed.

'What else? And now, I promise to stop being a sexist pig if you promise to stop being ultra-sensitive. Deal?' They shook hands solemnly. 'What I meant was that I was surprised at how much casual dress suits you. Quite a lot of PR ladies have applied so many layers of gloss that they couldn't ever swan around in jeans.'

'I'm human being first, career person second, Charles. Quite a few of my competitors would see that as an admission of failure.'

Charles turned slowly to watch the marina they had recently left grow increasingly distant.

'Where are we going?' Verry asked.

'I told you, we're following our friendly Arab.'

'Yes, but where to? We aren't just setting out to sea in

the vague hope of catching him up. You must have a plan.'

'A plan?' Charles seemed to consider the word. 'Yes, I have a plan. Come on, I think it's time to meet your fellow guest. He should have woken up by now.'

Verité was smiling happily as she followed Charles into the stateroom. The yacht was quite different seen in the daytime. She'd remembered it festooned with fairy lights, smelling of champagne and cigars, a place of dark, mysterious corners; but in the sunlight, with the sea curling away from the sharp white bow, it was clean, the surfaces shining, everything open to view and bathed in the clean tang of sea breeze.

'I think you know each other,' Charles said.

'Angus.' Verry's voice was flat. She felt as if the sun had suddenly gone in. 'What on earth are you doing here?'

Angus smiled around the cigarette hanging from the corner of his mouth. 'Well, nice to see you too. But I'm disappointed in you, Verry. I'd expected something more original, something like, "Of all the bars in all the world . . ."'

'That is the worst Bogart impression,' Charles laughed, 'that I have ever heard.'

Angus carried on with the phoney accent as he answered Verry's question. 'I'm here as a reporter, my dear. You may remember it's my job.'

'That was in the past. You're an editor now.'

'Busman's holiday.' Angus accepted the whisky Charles proffered. 'Couldn't resist the lure of dirty money deals.'

'If that's what it's all about then you should do well,' Verry said acidly. 'You certainly know all about dirt.'

'As you have cause to know,' Angus said, smiling. 'You see, I can even finish your sentences for you, Verry. I told you we knew each other well, didn't I, Charles?'

Verry spun on her heel and went quickly back out on

deck. How could she ever have thought that *Champers* was anything other than a stinking gin-palace?

'I'm sorry.' Charles followed her out on to the deck, proffering a glass of freshly squeezed orange juice as a peace offering. 'I should have warned you.'

Verry kept her eyes fixed firmly on the horizon and ignored the drink. 'You certainly should have. It would have saved you a lot of time and bother,' she said firmly. 'If Angus Mackay is involved in this, it'll just end up as another smear campaign. I'd like to get off at the next stop, port of call, or whatever you call it.'

'He's on your side,' Charles said softly.

'Crap.'

'Please don't get upset. It might be old-fashioned, but I really hate to hear a woman swear.'

'Tough luck, because I hate the bloody creep. You obviously know all about how he held me to ransom, threatening one stinking article after another. I was naive enough to think we'd done a deal, and then he made me feel cheap. I thought you wanted to help me.'

'And have you ever wondered why?' Charles asked softly.

Verry was still struggling to form an answer when a white-uniformed member of crew hurried up to inform them that their quarry was in sight.

Angus was laden down with cameras as he came out on to the deck. Several hung around his neck, and he held one in his hand. A metal case that he put down at his feet had a dozen or more assorted lenses on display.

'Overdoing it a bit, aren't you?' Verry said sarcastically. 'Worried you've forgotten how?'

'I save that kind of concern for my sex life,' Angus retorted briskly. He was peering through viewfinders, selecting the best equipment for the job. 'Talking of sex, how about a quick one? We won't catch up with Ahab for a few minutes.'

'You disgust me.'

'Sometimes,' Angus said enigmatically, 'I even manage to disgust myself.'

They were standing on deck, behind the tiered arrangement of saloon and bridge. Charles was at the wheel as they started to overhaul Salim's yacht.

'Time for me to do a bunk,' Angus said.

'You're not going to take any photos?' Verité asked, surprised.

'Not so as he can notice. Friend Charlie's sorted me out a cosy little hideaway. Fancy him, do you?'

'Don't you ever think about anything else?'

'Not often. Now don't go and fall overboard if the going gets rough. On second thoughts, if you do tumble into the briny, make sure you open your mouth nice and wide to yell. Otherwise your face'll be just a fat white blob on camera.'

'Oh, just go away,' Verry said in despair.

'Anything to oblige a lady, as the archbishop said.'

Charles had handed over the wheel to a member of the crew. 'Smile,' he said brightly as he approached Verry, 'I have a feeling we're on candid camera.' He turned to face the yacht that was now some hundred or so metres away on their starboard side.

'I thought we were going to get right up close,' Verry said. She stood beside Charles, both of them looking directly at *Aristotle*. Verry thought it must be a little smaller than Charles's yacht, although it looked as if it might be faster.

'This is close,' Charles drawled. 'For a meeting at sea it could almost be called intimate. Now, there's our fellow.' He raised an arm and waved in an exaggerated fashion.

Salim stood on his rear deck, a powerful set of binoculars held up to his eyes.

'Nice smile now, darling,' Charles instructed. 'Slip your arm round my waist. Come on, don't be coy. Let's at least act the part.'

Tentatively Verry slipped her arm around Charles's waist.

He gripped her firmly round the shoulders, squeezing her hard against him. 'Come on, sweetie, gaze up into my eyes. That's it. That's nice – that's very nice.' He was still waving with his free arm.

'Don't kiss me,' Verry said. Her lips were curved in a fixed smile for their audience. She was looking right into the blue eyes above her, the dangerous blue eyes that seemed to deepen before her gaze.

'I've done it before,' Charles said softly.

Verry nodded. Her throat was tight as she whispered, 'I remember.'

'So do I,' Charles said. He bent towards her, so that their lips were a few inches apart. 'I never kiss a woman against her will.'

There was the sound of the sea rushing beneath their feet. A short, sharp salute on the foghorn signalled that they had passed *Aristotle*.

Charles's grip loosened fractionally. 'We'll get into port ahead of him, just like the private detectives in the old-time black and white movies.'

Angus came noisily towards them. 'All ready,' he said. 'Later on I'll set up the night shots. When you two have finished snogging I could do with a drink.'

Charles laughed shortly as his arm slipped from Verry's shoulders. 'A journalist should check his facts, Angus. I didn't kiss the lady.'

'Facts have never bothered me, laddy.' Angus laughed. He thought it was such a funny remark that he was chortling all through his long, cool glass of scotch on the rocks.

## Chapter 12

Charles touched Verry lightly on the shoulder and she was awake in an instant. 'Did you get much sleep?' he asked.

She was lying stretched out on a comfortable sofa in the saloon, where she'd been since lunch. Glancing at her watch, she swung her legs on to the floor and slipped her feet back into their shoes. 'It's six-thirty. I've been asleep for hours,' she said, surprised.

'Sea air.' Charles smiled. 'It does the trick every time. We'll pop ashore and have something to eat before we set sail. You might like to freshen up first.'

Verry washed her face, cleaned her teeth, and began reapplying her make-up. She had already caught the sun, and laid aside her too-pale foundation. The bathroom was a masterpiece of design, every possible requirement fitted into a deceptively small space. There were strange chrome knobs and levers behind the bidet that she didn't intend to investigate, but at least the loo was self-explanatory.

Angus was nowhere in sight as they stepped ashore and strolled up the quayside. It seemed he was to stay hidden in the yacht. It was a warm evening. Cafés and bars were spilling yellow and pink light out on to the dusky esplanade.

'You might as well hold on to my arm,' Charles said. 'We're meant to be on a romantic cruise.'

'Is that an essential part of the subterfuge?' Verry asked as she did as he'd suggested. Charles just smiled. He was, Verry thought, being strangely distant. It made her uneasy. 'Is something the matter?'

'I don't think so. It's just – ' He stopped and began to

study the menu outside the brightly lit quayside restaurant in front of them. 'I think we may well decide to eat *chez nous* after all.' He shook his head at the maître d' hurrying towards them.

Angus was surprised to see them. 'Couldn't stand each other's company any longer?'

Charles smiled noncommittally and left them to go and chase up some supper.

'Bother ashore?' Angus queried.

Verry frowned. 'I'm not sure. Charles didn't say, but something made him change his mind.'

'Ahab's been busy. Taking on supplies by the look of it – stocking up for a long cruise, perhaps. Days and days of nothing but screwing his luscious bit of crumpet.'

Verry didn't bother to expostulate. 'How well do you know Charles?' she asked.

'Nosey little thing, aren't you? You know, you might have made quite a good journalist.'

'I might try it if things go wrong.'

'Worried they might?'

Verry shrugged. 'Sometimes it doesn't seem to matter how hard you work, things still go their own sweet way.'

'And sometimes it's not that sweet?'

She nodded agreement. 'I don't know why I'm talking to you like this, Angus. You'll probably manage to put it all out under some sleazy by-line tomorrow.'

'You're talking because you're on edge; I'm listening because I haven't had enough to drink yet. How's about we split a bottle of our host's best bubbly and cure both conditions?'

Charles came into the saloon, moving quickly, his face blank. 'We're off.' There was the sound of revving engines, and Verry felt the floor beneath her feet start to quiver. 'I want to be out there waiting when he makes the break.'

'He's loaded up?' Angus queried.

Verry looked from one man to the other. There was something she didn't know, some secret knowledge they were sharing. 'What is it?' she asked sharply.

Angus said, 'Ask the skipper,' and nodded in Charles's direction.

Charles smiled briefly, an expression that touched his lips but not his eyes. 'Sorry,' he lied, and then left them as quickly as he'd arrived.

'Me too,' Angus muttered. 'Bloody shame about the champagne.' Glancing balefully back at the drinks cabinet he stepped out on to the darkened deck, the oversized lens of the camera around his neck shining eerily like Cyclops's eye.

Above, the sky was a star-studded canopy of black; below, the whispering sea stretched to a far horizon soft as midnight velvet. A trail of phosphorescent gemstones churned behind them, as, like some exotic snail, *Champers* marked her passage.

Verry was sitting alone in the saloon, just as she had been for the last two hours. At first she had tried to amuse herself by flicking through the latest copy of *Vogue*, then she had considered giving herself a manicure, but nothing could hold her attention. Charles had changed. He was quick-spoken, authoritative, giving her instructions about how to act when they caught up with *Aristotle*. He wasn't playing games any more. She shivered despite the thick navy Guernsey of Charles's that she was wearing. He had insisted that she put it on and she was comforted by its warmth whilst disconcerted by the sense of his body wrapped around her.

Charles came swiftly in from the dark. 'We've picked him up again on the radar,' he said. He too was wearing a dark sweater, his eyes aquamarine in contrast. His hair was damp, his cheeks streaked with red; he must have been standing out on deck for a long time. 'I thought we'd lost contact, but we've been lucky.'

'Do we follow him?' Verry asked. She stood up and walked towards the drinks cupboard in case Charles wanted something.

'For as long as it takes.' His voice was low, as if he were talking to himself. He shook his head abruptly as he realized what Verry was offering. 'And don't let Angus get hold of any booze either. In fact, that's the most useful thing you can do for the moment: stand guard over the drinks cabinet.'

'You don't need me here,' Verry stated.

'Not right now,' Charles agreed impassively. 'But you were useful earlier. I would have been conspicuous if I'd been sailing around the Med on my own.'

'Not your image?'

Charles nodded, his mind clearly on other things. 'I'll tell you when to change.' Then he was gone.

They were going faster. Although she didn't need to, Verry found herself holding tightly to the back of a sofa. She felt off balance, as if she were falling through dark space. The thought, she knew, was silly. She would have a drink, relax and enjoy the sensation of the chase. But as she started to pour herself a brandy and the oily amber spirit trickled into the glass, she realized she wouldn't, couldn't, drink it. Why, she whispered to herself, had she ever got herself involved in this?

'Time for the next act.' When Charles came back he was breezy, cheerful. In his hands he held a flat-topped white and blue captain's cap. It was garnished with thick gold

and he was laughing as he put it on at a jaunty angle.
'Like the titfer?'

'Do you have one for me?' Verry smiled. She felt relaxed now that Charles was the showman again.

'You can wear this one later, if our fishing's been successful and we've landed our catch. Meanwhile I want glamour all the way. Let's see how far you can go, shall we? If you haven't got enough tinsel yourself you'll find an assortment of glitter in the guest cabin.'

'Your dressing-up box?'

'Let's just say spoils of war.'

Verry declined to touch Charles's 'spoils'. An entire two metres of fitted wardrobe was crammed with women's clothes: dresses, jackets, shawls. They were expensive pieces, and they made her wrinkle her nose in disgust. They smelt of a dozen couture perfumes, and reminded her irresistibly of the trophies of a big game hunter.

He had said she was to dress for a party. Her travel bag wasn't very big, but she had packed with care. The first thing she took from it was a generous metre-square silk scarf in fuchsia shot with purple, the second the bikini she'd bought during the Cannes film festival.

Angus was pinched with cold. He'd been hidden away in the very bows of the ship since they'd left shore. The cramped space had been built to house ropes and chains, not a middle-aged, desk-bound ex-journalist in search of a scoop.

The short respite standing up in the saloon was a lifeline.

'Good coffee?' Charles grinned wolfishly. The two men were side by side looking out into the dark. They were both holding mugs full of steaming hot, aromatic Arabica.

'My liver will go into spasm,' Angus growled.

'Your liver will bless me. Chin, chin,' Charles said, the

last word foreshortened as he almost choked on his scalding drink. 'My oh my oh my,' he crooned, staring over Angus's shoulder.

The newspaper man turned to look for himself. 'Bloody hell,' he said with feeling. 'Stuff the coffee. That's a sight to really warm a man up.'

'Verry,' Charles said with feeling, 'you look absolutely stunning.'

'Thank you.' Verry smiled archly. 'You said glamour, so . . .'

'You know,' Angus cupped his mug in his hands, 'I never really appreciated your body before, Verry.'

'And you needn't appreciate it now,' Verry said shortly. She had wanted to prove that she could look just as bright and glossy, as glamorous and artificial, as the Riviera starlets, but she felt acutely self-conscious.

The gold bikini was well made, the bra top cut to support and give lift, the briefs cut high at the sides, making her thighs look longer and slimmer. She had wrapped the giant scarf around her torso and then knotted it over one shoulder. A quick check in the mirror had confirmed that it hid her bottom. She had piled her hair up, catching it with multicoloured combs, and then put on her earrings, great moons of brass that swung on short chains. Finally she had slipped on a pair of pink high-heeled court shoes, and added the finishing touches: brown eyeliner, gold eyeshadow, and deep pink lipstick.

'You look like a Bond girl,' Charles said.

Angus had stepped towards Verry for a closer look. 'Less Bond, more bondage. Your mother wouldn't like it.'

Verry's face suffused with colour. 'Don't you dare mention my mother. Not after what you were prepared to do to her.'

'Hold on.' Angus raised a placating hand. 'Let's just

remember I'm only here to keep dear old Granny out of the shit. What happened before was business, so don't take it so personally. I just wanted the MP. He was a bloody charlatan masquerading as the people's hero. That kind of stuck-up git makes me want to puke.'

'Present company excepted,' Charles drawled.

'Naturally. Now come on, Verry.' Angus held his arms out. 'Give us a kiss. It's going to be a long cold night for yours truly.'

She hesitated. Angus was certainly suffering for his art.

'Go on, children,' Charles said impatiently, 'kiss and make-up. We don't have all night.'

Verry stepped close to Angus and kissed him on the cheek. He laid his hands gently on her shoulders.

'Good luck, lass,' he whispered.

'And you.' She found herself holding him tightly. 'Go for the jugular. Get some really good shots.'

It was very quiet after Angus had left. Charles went briefly to the bridge and then came back to the saloon. He perched on the arm of a sofa, his head tipped to one side as if he were listening for something. After a while he said conversationally, 'They've made contact. We picked up the second vessel a few minutes ago. We're just letting them get started.'

'Isn't it dangerous?' Verry asked suddenly. 'If we've been watching them, they must have been watching us.'

'Oh, yes, it's dangerous.' Charles's voice was calm, 'Of course they've been watching us, but they know who we are. I'm Champagne Charlie, remember? An armful of girls every night, parties by the score. Why do you think I told you to dress up? You said it yourself: women – glamorous women – are an essential part of my image.' He stood up. 'Time for the off. In case I forget to say so later, you do look very sexy. Almost delicious enough to take my mind off the chase in hand.'

Verry smiled wanly. She was beginning to feel seriously frightened. Looking out through the strengthened glass windows she could see the dim lights of their quarry, and she wondered who was aboard the second vessel and what Charles was letting them start to do.

Charles stepped behind her and went towards the music console built into the bulkhead. He pinched Verry's bottom as he passed behind her, a sharp, professional nip that made her jump and brought the colour to her face. He was laughing as he turned the sound system up to full, began flicking the switches that turned on lights all over the vessel, and finally activated the microphones that would fire the music out into the night. Right on cue *Champers* began to wander in its course, drifting in widening arcs, the meanderings of a water-borne palace dedicated to the pursuit of pleasure.

Salim hit out, his flat palm striking Shakira hard across the cheekbone. 'Get out,' he roared. 'I told you to stay in your cabin.'

'But, darling . . .' Shakira held her hand to her stinging face. 'I only thought – '

'Don't think!' Salim shouted, holding his hand up threateningly. 'I don't want you to think. Just do as you're told. Go!'

She turned and fled from the saloon. He had been angry with her before, but never had he seemed quite so beside himself. She had only wanted to find out what was happening on deck. There had been quite a bump when the vessel now moored alongside them had first arrived, and then the sound of many feet pattering above her head.

She threw herself down on the bed, revelling in the cool soft touch of the silk counterpane on her burning cheek. Pressing her hands over her ears she could cut out the noises that had tempted her out of the cabin. It was only a grubby little fishing boat tied up beside them anyway, so why the fuss? Later, he would punish her.

As she lay still, her breathing slowed. He would make her suffer; feel pain, perhaps, or humiliation. There had been a time when he had slapped her so hard on the buttocks that she had bled, the rings on his fingers leaving long blue weals on her soft skin. The reddened imprint of his hand had lasted for days. But then they had been making love, she sitting astride, savouring the approach of power, the smacking driving her on. She had gloried in the pain. It had been no punishment then.

In her waking doze she was aware, again, of the alien boat crashing against *Aristotle*'s thin hull. She felt no fear. The vessel could never sink because it belonged to Salim, and he was a powerful man. The sea had no control over him, with all his wealth. She was smiling, a beloved child waiting for chastisement, when she heard the music. She shook her head, thinking it was part of a dream and would fade, but instead it became louder, more distinct.

The soft carpet pushed between her toes as she stretched upwards to try to see through the porthole, but all was black. Disappointed, she stood very still, trying to get a fix on the throbbing music. Suddenly a flash of light shot through the darkness. There was a loud explosion and she stepped back in fear. Then she laughed, as a cascade of pink and white stars burst in the night. There was another loud bang, and then another. She wanted to run out on deck and watch, but Salim wouldn't like it. It would have been better if she had been alone.

Someone was having a party out there. She imagined the bright lights to go with the music, the crowd, the gaiety. There would be lovely food, and lots to drink. There would be handsome, admiring men. She closed her eyes, allowing herself to imagine the scene. What a pity it was that the men she needed – those with money – were often so unattractive. Another explosion, even louder than before, and Bruno's voice, swearing loudly as he ran along the deck. Salim was shouting into a megaphone. She couldn't distinguish the words, but the fury was clear. She hugged herself in excitement.

There was someone in the corridor outside. Turning swiftly, she threw herself full length, face down on the bed. She was asleep; she hadn't seen or heard anything. The door opened.

'That stupid bastard.' Salim's voice was high with anger. 'He is an idiot, a buffoon. If it was anyone else I would blow him out of the water.'

She rolled over slowly. 'I'm sorry. I was dozing . . .'

'Freeman. He is a fool. His boat is wallowing about like a pregnant pig, and he is letting off hundreds of pounds' worth of fireworks out here in the middle of the ocean. He's buggered off now, of course, but I've had to rush everything. He is a disgrace. I will never let him use my beautiful car, never.'

Charles Freeman, Shakira thought, was an exception. He was beautiful and he was rich. She closed her eyes and rolled seductively on to her back. 'Come here, my darling,' she murmured. 'Let me make you feel better, take all the tension away.' And all the time she was thinking about the man who liked fireworks.

The three of them had gathered in the saloon. With the lights on deck dimmed, and the music turned off, *Champers* felt once again like a luxurious floating apartment.

Angus was tired. His clothes were wet through with a chilling mixture of perspiration and salt spray, and his face was smeared with oil. He was, however, exultant. 'Bingo!' He waved his camera aloft. 'We really have got the goods on Mr Salim bloody Abu Dann. Enough to tuck him away for a long, long time. Jesus, have I got a thirst.'

Verry held a brimful glass of Foster's towards him. 'You've earned it,' she said.

'Come on, Charles.' Angus beamed. 'Let's really tie one on. Tequila slammers?'

'How do you make them?' Verry started checking through the comprehensive drinks cupboard. 'There's a half full bottle of Tequila in here. What else do we need?'

'Now, now,' Charles admonished. 'I'm looking to you to curb our associate's over-intimate relationship with the bottle, Verry, not encourage it.'

Angus drained his lager to the dregs and then wiped his lips on the back of his hand. 'I and the bottle have no problem at all, Charles. If you need restraining that's your affair. In the meantime, I and my lady friend would appreciate a bottle of lime cordial and a bottle of your finest champagne. I do think, in the circumstances, that wouldn't be an unreasonable strain on your hospitality.'

Verry pulled Charles's blue and white towelling dressing-gown more tightly around her. She had slipped it on as soon as the party charade was over. 'Come on, Charles,' she said. 'Don't be stuffy. I could certainly do with a drink.'

'We have to be on call in' – Charles looked down at his watch – 'four hours. Can you, as Angus puts it, tie one on, catch up on some sleep and surface in that time?'

Verry looked exasperated. 'Don't be silly. I only want one glass, not an entire bottle. What on earth's got into you?'

Charles had no idea why he felt the way he did. It may have been anticlimax, it may have been the fact that he'd been on the go for something like eighteen hours, or it may – and he had a sneaking suspicion that this was close to the truth – be the fact that in creating the phoney party, in setting the night sky alight with a small arsenal of fireworks and bombarding several square kilometres of ocean with music, he had only been recreating scenes from his life. 'I'll get the lime juice from the galley,' he said eventually. 'It's nicest freshly squeezed.'

'Nicest freshly squeezed,' Angus mimicked as Charles left. 'Top drawer, isn't he, lassy? The two of you should get on a treat.'

'Then why don't we?' Verry asked. There was something about Charles that kept her feeling on edge, sounding bitchy. What had she said to him earlier – don't be silly?

Angus's drink, which he laughingly called the 'real Mackay', was simplicity itself. A generous measure of Tequila in the bottom of a champagne flute, a shot of lime, and then the champagne, poured almost to the top of the glass. Verry picked hers up, but before she could taste it Charles put his hand on her wrist as Angus demonstrated the technique. Holding the glass by its stem, Angus slammed it down on to the table. At once the contents of the glass fizzed up, frothing over the edge in a silver stream. 'Down in one,' he instructed, and did just that.

Charles let go of Verry's hand and followed the newsman's example. Both men then turned to watch Verry.

Her cheeks were pink; she had been uncomfortably aware of the feel of Charles's warm skin. With a determined smile she crashed her glass down on to the table. Closing her eyes, as she always did when she drank Alka Seltzer – the only other drink she'd had that sent bubbles up her nose – she started to swallow. A warm glow burst in her stomach. She was gasping for air by the time she'd emptied the glass, but she was feeling good. 'Hit me again,' she laughed, and held out her glass for more.

\* \* \*

Dawn defined the line of the horizon, pencilling in in silver and grey the perfect horizontal of the sea, the sudden perpendicular of sheer cliff. The light turned to rose and the shadows to burnt umber as *Champers* hugged the shoreline.

Angus whispered, 'Won't be long now.' He was crouched on the deck, trying to keep out of the iced stream of early morning air that was whistling past his ears.

They were cruising at top speed, the sound of their engines reverberating back from the sandstone cliff, vibrating amongst the jagged rocks that primaeval forces had tumbled to the water's edge.

Verry huddled close to the journalist for warmth. It had been impossible for her to stay inside. Charles was constantly on the bridge, so Angus was the only human companionship she had access to. 'I just wish it was all over,' she said.

'So do I, lassy. So do I.'

She turned to scrutinize her companion. There had been an intensity in his tone that she found disturbing. A short while ago she had hated him, but now that he was frightened she wanted to help.

'I'll buy you supper at the Red Lion when we get home,' she said. 'Steak and kidney pie with all the trimmings.'

'You're on.' He picked his camera up and peered through the viewfinder at the coastline. 'I hope to Christ this works.'

Verry didn't ask if he meant the Leica or the entire final part of the plan. She heard a tapping and turned round. Charles was in the saloon behind them, knocking on the perspex, beckoning to her. She squeezed Angus's shoulder briefly as she stood up. It was as tense as steel.

'All going according to schedule,' Charles confirmed.

'About ten minutes until we round the point. Then we'll see them.'

'And they'll see us.'

Charles nodded. 'Frightened?' he asked.

'Yes.' There was no point in not telling the truth.

'Then use the fear. Channel it into a positive emotion. That way you'll find the primitive instinct for survival will take over.'

'You sound as if you've done this sort of thing before.'

Charles smiled. 'Crossing the road can be dangerous, Verry. Life is just a question of keeping things in perspective. I want you to stay in here. If there's any shooting' – he paused, gauging her reaction, finding her calmer than he'd expected – 'then lie down on the floor. No heroics. You stay there till I give the all-clear. Understand? This is my show, and you do as you're told.'

'Aye aye, sir.' She formed a sketchy salute. 'May I have permission to go to the little girl's room first?'

Shakira sat on the edge of the circular stool fixed in front of the built-in mahogany dressing-table. Slowly, carefully, she brushed her hair away from her face. The bruise on her cheekbone was a purple patch beneath the black circles under her eyes. It was just after seven in the morning, and she hadn't slept yet. Salim had been very demanding. She shifted a little on the stool; the insides of her thighs were also bruised.

The ring on the third finger of her left hand twinkled in the light cast by the crystal-shaded lamps. Shield shaped, almost three centimetres in length, and studded with diamonds, the engagement symbol was a visible proof of Salim's love.

She had been told, once again, to stay in the cabin. She pointed at her reflection, running a finger critically over her full lips. Life had been more amusing before they were engaged, in the days when she had been used as a business asset. She didn't mind making love with other men to oblige Salim, looking at it as her part of a bargain which yielded rich rewards.

Salim tapped on the door before coming in. 'Good morning, my darling,' he said smoothly. 'I had expected to find you asleep.'

Shakira smiled. 'I like the dawn,' she said. 'The start of a brand new day. I like to breathe in the fresh air.'

'No,' Salim snapped, the open expression on his face closing in an instant. 'You shall not go up on deck.'

'It's . . .' Shakira bit her lip. She had been going to say she was bored, but that would have been a big mistake. 'It's just that it gets stuffy in here.'

'Shakira.' He stepped towards her, burying his fingertips in her shoulders. 'Enough of this petulance. You of all people should know how to please a man.'

She wriggled under his grip. 'Is it nearly finished, your business?'

'My business?' Salim's voice was dangerously soft, and despite the increasing pressure of his fingers she stood quite still. 'What do you know of my business?'

She shook her head.

'I ask you again.' The fingers were now talons, pressing down. 'I will have an answer.'

The telephone rang shrilly. Shakira held her breath. It rang again and Salim released her abruptly. He held the receiver close to his ear and grunted a response, but the expression on his face cleared miraculously.

'You must be bored, my dear,' he said as he walked to the door. 'We will be in port this evening. Now, sleep, and you shall have fun tonight.'

He was gone. She sat down again on the stool, staring unseeingly at her reflection in the mirror, looking forward to the evening ahead. She could wear her new Dior jacket. She touched the red fingermarks at her throat. Salim would relax once his business was over. Or would he? She began to massage her neck. Life without affluence would be nothing for her. She squeezed a generous dollop of Estée Lauder's most restorative skin cream on to her hand and began applying it in increasingly wide circles. Cover-up make-up would conceal all the marks. She tried humming a little song, a tune they'd been playing in Cannes, something from a film.

She began thinking about the others: Fleur and Jesse, Dirk and Verité. The pearl-shaped tears rolled one after the other down the smooth planes either side of her perfect nose. Cannes had been such fun – the glamour, the excitement, even the drama when Jesse had been shot. Bruno wore his gun openly on board *Aristotle*. She had watched him take it from its sheath and clean it. Slowly, caressingly, as if it were some lethal phallic symbol, he oiled its secret parts then slid it lovingly home.

They were slowing down; the sound of the engines had become a thick throaty growl. There was shouting, a distant hail, that she thought must have come from the shore. She would have liked to look out of the porthole, but she didn't dare. Running feet sounded above her, dragging something heavy. She hoped they were being careful. The soft white wood of the deck was Salim's delight, and she was prepared to agonize for him should it be damaged. Was that a sign of love?

She slipped slowly between the cool sheets. It was important for her to love the man she would marry. She lay back, her eyes closed. He was powerful; that above all excited her. He was rich, an essential; at times he could be considerate. The fact that he could also be violent was proof that he cared, that his emotions were strong. She settled further down into the bed, willing her body to relax, instructing her limbs to lie limp. Sleep would come.

Her thoughts began to drift. She was in Cannes, suspended from the great, buzzing, mechanical insect that had carried her and Dirk to stardom. Dirk. She remembered the alpine chalet, could see his body, so slim, so hard and smooth.

The sudden shouts shattered the dream. She sat up, clutching the sheet to her naked breasts. When the shot sounded she cried out, and then she heard a scream, a drawn-out, wavering note of terror. It was a voice she knew. 'Verité,' she whispered, 'Verité,' and then she was out of bed, wrapping the sheet around her, stumbling as she ran towards the door.

There were men on the shore: that was the second thing Charles saw as they rounded the peninsula. The first was their prey, *Aristotle*, rocking gently, apparently moored to the sea anchor.

Charles checked the time on the bulkhead clock. It was five minutes to eight. He picked up the megaphone and stepped out on deck.

The arrival of *Champers* took Salim completely by surprise. There had been no trace of an approaching vessel on his radar. He realized almost instantly that her echo must have been masked by her proximity to the shoreline. There were still three wooden cases remaining on deck; the other twelve had already been off-loaded. Nine were stacked on the beach, three in the grey rubber inflatable dingy that was even now pulling away from his vessel's side.

'Ahoy!' Charles's voice echoed roundly through the megaphone. 'Ahoy, *Aristotle*.'

'Bruno,' Salim shouted, 'get rid of them, quick.' He gestured to the incriminating crates. 'Over the side. Quickly.'

There was a plume of sea water as a man dived

overboard. It was one of the team who had arrived that morning to unload. He was swimming hard for the shore. Bruno pulled out his automatic, aimed it at the centre of the dark-shirted back. But his employer shouted again, and with a shrug of his shoulders he reholstered the gun and began to run along the deck. The cases were heavy, he'd need help – he began shouting for assistance.

'Salim.' Charles's voice again. 'Just stay where you are, we're coming alongside.'

*Champers* was drawing closer to their quarry, Angus crouched on deck working flat out, dropping one camera as he finished the film it contained, picking up another from the selection hanging round his neck. He had taken yards of film. He was grinning, infected by the chase. He had incriminating evidence by the bucketful. He stood up to see more clearly, stepped towards the rail to get a better angle.

Eight o'clock on the dot. There was a shout from the beach as, with a clatter that carried clearly over the water, half a dozen carabineros raced down the cliff track to the beach. Chaos reigned as the handful of men clustered around the piled cases scattered. The one who had swum in from *Aristotle* ran back into the sea. He stood in water up to his chest, his hands pulling his hair in desperation, uncertain which way to flee.

Verry had heard the noise from the beach, and then the echoing Spanish voice issuing official-sounding instructions through another megaphone. She slipped silently out on to the deck to see what was going on.

'Angus,' she called softly.

He turned to face her, smiling, his face lined in relief. 'We did it,' he said. 'You owe me supper.'

Bruno shoved helplessly at the wooden cases. Each was so heavy he could move it only a few centimetres at a time. He glared over at the other yacht. That interfering playboy . . . He could see Charles Freeman, so upright, so idiotically handsome. He could also see a man with cameras, and the damning sight calmed Bruno so much that with an inspired shove he was able to shove one case into the water. He could do it. He looked quickly back at the shore. The carabineros were busy rounding up the beach party. The rubber dinghy had been let loose and was drifting away from the shore, towards them. He pushed at the second case, his strength now superhuman. It went swiftly into the water; the third followed. There was only one thing left to do. He stood up, aware that the muscles in his upper arms were shaking, but unconcerned. *Champers* was almost alongside. He stepped behind the shelter of the bridge, on the far side of the boat from the approaching invaders. He watched the woman walk towards the man with the cameras. He leaned his hands on the perspex sunguard where it ended in front of him. He smiled, spread his feet wide, and crouched a fraction. He could see in a perfect straight line, three point contact: his eye, the bead on his gun, and the beautifully targeted centre chest of his target. He squeezed, lovingly. There was hardly any recoil.

Verry screamed. Which had come first, the sharp crack of the explosion or Angus slumping against her, she didn't know. She struggled frantically to hold on to him as he staggered backwards away from her. He seemed to pause, to hang for a moment, and then he was falling, his arms out wide, his mouth open, red like the great gaping hole in his chest. There was a smack, like a fist hitting dough, as he hit the water.

Charles ran along the deck. He was wearing soft deck shoes that made no sound, and when he gripped Verry from behind she screamed again. She was leaning over the thin rail, staring down at the froth, at the bursting red bubbles. There was another splash, a cleaner, sharper sound, further away. Charles looked up as he jerked Verry back from the edge. He saw the figure in the sea, watched it swim the few short strokes to the rubber dinghy. Like an eel it squirmed out of the water, and within seconds the outboard had roared into life and the little craft was bounding away over the short waves.

There was a shout from the beach as the Spanish police gestured after their lost quarry. There was nothing Charles could do. He pulled Verry close to him but she struggled frantically out of his grip.

'We've got to save him,' she shouted. 'We've got to get Angus out of the sea. Don't you understand? We've got to pull him out of the water or he's going to drown.'

Charles shook his head sadly. 'No, he's not,' he said, and pulled Verry back into his arms. 'It's much too late for him to drown.' He watched as Shakira stepped out on to the deck opposite them.

She held her hand to her eyes to shield them from the sun. She stood still, a marble Aphrodite in a silken shroud.

Charles raised a hand in slow salute.

## Chapter 13

It seemed to take forever. The nightmare that had begun with Angus's body on the end of a boathook appeared to have no end.

The Spanish authorities were very correct, punctilious in their attention to detail. There was a great deal of form filling. Verry hadn't known that Charles spoke fluent Spanish. She had to struggle to make herself understood in a mixture of French and English.

There wasn't much, in any case, that she could say. They knew who had done the shooting, the man they knew as Bruno, and she kept asking why they hadn't set off after him. Charles told her that the coastguard had been informed of the fugitive, as had all ports of call along the coast. He didn't tell her that the shore was rich with landing places that never saw a member of the law enforcement services from one end of the year to the next. He also didn't tell her that the reason *Champers* hadn't set off in pursuit of the inflatable dinghy was because starting their engines would almost inevitably have sucked Angus's partially submerged corpse into the propellers.

Angus was put into a body bag. As the nylon zip slid closed Verité shivered convulsively, the noise grating on her nerves like chalk on a blackboard.

'What do we do now?' she whispered.

Charles said a few words to the departing carabinero captain as he stepped down into the tender, and then turned back slowly. He was tired, drained of energy. 'We just get on with our lives,' he said. 'Go back to square one.'

'But it can't all end there.'

'No, of course not. But these things take time.' He rubbed his forehead. 'I think we should have something to eat.'

Verry shook her head. 'I couldn't swallow a thing.'

'Somehow it doesn't seem right to suggest a drink.'

'It's what Angus would have done.' She smiled lopsidedly.

'I wish I'd never got involved in the damned business,' Charles said vehemently.

There was nothing Verry could say. She felt desperately guilty. Trying to save Sara's reputation had cost Angus his life.

'It wasn't worth it,' Charles said, as if he had read her thoughts.

'No. My grandmother would never have wanted . . .'

'I don't mean what we set out to do.' Charles was looking angry. 'I mean what that bloody madman with a gun did. He acted on his own initiative. Abu Dann would never have ordered the killing. He's in serious trouble now. A gun-running charge he could have crawled around somehow, but this – he's lucky they're not dragging him off to some bug-ridden local jail.'

'At least *he* can't escape. I counted at least half a dozen policemen going on board *Aristotle*.'

'We should be under way ourselves.' Charles listened intently. The engines had been started up a few minutes earlier, but it had taken several attempts to get one of them going and it was still not running smoothly.

It took over two hours to locate the source of the trouble: a few unidentifiable specks of dirt in a fuel line had clogged a valve. Verry spent the time packing her travel bag, taking everything out and rearranging it, twice. Her hands were still shaking; she kept seeing Angus's face as he'd hit the water. As they eventually left the rocky bay that would be imprinted on her mind for the rest of her life, there was a knock on the cabin door. It was Charles.

'There are sandwiches in the saloon,' he said.

Verry stood very still, her fingers squeezing the handle of the bag on the bunk in front of her. 'I can't bear it,' she whispered. 'I just can't bear it.'

He stepped forwards, laying his hands gently on her shaking shoulders. 'It wasn't your fault,' he said, his voice close to her ear.

'It was.' Verry turned quickly, burying her face in his warm, soft jumper. 'None of this would have happened if I hadn't set out to make a quick buck.'

'If it was anyone's fault' – Charles stroked her hair softly, nudging her face closer to his chest – 'it was mine. I was the one who knew what was going on, but I thought I could handle it. After the police arrived I relaxed, when I should have kept an eye on Angus. I should have insisted he stayed hidden to the end.'

Verry was sobbing now, her chest heaving, her breath coming in painful gulps. 'I saw my father die. I watched him die as well.'

Charles kept stroking her hair, leading her gently back so that they could sit down on the bunk. 'It's all right,' he whispered into her ear. 'Everything's all right now, I promise.'

'Please.' She looked up into his face. 'Please.'

He didn't know whether her words were a plea for comfort or for protection. Her lips were swollen and red. 'Don't cry,' he said. 'Don't cry, baby.' He kissed her gently, tasting the perfume of her lipstick, the salt of her tears.

She slid her arms up to his neck, holding him tightly to her. He couldn't hear what she was saying, but between the light kisses her lips were moving. Her eyes were closed as she pressed against him, and he could feel her need.

'It's all right,' he murmured. He pushed her jumper up, stroking the warmth of her skin, feeling her shiver with the cold of his hands.

'Please,' she whispered again.

He was touching her breasts, kneading them gently. His hand slipped inside her brassiere and she tipped her head, her lips parting. She lay back, and he followed her with his body. Their mouths locked, he ran his hand over her stomach, over the tight denim jeans she was wearing.

Everything was sensation. She had been cold, that was all she knew, and she was so desperate to be warm. She existed in a world of grey, her eyelids flickering but never opening. She was aware of the moving hands, adjusting herself to his touch; aware of her clothes being slipped off, conscious of helping him. Then he was on top of her, and she spread her legs wide, wrapped them around him as he entered her and a void was filled.

He left her sleeping, first covering her gently with a duvet and laying a travel rug on top of that. The sandwiches were still in the saloon, and he began to eat mechanically. There would be a lot to do in the next few days. The police would expect more statements, there would be the press to face, a complete strip down of *Champers*'s engine. He didn't want any more problems.

And there would be Verité.

Verry stepped out on to the deck. The erratic beat of an engine had woken her. Dressing quickly, she had refused to let herself consider the implications of what had happened earlier.

They were approaching port. The harbour lay open before them, and there was a strong smell of diesel. Leaning over the rail, she could see a trail of grey exhaust fumes hanging behind them on the churning blue water. There was a small crowd waiting on shore. She pushed her hair off her face, then kept her hand on her forehead to stop the wind blowing it back into her stinging eyes.

A solitary figure stood on the very edge of the quay, wrapped in a short scarlet coat. A few metres away a gaggle of enthusiastic pressmen were gathered together in pursuit of hot news.

'The vultures are circling over the kill.' Charles had come up silently behind her.

'It's only to be expected.' Verry spoke shortly, her words clipped and precise.

The red jacket began to move animatedly as an arm was raised and waved frantically.

'I think we can all make an educated guess as to who that is,' Charles said drily.

'Something else that was to be expected.'

Shakira waved again. She was oblivious of the chatter behind her. All her attention was focused on the approaching vessel. 'Verité,' she called out, the word whipped away by the sea breeze.

'It's all right,' Verry soothed. She held Shakira close, comforting the distraught girl.

They were standing on the stone quay. Shakira's face was pressed into her agent's shoulder; over the quivering raven locks, Verry's gaze caught Charles's almost amused expression. He was giving an interview in professional style, the journalist jotting down the words as they fell from his well-formed lips.

'Salim ripped the ring right off,' Shakira complained bitterly. 'Look.' She held out her hand. A red graze extended the length of her ring finger.

'You're better off away from him,' Verry said. She was

aware of her words being noted down around her. 'He's a very unpleasant man.' Her words were careful and considered.

'He's vile,' Shakira burst out. 'The terrible things he made me do . . .'

There was an expectant pause that Verry broke. 'We can talk about that later,' she said. 'When we get home.'

'Home?' Shakira's voice was hollow, her eyes desolate. 'I have no home now. He will have taken everything.'

'We'll sort something out.'

The two women stayed one night in a modern international hotel poised on the cliff top. They took little notice of the breathtaking view, although Shakira's eyes were drawn more than once to the beautiful white yacht moored all alone close to the dry dock. *Champers* was longer than *Aristotle*, and also, she had gathered, a little slower – as would be, she was sure, the sexual performance of its owner. As an experienced lover Shakira appreciated that both the speed and the size she attributed to Charles would please her enormously.

The plane to Heathrow took off on time and landed slightly ahead of schedule because of a tail wind. Verry noticed on the flight how Shakira kept steering the conversation around to Charles. It was only to be expected, she thought. Once Shakira had developed a taste for cruising Charles was a natural provider. He had come to see them off at the airport and kissed them both goodbye: a kiss on each cheek, a brief squeeze of the arm, no partiality. He had said he would telephone Verry to tell her how things were progressing with the search for Bruno. That had made Shakira start to cry again and, always the perfect gentleman, he had put his arm around the girl and comforted her until their flight was called.

Customs at Heathrow was a mere formality. They both

put on dark glasses to push their way through the waiting cameramen. The taxi was a haven of peace. Verry would have to announce to her mother and grandmother that Shakira was going to spend a few days at the cottage. It was essential; she couldn't let the girl go off on her own to be hounded by the press. It would be, she thought, not quite a case of putting the cat amongst the pigeons, but rather letting the predatory puss loose amongst domesticated ones.

'Of course I don't like her staying here,' Angelique said loudly. 'She's nothing but a tart. Your father would never have allowed her to enter the same house as me.'

'Mother, please,' Verry said in exasperation. 'If you have to keep going on about Shakira at least lower your voice. It's not fair to upset her any more than she is.'

They were standing in the hallway between the kitchen and the drawing room. Angelique, Verry was convinced, had chosen the spot for the confrontation with her daughter because their voices would carry upstairs to Shakira in the guest bedroom.

'She's upset?' Angelique flounced. 'What about me? I need peace and quiet. You know the doctor said so.'

'That was weeks ago. You're fine now.' Verry didn't go on to say that if her mother was fit enough to be out until all hours at night she was fit enough to put up with a house guest.

'And she used up all the hot water this morning.' It was Angelique's ultimate argument. 'My bath was icy cold.'

'Would you like some coffee?' Verry stepped determinedly into the kitchen. 'I have time to make you one before I leave.'

'You're not going out? Not leaving me alone with that slut?'

'You're not alone. Grandma will be downstairs soon,

and I wish I knew what you think Shakira is going to do to you. She's been as quiet as a mouse since she arrived. All she wants is somewhere tucked away where she can get some peace.'

For two days Verry's guest had kept mainly to her bedroom, venturing downstairs only to eat a couple of bowls of cereal and a boiled egg. The only emotion she'd shown was when Verry told her about Charles's phone call, but whether the sudden light in her eyes had been due to the news of Abu Dann's being made persona non grata in Spain or the fact that Charles had sent his regards, Verry couldn't tell. Bruno seemed to have disappeared completely. Charles had said it was just what he'd expected. He hadn't said if he would phone again.

'I'm going to a meeting with a firm of accountants,' Verry said placatingly. 'They've seen my proposal for the *Europa* film, and they seem to think they might be able to raise the finance. You can't possibly want me to stay here and miss that chance.'

Angelique did not want the film discarded. Dirk was convinced that it would be a great success. It had been agreed that he would perform six of the eight songs it would feature. He would be paid his fee, but he was also going to get twenty per cent of the profits of the CD that was in the planning. It could be a lot of money; but then, as he would have said himself, he was a star. 'How much have you said you will put in yourself?' she asked.

'It isn't finally agreed, but it will have to be somewhere around a hundred thousand pounds. We're trying to raise a million. As films go, *Europa*'s low budget, but then that was the original appeal of the whole story.'

'And you have the hundred thousand?'

'Of course I don't,' Verry said shortly. 'And I shan't even try to raise it until the million is a real possibility.'

'"Try?" You mean you're not sure you'll be able to get it?'

'Mother.' Verry busied herself spooning finely ground Blue Mountain into a two-cup cafetière. 'How many times do I have to say this? I am borrowed right up to the hilt. I have no more security to offer. There may be something I can do on the music side, presell the rights or something. I don't know. But I'm certainly not going to give up the chance of raising the big money because I don't have what it needs to prime the pump. If I did that I'd be an idiot.'

'You can have the money,' Angelique said grandly.

Verry almost let the Bodum glass mug slip through her fingers. 'I beg your pardon?' she said slowly. 'I don't think I quite caught that.'

'I said you may have the money.' Angelique perched on the bar stool in front of the breakfast counter, adjusting the full skirt of her housecoat so that her knee peeped through.

'But you said . . .' Angelique had told Verry she had twenty-five thousand pounds left from her inheritance, after paying for Dirk's stunt.

'Don't nitpick, darling. It's not lady-like. Just smile sweetly and say thank you. As soon as you have written confirmation that you can go ahead with the film on production of one hundred thousand, then you shall have it. Now, hurry up with my coffee, or you'll be late for your meeting. And don't forget the thank you.'

'Thank you, Mother,' Verry whispered. She was stunned. Her overwhelming emotion was one of amazement, heavily tinged with relief. She'd had serious doubts about being able to raise the money. She smiled genuinely at her mother sitting there so pertly, so pleased with herself. There was no point in being angry about the lie she'd been told. Angelique was not like other people.

'And don't forget,' Angelique called at the top of her voice as Verry opened the front door, 'I want that slut out of the house before this evening.'

Sara tapped on the door of Verry's bedroom. In her hand she held half a dozen letters. She looked worried.

'Come in,' Verry called. She was sitting at her dressing-table putting on Estée Lauder's Lucidity reflective foundation. She needed the coverage. Her skin was blotchy because she'd been skipping meals and eating too many chocolate bars.

'Nice to see you sitting down for a change,' Sara said tartly. She was concerned. There had been no chance for a real talk since Verry had come back from Spain.

'I'm not going anywhere until this afternoon. I've actually managed to catch up on some paperwork, even if I had to spend the past couple of hours sitting up in bed to do it. I thought I would go out for some lunch soon. I'd like to try that new wine bar round the corner. Do you feel like joining me?'

Sara nodded noncommittally. She had every reason to suppose that Verry's plan for the day was about to change. 'Some more post came while you were away,' she said. 'I didn't give it to you with the other letters because I felt that you'd need time to deal with it. Here. They're in order of arrival.'

Verry could see the orange flashes on the envelopes. They were all recorded deliveries. 'From the bank?'

'Yes, from the bank. Did you expect them?'

'It depends on what they say – I knew they were going to set something in motion.' She quickly skimmed the initial few lines of the first letter, then went on to the second. 'You've read them?'

'I'm sorry, Verry. You've tried so hard.'

'Why on earth couldn't they have waited?' Verry stood

up. 'I'm almost there. The accountants think they can get the money to make the film. I can offer different security as soon as it's in motion, tie the house in as well. Why couldn't they wait? A possession order is so final.'

'What about your mother? How much has she actually got? Couldn't she put some money into the house?'

'She's already offered me the hundred thousand pounds I need for the film project, and I believe her when she says that takes her close to the edge. I'll have to sell.'

'But can you?' The market was bad; half the street seemed to be littered with 'For Sale' boards.

'That's the point, isn't it? I'll probably lose tens of thousands of pounds. Then we'll have to rent somewhere to live, and that will eat up whatever else I could have used to pay the bank back the inevitable shortfall. Oh, God.' She looked out of the window, at the grey skies, the chilly pedestrians drifting past like blown leaves. 'Autumn's an awful time of the year to have to sell.'

'What about your share of the flat? I thought Sam had agreed to buy you out.'

'He can't. His business is in trouble. He wants to sell up himself, but what we stand to get in this market will only just cover what we owe on it. It's all such a mess.'

'I just wish there was something I could do. If only those publishers would come through. But they're insisting on proof that the film will go ahead before they commit themselves. It's a vicious circle, and there doesn't seem to be any way to break through.'

'There has to be,' Verry still stood facing the window, but her eyes were closed. She was desperately trying to concentrate. 'I refuse to give up now.'

'That's the spirit.' Sara spoke admiringly, but she could feel no confidence. 'I'll come with you to court,' she said.

'I don't suppose it'll actually get there. They were asking me to sign a voluntary possession order before I left. This is just to force my hand.' She had an almost overwhelming desire to slump down with her head in her hands, but that would be to admit defeat and that was inconceivable. There was too good a future on the horizon if only she could hold on.

'There are some very nice places to rent,' Sara volunteered.

'Wasted money. Somehow I have to hang on here. I'll have to work even harder. I'm afraid our lunch is off.'

'That's no great surprise.'

'I suppose not.'

'Did I do the right thing, not giving these to you as soon as you came home? I was worried I might be making the situation worse; on the other hand I didn't want you overwhelmed.'

'No, you did the right thing, Grandma. I wouldn't have been able to think straight to begin with. I was just relieved that there wasn't anything from the bank waiting for my return. It'll be all right in the end. I just have to make everything happen faster.'

'Take care, darling. Your health matters more than anything. I'm worried you're taking too much on. I just wish . . .'

'I have a wish too, Grandma. I wish you'd go downstairs and make me a sandwich. I'll have that and a glass of milk, and then I'll get going. It'll be a case of clearing the decks for action. I have to see my foursome and find out exactly what they intend to do, then I'll chase up the accountants, and after that I'll have to work out some publicity stunt, something to get us more coverage, get the film mentioned in the press again. That should help me pick up a distribution deal, which is what I need next. I have to be able to deal with the bank from a position of strength.'

Sara dabbed at the corners of her eyes. 'Your grandfather would have been so proud of you.'

'He'd only have been proud if I'd succeeded. Now, are you going to get me that sandwich?' She was pulling off her dressing gown. She wanted to get on with the day.

Pencombe Place was dressed in its most elegant coat. An early, crisp white frost was dredged like thick icing sugar over the formal lawns and close-cut yews, and scarlet hips cast a blush of colour over wind-scoured hedges. The River Medway flowed slowly, steel grey; low between its ice-rimmed banks it revealed the myriad tiny tunnels that were home to countless voles and other furry water creatures.

Fleur walked the riverbank. Wearing country green – an old Barbour jacket, corduroy trousers tucked into her wellington boots and an ancient flat cap – she looked more like a gangling youth than a fashion model. Her fame had flared even brighter since Jesse's shooting. There had been more coverage about her private life than ever before and she felt somehow violated. Her husband was now totally well, and quite proud of the jagged purple scar across his chest. In training for his next fight, a fill-in to replace the British title bout he'd missed after his accident, he had welcomed Fleur's suggestion that she spend a few days at her childhood home.

There were horses ahead. She couldn't see them yet, but the drumming of hooves carried clearly over the ploughed field. The first appeared suddenly, a few hundred yards ahead of her as it broached the low summit of a fold of country that swept down from the higher Wealden ridge.

The peak of her flat cap shielded Fleur's eyes from the sharp sunlight and she recognized Bengy instantly. He was riding Thunder, a horse that belonged to a local farmer with ambitions to race it on the point-to-point circuit. Fleur stepped off the narrow track beaten by fishermen and walkers and waited. She was close to the bank where it crumbled down into the river. There were five riders in all, their mounts puffing out clouds of steam and stamping iron-shod feet as they were pulled up.

There was a short conference, the resonant notes of the voices carrying to Fleur, but not the words. Then the group was coming on, cantering towards her. Bengy was holding his mount in, keeping to the rear. The horse was throwing its head, irritated by the harsh feel of the bit, wanting to get to the front, a natural leader. Fleur smiled politely as the riders began to pass. A woman waved briefly in recognition, a man grinned whilst keeping both hands on the reins, Bengy was slowing down. A few feet in front of her he stopped.

'Fleur.' He touched his whip to his hard hat, the only visible concession he made to his accident. She couldn't ever remember having seen him wear anything on his head for exercising before.

'Hello, Bengy.' Their last meeting had been so awful. 'What's he like?' She gestured towards the horse.

'Bloody obstinate.' Without apparent effort Bengy controlled the animal's attempt to crab-step sideways, away from the sound of running water.

'I hear you're opening up the stables again.'

'Bad news always travels fast.'

'Bad?'

'Bad for you. I expect you thought I'd sell up and move away rather than embarrass you. Well, I'm sorry to disenchant you, but I'm not going to act the gentleman this time.'

Fleur smiled wryly. 'I never thought of it as an act, Bengy.'

'Very clever.' His voice was bitter, his expression hard,

uncompromising. 'Such a pity you're so thick in other ways.'

Fleur was suddenly aware how cold it was. A solid chill was creeping up through her boots. 'I don't think we have anything left to say to each other. Why don't you join your friends? They're waiting.' Turning round, she could see the others clustered around the gate leading to the bridletrack.

It was as if he hadn't heard her. 'Mrs Standing,' he sneered. 'The name could have been worse, I suppose. It could have been Mrs Sitting, or Lying. That would have been much more suitable. Mrs Lying on her back for any common scum to have his way with.'

'Bengy,' Fleur said despairingly, 'just go away. This is as difficult for you as it is for me. You're destroying yourself.'

He laughed harshly. 'I'm destroying myself, am I? That's a good one. You've made me the joke of the country, the poor lame bastard who couldn't keep his woman. Who was obviously so bad in bed that she rushed into the arms of some stinking boxer. You enjoy that, do you, Fleur? The sweat and the blood? I suppose that's what it takes to turn on a frigid bitch like you.'

She stepped out on to the ploughed earth. She would never turn her back and walk away, but she could walk around him.

'Stay!' Bengy snapped. 'Stay right where you are. I haven't finished yet.'

'But I have,' she said softly but firmly.

'You bitch.' He raised his whip, held it aloft so that the metal tip caught the lemon-white sunlight. 'You need a good beating. Just like any bitch on heat, you need to be taught control.'

She kept walking at right angles to the path, away from

the river. Ahead of her the ground began to slope upwards.

'You won't get away from me.' Bengy was using his legs, squeezing his mount tightly around the girth, and all the time he held the whip aloft, both reins in one hand. 'Your common little lover isn't here to save you now. Look at me. Look at me, by Christ, or I'll . . .'

'Or you'll what?' Fleur spun round furiously. 'You'll beat me, will you? And then what? Will that alter what's being said about you? Seeing that's what seems to matter most to you, you'd better consider what the county will make of you beating a defenceless woman. Go on, what are you waiting for? There's no Sir Galahad to come rushing to my rescue. Go on, hit me.'

Bengy's mouth was working furiously, chewing on his bottom lip in rage. He had never felt such red-hot anger, and all because of the pale-faced chit standing her ground before him. He impelled his mount forward despite its attempts to resist. It wanted to catch up with the others.

'What are you waiting for?' Fleur taunted, her eyes glittering. She felt no fear.

Bengy kicked savagely with his heels. His short spurs dug into warm, soft flank, and at last Thunder rebelled with strength. The horse reared up: prevented from escaping forwards by the all-controlling reins, and impelled by strong legs to move where it had no intention of going, it screamed out in protest.

Involuntarily Fleur stepped back as the flying hooves threshed the air in front of her. The very real possibility of being kicked cooled her anger and made her realize how much she was in danger.

Bengy was fighting the horse. Confident of victory, his legs clasped even more tightly around the soft belly, he leaned forwards in the saddle, smiling grimly. There was a distant shout as his companions saw he might be in trouble.

Fleur struggled to control her panic. The horse's eyes were rolling wildly. It was twisting and turning, throwing its head up and back, determined to get rid of its rider, just as Bengy was now determined to ride Fleur down. She ran a few steps, but she had to keep looking back over her shoulder. The animal would move so much faster than she could. After a few more steps the mud was clinging to her boots, slowing her to a stumble.

The flush of victory was building on Bengy's face. He was the master. The horse was starting to respond, its bucks shorter, the tossing mane lower. He pulled savagely on the reins, twisting the fine head round to face his prey. He was so absorbed, so unprepared for the sudden pain in his hip that he shouted out. It was a roar of fury. His disability had struck at the climax of his power. The muscles in his leg turned to water, he trod down hard on the stirrup for balance, and his seat shifted violently on the saddle.

Thunder realized instinctively that this was his opportunity. With a final squeal of victory he cavorted joyfully and Bengy had no chance as he began to slip ignominiously sideways. For a moment it seemed his foot might get caught in the stirrup and he would be dragged lethally by the bolting horse, but as it was he fell heavily, safely, on to the thick, shock-absorbing brown mud. Thunder and Fleur, at the same moment, began their runs to freedom.

## Chapter 14

'Hey,' Jesse boomed down the phone, 'I was just going to call you, Verité. I want to confirm you're coming out to watch my Las Vegas fight next week. I'm going to be second on the bill. The main bout's being screened by HBO, and they reckon they're going to show mine as well. You do realize what that means, I hope?'

Verry relaxed a fraction and laughed. The boxer's enthusiasm was contagious. 'You're a star?' she asked.

'On my way, babe, and it won't do your film any harm either. I can just see the spiel. The great American Home Box Office corporation invites you to watch its latest discovery – or something like that.' He chuckled. 'You can tell I don't suffer from false modesty.'

'I've never thought that was your problem.'

'You're not subtly trying to tell me I actually have problems?' Jesse's voice was still charged with enthusiasm. He was pumping it up, forcing himself past the disappointment of missing his crack at the UK Championship.

Verry thought it seemed a shame to spoil the atmosphere. She said, 'No, it's only me that has the problems, Jesse. And they're nothing much, just the usual hassles of a great mogul.'

'Sure.'

They'd developed a solid relationship whilst Jesse had been recuperating. Their talk was based on banter, but they shared a mutual respect. From the day he had first signed up with Verité the boxer had felt somehow responsible for his agent, because, as he appreciated, he was old-fashioned in his attitude to women and thought they needed protection. She had the ability to get him a new kind of publicity and he thought that if anyone could get him into films she could, but it didn't stop him wondering if she wasn't out of her depth moneywise.

'The week after your fight, I want to schedule a press conference in London. Something really glitzy, so that we'll get a load of the press there.'

'You want to ask a few of the boxing correspondents as well as your usual media crowd. They'll turn up as long as it doesn't clash with anything special on the sports side, and it would give them an opportunity to widen their coverage on me, get a bit of a new slant.'

'Give me a list of names. I'm going to do it in style: glossy printed invitations going out in a couple of days, telephone follow-up a week before the call, fax at breakfast on the actual day.'

'Do we performers get a game plan?'

'Just like the punters, you get told when to turn up and where. You also get told to look seriously flash.'

'Is this the four of us?'

'Do you think Fleur will want to be involved?' The model still hadn't said if she was going to carry on with Goode as Golde.

Jesse thought for a while. 'I think so. She had a problem at home the other day. Another run-in with that jerk.'

'The man she was engaged to?'

'Yeah. I wanted to go down and punch his head in, but she wouldn't let me.' He sounded wistful.

'I think you should talk to a lawyer. He should be warned off.'

'You might be right. We'll do something when this fight is out of the way. Are you going to call Fleur about the press conference, or shall I tell her?'

'I'll speak to her myself. Meanwhile, keep up the good work. I'll see you in the States. I'll try and get in early enough to wish you good luck in person.' She placed the receiver back in its cradle. There were too few days in the week. She began to dial Dirk's number.

He answered after half a dozen rings, 'Hi!' He sounded breathless.

'It's Verité.' That was one good thing about having an unusual first name: she rarely had to give her surname on the phone to identify herself to people she knew.

'Talk of the devil.'

'I suppose that means my mother is with you.'

'This is true.' Dirk's voice had regained its usual drawling tone. 'How did you know that? Have your ears been burning?'

'No more than usual. I've just been speaking to Jesse. Are you going to the fight?'

'You try and stop me. I'm hoping to persuade Angelique to come as well.'

Verry closed her eyes in exasperation. She had intended to make a quick in and out trip to the States. With her mother in tow everything would have to be very leisurely. 'Would she be travelling with you?' she asked, crossing her fingers for an affirmative.

'No. You know I've got that gig in the Big Apple a couple of days before. I don't think she'd enjoy that – too chaotic.'

Too many bimbettes, Verry thought acidly. 'How about on the way back?'

'I thought we'd stay on. A week or so in Acapulco sounds tempting to me, and from the look on Ange's face I'd say she fancies it too.'

'I need you back in England for the twenty-eighth.' The press conference was scheduled for the thirtieth, which meant Dirk could be two days late without it mattering.

Dirk was silent, whether sulking or communicating with Angelique it was impossible to discern. Eventually he said, 'What for, o glorious leader, or are we minions not meant to ask?'

'To meet your adoring press,' she said sarcastically, 'Lots of pretty pickies to tempt our friends with the power to make or break.'

Dirk appreciated Verry's success rate at getting coverage. 'Will Shakira be there?' he asked.

'I should think so, and Jesse, and Fleur.'

'I suppose Acapulco can wait a while.' Dirk's voice began to contain a tinge of enthusiasm. 'You doing something special?'

'You could say that. And it's going to be as big a surprise to you as it is to the press boys. That way it'll be spontaneous.' She rang off with Dirk's avowal that he wouldn't miss it for the world still ringing in her ears.

Shakira's line was engaged. Verry began to dial Pencombe Place. The press conference must be brilliant, sparkling, a gem of a hype. The fact that she hadn't yet worked out the magic ingredient that would get her front page coverage didn't worry her – not yet. But she did want the invitation cards printed. She wanted them available tomorrow at the latest, because she wanted to be able to prove to the court that she needed a postponement of the possession order scheduled for the thirtieth. She remembered reading somewhere that the courts had a minimum six-week backlog for that kind of hearing. Six weeks that in her case might just wind up being worth a fortune.

Angelique opened the front door of the cottage, leaving the security chain attached. Peering through the narrow crack gave her a novel perspective; Shakira looked taller, slimmer, older.

'Hello, Angelique. Is Verité there?'

'Shakira.' The older woman's voice was harsh. 'I didn't

expect to see you here again.'

The weather was bleak. A cold wind blew across the tiny, bare front gardens, and Shakira stamped her feet to warm them. 'Is she there?' she asked again.

The door closed silently.

'Angelique!' She banged on the door with her fist. 'I want to talk to Verité. Open the door, for heaven's sake.'

In the hallway Angelique stood resolute, arms folded across her chest as she barred her daughter's way to the door.

'Mother,' Verry said patiently. 'There really isn't any harm in her. Let me past, please. I want to see her.'

Angelique was silent. She hadn't yet decided what her course of action should be. At the thundering on the door behind her an unbidden smile crept to her rose-pink lips. 'She's certainly keen to see you,' she said.

Verry gently pushed her mother aside, slipped the chain off the door and opened it wide. 'Come inside,' she said. 'I think we've provided the street with enough amusement for one day.'

'It was your mother's fault,' Shakira said, glaring at her persecutor still standing in the hallway. 'I can't understand why she's so unkind to me.'

Satisfaction coloured Angelique's porcelain cheeks. 'You wouldn't understand human kindness if it jumped out and stroked you,' she said smugly.

Verry began to whistle soundlessly as she led Shakira through to the drawing room. She was learning not to react to other people's moods. The only supercharged emotions she had the strength to cope with were her own.

Shakira's first question was enlightening. 'Have you heard from Charles lately?'

'No.' Verry sat down at the dining-table, which she had started to use as a desk for business meetings. 'Have you?'

The girl looked flustered. 'No, and I wouldn't expect

to. I only meant . . .' Her words drifted off.

Verry was tempted to ask exactly what she did mean, but she didn't have the time to give in to temptation. 'Are you coming to Las Vegas next week?'

'For Jesse's fight? It doesn't count as an expense that you pay, does it?' In response to Verry's quick shake of the head she carried on, 'I'm not sure. It will be expensive: the flight, the hotel and everything.'

'It might be money well spent. Dirk will be going; you could pick up some useful publicity.'

'I don't want to pretend to be his woman any more. It's demeaning.'

Verry breathed in slowly. She thought it was a little late for Shakira to start acting coy.

'I might ring round and see if any of my friends are going.'

'Fleur will be there, and so will I.'

'I didn't mean friends like you. I meant friends who will be going in style, people who'd be happy to have me along for the trip in their private jet. People who, for the sake of my amusing company, would be happy to pay my hotel bill.'

'I thought that after your experience with Abu Dann you might be more wary of that sort, Shakira.'

The girl smiled. 'I'm a quick learner,' she said. 'I made some mistakes I won't make again, but I have no intention of changing the way I live. Why should I? Even if the film does take off, and I become a big star, I still don't see why I should use money I earn to pay for things someone else would be more than happy to provide me with for free.'

'It's not up to me to tell you how to live your life. But –'

'Nobody has the right to do that,' Shakira said quickly. 'I know you think I'm an immoral alley cat, but I assure you, the alleys I frequent are very exclusive, and the food I scavenge is only the best. If in exchange I sometimes have to endure the attentions of a prowling tom, then I won't complain.' She laughed, apparently happily.

Verry looked down at the typewritten pages in front of her. Shakira, she was convinced, was whistling in the dark. She was frightened but she wouldn't admit it. 'Let's just say that if you find at the last minute that you'd like to travel with us, we'd be more than happy to have your company. Now, I want you to be free on the thirtieth of this month. I'm giving a press conference about the film.'

'Really? It's got that far?' Enthusiasm gave new life to Shakira's eyes. 'I wondered . . . I mean, I thought that perhaps with everything that's happened, Jesse getting shot, Fleur getting married . . . oh, I don't know what I thought, really. What shall I wear? Where will it be?' The questions tumbled out, the veneer of sophistication filed away for another day.

'Here's a draft of the invitation.' Verry handed over a flimsy sheet of paper. Inside an A6 rectangle was the formal wording: 'Verité Goode, Managing Director of Goode as Golde, requests the pleasure of your company . . .' It went on to name the venue: the Tower Hotel, London; the date: the thirtieth of March; and the time: twelve noon. The reason for the reception was the announcement of a new film, a joint French and British production, to start shooting in late April. It listed the four stars, and then there was a space.

'What's this gap for?'

'I'm going to write in that by hand, use it as my place to lay the bait. What the press wants more than anything else is a good photo-opportunity, and you can rest assured that's what we'll give them.'

'You're so clever, Verité,' Shakira enthused. 'I wouldn't know where to begin with something like this.'

'I have a shrewd idea that there are areas of life where you could teach me some useful lessons.'

Shakira laughed. 'I don't suppose you'd ever practise what I preached. Charles Freeman, for example.' She smiled at Verry. 'If I wanted him I could have him.'

'And on that interesting note' – Verry stood up – 'I'm afraid we have to part. I have a lot to get through in the next few days. Don't forget to let me know if you want to join us on the trip to Vegas.'

The glamorous crowd was determined to enjoy its evening. Like waves in a multi-coloured sea, tuxedoed men and bare-shouldered women swept from dinner table to casino to sporting hall.

'Isn't it exciting?' Angelique sparkled. She was dressed in buttermilk crepe, a full-length sheath that stretched from just under her chin to her ankles, its tightly swathed sleeves reaching to her finger tips. Her figure was that of a young girl, her face had been expertly made-up, and her hair shone with gloss. She didn't look a day over thirty.

'That's the good old dependable USA for you – entertainment with a capital e.' Dirk wore a silver jacket cut in dinner-suit style. His shirt was American white, his bow tie black.

Verry had little time to spare for her mother and her escort. She was concerned about Fleur who, as the time for the flight came closer, was growing progressively more nervous. The model was wearing a floating evening dress in rose print chiffon. Her hair fell in soft curls, she wore several strands of long pearls, and her whole appearance was very English. At Verry's suggestion she was using the evening as one of her agreed international appearances in the Fleur perfume image.

Dirk turned to the model. 'You sure you can't pull some strings and get us in to see Jesse?' he asked. 'I reckon the atmosphere in that dressing room has to be manic.'

'No.' Fleur shook her head emphatically. 'He doesn't want to see anyone, not even me.'

'Well, you know how it is.' Dirk laughed coarsely. 'No screwing allowed for weeks. He must be horny as hell, and they're not gonna want him jumping you just before the big fight.'

'Stop it, Dirk,' Verry said shortly. 'Why don't you go and get us a drink or something?'

He leered, rubbing the side of his nose suggestively, making Angelique giggle convulsively. 'More than happy to oblige with the "something". I could do with a snort myself.'

Verry gritted her teeth. Dirk's predictable showing-off she could cope with, but her mother's schoolgirl behaviour was something else. 'Let's just make for our seats. It'll take ages to get through this crush to the front row.'

'My, Verité, you're . . .' Dirk began, and then suddenly stood up on tiptoe to see over the mass of heads around them. 'I thought you said Shakira wasn't going to turn up? That's her going in now, and who do you think she's with?' He bent down to look closely into Verité's eyes. 'Something tells me you aren't going to appreciate my news.'

She held her breath, struggling to suppress the thought that had come to her with Dirk's words. What she had half expected had obviously happened.

'You've got to hand it to Shakira,' Dirk said, turning to speak to Angelique. 'She's got one hell of a track record, and the latest car putting the miles on her circuit is none other than our long-lost pal Charles Freeman. It seems that even the old school tie brigade falls for her charms. I don't know what she's got, babe, but whatever it is has got to be something special.'

Fleur glared at him. She was furious with the singer for telling Verité who Shakira was with, and equally infuriated by his pretending he hadn't had intimate knowledge of Shakira's particular brand of charm.

'We really must go in now,' Verry said. She felt numb. Everything was working out as she'd expected, but nothing had prepared her for the sense of loss she felt. 'Mother, will you go with Fleur? I won't be long, but I just have to go to the ladies.' If only she could hold on. She couldn't break down and cry, it would be too embarrassing. They'd all know why, and it would be such a loss of face. She began to lecture herself, a self-defence mechanism she'd developed as a child. All the way to the powder room she was instructing herself not to snivel, and reminding herself that she couldn't risk ruining her make-up.

Her timing was perfect. The last female fight fan had left and the ultra-luxurious sanctuary was almost deserted. She stepped into a cubicle and pulled the door closed behind her. Sitting down on the seat, she put the backs of her hands to her eyes. They were burning, as were her cheeks. She couldn't face the others. She wasn't some lovesick teenager to be sympathized with, she was a grown woman who should know better, be able to control her feelings. She would run cold water over the backs of her hands, a trick of the trade she'd known for years. It cooled down your face in a crisis, helped you look neat and effective, at all times.

By the time the water trick had worked, it was too late for her to get into the hall. The fight had started. Fleur would have to watch with Angelique and Dirk. Verry felt guilty. She had responsibilities to consider. She wandered aimlessly, her thoughts jumbled. Shakira should have phoned her. They could have arranged to meet up before the fight. All the normal, civilized rules of society conspired to make her feel worse. She was startled by a sudden outburst of cheering from the hall.

'Verry!'

She spun round.

'Where on earth have you been?' Charles demanded smilingly. 'I've searched everywhere for you. Why aren't you watching the fight?' His expression softened. 'You're not against blood sports, are you? I hadn't put you down as being squeamish.'

'Charles.' She held out her hand, forcing a smile. 'How nice to see you. I didn't know you were coming over for the fight.'

'I thought you might be pleased to see me, but I have to admit, I've had warmer welcomes.' He looked puzzled. 'What's the matter? I forgot to write, I didn't send flowers? Don't I even rate a kiss hello?'

She leaned forward and touched his smooth cheek briefly, coolly, with her own.

'I suppose that's better than nothing.' He took hold of her arm. 'How about a drink? I've no idea how long the fight'll last, but when it's over that crowd is going to pour out like a load of thirsty Arabs in search of an oasis. Which reminds me . . .' He stopped talking abruptly as a thunderous roar sounded behind them.

Verry turned round, looking back to where, behind closed doors, a drama was being played out that she should have been part of, where Fleur could well be in need of her.

'Jesse going in for the kill, or the other guy?' Charles wondered. 'Who's your money on?'

'I never make bets,' Verry said softly, her thoughts clearly elsewhere. 'I just hope to God . . .' She didn't finish her sentence, just stood very still.

* * *

'Jesse.' Fleur had managed, somehow, to push her way to the ringside. 'Jesse.' The faces around her were a blur. There were heavy men in DJs pushing her back, and she was hardly aware of Dirk beside her, shouting who she was.

The fighter was curled up like a sleeping baby. Fleur was desperate to reach him, but it was a man's world her husband lay in. The quickly moving black-shod feet around his body were all male, as was the voice on the microphone calling for calm, the doctor forcing a tube down the unresisting throat.

'Jesse.' Fleur had her hands on the swaying bottom rope. She held on to it desperately, willing her voice across the few, unsurmountable metres that separated her from her husband.

Dirk was fighting off the mindless minions determined to clear the ringside. He looked like a wild animal at bay as around the silently weeping woman he fought for, and won, an island of space.

Heathrow was jam-packed. There had been a lightning strike of air traffic controllers in the States and the backlog of flights was building up.

Fleur walked behind the wheelchair bearing Jesse, flanked by Dirk and Verité. She wore dark glasses, a scarf wound high round her chin and a belted raincoat. She was every inch the star and loathing her role as the anxious wife.

Shakira had made her way through the press gauntlet a few minutes earlier. Holding tightly on to Charles's sleeve she had smiled brightly but tautly. She wanted to get over the message that she was concerned about her future co-star. She had personally begged him never to fight again, she informed the reporter from the *Daily Mirror*.

* * *

'Verry?' Charles's voice was loud, magnified by the telephone. 'I'm sorry we lost touch at the airport.'

'We left in a private ambulance,' she said. 'Jesse has to spend a night under observation.'

'How's Fleur now?'

'Much better. She's still vowing to leave Jesse if he fights again, but she's a lot calmer. I don't know about the boxing. I'm not sure if Jesse could give it up unless he's medically forced to, but it's something they have to sort out for themselves.'

'I wanted to explain about Shakira.'

'You don't owe me any explanations. I'm glad you were with her; she wouldn't have enjoyed the flight home otherwise. She's used to a more exclusive form of travel,' Verry finished tartly. 'Now, if you'll excuse me, I have a lot to do. We've a major press conference next week. I was just about to leave the house when you rang. I'm going to the hotel to check their facilities.'

'I heard about your bash,' Charles said equably. 'That was part of the reason why I rang. I thought I might be able to help.'

'You?' Verry's voice was scornful.

'If you're using the Tower Hotel I thought you might find *Champers* useful. She's moored at St Katharine's Dock, right beside . . .'

'I know where St Katharine's Dock is, thank you.'

'I thought you just might. It strikes me it's your sort of place.'

'And what does that mean?'

'Glossy, but functional.'

The sarcasm was heavy in Verry's response. 'Thank you so much.'

'But that's what you want to be, isn't it? The total professional; modernism as a way of life. Everything clean-cut and shiny, no room for sentimentalism, no place for dust.'

'Why do I have the feeling you're insulting me?'

'I'm not insulting you, Verry, I'm just providing you with a mirror to see yourself in. You can have fun, you know. It's not immoral, or illegal, or even, in that hairy old line, fattening.'

'Is that all you wanted to say?'

'I suppose so.' He sounded contemplative. 'Apart from adding that you might like to watch out for a bit of my own publicity rousing. When you're doing your quick skim of the financial pages over your weight watcher's breakfast complete with decaffeinated coffee, my name might just pop up and surprise you. Meanwhile, think about *Champers*. She's yours for the day on the thirtieth, if you'd like. Since you're such a busy lady I won't insult you by suggesting you might have time to spare for dinner this evening. *A bientôt.*'

He was gone, leaving her fuming with herself. Why had she not let him at least try to make some lame excuse for having fallen for Shakira's more than obvious charms? Not that he needed an excuse, she reminded herself crossly, slamming the door of the cottage closed behind her.

'How does this look?' Angelique did a quick pirouette. The skirt of her dress swirled out like the aubergine flute of some exotic flower.

'Great legs,' Dirk said appreciatively. He was sprawled on his bed, watching the private fashion show. 'Now, take your knickers off and give us another twirl.'

Angelique flushed. 'Don't be silly,' she giggled.

'No, seriously,' Dirk scowled. 'I like you without anything on, I like to feel you're always accessible. I don't want you hiding anything from me, ever.'

Angelique stood uncertainly in front of the full-length mirror. She found it hard at times to work out whether Dirk was serious or joking. 'I will, if you want,' she said tentatively. 'Take them off, I mean.'

'Yeah, you do just that. And put on those other shoes, the really high-heeled ones. I like that too. Then you look like you've got legs right up to your middle.'

She went into the bathroom to slip off her tights and Janet Reger panties. Her hands were trembling, and she felt breathless. She sipped a few mouthfuls of water from the toothmug and waited a few moments until she was calmer.

'All ready, then?' Dirk asked. He was still lying back, a couple of pillows propped behind his head. 'Now go on, nice and slow. Put on a real show.'

Angelique turned slowly. She was well balanced on the four-inch heels, her weight all on her toes; she was, after all, a trained dancer. In her head she could hear the Nutcracker Suite. She hummed softly, began to use her arms.

'Hold your skirt up.'

The instruction broke her concentration. She paused, her arms stretched above her head in a perfect arc.

'Come on.' Dirk was rubbing the front of his trousers, massaging the bulging zip. 'Hold it up and spin. I want to see you.'

She felt embarrassed, and knew that a red flush warmed her chest. It was a relief that the neck of her dress was high cut.

'Legs apart,' Dirk said loudly. 'Spread them, come on. Face me, baby.'

Her eyes were frantic. She felt exposed, excited, a chaos of emotions. She couldn't think where to look, couldn't face the man sprawled on the bed. She was aware of him moving, coming towards her.

'Want it?' he whispered close to her ear. 'Want it, do you, baby?' He put his hands on her hips and slid them up around her tiny waist.

'Dirk?'

'Like it?' He had turned her round so that she faced the mirror, saw the furry triangle she'd revealed. 'You're beautiful,' he crooned.

She felt the glow build from deep inside, low in her stomach. She was loved, wanted and admired.

'Just beautiful,' he said again. 'And now' – he slapped her hard on the bare buttocks, pulled the skirt sharply out of her hands so that it fell demurely – 'Now your man is hungry. Go make food for your man, baby.'

She went downstairs in a daze. It was almost five minutes later, with the bacon sizzling under the grill along with tomatoes and a slice of his favourite pineapple, french toast frazzling in a frying pan and the kettle hissing merrily, that she remembered she still had no underwear on. She remembered because Dirk came up behind her and proved the fact.

## Chapter 15

Sara slowly made her way to the front door. It was a damp, misty day, and her joints were even stiffer than usual. If the caller had arrived a few minutes earlier it could have been attended to by Angelique, but she had just gone off somewhere with her amorous pop singer. 'I'm coming,' Sara called out again. With any luck, whoever it was would give up waiting and go away.

'Mrs Goode.' The dark-skinned, cashmere-coated man standing on the doorstep smiled expansively. 'After all this time, how nice to see you again.' He extended a hand, which she hesitantly took. She couldn't quite remember who he was. This age business was so irritating.

'Mr – '. She paused, willing him to fill the gap.

'Muhammad, my dear Mrs Goode, but of course you must call me Muhammad. You remember how your dear David used to joke, to tease me about my rather famous name, though of course I never minded.'

'Of course.' Sara nodded uncertainly. It really was too bad; these memory blanks were getting worse. 'Do come in. Can I get you some coffee?' It was a windy day; the least she could do for an old friend of David's was give him a hot drink.

'No, no, I wouldn't dream of putting you to any trouble. In fact, I came to invite you out for a little lunch, for old time's sake. I'm so glad I caught you in England. I'm very rarely in the States these days, and the years just seem to fly by.'

Sara nodded. It would be pleasant to go out. She could see what must be his car, a big black shiny saloon. The engine was still running; he had a chauffeur, she thought. How nice it would be not to have to spend a long day on her own, how lovely to be bought lunch. 'I'll just get my coat.' There was no need to leave a note. She'd be back home hours before the others.

'Gran?' Verry called. She'd been surprised that there were no lights on in the drawing room. As she'd walked up the front path she'd looked up to the bedroom windows. There were no curtains drawn closed, no lights on anywhere although it was past seven o'clock.

It took only a few minutes for her to check all the rooms. By the time she got to the last, Angelique's bedroom, she was convinced that she was going to find Sara collapsed on the floor. It was such a relief to find the room empty that for an instant she forgot to be concerned.

There was no note in the usual place on the kitchen counter, nothing to give a clue to Sara's whereabouts except the fact that her thick blue tweed coat was missing from the understairs cupboard. Verry put the kettle on and spooned coffee into a mug. Sara didn't know anyone in the street. If she'd gone out with Angelique surely they would have left a message. The sound of the key in the lock made her run into the hall.

'It's freezing out there.' Angelique was red-cheeked. Wrapped up in an all-enveloping scarlet swing coat and black and white checked wrap, she looked warm and happy.

'Is Grandma with you?'

'Sara?' Angelique frowned. 'Of course she's not with me. I've been dry-skiing.' She slipped out of her coat and began pulling off her boots to reveal skin tight black stretch ski pants. 'Somehow I don't see that as her scene.'

'Do you know where she is? Had she planned to go out anywhere this evening?'

'No.' Angelique was inspecting a deep scratch on the heel of her leather boot. 'Damn,' she said. Then, looking up, she continued, 'God, she's not gone completely gaga at last, has she? She hasn't taken to wandering the streets in her nightie and accosting strange men?'

'Don't be ridiculous,' Verry snapped.

They stood looking at each other, both, in their own ways, concerned, both wondering what to do next. When the telephone rang they both tried to be first to answer it.

Verry won. 'Hello?' she said quickly.

There was a faint rustling, and then, 'Verité?' It was a male voice, one she didn't instantly recognize.

'Yes, this is Verité Goode speaking.'

'So – I hope you are well.'

'Who is this?'

'You disappoint me, Verité. I thought you might have guessed. You have, after all, been home quite long enough to find that your beloved grandmother is missing. You have had time to wonder where she might be, whom she might be with.'

'Salim!' She breathed the name disbelievingly.

'Ten out of ten. And now, can you make some more guesses? The who, the why, the wherefore?'

'What do you want? Where is my grandmother?' Verry almost screamed into the telephone.

'So, you won't play my little game? What a pity. Still, *tant pis*, as they say in France. You do remember France, don't you, Verité? Our charming morning in the chalet, the party on board your friend's yacht at Cannes? Such a glittering life we all lead. And it is so important to be able to sparkle, to have fun. I should not like that to alter for me or my friends.' His voice was still pleasant, ostentatiously conversational, but something about it chilled Verry to the bone.

'What do you want?' she asked again.

'I want guarantees from you and your associate. I also want all the photographs that man took, the negatives as well as the prints, you understand. I will not be fobbed off with anything less.'

'There were no photographs. They were all ruined by the sea water – you must know that.'

'I'm not a child, Ms Goode; please don't treat me as such. I am perfectly aware that Charles has had them developed.'

'I didn't know.' Charles had said nothing, and she had assumed that Angus's efforts had been in vain.

'I am especially keen to have the night-time shots. I'm sure that your fireworks make a spectacular background for *Aristotle* at sea. I shall have the best one mounted and hung in the saloon.'

'Where is my grandmother?'

'She is here with me. She is very happy. Very, very happy, if you understand me. Euphoric, you might say.'

'If you hurt her . . .' Verry was white with fury, her jaws clenched tightly so that she had to almost spit the words out. 'If you even touch her, I will . . .'

'You will what?' he mocked. 'Please, Ms Goode, do us all a favour and act realistically. Call your friend Charles and tell him what I want. He will be most understanding. He is, despite his puerile posturing, a man of the world.'

'What do you want me to do with the photographs?'

'You are a busy lady. You have an important press conference tomorrow, I believe?'

Verry put her hand up to her forehead. She had forgotten all about it. She would have to cancel – somehow she would have to contact everyone.

'Take the photographs with you to the Tower Hotel. I will get instructions to you as to what must happen next. I expect Charles to be there, of course. I understand you will be using his yacht – it is moored so conveniently for you.'

'I want you to bring my grandmother home, now. Then I will do as you say.'

Salim laughed. 'That would be very silly of me, and I think you would be the first to agree that I am not stupid. Do give my love to Shakira, and wish her all the best for tomorrow. I know how much she is looking forward to playing a starring role.'

'Please,' Verry said softly. 'She is a very old lady. Please let her come home now.'

The click of the disconnection was very loud in her ear.

Charles Freeman ran easily up the flight of Wilton carpeted steps leading to the Tower Hotel's Riverside suite. It was just before ten; the morning press-call was scheduled for twelve.

Verry had arrived before him. She stood forlornly looking out through the picture windows that made up one wall of the large, airy, lime-panelled room. It was a fine day outside, a bright sun sparkling off the choppy, blue-grey waters of the Thames that flowed swiftly less than a hundred yards in front of her.

'Verry.' He touched her gently on the shoulder and was instantly aware of the tension that was making her pale and drawn beneath the inevitably perfect make-up.

'Thank you for coming,' she said dully. 'I did as you said and made my mother promise to stay at home. She didn't like it.'

He turned her around to face him. 'It will be all right, Verry. We'll get your grandmother back safe and sound. There's no point in harming her.'

'Does he have to have a reason?' Her eyes seemed glazed.

'Of course. This is his way of buying his safety. It's quite logical, if you look at it from his point of view.'

Anger flashed suddenly, snapping her out of her daze. 'Which I will never do. I want him brought down, I want him to suffer, I want him in prison.'

'We had a conversation once before that contained a lot of "wants". As I recall, that time I said something like "Gimme gimme doesn't get".'

'And I said "Those who don't ask don't get", and in the end you agreed with me. Salim seemed to think you would know what to do. Do you? Are you going to do everything he asks?'

She was overwrought. He had just pulled her close to him when a white-jacketed waiter appeared. He handed over a fax headed 'To Verité Goode, Goode as Golde.' It was, it proclaimed, from 'a Greek bearing gifts'.

She held the single page out so that they could read it together. The instructions were simple. The photographs were to be left at the hotel reception in an envelope addressed to Aristotle, as were signed copies of the other faxes that would follow shortly. Charles and Verité were then to go aboard *Champers*. They were to leave St Katharine's Dock and set off slowly up river, moving at little more than a crawl. Before they reached Tower Bridge they would be given instructions on where to pick up Sara if what they had left at reception was found to be satisfactory.

In the event, there were no more faxes. That method of communication was too public a medium for some messages. Instead a brown envelope was handed in at the porter's lodge by a motor cycle courier service. It arrived at half past eleven. Several cameramen were already helping themselves to coffee from the damask-covered buffet. The journalist from *The Times*, who was to do an in-depth article on Verité as the new breed of film producer, kept looking down at his watch. He wanted to be away before twelve. He didn't enjoy publicity bunfights.

Charles and Verry took the envelope to the open-plan hotel foyer. There they sat on high-backed, faux Louis Seize chairs set around a small table. It was like a dream, Verry thought. Life was going on around them as usual. Tourists were checking in at the reception desk. Shakira arrived by taxi, wearing a vivid lime-green jump suit and a shocking pink matador cape. A few minutes later Jesse drove up, Fleur beside him in the passenger seat. They were chatting happily as they looked for a parking place. She and Charles were isolated from the excitement by their concern.

Charles looked grim. 'You have to hand it to Salim,' he said. 'He's certainly a clever devil.'

'Will you sign?'

'Of course. You know me.' He laughed shortly. 'I'll do anything for a free drink. You are laying on drinks here later, aren't you?'

She nodded, puzzled. 'But we won't be here. We'll be on board *Champers*.'

'If you say so.'

'But Salim's instructions were that we were both to get on the boat. What's the matter, Charles? Aren't you going to go through with it after all?'

He looked at her intently. 'I'd prefer you to stay on shore. I'd be happier if you weren't with me.'

'But of course I have to come. I have to be there for Sara. God knows what condition she'll be in. She's an old lady, and she's been frightened.'

'I don't think Sara will come on board *Champers*. Think it out for yourself. No one in their right mind is going to try to manhandle your grandmother into some nippy little boat that could power up beside us and then cream off again. And I can't see them taking her to a wharf – that would be far too conspicuous. Besides . . .' He paused, looked at the taxi depositing Dirk, and then continued, 'I just have a feeling.'

'That?' she prompted.

'A feeling that you should stay on shore.'

'No,' she said shortly.

'How did I know you were going to say that? OK.' He seemed to brighten up. 'Let's get on with this. You sign here, and then I'll do my bit. It appears that between us we're ordering enough guns to fuel the entire Arab-Israeli conflict. Let's just hope Salim remembers that these orders are his guarantees, and not for real, or we could end up owing a fortune. Waiter?' he called. 'Will you come and witness these for us?' As he spoke, he was flicking through his wallet, looking for a five-pound note to give as a tip.

Shakira swept up the stairs towards the beckoning noise. She adored the sound of success – of glasses chinking, of voices raised in expectation. The brief hush of admiration as she reached the assembled press was everything she could have wished. She recognized Pam Stiles, a journalist with one of the weekend supplements, and with a beaming smile she went forward to meet her adoring fans.

Jesse told Fleur to go on ahead of him. They'd entered the hotel together, just as they'd walked the corridor leading to the Riverside suite hand in hand, but it didn't seem right, he thought, for them actually to arrive *à deux*. The first thing he noticed as he reached the gathering was that Verité wasn't there. The second was that his wife was with Shakira. He felt a glow of renewed pride in his woman's appearance. The cream and white Chanel jacket and rows of swinging pearls teamed with a short, short skirt and flat pumps was jaunty but ultra-ladylike. He gave the exotically clad Shakira an enthusiastic hug. He loved it when she lived up to his expectations.

'Ladies and gentlemen.' Verry clapped her hands as she arrived at the top of the stairs, smiling widely. In her navy and white sailor jacket and matching knee-length shorts she looked *très sportif*. 'I hope you've all had a warming cup of coffee, because let me warn you, you're going to need it.' She laughed infectiously.

Dirk appeared at her back, his leather jacket swinging loosely over one shoulder, his white open-necked silk shirt underlining the healthy glow of his skin, his tight palomino suede trousers the masculinity of his new, cleaner image. He put an arm around Verry's waist and squeezed her against him. 'Isn't she just great?' he grinned.

Verry carried on with her patter, issuing her instructions in a light, bouncy tone. The four stars were to take their places at the riverside. There was ultra-picturesque Tower Bridge in the background, it was a glorious day, the sea gulls were swooping. And just in case the cameramen needed more, there would be, as a backdrop, the most glamorous yacht to grace the Thames in ages, complete with resident playboy and – raising a small cheer – the hypiest hypester around as crew: Verry Goode, of Goode as Golde. There was a pile of press releases on the buffet table, she reminded them. There would be time afterwards for interviews, just as there would be lots of food and something a bit stronger than coffee.

She ran down the stairs, looking eager and enthusiastic and ready for the off. Her smile lasted until the swing doors closed behind her, and then she ran in earnest. She was heading for the marina, where Charles was waiting on *Champers*. The yacht was ready.

Bruno smiled. Slowly, caressingly, he ran his hand along the icy, steel-blue barrel of his rifle. It was an old friend, its killing power an extension of his own.

His hair was slicked back firmly, his clothes dark, well cut, elegant yet purposeful from navy thermal polo-necked jumper to matching ski trousers and lightweight black leather trainers with anti-skid soles. His vantage point was a windswept eyrie: a painter's cradle hung high beneath the massive iron roadway of Tower Bridge. It was tucked against the antique stonework of the bridge's south tower, and gave him a clear view of the river, the Tower of London and the riverside walkways. He could also look with ease into the many windows of the Tower Hotel.

He breathed in appreciatively. The Thames was putting on its finest show for him. It was high tide and the filthy mud was covered. Turning his head slowly, he looked around him. To his left the oatmeal-coloured walls of the Tower shone in the sunlight. He adjusted the specially-made dark glasses more exactly. They were Swiss, and fitted him perfectly.

Almost on a level with the moving water, where modern flagstones created a mock quay, a lime-coloured figure posed, stretched and danced with three other doll-like figures. On the far side of them, intent on the performance, a grey and black jumble of humanity swept slowly from side to side like some fat caterpillar as the cameramen had a field day.

Bruno watched it all. Then, slowly, carefully, he raised the sight of his rifle and laid his shielded eye against the freezing lens. In an instant Shakira seemed no more than a few feet away from him, her face filling his vision as she turned towards the river. He saw her verve, her zest for life. This was the moment he enjoyed best, when his senses were most acute. He was aware of his finger curved sculpturally around the trigger, he could sense the finely stretched skin, feel the tightening tendon. He was so tuned in to his body that he could sense the rhythmic whorls imprinted on his finger tips, the symbols of uniqueness.

Time waited on him. It was his to control, and there was more to see. Smoothly swinging from the hips he traversed the stage before him. There was oily water, a floating, bobbing seagull ridiculously white on the summit of a grey-brown wave. He panned further to the right, seeking landmarks. He inched his foot slowly sideways; he was secure where he was, the planning had been meticulous. His escape route was foolproof. More than that, it was flamboyant, and that amused him. He was developing his trademark. He thought back to the first time, to his escape by water: the scudding rubber dinghy that had spirited him to safety. And all the time he was quartering the water, backwards and forwards, from side to side. He could have looked away from the viewfinder, have surveyed the river with his own eyes, with the larger vision of man, but he relished challenge.

He swung back swiftly, wanting to keep an eye on the photo-shoot. He, like the four dolls, was a born star. Soon, he would be revealed as the maestro, wiping their efforts, stillborn, off all the front pages. The painters who should have been working in the cradle were in their Ford Transit van, bound securely with vinyl tape. He had hit the older man a fraction too hard, and it displeased his sense of artistry. It had not been necessary for them to die.

*Champers* moved effortlessly, her engines churning life into the thick water, even at less than half throttle treating the current spinning off the bridge with contempt. With a sense of destiny Charles had turned on the sound system. To a background of the haunting cries of gulls, Verry's father's music began to swell.

* * *

Sara rubbed her face wearily. There was a nasty taste in her mouth and a dull pain at the base of her neck. She shifted her position on the slippery leather seat, trying to get comfortable. 'You know,' she said, 'that's the first time in my life I've spent the whole night in a car. It's good to know that even at my age there are still new sensations to experience.'

'I admire your spirit, Mrs Goode.'

Sara nodded an acknowledgement of the compliment even though the man she now knew to be Salim Abu Dann wasn't, for the moment, watching her every movement. Sitting in front of her in the driving seat of his car, he was looking out through the dust-streaked windscreen. She couldn't understand what she was doing there, why he was her granddaughter's enemy.

The wasteland around them was bathed in sunlight. There were a few scrubby bushes, a couple of piles of rotted rubbish, but in the main it was wind-dried mud criss-crossed by apparently aimless tracks of concrete. However desolate it was, it looked much more hospitable than it had seemed when they had arrived late last night in the dark.

Sara sniffed. She thought she might be going to get a cold. 'You know, you were lucky some local gang didn't find us last night. They would have made a mess of your car.'

'I think not.' Salim seemed deep in thought. 'Bruno would have seen them off.'

'Maybe, maybe not. Anyhow, wherever he's gone to now I hope he'll bring us back some breakfast. I'm absolutely famished.' It wasn't true; she was still feeling queasy from whatever drug he'd slipped in her drink yesterday, but she was determined to maintain her self-control. That reminded her of something she wanted to say to her captor. 'You're lucky I don't have a weak bladder. Most old ladies have to go to the bathroom several times during the night.'

Salim turned right round to face her. 'That wouldn't have been my problem, Mrs Goode, it would have been yours. However, I believe the tranquillizers have, let us say, a drying-up effect, similar to the shot they give you before an operation. So you see, I have thought of everything.'

Sara forced a smile. She wasn't feeling anything like as confident as she was acting. If she hadn't been so old, and had such a good, full life, she would have been very frightened. The voice inside her head, the one that in years gone by had been her conscience, and was now her confidant, tried to contradict her, but she quashed it firmly. She wasn't frightened. Fear would be debilitating.

The low ringing of the car phone broke into her thoughts. Salim picked it up. He didn't say anything, just listened. As he put it back on to its rest he was reaching forward to start the engine. '*En avant*,' he said triumphantly. 'You will be relieved to know that your granddaughter seems to want you back.'

The car jolted over a succession of ruts and Sara clutched at the back of the seat in front of her to keep her balance. She looked about her. There were what she thought must be cranes against the skyline, vertical smoke plumes from factory chimneys. A final jolt and they were on a tarmacadamed road. Salim drove around the dilapidated warehouse that must once have provided the reason for the existence of the rusting chainlink fence ahead, and the sagging gateway that they finally drove through.

'Such a shame,' Salim said conversationally. 'All this land would have been developed but for the recession.' He shrugged expressively. 'The iron lady had a lot to answer for.'

'Do you have business interests in England? Do you spend a lot of your time here?' Sara asked. She'd read that one should try to get alongside a kidnapper, make him believe one was genuinely interested in him and his affairs.

'Business? I have business interests everywhere. England I enjoy. At times it is the most civilized place in the world to be. Ascot, Wimbledon, Henley – I love them all. I enjoy tradition.' He swung the car out on to a main road. The traffic they entered was heavy but fast moving, mostly lorries and vans interspersed with cars.

Sara looked around as quickly as her stiff neck allowed, searching for road signs. They would have to be big for her to be able to read the names without her glasses. She peered at a seedy row of shops as they sped past.

'We are about to enter Wapping,' Salim said, his voice tinged with amusement. 'There is no secrecy about our whereabouts today. In a little while I will give you back your handbag. We are going to town, and I think for that you might like to put some lipstick on.'

Verry shivered violently. She was so cold that she had to clench her teeth together to stop them chattering.

*Champers* was under way. They had left St Katharine's Dock behind them and were pulling out into the river itself. Charles and Verry stood side by side on the elevated deck a few feet in front of the sloping tinted glass that made up the yacht's windscreen. They looked like a fashion plate from *Vogue*. The wind was whipping their hair back, and their clothes were clamped tightly against their bodies. They were both dressed in dark blue and white, Charles in a navy blazer and light worsted trousers, Verry in her sailor suit. Charles, as had been instructed, held a mobile phone. They were approaching Tower Bridge, which reared up ahead, dwarfing them by its size, dominating even the mighty river. Verry tipped her head back and gazed up at the ornamented railings, the castellated towers. She swallowed convulsively as a succession of powder-puff clouds chased each other across the high azure sky, making her feel giddy.

Bruno had seen them as soon as the yacht nosed out into the mainstream. His gunsight raked the snow-white deck, lingered on the woman, panned to the man. The headphones he was wearing were small, beautifully engineered. They were attached by wires to a small power pack at his waist. Right on cue, as *Champers* straightened her bow towards him, a muted bell rang in his ear. At the flick of a miniature switch Salim's voice came through clearly.

'*Ça va.*'

That was all. That was enough.

Shakira was glowing with excitement. It was such fun and they were so happy together. She had linked arms with Jesse and Dirk, Fleur was holding on to her husband on the end of the line, and they were all laughing and singing.

On the river behind them, *Champers* floated majestically, a giant seabird in its natural element. It had been the ideal lure to get the press photographers turning out in force. A crowd of sightseers had formed to one side of the cameramen, cheering each new antic the foursome performed. When Dirk started to dance an accelerated version of the can-can even the hardened cameramen laughed. Shakira turned, once more, to look at her agent standing on the prow of the boat. Charles was with her. Shakira couldn't wait to meet the delectable jetsetter again. He was sure to adore her outfit. Life was fantastic, exhilarating . . . She looked up at the bridge. It was a magnificent frame for them all and she grinned in appreciation.

The marksman breathed in sharply – how could she have seen him? The beaming smile was straight into his eyes, but why? What would make a woman welcome certain death? For a moment he was confused. He felt sweat break out across his chest, the thermal knitwear increasing the heat until he felt drenched and stinking. He understood suddenly that she had not seen him at all; she was happy because she was unaware of his existence. 'Bitch,' he swore viciously. He would blow the smile off her face, ram the flashing teeth down her bloody throat. But not yet. He swung the gun again, back to focus on the yacht. He would deal with the whore later, after he had earned his money.

One final sweep across the river. Everything must be in its place; above all he wanted to leave his kill in style. His escape route would provide him with a major part of his satisfaction. There was a distracting flash of colour on the river almost directly beneath his feet, and he lowered the head of the rifle, jerking it down in search of possible danger. He breathed out slowly through his nose. A vessel was coming out from under the bridge. It would pass *Champers* as she wallowed, waiting for instructions.

He would have to wait until the new boat had gone by, then he would have to allow for the wake that would hit the yacht. He swore again as *Champers*'s helmsman took what the marksman saw as unnecessary action, slipping the boat sideways to give more room to what Bruno could now identify as a tugboat. A sudden stench of rubbish was borne up to him on the wind, a sweet reek that hit him low in the stomach. He understood instantly that the tug would be towing a loaded rubbish lighter. It was disgusting, uncivilized, to drag such a foul stinking mess through the heart of a great city.

In its new position he could no longer focus on the yacht. He would have to move. It was unbelievable – all his planning, the hours he had spent familiarizing himself with the angles, and at the last minute he was going to have to shift several feet to the right. He was still determined not to take his eye from the sight, his focus was so perfectly adjusted. He edged slowly sideways, his hand touching the chill metal rail, a little further. The stern of the tugboat crept slowly into his field of vision, and he tilted the gunsight a fraction. There was a cheerful toot of foghorn beneath him. The tug was through, and he just had to allow time for the barge to follow suit.

His foot touched something and for a moment he paused. Tentatively he explored the alien object with his foot, and then he smiled. It was the rope, the few metres of slack that he had coiled neatly, ready for his escape. His experience in the mountains had given him the idea – he would abseil his way to freedom. The lightweight mountaineer's rope had been simplicity itself to handle. One end was secured to the side of the cradle, the other to the small, smooth-skinned rubber dinghy that at this moment would be nudging gently against the stone pillar beside him. The motor in the miniature vessel was fast and reliable, as was the silver-grey BMW saloon parked on a convenient meter some twenty or so strides from the river steps that were less than a quarter of a mile downstream from the Tower.

London would provide him with his most spectacular kill to date. Even the weather was perfect, and the watching press would obtain pictures that would travel the news agencies of the world.

His foot slid the necessary fraction further; he altered his balance. Perfect.

Sara sighed fretfully. She was doing exactly what Salim had told her to do, waiting in his car while he went into the Tower Hotel. If only she was younger, she kept thinking, she could have trusted herself to do something inspired.

Salim walked jauntily back to her. He was smiling broadly as he opened the car door. The first thing he did was make a call on his mobile phone. '*Ça va*,' he said briefly into the mouthpiece, and then carefully, reverentially, locked a brown envelope away in the glove compartment.

'You look very pleased with yourself,' Sara said. 'Does that mean I'm free to go? I'd really quite like to get out of the car. I'm so stiff, and I would just love a hot bath.'

'You are to stay exactly where you are.' Salim twisted round on his seat. 'I have told you already, I hold your granddaughter in the palm of my hand. If you irritate me now I shall have her killed, like that!' He made a tightly clenched fist and slammed it down on the leather seat.

The explosive sound made Sara recoil. 'You don't have to get so worked up,' she whispered. 'I'll do whatever you want me to.'

He nodded abruptly. 'Now, we will go together to where we can watch the action.'

It took only a few minutes to park the car in the hotel car park that overlooked the yachts moored in St Katharine's Dock. For a moment Sara thought that the Arab was going to take her to one of the flats in the elegant riverside development, but instead they began to walk arm in arm towards the river. Salim, it would appear to a casual observer, was being solicitous to an old lady whose fragility was clear to see.

'The beautiful Shakira,' Salim breathed. He could see the group still posing for the cameramen.

They walked to the river's edge.

Sara was trembling all over. She was so weak that simply breathing in the cold air seemed too much of an effort. 'I shall have to sit down,' she said feebly.

'No.' Salim spoke softly. He was smiling, maintaining the illusion of care for the non-existent watcher. 'You will stand here, where you can watch it all.'

A wave of dizziness swept over her. She could see the river only as a grey blur. They were close to the water, their feet at the very edge of the wharf.

'Look at the bridge.' Salim swept an arm out, encompassing the brick and iron celebration of Victoriana. 'I want you to concentrate on that – and on the yacht ahead of us, of course. Your granddaughter must be feeling the cold out there. It is as well it is almost time.' He glanced down at his watch.

Slowly, Sara's eyes were starting to focus. They had always been better at a distance; today – she blinked back the tears brought on by the watery breeze – today she couldn't have read even the largest print close up. But she was beginning to sort things out. Ahead of her the bridge was a great multicoloured letter H; the boat was sparkling white on dark water. With an effort she could even distinguish two small figures on the deck.

'Twenty, nineteen . . .' Salim's voice was charged with excitement. 'We are almost there. That rubbish lighter is so nearly through that we will still be on schedule. Fifteen, fourteen . . .'

On board the London registered tug, *River Dog*, skipper Fred Thomas glanced behind him and swore. He'd been looking forward to an uneventful trip. Thanks to the work going on on Tower Bridge there would be no big vessels on the move – they couldn't raise the road with union-protected labourers hanging under it. He spat over the side in disgust. It was just his luck that the barge he was towing had picked something up again. Last week it had been a twenty-foot baulk of timber that had narrowly missed his tug's propellers. This time it was a rope. He held his binoculars up to his eyes. The rope stretched tightly at an angle across the stubby lighter's bow was new and nylon, and attached to something he couldn't see that was being dragged along behind. He had no idea what its breaking point would be but he did know that if it got caught up around his prop shaft it would cause no end of damage. As soon as he was past the tart's delight of a cruiser that was wallowing like a pig alongside, he'd slow down and see if he couldn't slip it off.

'Ten, nine . . .' Salim's grip on Sara's arm was so tight it was affecting her circulation. She wriggled ineffectively.

Bruno was also counting, mouthing the numbers silently: 'Six, five, four . . .'

The lighter seemed to check for an instant and Fred shook his head. Turning to scan the water behind him, he reached for the lever to throw the engines into reverse.

The rope coiled beside Bruno slithered silently. It unleashed itself steadily, letting out the slack that the incessant force of the lighter demanded.

The gunman breathed in lightly, held the breath at its zenith as he began to squeeze the trigger.

The final curl of rope slipped soundlessly down, and suddenly it was stretched taut. Without warning, a savage, numbing pain struck Bruno around the ankle. At the same instant, the picture within his lens tilted manically. Charles Freeman spun out of sight, and there was the briefest glimpse of Verité Goode, the deck, the river. The gunman was screaming in pain as his finger tightened convulsively.

The noose around his leg had bitten in to the bone, the short end that was still attached to the cradle vibrating like catgut. The force of the tug was inexorable, and the breaking point came swiftly. The scream lasted for only as long as Bruno spun, head over heels, towards the water.

The sound of the shot had stopped them all. Shakira and Dirk were caught, Jesse and Fleur frozen, in a parody of dance. Salim stopped breathing, his mouth agape as he watched the spinning figure hurtle to the water. Only Sara seemed to come alive with the report. Wrenching her arm from the detested grip, she pushed hard. With every last remaining ounce of her strength she pushed Salim over the edge and into the river. Then she tottered, almost following him into the churning brown waters, before slumping heavily to the ground.

The frenzy of clicking cameras, an orchestration of cicadas, seemed far louder than Verry's high-pitched cry of concern.

The midnight blue Rolls Royce convertible pulled to a smooth halt in the Chelsea sidestreet. There was scarcely a sound as the beautifully engineered passenger door swung open on perfectly balanced hinges. In one fluid, graceful movement, Angelique swung her slender legs out on to the pavement and stood up. Without a backward glance she made her way up the short path leading to the front door of her home. As she turned the key in the lock she was aware of the car pulling away behind her.

At the sound of footsteps in the hall, Verry looked up from her seat at the round table in the drawing room.

'If Dirk should phone,' Angelique called out as she began to climb the stairs, 'I'm not at home.'

It was the third time in under a week that her mother had issued those instructions. Verry sucked contemplatively at the end of her ballpoint. Her own love-life was non-existent, her relationship with Sam as cold as yesterday's Wiener Schnitzel, her affair with Charles apparently destined never to progress past stage one. He was, as far as she was aware, back in the Mediterranean. The aftermath of Sara's kidnapping had left the Goode family in emotional turmoil. By the time Verry had calmed down enough to realize that she was in love with Charles, he had gone. She had driven him away with her overwrought emotions.

The telephone rang and she waited a few seconds before grudgingly lifting the receiver. She hoped it wasn't Dirk.

'Ms Goode?' The voice was female, middle-aged, efficient, and it had a strong foreign accent.

'Speaking.'

'I am calling on behalf of Mr Thomson of Funda Europa. He wished me to check with you before sending confidential information through the fax.'

'That's fine.' Verry was suddenly breathless. 'My line is secure.'

With a brief salutation Carl Thomson's secretary severed the international connection and Verry's attention switched to the fax machine on the small Georgian side table against the wall. Within seconds it burst into life. She read the words as they appeared, mouthing them silently.

'. . . funding for the film *Viva Europa* . . .'

She had it all.

'Mother!' she shouted as she began running up the stairs, two steps at a time. 'Mother, we've got it!'

'Fleur.' Verry raised her champagne glass. 'Here's to you, and to Jesse.'

The ex-boxer nodded in appreciation of the toast.

'And to Dirk, and finally, of course, to Shakira. I salute you all. You've done magnificently. We start shooting in less than a month, and I'm convinced that each of you is going to be a brilliant success on screen.'

Jesse pushed back his chair and stood, and the other three of the 'famous foursome' followed suit. There was a murmur of amusement from neighbouring diners in the elegant riverside restaurant of the Savoy.

'To Verité,' Dirk said, and they all drank.

'More champagne?' a voice whispered close to Verry's ear and she nodded agreement without even checking the state of the bottle in the ice-bucket. Of course the waiter should bring more. They were really going to celebrate. Her eyes were full of tears. It was actually going to happen – she was going to be a film producer, albeit to begin with in name only. The man behind the money had insisted on experienced hands manning the till.

The new bottle of bubbly opened with a bang behind her, and a surprisingly elegantly cuffed arm appeared to pour the foaming liquid into her glass. 'Congratulations,' Charles drawled as he kissed her on the cheek. She turned to face him, and he embraced her properly, his mouth covering hers, his arms tight around her. This time the reaction of the diners around them was less restrained; this time there was actual applause.

'I think I've had a bit too much to drink.' Verry leaned her head on Charles's shoulder. The motion of the taxi was making her feel dizzy, slightly sick.

'I think we all did!'

'It was such a surprise, your suddenly being there.'

Charles put his finger under her chin and tilted her face towards him. 'You do something strange to me, do you know that? I can't stop thinking about you.'

Words she hadn't even been thinking spilled out. 'Even with all your lovely starlets in tow?' She'd seen the piece in Nigel Dempster's column. Four different girls in as many nights. Champagne Charlie had been living it up even by jet-setting standards.

'Did you mind?'

It wasn't her place to mind. She was sobering up quickly; she couldn't let him mean too much to her. 'I don't know if we can still use the Bugatti in the film. Bugsy says . . .'

Charles leaned forwards to talk to the driver. 'Right on through to the marina.'

She'd imagined he was taking her to his hotel. 'I thought you'd taken *Champers* back to the Med?'

'No, she's been in dry dock.' He turned to look at her, amused. 'So, you checked up on me, did you?'

Despite her intention to remain calm and collected, Verry felt herself blushing. It had been such a wonderful evening that she'd almost forgotten how hurt she'd been when he'd left England with the most casual of goodbyes. She had to stay in command of her emotions, be adult.

They walked the short distance to the yacht. *Champers* was exotically glamorous in the midnight blue air; a subdued glow of orange light shone from her myriad portholes.

Verry stepped into the saloon. After the chill outside, the air was warm and comforting. There was background music, there were roses. 'Something's different in here.' It was somehow more solid, more luxurious, less frivolous.

'I had work done on the interior while the engines were being stripped down. It was time for a change. Like a drink?' He gestured towards the dark teak fitments which had replaced the limed oak that once covered the bulkhead.

'No, I'm fine.' She shivered, huddling deeper into her white mohair evening coat. 'I'm just tired.' A great sense of anticlimax was threatening to overwhelm her.

'How about a hot shower? That would warm you up,

clear the gremlins out of the system.' He was standing a few feet away from her, appearing relaxed and considerate. Had he really said he hadn't been able to stop thinking about her? It was probably one of his standard come on lines.

'That might be a good idea.' She wasn't sure that it was, but she knew that to leave *Champers* now would be to push Charles out of her life for ever. That would be disastrous, because she was sure she would never get him out of her system until she could prove that she could enjoy his undoubted physical talents and then walk away.

'Use the guest cabin. You'll see I've made some changes in there, too.' He sat down and picked up the telephone, pressed a button and asked, 'Any messages?' He was absorbed, jotting down notes on a small leather-bound pad, as she stepped down into the companionway.

The wardrobe doors were open, folded back; it was quite empty. The expensive women's clothes that he'd called his 'spoils of war' were gone, the shelves lined with pristine white paper. Even the bed cover was different, a mass of pink and white peonies. The cabin had been anglicized; it was pure Colefax and Fowler.

Verry quickly slipped off her coat, unzipped her Jean Muir bias-cut crepe slip. She would shower, and then get dressed again. When she felt fresher she might find it easier to deal with Charles.

The water foamed enthusiastically out of the five-inch shower head. It was a touch too hot and she adjusted the controls until, with a fresh surge of bubbles, the temperature was perfect.

She felt better already. Tilting her head back, she could keep her hair out of the stream of water that surged over her shoulders to run in shining rivulets between her breasts. She would use Charles as he used women, and then get back, refreshed and reinvigorated, to her film business.

She wasn't really surprised when a hand appeared beside her holding a champagne glass. She was, however, slightly puzzled by the fact that the glass was empty.

'Cheers.' A naked Charles stepped swiftly into the shower cabinet beside her. He lifted the glass, now full of water from the shower, to his lips.

It was subtly erotic, his drinking the liquid she was washing in, and she laughed, feeling the warmth build at her throat. She was working hard on maintaining eye contact; she wanted to stay in control.

He put the glass to her lips, and tentatively she sipped.

'Champagne!'

'What else?'

Verry tipped her head back to look up at the liquid flooding out above her. There must be gallons and gallons of it. She began to laugh. Her hair was wet now, and she lifted her hands up to run her fingers through the strands.

Charles was kissing her throat, running his hands gently, tantalizingly slowly, down her back, and all the time the bubbles tickled and sparkled on their skin. His mouth was on her breast, his teeth nipped and she opened her mouth to cry out but the champagne flooded over her lips so that she began to laugh again. He was stroking her buttocks and it was like the touch of silk as his hands slipped round and round. She started moving her hips, to sway from side to side. He was towering above her and she reached up to him, her hands in his hair, pulling his mouth down to hers.

The champagne was forcing a way between them, pouring over his shoulders, splashing her erect nipples, forming a torrent to run down her thighs. He knelt swiftly, and her hands were in his hair again, pushing his mouth against her as he licked at the warm, sweet wine. His tongue flicked briefly in and out, once, twice, and she was spreading her feet, willing him to fill her. He stood again, lifting her easily, his fingers squeezing into her slippery skin as she wrapped her legs around his waist. With a lunge he was inside her. All restraint was gone, and she released herself to his will. With strength and power he used her body, moving her with ease to bring himself and her to the verge of ecstasy, until, with one final plunge, they soared over the edge.

It seemed a long time later that she slipped away from him, leaving the bed for the bathroom. She wanted to use the bidet. It was, as she'd remembered, controlled by several chromium taps. She flicked at them all, and in a short while warm water was bubbling up enthusiastically from the centre spray. She sat down on the cool porcelain, positioning herself carefully. The water stung, making her gasp. A thought struck her, and she reached between her thighs to put her fingers into the spray, then licked at them.

'Very kinky.' Charles stood in the doorway, stark naked, and beautiful.

Verry remained frozen like stone, she couldn't decide what to do: to get up, or stay where she was.

'You're quite right of course, it is champagne. It's everywhere, filling the entire water system. I have to admit, the coffee is disgusting.'

'You're mad,' she whispered.

He nodded. 'Come back to bed, and I'll prove just how mad I can really get.'

It was an offer she couldn't refuse.

The snow was a crisp white, the air sparkling blue. The French press were present in abundance. Shakira was posed artistically on the bonnet of the Bugatti. She was wearing very little – a few pieces of turquoise silk, a sliver of net – but what there was was very expensive, very designer. The press-call for *Viva Europa*'s mid-production publicity was going well, and the hype was in full swing. A week earlier there had been a staged middle-of-the-night 'accident' in the vintage car that had tickled the public's imagination by exposing the recently married English aristocrat in the private company of the outrageous American pop-star whose latest leisure activities were skating close to the edge of the law. Jesse's 'revenge' had given the singer a very picturesque black eye that he was moodily showing off to the cameramen. The press release said that the husband now accepted the innocent explanation for what one particularly sparky French journalist had referred to as the '*liaison dangereuse*'.

'When do you expect Charles to arrive?' Sara asked her granddaughter. The older woman was wrapped in swathes of fake fur, complete with a vast circular padded hat. She looked like a modern-day equivalent of Catherine the Great. At her side, Verry in a fitted sugar-almond beige snowsuit looked slim and sophisticated.

'Tonight, or perhaps tomorrow. He's in the middle of some property deal.'

They'd had so little time together, less than a week before his business interests had taken him away. But, as he'd said to her, it was the price they had to pay for his reformed love-life.

The press were getting restless, looking for new angles to photograph. They shouted instructions in half a dozen languages, eventually succeeding in posing the two female stars of *Viva Europa* against the background of the vividly striped hot air balloon drifting round the edge of the mountain towards them. Shakira was well aware of the wooden knob of the gearstick positioned suggestively between her thighs, but her wide eyes feigned innocence. Dirk laughed and she winked at him conspiratorially.

Sara was enjoying the scene. She liked watching the fuss the Continentals made, their extravagant gestures. Soon, she would fly home to America. The Chelsea cottage would provide her granddaughter with the ideal base for her UK operations – the deal with Funda Europa had tied that in nicely. Verry no longer had her mother to worry about; Angelique was safe in the affluent arms of the one-time British ambassador in Vienna. The Austrian capital was where the silver-haired diplomat had first met David Goode's exquisite wife, and the memory had lingered – through his own bereavement, and Angelique's widowhood. He had bided his time, for decency's sake, and then, as he was convinced fate had for so many years intended, had made his sublimely orchestrated move.

The cameramen began to scatter and Jesse shouted at Fleur to run out of the way as the hot air balloon swooped towards them. It seemed to hover, for a moment, close to the car, and then gently touched down on the trodden snow.

'Quick!' Charles shouted from his position in the basket. 'Over here, Verry.'

She glanced at her grandmother, looked over at the four young stars; they were all laughing. For a moment she hesitated, remembering her last trip in a balloon, but Charles had explained that she had blown that out of all proportion. Besides, this time she would be with the man she loved. She began to run.

They floated effortlessly higher in the champagne air. There were mountains everywhere, beneath and beside them as they skimmed over the world of white. The tiny pine trees decorating icy slopes were like the ones Verry remembered on childhood Christmas cakes; they passed over the occasional lodge, each miniature alpine dwelling looking like something out of a fairy tale. She held tightly on to Charles's leather-clad arm. He was wearing a flying helmet and jacket, and he was grinning, peering every now and again over the side of the basket. She had the feeling they weren't simply on a pleasure trip, but were making for somewhere special.

It was the largest lodge of all. Verry saw the sweep of the driveway marked as a smooth white path in the snow; the balloon dropped lower until she could see the miniature balconies. 'But it's . . .'

'No, not "Edelweiss",' Charles laughed. 'At least not any more. You can choose the name – after all, you're in the image business.'

She looked at him, puzzled. 'Why are we going there?'

'Because it's ours. I've bought it. I told you I was turning over a new leaf, and part of that was going land-based. It was a good buy – a brilliant buy, in fact. Shakira's ex-buddy had only leased it, and the owner was delighted with an outright sale.'

'But whatever will you do with it?'

'I thought the kids might like it – you can't get them on skis early enough these days – and of course you can entertain your people there, use it if and when they change the film festival to September. Movie moguls do that, you know, take half a dozen of their . . .'

'What kids?' Verry had to shout. They were close to the ground, and Charles had let off a burst of gas to slow their descent.

'Ours,' he bellowed. 'Yours and mine.'

The basket touched down gently on the snow.

'"*Champers 2*",' Verry said in the sudden hush. 'Pure Hollywood. We'll call it "*Champers 2*".'

'Very movie mogul.'

She tried to say 'Very' herself, but she couldn't, because Charles was kissing her, and they were in the middle of nowhere, and there was nowhere else on earth that she would rather be.